D1645582

CONFLICT
OF
INTEREST

TERRY LEWIS

Pinnacle Books
Kensington Publishing Corp.
http://www.pinnaclebooks.com

To my two girls, Fran and Angie,
lights of my life

ONE

Tuesday—July 9th

My head pounds; my stomach tightens with every step up the stairs: reminders of last night's excess. I have taken the stairs, not wanting to wait on the elevator, which is often interminably slow at this time in the morning. I glance at my watch: 9:02 A.M. It's fast, I remind myself, set ahead on purpose, a concession to the narrow margin of error in which I generally operate. I charge through the stairwell door onto the third floor, headed for the courtroom, slow my pace, try to catch my breath, not wanting to appear rushed.

Though I have not yet arrived at the courtroom, I can picture the scene clearly. It is sentencing day. That mass of humanity which is fodder to the wheels of justice gathers in and about the courtroom. Lawyers hammer out last-minute plea agreements. The clients, some hopeful, others hopeless, wait to learn their fates. The hopefuls, dressed in their Sunday best sit neatly and quietly on court benches which are, ironically, much like church pews. Accompanied by a smattering of family and character witnesses, they adopt a practiced hat-in-hand demeanor which their attorneys hope will seem sincere.

The hopeless also stand out. Some are old men, alcoholics and drug abusers, street people. Their faces are as worn as their clothing. Their eyes show disinterest, apathy, defeat. Some are young black men. They wear high tops, Reebok or Nike, untied, and T-shirts of their favorite sports teams. They joke and tease each other. Their walk, their gestures, are like a ritual dance that confirms their sentence as a rite of passage. They show not so much their ignorance of the game, but their indifference to its rules.

The deputy clerks and the court reporters ready themselves. The bailiffs escort the prisoners from their holding cells to the long bench on the side of the courtroom. People stare at these men dressed in the drab olive-green prison garb shuffling across the floor, their ankle irons clanging with each step, their jail-issued slippers ludicrously casual, as if they had all been watching television in their pajamas and hadn't bothered to change.

The victims are there too. They sit mostly in the back of the courtroom. Some are alone. Some sit with friends or family, or victim advocates. Most are as anxious as the defendants, intimidated not only by their assailants, but also by an impersonal, insensitive system. It shows in the ashen faces, grim and set, the white knuckles clinched around tissue.

Though there is a certain exhilaration in playing it so close, I am relieved to see that flashing red light over the doorway as I turn the corner—the signal that the judge has left his chambers en route to the courtroom. It means that I am not late. Almost everyone has entered the courtroom by now and the clacking of my heels on the terrazzo floor makes an eerie, hollow sound. I enter from the side door, stage right.

Courtroom 3A is a relic, a throwback to a time when people were appropriately awed by its majesty, its mystique. It has the feel of both a theater and a church. The ceiling rises to a cathedral-like twenty-four feet, framed by a border of burled walnut. The same paneling covers the bottom half of the walls except behind the judge's bench, where it makes a huge arch, reaching within a few feet of the ceiling. Lighting is provided by three round light fixtures which hang from long brass rods in the center of the courtroom. The judge's bench is massive and raised appropriately to give the judge that hint of omnipotence. The public benches, or pews, are separated by a wide aisle in the middle and two more narrow ones on the sides.

I walk over and ease myself onto one of the benches just inside the railing. An assistant public defender, who is seated next to me, gives me a quick look, a mix of contempt and pity, it seems. She mouths an innocuous hello, though, and gives me a half-smile. Some of the other lawyers nod as well. I grab a copy of the docket and quickly review it. There are approximately sixty cases in all, three of which are mine, starting about midway down. I look up and steal a sideways glance at the assistant public defender again. She looks my way as if she can feel my eyes, and I quickly look away.

Suddenly, I feel very self-conscious. There had been no time to shave this morning, or shower, and I know that my suit is in need of cleaning. I straighten my tie, run my fingers through my hair, realizing it hasn't been washed in a couple of days. I scratch on my day-old beard. Fragments of dead skin, matted by dirt and oil, come loose underneath my fingernails, and I clean them absently while I look at my files.

"All rise."

I stand instinctively along with the rest of the courtroom with this command from the bailiff.

"The Circuit Court of the Second Judicial Circuit in and for Leon County, Florida, is now in session, the Honorable John A. Rowe presiding."

Judge Rowe is an imposing figure even without the trap-

pings of his office. Although the trademark flattop is gray
now, he still looks as solid as he did when he played defensive end for the University of Florida. Those who don't
know better say that his nickname, Gator, is a reference to
his alma mater. In truth, it has more to do with his personality.

He strides into the courtroom and onto the bench with
an imperiousness that twenty years as a circuit judge can
foster. His steely blue eyes survey the crowded courtroom
briefly as he takes his seat. Rowe moves through his docket
quickly.

On two of the three cases that I have scheduled this
morning I ask for continuances, which are granted without
objection by the state.

My last case is Danny Wells. I spot him, make eye contact,
and squeeze into the bench next to him. Danny is young,
about twenty-five, thin, with the slouch of a loser. He fidg-
ets with his hands and gives me a nervous smile, showing
cigarette-stained, rotten teeth. Years of drug abuse have
taken their toll. The realization that he is about to be sentenced to three years in the Department of Corrections
has just about done him in. I am thinking that, ironically,
a little dope might have been a good idea today for Danny.
I touch him on the shoulder for a moment. It is not
enough, I know, but it does seem to calm him a bit. I can
almost hear his heart beating when Rowe calls out the case
and we walk to the podium together.

Rowe's baritone voice is robotic, impersonal. "Mr. Wells,
having previously entered a plea of nolo contendere to the
charge of possession of a controlled substance, to wit, cocaine, is there any legal reason why judgment and sentence
should not now be imposed?"

"No, Your Honor," I answer.

"I have reviewed the presentence investigation report,"
Rowe continues. "Are there any errors that you would like

to note, or is there anything further that you or your client wish to say before sentence is announced, Mr. Stevens?"

"The PSI appears to be correct, Your Honor. On Mr. Wells' behalf, however, I would like to point out a few things to the Court." I give the usual dog-and-pony show, talk about the terrible addiction that had, in fact, doomed Danny to fail in his efforts to stay straight. I point out that at least he is not dealing, that he is young, that prison is not a place for him, etc., etc., etc. The trouble is, it is the same argument I had made two years earlier.

When Rowe had placed Danny on probation then, he had promised him, "Mess up, Mr. Wells, and I'll give you the max. Understand?" Danny had nodded, but he didn't understand, not really. In the interim, Danny had beaten a violation of probation charge because of some sloppy police work, a sharp defense attorney (me), and a bit of luck.

He had not been so lucky this time. Stopped on a minor traffic infraction, he had been arrested when a DMV records check revealed that he was driving on a DUI suspended license. A search of his person had produced various and sundry illegal drugs. A trial would have been a waste of time, delaying the inevitable, so Danny had entered his plea of no contest six weeks ago. Now, the prosecutor responds briefly to my argument, reminding the judge of his promise to Wells two years before. Then, Rowe keeps his promise.

I stand aside as Danny is led away by the bailiff to sit on the benches with the other sentenced prisoners. He will be fingerprinted, and then the judge will give a mass advisory to all of those sentenced of their right to appeal within thirty days from the date of the judgment and sentence and their right to have court-appointed counsel in the event that they are unable to retain private counsel. Danny knows, of course, that there is nothing to appeal. All I can do is to mouth some more useless words, assuring Danny that if there is anything I can do, telling him to stay in touch, etc. It is awkward. I know what is in store for Danny in state prison. I don't think Danny has fully comprehended it. But as I give my client one final nod and make my way to the back of the courtroom, I am already putting Danny Wells out of my mind—a practiced skill, an occupational necessity. I quietly slip out of the courtroom and head back to my office, paddling furiously upstream just to keep afloat.

"Mr. Stevens."

I am standing, waiting for an elevator when I hear the voice behind me. When I turn around I see no one at first, though I hear footsteps in the hallway. A couple of seconds later, Rusty Campbell has rounded the corner.

"Good. Glad I caught you." Rusty is Judge Rowe's bailiff. He is about sixty and the short sprint down the hallway has left him a bit out of breath.

"Hey, Rusty. What's up?"

"Judge Rowe wants to see you in his office. He's going to take a break in about ten to fifteen minutes, if you can wait."

"What's it about?" My mind is suddenly racing through all of the possibilities, none of them positive. Rusty simply shrugs his shoulders.

"Okay. Thanks," I say, looking at my watch. "I'll be there." Time enough for some coffee, black, I think to myself as I step into the open elevator.

I get my coffee to go, drink it outside the courtroom. I pace nervously, trying not to speculate on his purpose in wanting to see me.

The courtroom begins to empty and I see Rowe exit a side door and make his way down the hallway towards his office. Rusty is in front, and two lawyers, a prosecutor and an assistant public defender, are on either side. They have to walk quickly to keep up with Rowe.

I throw my coffee cup into a nearby trashcan and follow the group, unobtrusively, from a distance. As the two lawyers follow Rowe into his private office, I hesitate a few moments more and then step into the outer office to find myself standing in front of Rowe's secretary, Eva Sturgiss.

"Mr. Stevens," she says with a smile, "good to see you again. Judge Rowe has someone with him right now but he should be through in a minute. How have you been?"

I want to tell her that my life is going to hell in a handbasket, thank you very much, but instead I say, "I'm fine, thanks, Eva."

She looks at me for a moment as if she has heard my thoughts rather than my words, but all she says is "Good."

I have known Eva Sturgiss now for about eight years and she has always called me Mr. Stevens. I have tried to get her to call me Ted. Each time, she nods politely and says something like, "as you wish," but the next time it is Mr. Stevens again. I have long since given up.

"Do you know what he wants to see me about?"

"Perhaps he should tell you himself. I believe it is about a conflict appointment."

I ponder Eva's words for a moment. Normally, the public defender's office represents indigent criminal defendants. Sometimes, however, there is a conflict of interest in representing a particular client. There might be, for example, codefendants who point the finger at each other, or perhaps a witness for the state in one case is also a public defender client in another. In those instances, the public defender's office withdraws and a private attorney is appointed by the court, paid by the county at a reduced rate.

I have been on the conflict list, as it is called, ever since I left the state attorney's office three years ago. Being a conflict attorney is not a real lucrative proposition but it has been good for business. It keeps me in practice and in touch with all of the players on a regular basis. It keeps my name out there. It was unusual, however, for Rowe to want to speak to me about a particular appointment. Usually you just receive a copy of the order by mail.

"Please, Mr. Stevens, have a seat."

"Thank you," I say. As I settle into one of the chairs along the side wall, looking anxiously toward Rowe's closed door, I remember the first time I was in this office.

It was during my third year of law school. I was interning with the public defender's office. During my first week, my supervising attorney, Rick Hauser, sent me to Gator's office to obtain his signature on an uncontested order. When I eased into the outer office the secretary was not there. Just as well, I thought. I'll just leave it on her desk with a note to call when the order has been signed. Suddenly a voice boomed.

"Eva! Is that you?"

I stuck my head past the door jamb to Rowe's office, looking a little sheepish, I suppose. It was pretty obvious that I was not Eva, who I presumed was his secretary, but I was not quite sure what to say or to do.

Rowe was seated behind a magnificent antique oak desk with intricate carvings on the front and the legs, a fat cigar sticking out of the side of his mouth. Abutting the desk was a long conference table with three chairs on either side and a seventh on the end. The only other thing that struck me at this time, because I didn't want to take the time, or the chance, to look at much else in the office, was the fact that his desk was virtually clutter-free, except for the file he was reviewing in front of him.

He looked up at me with an icy stare, then bellowed, "You're not Eva!"

I wanted to come back with a quick sarcastic reply, but

I also wanted to live, so instead I replied, "Ted Stevens, Your Honor. I'm interning with the public defender's office."

I tried my best to act nonchalantly but, in truth, I was more than a little intimidated by this grizzled jurist who, I had been told, ate new lawyers for lunch. I faced my fear and continued, as steadily as I could. "I've just brought this order in the Greg Turner case."

"What order?" he spat.

"It's an order authorizing a psychological exam. I understand it was uncontested." My words were as much a question as a statement.

He looked at me oddly for what seemed an eternity. From the scowl on his face I almost expected him to leap across the table and pounce on me like some pumped-up linebacker on a quarterback sack. Instead, he said, "Well, you want me to sign it, or just look at it from a distance?"

I fumbled my way over to him, mumbling something like, "Of course. Sorry," and handed him the papers. I could feel my facade crumbling.

Rowe quickly reviewed the order, signed it, and then pushed it back in my direction, adding gratuitously, "You'd better get a haircut if you want to be a lawyer in my court."

My face burned. Flustered, I edged silently towards the door, aching to get away from this arrogant asshole, anxious to avoid saying something that would brand me forever in his mind as either a wimp or a jackass.

Just as I reached the door, Rowe boomed, "Mr. Stevens!" I turned to face the expected insult but instead the Gator was smiling a big toothy grin, and in his most Southern gentlemanly voice he said, "So nice to have made your acquaintance. You stay close with Rick Hauser and you'll learn a lot about this business. Good luck with your internship."

* * *

"It shouldn't be much longer."

Eva's words bring me out of my daydream. She is the perfect secretary for John Rowe. Her polite formality is in sharp contrast to his redneck abrasiveness. She looks to be in her mid-forties. Though attractive, she seems to purposely try to make herself dowdy in appearance. She has never married, to my knowledge, though I can't be sure. I know very little about her personal life, as she has always been very reluctant to talk of herself. I sit quietly while she works on her typing, interrupted occasionally by the phone.

In just a few minutes, the door to Rowe's office opens and the two lawyers stand in the doorway.

"See you, Judge," one says.

"See you later," joins the other.

"Humph" is all they get from Rowe. The two look in my direction, the defense attorney rolling her eyes. When she gets closer, she whispers to me, out of Eva's earshot, "Hope you don't have a defense motion today. I don't think the old fart knows what 'suppression' means."

The prosecutor chips in, also in a whisper, "Sure he does, it's that popsicle stick thing that the doctor puts on your tongue when he wants you to say 'ahh.' " The other lawyer smiles involuntarily and I join her. The prosecutor directs his thumb in her direction. "What a poor loser. Hey, by the way, I need to talk to you about your man McVoy." Then, in his best godfather impersonation, "I've got an offer you can't refuse."

"Those are the kind I like to get. I'll try to call you this afternoon. You'll be in?"

"Yeah, well, as you know, we state workers usually get off about noon, but I'll make an exception if you're going to call." He smiles again and then, "What you got with the Gator?"

"Don't know. He just wanted to see me." Both lawyers

look at me with a touch of surprise and sympathy; both silently mouth good luck as they leave the office.

Eva speaks into her intercom. "Judge Rowe, Mr. Stevens is here to see you." We can hear Rowe's response without the necessity of mechanical assistance.

"What's he want?"

"He's responding to your request that he come over." She smiles at me.

"Well, tell him to come in, then. I got things to do." Rowe knows, of course, why I am here, but it is obvious that he enjoys his carefully formed image, and he always likes to keep in practice.

I step inside, not sure whether I should close the door or leave it open. I ask. Rowe does not respond, motioning me to take a seat at the long library table that runs perpendicular to his desk. I leave the door open. Rowe, meanwhile, is reading some papers and does not look like he wants to be disturbed, so I stand quietly for several seconds until he looks back up. The walls have an earthy feel about them, lined with photos of family, awards, images of hunting and fishing, as well as reminders of his former football days. As usual, the only things on his desk are the file in front of him and an ashtray containing a half-smoked cigar. Finally, when he looks up at me he stares for a couple of seconds and says, "You look like shit."

"Thanks," I respond curtly. I know, after several years, how to play the Rowe game. You don't want to back down, but you have to be careful not to give too much of a challenge, or an opening, either.

Rowe seems to accept my response. He softens noticeably in tone and volume. "You making any money yet?"

"I'm doing all right."

He looks at me, assessingly, for a couple of moments. He is not one for small talk, so he gets to the point of the meeting. "Remember the lady reporter who got killed a few weeks ago?"

His words hit me like a hammer. My stomach goes up to my throat and then slams back down with such force that I think Rowe must be able to hear it. I twitch involuntarily, feel the sweat form under my arms and roll down the sides, before it can be absorbed by my T-shirt. What does he know? I study his face, can detect nothing.

"Yeah, Patty Stiles, you mean," a half-statement, half-question. I wonder if I look as nervous as I feel.

He looks at me. "You okay?"

"Yeah, sure. A touch of flu, maybe," I say, knowing it's not.

"Yeah, Patty Stiles, that's the one. They made an arrest last night. Kid named Bobby Jackson. You probably heard about it on the radio."

I hadn't, but I nodded.

"The P.D.'s got a conflict they tell me, say they represent one of the potential witnesses for the state. I was gonna appoint you to the case, since you're up next. But the P.D. told me you might have a conflict yourself, that you might have known the victim. Former client, maybe?"

Rowe is looking at me intently now, his eyes narrowing. Get a grip, I tell myself. I fight for control, feel it returning. I can't block out the images, though. Auburn hair, a massive, curly mane atop a thin, tall frame. Large blue eyes. A smile that could move easily from innocent, to seductive, to sneering. I refocus, concentrate all my strength and energy, compose myself before answering.

"Yeah, as a matter of fact. I represented her in her divorce about a year ago." I look at him, anxious, but trying not to appear so.

"Strictly business, I assume?" Rowe looks at me sideways, as if he isn't too interested in my response—or already knows the answer. I hesitate—a lie could get me in trouble if Rowe knows, or finds out, the truth. How do I respond without lying but also without revealing the truth?

"I did see a good bit of her because it turned out to be a sticky case. I had to get a restraining order against her husband for slapping her around a bit, harassing her, that kind of stuff. But she was not an easy person to know." This, of course, is very true. I congratulate myself.

"I won't make you represent a person accused of murdering a former client if you're not okay with it. What do you think, do you see a problem?"

The coincidence, the irony, is just too remarkable. I fight back a crazed smile. Do I see a problem? I should see a big problem. A small voice inside me is screaming no, don't take this case. Stay the hell away from it. But I ignore it. Sure, I should see a problem. But I see only opportunity instead. What better way to have legitimate access to whatever the police have uncovered? What better way to throw suspicion elsewhere? Not to mention my chance for the spotlight, out from the shadow of my partner for a change.

"No, I don't see a problem," I say finally.

Rowe looks at me for several more seconds as though he expects me to say something else. Then, with obvious reluctance, he continues.

"Also, um, sorry to hear about your, um, family troubles. Now, I'm not one to pry into somebody's personal affairs, but, I was thinking, maybe you don't want something like this on your plate just now. I'm sure you've got plenty on your mind already these days. If you'd rather not take this on, I'd understand."

Rowe's words trigger images, painful and vivid: Beth's dark eyes flashing with anger and hurt, her voice getting louder and louder. "Who is she?" she demanded. She had received a phone call—anonymous. The caller, a woman, had told her that I did not deserve either one of them. Told her she'd be sending her some photographs and that

they would talk later. I assured Beth it was a prank, someone's cruel idea of a joke. There was no one else, I assured
her. She was not convinced. My daughter, Annie, didn't
know what was wrong, only that something was. Her eyes
were filled with confusion, sadness. I waved to her sadly as
she and Beth pulled out of the driveway, car packed,
headed for Beth's parents in Panama City. A few days, Beth
said, just to sort things out. "I need to be away from you
right now, Ted." The divorce papers were served on me a
week later.

I realize that I have been hesitating too long before responding. Rowe has given me plenty of opportunity to
gracefully back out. I should, I know. It would be the wise
move.

"I appreciate the concern, sir, but I'm doing all right.
Actually, the more work I've got, the better I feel."

Rowe seems pleased with this response, though it is hard
to tell. He looks at me directly again. "I know this boy, Ted.
At least, I know his mother. She used to work at my
brother's store. I told her I'd make sure her son got a good
lawyer." He hesitates for a moment and then adds, "I guess
he's stuck with you though." He gives me one of those
toothy Gator grins and I smile back. Despite everything,
for one brief moment, I feel good about myself.

"Well, Eva's got a copy of the order appointing you.
Good luck." And with that he is back to his papers, a mo-
mentary chink in the armor now closed. Realizing that the
conversation has ended, I back out of the doorway, pick
up the paperwork from Eva, mutter my goodbyes and go
to meet my new client.

TWO

Outside it is like a steam bath. Though it's only mid-morning and the sun is hidden by clouds, the temperature already is close to ninety degrees. The air is still, heavy, a haze so thick it seems I can push it away with my hand. Instinctively I remove my coat, loosen my tie. I remember an observation made once by my brother, Charlie, who now makes his home in Arizona. Tucson heat, he said, is like a fat lady slapping you in the face. Tallahassee heat, on the other hand, is like a fat lady sitting on your face. Yes, I think, exactly.

Small beads of sweat form on my forehead within seconds as I begin to cross the street. By the time I turn the corner onto College Avenue, I am perspiring profusely, my shirt damp, sticking to me. It is a sour-smelling sweat, a mix of last night's Scotch and this morning's breakfast sausage. I wipe my forehead with my finger, shake the accumulated perspiration onto the sidewalk, and wipe my hands on my pants leg.

Elliott, standing outside his Monroe Street store, smiles at me as I approach. He's okay, Elliott, has owned The Haberdashery for as many years as I can remember. He kids me good-naturedly about my cheap suits. Sometimes

I stop and chat, but not today. Today I just wave and say, "How's it going?" "Fine, Teddy," he says back. He always says fine.

I pass on by quickly. It is too hot today for even brief conversation on the street. Half a block later I reach my destination, pause briefly in front of the tall mahogany-framed French doors, checking my reflection in the glass, then enter gratefully into the air-conditioned space.

The building has housed the firm of Morganstein & Stevens since its formation three years ago. Paul Morganstein, my partner, had bought the building the year before. It had previously been owned and occupied by two sisters, Rose and Catherine Green, who had opened a woman's clothier in 1938 called simply The Rose, its emblem and trademark a long-stemmed single rose.

For more than fifty years the store had been a fixture of downtown Tallahassee, until it became a victim of the malls and the inability, or unwillingness, of the two sisters to keep up with changing styles and fashions. When Rose died in the late 1980s her sister Catherine decided she had neither the ability nor the motivation to continue and closed the shop within a year. The building sat vacant for quite some time, Catherine being a bit of a crotchety old lady with no real need to sell the place. Somehow Paul, who can be a real charmer when he wants to, convinced her otherwise, and on fairly favorable terms. I suspect that Miss Green had been persuaded by Paul and his sense of history, concluding that The Rose would be appreciated by Paul.

And it was. Paul restored and remodeled the Victorian front and completely refurbished the interior, furnishing it with antiques, Persian rugs, brass fittings, rich cherry wood trim, and legal-themed prints and paintings. Just above the entrance is a gray and pink marble crest depicting a single rose. To be honest, it's all a bit ostentatious for my taste, but I am more the silent-partner type when it comes to those things. Underneath I understand that it is the type of image that brings in the big-paying clients.

"Good morning, Mr. Stevens." Adrienne, our new receptionist, beams at me from her control station. Jesus, the lady is too cheerful. She's also too good-looking and too smart. She must be a real bitch at home, I think. It gives me some consolation, so I give her some slack.

"Good morning back at you. And, Adrienne, it's Ted."

She smiles again, a little more shyly now. "Okay . . . Ted."

I nod my approval and walk past her, heading for the stairs that wind up and behind the reception area. My partner's office is downstairs, as is that of his secretary, Cathy. Downstairs also includes the law library, kitchenette, shower, and conference room. My secretary, Janice, and I are upstairs, along with a few extra rooms for possible expansion. Paul, my partner, got his pick of offices—it is, after all, his building—and his office is nice, larger than mine, and it looks out onto a private courtyard which is used sometimes for entertaining. It also means that he does not have to climb the stairs. But I like my office better. I can look out on the traffic below, and out on the balcony, I can see up College Avenue all the way to the entrance of the FSU campus.

Janice looks up from her typing as I reach the second-floor landing. "Oh, is it raining outside?" A slight smirk on her face. Smart ass, I think, but I say, "Yeah, just a light drizzle." She looks out the window quickly again and then back at me. Got you, I thought. Janice can hold her own against anybody, but I give her plenty of practice.

I put my jacket on the coat rack, grab the message slips from my slot on Janice's desk, and go past her into my office. I roll up my sleeves and take a Coke out of the mini-fridge which I keep in the corner, take a big swig, sit down behind the library table that I use as a desk, and begin going through the messages. Janice appears at the door. One message is from Robert Lamb, who wants an extension of time to serve answers to interrogatories in a case—can he have an extra week? I look up at Janice.

"Call Rob back and tell him no problem."

I look at the next message. Sandra Jenkins called, please call back. I groan inwardly just seeing the name. It is one of those divorce cases that never die. She and her ex have too much bitterness, too much money, to let it go. What is scary, though, is I can see Beth and me like this. Of course, if you had asked me two years ago, hell, even two months ago, I would have said no, impossible. Things seem to be getting out of control though now. Forget it, Ted. Back to business. The message says her ex is not returning the kids on time after weekend visitation.

"What else did she say?" I asked.

"Well, she ranted and raved for a good five or ten minutes and I don't think you want to hear it all. The general impression was that she thought this should be a jailable offense."

"Oh well, call her back and tell her to just keep a journal of any similar transgressions. Tell her we need to have a pattern over a period of time before we bother the judge with this." I look up at Janice who dutifully nods her head, but her eyes are doubtful.

"Never mind," I say. "I'd better call her myself."

I check to see if my partner is in. He is not. I leave him a note about the appointment on the Jackson case, brief Jan about it, and tell her I'm headed out to the jail. I take the time for a quick shave in the office, stop by Elliott's store for a shirt. A trip to the clerk's office produces copies of the probable cause affidavit, offense report, and other papers in the newly created court file. Thus armed and somewhat rejuvenated, I bounce out of the door and within sixty seconds I am wheeling my car out of the parking garage. Fifteen minutes later I pull into the parking lot of the county jail.

The Leon County Correctional Facility is a massive building, some architect's vision of aesthetic perfection. Unfortunately, it is also a tribute to incompetence in functional design, eighteen months beyond completion date, and several million dollars over budget. The staff has been forced to move in early, and the resulting problems encountered in operations have led many to conclude that the term "correctional" is an appropriate adjective.

Sheriff Woodrow "Woody" Hall, whose job it is to run the place, is good-natured and philosophical when listening to complaints about the new jail. He just nods his head in agreement and then says, "Yeah, but it shore is pretty, ain't it?" Hall's folksy manner masks a progressive law enforcement leader who stays on the cutting edge of new theories, techniques, and technologies. His easy going, hands-on management style and political savvy have kept him in office for sixteen years with no signs of trouble on the horizon. With some notable exceptions, the jail staff reflects the professionalism of the boss.

Three years ago I got a career boost when I represented Woody's son in his divorce. It was one of my first cases as a private lawyer. Having handled only criminal cases for the five years before, I was not exactly overconfident, but my partner, Paul, had been too busy to handle it and referred the case to me. The son was a bit of a hothead, and early on in the representation, when I balked at certain strategies that Woody Jr. suggested, he had walked out in a huff. A couple of days later, however, after a chat with his dad, Junior was back, with a better attitude. We ended up getting along quite well. We also ended up with some very good results in the divorce. Though I am sure these results were more attributable to favorable facts, a fair judge, and beginner's luck, I did not protest too much when both father and son sang my praises to everyone they knew. Since then, I have handled a lot of cases for other law enforcement officers, divorce and otherwise.

Another benefit of this relationship is the fact that I now enjoy various and subtle courtesies at the jail which are not always available to other criminal defense lawyers. This not only makes my job easier but is also of benefit to my clients. I have taken advantage of those courtesies today, coming to visit a client during mealtime and receiving permission to interview my new client in a separate interview room, face to face. Often, lawyers speak with their clients via phone separated by a half wall of thick glass, an adequate arrangement for most purposes, but it does not provide you with the opportunity to "read" a client.

The jail has five floors. Most of the phone interview rooms are on the first floor. The interview room to which I am taken is on the second. I am given only a cursory search before being led up.

The room is fairly large, approximately twenty-five by thirty, and is apparently used as a classroom. There is a small desk in front, presumably for the instructor, but no chair. There is a marker board rather than a chalkboard on the front wall, but no markers. Correctional personnel are usually wary (some would say paranoid), about any extraneous implement that might be used in an inappropriate manner. A similar philosophy has produced your basic correctional facility decorating package: rubber tile floors, cement block walls painted the same color as the baseboard and trim, a dull, washable yellow. The same color is used in every room and every hallway on every floor of the jail. No plants, no paintings, no objets d' art anywhere to be found. All of the doors are standard, solid, heavy metal.

I can't argue with this approach from a management

perspective. It doesn't take too many times of arrestees uri-
nating on the walls or throwing up on the floor or kicking
cell doors over and over again, until one very quickly is
willing to sacrifice aesthetics for utility. It is a hell of a lot
easier to clean up a tile floor than carpeting. This place is,
if nothing else, clean. And, under the circumstances, I suppose that is saying a bit.

As I wait, I read the offense report again, a little more
carefully. The victim had died from multiple stab wounds
to the chest, throat, back, and head. The suspected murder
weapon, a butcher knife, was found in the bushes approximately fifty yards from the house alongside a pathway. La-
tent prints, taken from the victim's home in various places,
including the kitchen, matched those of Bobby Jackson.
Neighbors said that Bobby had visited her on other occasions. One of those neighbors had called the police upon
hearing screams just before midnight. Another saw someone who looked like Jackson run from the back of the victim's house down the same pathway where the supposed
murder weapon had been found. That person was dressed
similarly to the way Bobby Jackson had been dressed that
night, according to his coworkers at the restaurant where
he had gotten off work at approximately 10:45 P.M.

A search warrant executed at Bobby Jackson's home,
where he lived with his mother, had uncovered a pair of
sneakers with some small bloodstains which were the same
blood type as the victim's (though apparently the victim
and Bobby Jackson have the same blood type). When officers came to arrest Bobby, he was found hiding in the bedroom closet.

In earlier questioning Jackson admitted knowing the victim but denied going to the victim's house. He insisted that
he had walked directly home from work, but refused any
further detailed questioning.

I hear the clicking of the guard's heels on the tile floor

and the shuffling of my client's flip-flops along the hall several seconds before they appear at the entrance. The guard ushers Bobby Jackson into the room.

"Just call when you're ready to leave," he says to me, pointing at a phone on the wall next to the marker board. Then he closes the door and walks on down the hall.

Jackson is smaller than I had, for some reason, expected. He looks to be about five-nine and approximately a hundred and fifty pounds. He has a handsome, clean cut, athletic look about him. His hair is short, and he has no facial hair. His skin color and features suggest an Asian influence with the African. I find myself already thinking of how a jury would see him, concluding that he exudes a confident, nonthreatening image which I think would be favorably received. He doesn't look like a murderer. I am half-sitting, half-leaning against the front desk. He remains just inside the door entrance, looking at me with what seems like a mixture of anxiety and detached curiosity. I decide to play it formal, professional.

"Mr. Jackson, my name is Ted Stevens. I am an attorney, and I have been appointed to represent you in this case." I do not offer my hand, nor does he.

"You a public defender?"

"No, I'm private. The public defender's office has a conflict in your case. They already represent one of the people that will be a state witness in your case, one of Patty Stiles' neighbors. So, the judge appointed me."

If I have been sizing him up, I am sure that he is doing the same with me. For his part, he sees a fairly large man by comparison—approximately six-three, around two hundred twenty pounds (up from my usual one ninety-five), mid to late thirties, longish dirty-blond hair, clean-shaven (at the moment). Jackson finally breaks the silence.

"Can you get me outa here, man?"

I suspect that my answer to his question is the most important factor to him in his evaluation of my competence at this moment.

"We're going to talk about that. We have many things to talk about, Mr. Jackson, and one of them is bail. I want us to spend the next hour or so learning about each other, discussing some of the theories or strategies that might be appropriate in your case, and figure out how we can best help each other. And that includes getting you out of here on bail so you can help me with your case." I don't tell him, that in murder cases, it is very much the exception rather than the rule that the accused is released on bail. You don't want to start out being pessimistic.

"Now, before we start, I need you to listen close. I need to tell you a little bit about myself and where I'm coming from, so you can decide how you want to go." He is still plainly agitated but nods at me silently to go on.

I explain to him about attorney/client confidentiality, that anything and everything he tells me is privileged information. "I cannot, I will not, without your permission, tell it to anyone. You don't have to confide in me; you don't have to tell me the truth. Hell, you don't even have to talk to me or cooperate with me at all. Of course, if you don't, it will make my job a hell of a lot harder, and your chances of beating this thing a lot slimmer." Jackson starts up but I wave him off. "I've been a lawyer for eight years. For the first five years I was an assistant state attorney. The last three I've been in private practice and have done a good bit of defense work. Point is, I'm not a novice, Mr. Jackson, and I think that if you check around you'll get a fairly favorable impression of my abilities as a lawyer. But I also have to tell you I've only handled one other murder case. That was two years ago."

"Did you win or lose?"

"Depends on how you look at it. My client was found guilty, but he got a life sentence instead of the death penalty, which the state was seeking. I considered it a win under the circumstances. I believe he did too."

"What are the 'circumstances' in my case?" A hint of sarcasm.

"I don't know yet."

My new client looks at me closely, as if he is trying to get a read on me but can't. I continue.

"The way I see my job, I give you the benefit of what knowledge, skill, and experience I have so that you can make the best decision in maneuvering through a some-times complex legal process, to decide what's best for you. It's not for me to judge. It's not for me to preach or tell you what you should do. What I try to do is put myself in my client's shoes and, given that situation, try to determine what I'd do and how I'd go about it and advise you accord-ingly.

"There is one thing, though. I am not in your shoes, and I don't want to be in your shoes. I am an officer of the court and I cannot do anything illegal nor allow you to do so. For example, if you tell me today that you killed Patty Stiles, I couldn't put you on the stand and let you commit perjury by saying you didn't. If you want to talk hypotheti-cally, that's okay, but once you tell me something for real, it's there. On the other hand, if you lie to me today or throughout my representation of you, and I rely on it, it can be disastrous if I get blindsided. Understood?"

Jackson looks at me thoughtfully, asks a few more ques-tions, making sure that he understands the concept. Finally he says, "Yeah, man, I'm cool, so let's talk, hypothetically."

"Okay, let me tell you what they've got, at least what they say they've got, so far."

I tell him what is in the probable cause affidavit and the arrest report, looking at him, trying to gauge his reaction. I expect either a hangdog, guilty look, or righteous indig-nation. I get neither. His intense calmness could mask a cold, calculating mind or reflect the naive confidence of an innocent man. He answers my questions directly and asks a lot of questions in turn. I conclude very quickly that he is both intelligent and sophisticated about legal issues. I don't know if that is good or bad.

After a while he says, "Looks like it's all circumstantial to me, Counselor."

"Well, it is all circumstantial evidence, but it's pretty strong circumstantial evidence. Of course, there are bound to be supplemental reports and additional information that we're not yet aware of. The cops usually don't like to play their entire hand simply to get an arrest or search warrant. But let's deal with what we do know, and what innocent explanation there may be for these circumstances.

"Your fingerprints in the house, for example. If you were, in fact, a friend or acquaintance of the victim and had visited her in her house on occasions in the past, that would explain how your fingerprints could have been there, without your having been there the night that she was murdered. So, you knew Ms. Stiles I assume?"

"Yeah. I met her two or three months ago and we had gotten to be pretty tight." Jackson looks at me, satisfied that I understood his meaning, but I press it nevertheless.

"You had sexual relations with her, then?"

"Yeah," he replies simply, amazed at my apparent denseness.

"How often?"

"Man, what's it matter? I don't know, several times. I wasn't counting—why you want to know all the details?"

"Everything is important, Mr. Jackson. Every detail I don't know at this point may or may not be of use."

He relents and tells me that he and Stiles had met at a night club. They hit it off pretty good, smoked a little dope together, ended up at her place in bed. He said he thought that maybe she had a thing for black men. At least that's what he had heard around. Part of it, he conceded, was probably that she was working on some story. What she called a "glimpse into the drug subculture in the black community." I could tell by his expression and tone that he was being a little derisive.

"But hell, she was a pretty hot white chick. She was pumping me for information, so I was pumping her for fun." He smiles, pleased with himself.

"You told the cops you got off work at about ten forty-five and walked straight home."

"That's right."

"You didn't stop off at Patty's on the way?" He looks a little surprised at my use of her first name.

"No, man, I didn't go by there that night." Jackson shifts uneasily in his chair.

"Okay." I continue to make notes while we talk. "Did you stop anywhere on the way, or see anybody that you know?"

"Like I said, I walked straight home. I didn't go anywhere else."

"When did you get home?"

"Just before twelve, about eleven forty-five."

"Took you an hour to walk home?"

"I wasn't walking real fast—but that's good time anyway."

"What about your mother, was she there when you got home?"

"Yeah."

"Can she verify what time you came home?"

"Probably—I mean I don't know for sure 'cause she was asleep, but usually, no matter how quiet I am, she hears me anyway. She's a pretty light sleeper. 'Cause I mean she's always giving me a hard time the next morning when I'm out a little late." My hopes are raised just a bit, and I get the details of his mother's name, address, and phone number.

"Isn't that good?" he asks. "I mean if Mama says I was home when she, Patty, was killed, won't that clear me?"

"Well, a lot's going to depend on how sure the neighbor is, and, how firm your alibi is. Of course, even if your mom swears up and down that you were home, the jury might not believe her. After all, you are her son and mamas will do just about anything to protect their children." Especially, I think, a son who is still living at home at twenty-eight years old, who can pull the wool over a trusting mom's eyes or manipulate her, get her to lie or stretch the truth a little. She would believe him if he professed his innocence. I have to admit that if he is lying to me, and I think that he probably is, at least partly, he is pretty convincing—how much more so to a mother who wants desperately to believe him?

"What about the blood on your shoes?"

"That was my blood. I cut myself shucking oysters at work." He shows me a small, almost healed puncture wound between his left thumb and forefinger which looks to be maybe two to three weeks old. Then he looks back to me and says, "Accidents happen, you know. Looks like you tangled with someone yourself." He points to some deep scratch marks on my wrist.

"Yeah, result of a not-so-friendly game of round ball a couple of weeks ago," I say looking at the scratches. "I play at the Baptist church downtown sometimes."

He assesses me briefly, wondering if I know anything about B-ball, apparently giving me the benefit of the doubt. "Well, looks like some dude needs to trim his fingernails."

I change the subject. "One thing you need to know before we go any further. Patty Stiles used to be my client. I represented her in a divorce case about a year ago." I have waited to bring this up, hoping that it will seem less objectionable now.

"Yeah." His face lights up a bit. "Patty talked to me about that once—bad scene. Her ex is apparently a real dick, wouldn't leave her alone. I thought your name sounded familiar. Ain't this a coincidence."

"Some people might question my ability to represent someone charged with the murder of a former client."

"You got a problem with it?" he asks.

"No," I answer, without hesitation.

"Then it don't bother me neither. Now, let's talk about getting me outa here."

We do talk about bail, a bit about defense strategies, but there isn't a whole lot to decide so early on. I ask him a lot more questions—about the case and also about him, his childhood, his family, his habits. It seems that he talks openly and freely. I begin to become aware of an easygoing charm and confidence that I imagine is never too far removed from his personality, whatever the situation. It's a trait often attributable to liars, very good liars.

Some lawyers and law enforcement types, borrowing as they often do from old movie jargon, insist that things just don't "smell" right. Or, they say they have a "gut feeling." Preposterous thoughts perhaps, but I do believe we all assimilate, analyze, and act on a variety of types of sensory information without consciously understanding how. This way of perception is either innate or a product of one's training and formative years, a trait that in some people's cases serves them well and earns their trust, and in other's causes confusion and uncertainty. Whatever you call it though, I sense it here, a bad feeling, a feeling that there is something wrong, something beneath the surface that I am barely aware of. There is a faint voice telling me not to take the case.

It would not, of course, be unusual for me to decline the representation, and no one would think it particularly odd. Indeed, I suspect that most people would look at the situation much the same as my secretary, Jan, when I told her where I was going and why. She had wrinkled her face, stifled a small gasp, and stared at me for a few moments before responding. She spoke from a position of knowledge of my professional and personal life that extends at least as far as propriety will allow, perhaps a little farther.

"Isn't there some kind of problem with representing a person who is accused of murdering your—" she hesitated, "—client? Isn't there a rule or something?"

"Former client," I corrected. "And no, there is no rule. There is no way that anything I learned when representing Patty could be used to her detriment now. There is no way it could be construed as betraying a confidence. After all, she is dead, and any attorney/client privilege died with her. The state of Florida sure as hell can't claim it on her behalf. On the other hand, my knowledge of my former client might in some way prove useful in defending my new client."

My response was a little too pat, and I don't think she bought it, but she didn't press it. Still, it made me feel a little unsure about the whole thing.

Now those doubts are trying to push to the surface again, but to no avail. By the time I'm ready to go, my client and I are on a first-name basis, and that little voice that had warned me before is not to be heard.

THREE

The Sunset Motor Inn is one of several small motels that fit in nicely between the countless car lots and mobile home dealerships that beckon to travelers along U.S. 90 West with their loud tacky signs and fluorescent-colored banners. It is a one-story stucco building painted mustard yellow and consists of an office on the east end with ten units toward the west. Though the rooms are small, the place is clean, it's cheap, and it rents by the week. It allows me the illusion that my arrangements are only temporary.

It's about 7:00 P.M. as I pull into the parking space in front of unit number four. The heat has lessened a bit, but not much. I have been running my a.c. full blast in my Honda Accord. When I get out, it's like I've opened the door to an oven. The motel is owned by an Indian family, headed by Ami Majeed. I can see him behind the desk as I move toward my room and give him a wave, which he returns. He does not, I am sure, completely approve of some of my habits. But I am not loud, and I pay my rent on time. He is polite, but not overly friendly.

Though my room is small, the space is well organized. There is a small stove, a mini-fridge, a sink and two cabinets, a small table, an alcove for hang-up clothes, and a dresser for the others. On top of the dresser sits a TV. No cable, no remote. There is one double bed in the room. When Annie is over, I rent a fold-up cot from Ami. I rarely use the stove, opting instead for a lot of pizza deliveries, take-home sandwiches, and eating out before I get home. To-night the menu is roast beef sandwich and beer, heavy on the beer.

I have brought some files with me to look over, including my newly opened Bobby Jackson file. Reviewing his crimi-nal record, I see that he has two prior drug-related charges, including the one for which he was on probation at the time of his arrest. I also see a prior domestic battery charge. I make a note to find out the circumstances surrounding that case. I want to make sure that this doesn't somehow become evidence for the state.

Then there is the statement. There is no question that it was given before Bobby was advised of his Miranda rights. The state will argue that Bobby was not a suspect at that time, that they were merely asking routine questions at the beginning of an investigation. I suspect, however, that they had already gotten the statement from the neighbor iden-tifying Bobby and were looking hard at him as a suspect. If so, Miranda would apply because he was definitely in custody at the time. I make a note to do some research or this area for a possible motion to suppress.

About half an hour into my review the phone rings.

"Teddy?"

I recognize the voice immediately. "Mother, what a pleas ant surprise," I lie.

"Teddy, I tried to get you at your office. I've been worried about you. I haven't heard from you in so long."

I can hear the booze in her voice. "We talked last week, Mom. Remember? I called on the Fourth. You know, Inde-pendence Day, all that stuff?"

There is an embarrassed silence on the other end of the

line, followed by a short giggle. "Well, it seems like forever," she says. "Anyway, I still wish you would have come down for the holiday. Charlie hated missing you. He came all the way from Arizona, you know."

"And the least I could have done was to travel that short little distance from Tallahassee to Miami."

"I didn't say that, Teddy." Annoyance now creeping into her voice.

Yes, she did, I think to myself. That's just what she said one week ago. But she was so drunk she doesn't remember it.

"It's just that I like having my boys with me together."

She means well, I tell myself—or does she? I tell my mother what I told her a week before. That I wish I could have gone down, but it's been really hectic here with work—and the separation has been tough. (I don't like the word divorce.) I had Annie for the weekend and didn't want to spend it on the road. So fly, she had said. She and Robert would pay for it if money was a problem. Sure, I thought, they would have paid and never let me forget it either.

"And how is my little Annie?" It sounds like she is talking about a pet dog.

"She's doing okay, I guess. Beth's got it where I only see her every other weekend and once during the week."

"Oh, listen, Teddy. We're worried about you living in that dump up there." She changes the subject abruptly. "Robert's got some friend or something up there who's got an apartment. He can get you in there. Let me let you talk to him."

"No, Mother, I don't need to—"

"Hello, Ted. How are you?" My stepfather has already taken the phone.

"Hey, Robert. I'm doing okay. How's it going with you?"

"Oh, can't complain. Nobody would listen if I did anyway." A loud belly laugh on the other end. It's obvious that my stepfather is about as fried as my mother. Robert has become fairly wealthy as a real estate broker and investor in Miami. Everything about him is superficial. I think that's what makes him tolerable to me. I get along fine with Robert, as long as I don't have to speak to him for more than two minutes at a time.

"Yeah, Ted. A friend of mine owns an apartment complex up there. Called Oak Ridge, Oak Hill, something like that."

"There's an Oak Hill on Miccosukee Road."

"That's it. I remember it was some Indian-sounding name. Anyway, he owes me a favor and he's got a unit up there that he'll let you have at a discount. Of course, on paper he'll charge you full rate. That ought to help you a little bit in the divorce." I can visualize the wink of his eye when he says this.

"Robert, I appreciate your help. I don't think there's any need to . . ."

"Listen, son." I always hate it when he calls me son, but I say nothing. "I know what I'm talking about here. You forget I had a pretty nasty experience in the divorce area myself."

I let him drone on for a bit longer. Just before my two-minute limit is up I cut him off.

"Thanks, Robert. I'll give him a call." It's a lie. I have no intention of taking any help from my stepfather, but it's easier to put him off this way.

"All right, now you take good care of yourself, Ted. Here's your mom again."

My mother spends a few more minutes rambling on until I make some excuse and get her off the line. I hang up the phone feeling both drained and agitated at the same time. I take out another beer from the mini-fridge and down about half of it at one time. Like mother like son, I say to myself.

I take another large swallow and try to take my mind off

my mother by getting back to my files. The first one I look at is a new divorce case though, and it triggers thoughts of my own divorce case. The nightmare began the night I was served with a copy of Beth's divorce petition and Judge Miller's order of temporary relief which, in effect, kicked me out of my house and gave sole temporary custody of our six-year-old daughter to my wife.

The deputy sheriff who served it on me was understanding, almost apologetic. I had been too much in shock initially to be angry. As I read the paperwork, the anger began to rise to the surface, striving to join the other companionable emotions—hurt, embarrassment, confusion, humiliation. I fought them all back, maintaining a calm, almost detached exterior. I gave no indication as to what I was feeling, what I was thinking. This practiced skill is why I often win at poker.

And later, after I had checked into the Sunset Motor Inn with the few essentials I was able to pack into a suitcase, after I had finished the first of what would be many Budweisers that evening, I read the petition and the order again with a touch of ironic bemusement. My wife, Beth, was doing just what I would have advised her if she had been my client. A hundred times I have crafted similar petitions and other legal pleadings, carefully choosing the words, the phrases that, though factual, are nevertheless half-truths by virtue of what is not said. We lawyers like our legalese: phrases set in an official, solemn format, the terms archaic, all designed to perpetuate the mystique of the law.

Even for someone as jaded as I am—as intimately familiar with the rules of the game as I am, with the posturing that is routine in such things—I felt both anger and fear as I read the formal, accusatory language: "Petition for Dissolution of Marriage. Petitioner, Elizabeth Arden Stevens, files this petition regarding her marriage to the Respondent, Theodore Allen Stevens, and alleges as follows . . ." There were allegations of residency, the date of marriage, that there had been "one minor child born of the parties, to wit, Elizabeth Annette Stevens, age six years. . . ." And further down: "Respondent is not a fit and proper person to have custody of the minor child and his visitation with the minor child should be supervised . . . pattern of physical and emotional abuse . . . the marriage between the parties has become irretrievably broken . . . parties have acquired during the marriage certain real and personal property which should be equitably divided by the court . . . petitioner and minor child in need of financial support. . . ."

There was the request for an injunction for protection. It had been issued "ex parte," that is, without giving the other side, me, prior notice. This can be done only if there is some compelling reason. My wife's petition read: "Because of the Respondent's past conduct and his threats of future harm, the Petitioner has a reasonable fear that to give notice to the Respondent of the Petitioner's request for such an order of protection will exacerbate an already volatile situation."

I had of course never hit Beth, nor harmed her in any way. I may have broken a couple of items of personal property, yelled a few times, but the petition made it sound like I was a real brute, a violent, crazy person. Why I should be surprised, I don't know. We lawyers are good at making the innocent appear guilty, and vice versa.

When I saw the signature of the attorney, I groaned. Don Carey was one of the most expensive, if not the best, divorce lawyers in town. I had been on the opposite side a few times in divorce cases, and he had been a real pain in the ass.

I had to admit though that he and my wife had set me up but good. I wondered when she had gone to him. She had never mentioned divorce before, never mentioned seeing a lawyer. Of course not, that's the way she would think and Carey would advise. There will probably be a charge on my Visa account next month for his retainer too. It was a common strategy. Why wait for a judge to maybe award temporary attorney's fees several weeks later? Charge it to the husband's credit card and you have a de facto award of attorney's fees before the case even begins. Similarly, I could expect to find our joint bank account lowered considerably. Not cleaned out. That would look too greedy, too cruel.

I had tried several times to call Beth that night. Her father in Panama City lied and said she wasn't there. None of her friends would own up that they knew anything either. If Panama City had not been so far, and I had not been so drunk, I might've made the trip over, confronted her, and her father—which is another story entirely. But I settled for cursing her silently—her father not so silently—and drowning my sorrows in beer.

Beth is now back in our house, with our child. Her parents stay there occasionally, alternating between Tallahassee and Panama City as their business will allow. And here I am, living out of my suitcase. I am thinking that if I can only get Beth alone for just a while, talk some sense into her. I down the last of another bottle of beer and lift up the receiver of the phone, then think better of it. I wouldn't want anybody to have a record of my phone call. I walk to the convenience store down the road, put a quarter in the pay phone, and dial the number. She picks up on the third ring.

"Hello."

"Hey, Beth."

Uneasy silence.

"Beth?"

"Ted, you're not supposed to be calling me. You know that." There is a tremble in her voice, like she is the one doing something wrong.

"I can't believe that's your idea," I say. "Tell me it's Dandy Don's. Or tell me your dad is behind it. That I'll believe. What I can't believe is you would try to keep Annie away from me."

"It's not like that, Ted," she says. "I don't want to get into this now. You've been drinking." Exasperation in her voice.

"No shit, Sherlock."

"I don't want to talk to you now."

"That's okay, sweetie," I say. "I really only wanted to talk to Annie. So put her on. I am allowed to talk with my daughter, aren't I?"

Her sigh is long and audible. "Ted, it's almost ten o'clock. Annie is in bed. Now, I'm going to hang up. Maybe we can talk later when you are in a little better condition. When you're sober."

"No, listen, Beth. I'm sorry. I—"

"Who is it, dear?" I hear a voice in the background.

"Bye-bye. Talk to you later." Beth disconnects.

I put in another quarter, dial again. On the second ring I hear the click of the receiver and a male's voice. "Hello." I hesitate a few moments. "Hello?" the voice says again. There is no mistake. It's my father-in-law. I hang up the phone. Son of a bitch, I say to myself, as I head back to my room, and my beer.

FOUR

Wednesday—July 10th

I am dreaming. Somewhere in the distance there is a faint, buzzing sound. It must be getting closer, though, because it is getting louder. Somehow I begin to realize it is my alarm clock that I hear. Fighting the effects of last night's beer, I slowly arrive at full consciousness, turn off the alarm, ease myself up from the bed, and head into the bathroom.

A hot shower and shave brings me most of the way back. I put on my armor for another day's battle. White shirt, gray suit with subtle burgundy stripes, paisley tie, cordovan wing tips. By the time I reach the office I present a fairly convincing picture of the hardworking professional, perhaps a little overworked, but presentable, ready to shrug off whatever had worn me down the day before.

Janice has a cup of coffee and phone messages for me, the first of which I eagerly accept. She also has her tickler calendar and corresponding files waiting for me at my desk. She gives me a look that tells me she knows what I did last night. Not the details, mind you, but the general gist of it. It is pretty much the same as I have done for what seems like a very long time now. I give her a look back that says leave it alone, I don't need your crap this morning, and she gives me a silent acknowledgment, message received. I sit back in my chair and listen to her recite the schedule: two appointments with potential clients this morning, deposition in the afternoon. She also reminds me that interrogatories are due in a divorce case I'm handling. It reminds me that I am set to give a deposition in my own divorce case two days from now.

"By the way, Paul said he wants to see you when you get in."

I shrug my shoulders. "Well, let me see what the big cheese is up to."

Paul is on the phone, pacing, when I appear at his open door. His jacket is removed to reveal the ever-present suspenders. He wears a bow tie which also sets him apart, but in a distinctive way. He is a short man, about five-eight, and considerably overweight. He motions me in.

My partner is a walking, talking anomaly, a man of sometimes outrageous contradictions. He is a former assistant public defender who looks and talks like a conservative prosecutor. He is a Jew from a small north Florida town who married an Italian Catholic from south Florida. He is a graduate of the University of Florida Law School but is one of the biggest Seminole boosters in Tallahassee. He was a civil rights activist in the sixties, champion and defender of the poor and disadvantaged. Now, his clients are mostly rich and very much advantaged. He has quickly become one of the most influential lobbyists in Tallahassee. He does almost no criminal work anymore.

I suppose that's one of the reasons he took me in and keeps me on as a partner. Though I bring in a fair amount of business, my cases are generally not the high-powered, big-money type. Paul Morganstein is definitely the rainmaker in this outfit. He brings in more business than we can handle. Though I have argued against it, not at all sure that bigger is better, we will be hiring an associate very shortly. I have deferred to Paul on this, as I always do on questions of firm business.

Paul is five years my senior. When I first met him, he was a few months away from leaving the public defender's office, and I had only recently started with the state attorney. We worked opposite each other on several cases and developed a mutual respect for each other's abilities and sense of fair play. Our professional relationship turned into personal friendship.

Paul had been chief deputy assistant and handled all of the administrative functions that his boss, Bill Melton, had neither the desire nor the aptitude for. When Melton lost the election in 1990, Paul saw the writing on the wall and resigned to go into private practice.

He quickly built a successful practice. Though he is a walking encyclopedia when it comes to criminal law, and a skilled trial lawyer, his efforts in lobbying on behalf of the public defender's office were what gave him the base for his new clientele. He earned high marks in that position, and before long he attracted clients who were happy to pay him large sums of money to do what he once did for a state salary.

When Paul generously offered me a partnership three years ago, it was too good to pass up. It meant an immediate boost in income; I knew I could get along with Paul; and I would be able to expand beyond criminal law.

All in all, it has turned out well. We are counterbalanced. Where he is the former public defender who looks like a state attorney, I am the former state attorney who looks like a P.D. Where he is meticulous, organized, ordered, I tend to be a bit impulsive, haphazard. But I think I have an intensity, even with my present distractions, that my partner has somehow left behind for the comfort of security.

Paul is holding the receiver several inches from his ear and moving his index finger and thumb in an open and close motion, the universal symbol for yacker. He moves the receiver back and speaks into the mouthpiece.

"I appreciate you talking with me, Senator, and thank you for your leadership on this issue. With you spearheading the push, I am sure we are in good hands. Thanks again, and let's stay in touch. Bye now." Paul hangs up the receiver and looks at me, a bit of amusement in his eyes. "What a dickhead. He wouldn't know the truth if it bit him on the ass. Come on in, Ted. How'd it go with Bobby Jackson yesterday?"

"Looks like I'm going to have my hands full."

"Did you tell him about the victim being a firm client?"

"Yeah. It doesn't seem to bother him. But what about you? I could decline the appointment if you want," I said, knowing he doesn't.

"Of course not. It's just something you have to let him know. This could be a good case for you, and for the firm,"—he hesitates and then looks at me—"if it's handled right. There's going to be a lot of opportunities to fuck up on this one. And the media's going to be waiting to pounce on it. Let's see, now. We've got a young, attractive, provocative white lady, freelancer for the local newspaper. We've got drugs. The accused killer is a black man. Then, if they get wind of any relationship between the victim and the defendant's lawyer . . ." He pauses. "Hello, *National Enquirer?*"

I had thought about those things in a vague, general way. But somehow, Paul's words make my stomach churn. When I don't respond to his rhetorical question, he grins at me for a moment. "Maybe I should work with you, second chair. I could help handle the press, you know, things like that." It's obvious that Paul does not expect to be contradicted.

"Yeah, sure," I say. I am a little resentful about Paul's presumptions, but I know he is right. I never have liked all that publicity shit anyway, and Paul plays the press like a violin. You can be sure though that I will do the work on the case. Whatever Paul does, it will be just for show.

"Well, keep me posted on this thing and let me know when the court dates are scheduled so I can put it on my calendar. Use me as a sounding board. Don't be afraid to ask for help—that's what partners are for."

As I say, I know who will do the work on this case.

Paul shifts gears. "How's it going with the divorce?" His eyes reflect genuine concern.

"Well, you know they say life's a bitch—well so's my wife, and her lawyer. Carey's got me scheduled for a deposition the day after tomorrow. I feel like I'm getting ready to go in for major surgery."

"Well, knowing Don, you probably are. But at least you got somebody to help stop the bleeding. Denise Wilkerson is no slouch as a lawyer. She'll do you right."

"Yeah, I'm sure it'll turn out okay." My words must sound as hollow as they feel as I back toward the doorway.

"Hey, listen, Ted. How 'bout dinner at our house Saturday night? You can recuperate from surgery."

"Paul, man. Don't you ever check with your wife first? That's a major no-no."

"Not with Anna. Not with you."

"Okay. Sounds good. I'll bring some wine."

The rest of the day goes by quickly. Both of my morning appointments convert into new divorce clients. Ironically, my divorce caseload seems to be expanding exponentially as I go through my own "divorce from hell." Oh well, I have to say it makes me a little more attuned, sympathetic to my clients' troubles.

One of my new clients rants and raves about her husband's infidelity, his insensitivity. I explain to her the concept of no-fault divorce, that evidence of boorish and obnoxious behavior, even adultery, is not relevant or admissible in a dissolution action, unless the behavior can be shown to have some detrimental effect on marital assets. She is disappointed.

The trick, I tell her, is to find a way to let the judge know what an asshole her husband is without coming right out and saying it. She must learn to hide her hate, control her emotions. The most satisfying revenge, legal and otherwise, requires a calm and controlled mind, a deliberative approach. I believe this now more than ever. I think my client will, with proper coaching, make a good victim, and I assure her that everything will turn out all right.

A little after five I finish up some interrogatories that are due in a case next week and place them on Jan's desk. I gather up my new, but quickly expanding, file on Bobby Jackson for review this evening and head for the gym.

My jersey is completely soaked. I feel the sweat roll down my forehead, watch it drop from my nose. I am sitting on the first row of bleachers, my elbows resting on my knees, my head bent, looking at the floor. God, am I out of shape! A couple of half-court basketball games and I'm sucking air.

For years I have exercised vigorously and regularly, which has tended to compensate for the fact that I eat and drink pretty much what I want. This formula, however, is no longer working, which is no surprise given the incredible amount of alcohol I have consumed in the last several weeks. I just can't seem to get rid of the poison quick enough. I tell myself that I just need to work harder, cut back on the booze a bit, lose a few of these extra pounds I have recently acquired. My little voice tells me, though, that it is not as simple as a lapse of self-discipline, that there is a much stronger demon latched onto my soul. But the voice is faint, a distant radio signal. I ignore it.

The First Baptist Church sits on an entire city block, its fitness center taking up half of it. Besides the gym, there are racquetball courts, pool tables, a swimming pool, and a weight room. I have been coming here for years, ever since I started with the state attorney's office. From about 4:30 P.M. on each weekday, the center opens the gym for pickup games. It's a great way to unwind while the rush hour traffic trudges along outside.

Among the regulars there is a kindred spirit of sorts, a basis for a few friendships that extend beyond the court. But mostly, it is group therapy, all of us using each other to get rid of frustrations and stresses that have built up during the day. There is nothing quite like the reckless abandon of several large male animals of questionable co-ordination charging in and up for a rebound. There are some, of course, who are very good players, those who have a touch of artistry. For most of us, however, it is a sanctioned, civilized outlet for aggressive behavior.

It has been three weeks since I have played ball. The last time I was here things had not gone well. In fact, it had been a bad day all around—the day after I'd been served with Beth's divorce petition. I had a terrible hangover and was deeply depressed. But I knew I needed to maintain control, act as normal as possible. I went to work as usual. Didn't say anything to Paul or the others about what had happened, and at the end of a pretty bad day, thought a few games of basketball might makes things better.

But, as Murphy's Law would dictate, I couldn't seem to do anything right. I missed easy shots, threw the ball away, getting more and more frustrated. The guy who was guarding me, John Henry, unwittingly made a serious error in judgment when he decided to take a charge as I drove for the basket. I saw him clearly planted, had time to stop or go around, but I just didn't want to. I wanted to run right over him as hard and as fast as I could. And I did.

When John called me for the foul, I went berserk, threw the ball directly into his face as hard as I could. As it had been all day, however, my aim was not all that good and I only grazed the top of his head. But my intent had been clear, and John quickly came toward me, bowed up.

I knew John didn't intend to harm me. I knew he would hit me only in self defense. But, I swung hard with my fist toward his face. Given my percentage that day, I should've known better. I missed cleanly and he popped me good, right in the nose.

The other guys separated us before any real damage could be done. The director of the center had witnessed the entire incident and knew who was to blame; nevertheless, he brought both of us into his office, like we were school children and he the principal. It was not, he had told us, the kind of Christian behavior that was expected at the center. We had both agreed, heads down, eyes on the floor, looking and feeling guilty. I started to explain about Beth, the divorce, but it wasn't any of their business. And, besides, it wasn't really the point here. I did apologize, sincerely, to John, and he graciously accepted.

I was put on a probation of sorts as a result of my outburst. Still, though I was permitted to play ball, I had not felt like coming back. Instead, I had done a little jogging, some swimming, worked with the weights a bit, and done a lot more drinking. Now, despite my fatigue and frustration, I realize how much I have missed this particular outlet.

"Hey, Teddy Bear." The familiar voice, strong north Florida backwoods accent, comes from my side. I look up to see Albert "Bert" Murphy just inside the gym door. He is dressed in street clothes, duffel bag slung over his shoulder, wide smile spread across his face. Bert is ruggedly handsome with short, light brown hair which never seems to be out of place, a strong, chiseled face and the body of a weight lifter. His posture and movements suggest both power and quickness.

"Hey, Bert. Long time no see. You coming or going?"

"Comin'. Looks like you've just about gone, though," he says. He gives me that combination look of sympathy and righteous smugness that is the province of the well-conditioned athlete.

"Man, I'm dying."

"I know I ain't seen ya up here much lately. What, too busy makin' the big bucks?"

He probably knows about Beth and the divorce, the fight with John Henry. Bert Murphy, private eye extraordinaire, seems to know just about everything that goes on in this town. It's uncanny and has helped to create a reputation that makes him a sought-after investigator.

If he does know, though, he doesn't let on, so I don't either.

"Yeah, right. You're the one making the big bucks. I saw you the other day in your new toy, didn't I? What is it, a sixty-seven?"

"Very good. You know your Vettes. But, Teddy Bear, this ain't no toy, son. This is an investment. Everything's original. All the numbers match. It's got a four-twenty-seven engine, knock-offs, a.c., power everything. It's got the original paint, twenty-seven thousand original miles. I only drive it to keep it happy."

"What is that, four now?"

"Three. I've got the fifty-seven fuely, and the seventy sportster. I got rid of the sixty-three split-window coupe."

"You want to give me the test drive now or later?"

"Well, it'll have to be later, 'cause I'm drivin' the El today." The "El" was a 1968 El Camino which was Bert's primary vehicle.

"You'd better hurry if you want to get some ball in today."

"Nah, I'm just gonna pump some. By the way, I hear you're gonna be representin' Bobby Jackson in that murder case."

He startles me. "Yeah, I just got appointed yesterday. How'd you find out so quickly?"

"It's my job to find out things, Teddy Bear—and I'm real good at my job." He gives me a big grin, like he's a little embarrassed to be stating such a simple truth. "That's why you're gonna want me on this case."

"Right, maybe you weren't listening. I said I got appointed on the case, as in low budget, state-rate pay and expenses. I can probably get court approval for an investigator, but it's not going to be a big budget. I know what you charge, Bert."

"Hey, listen, I'll give you a break, charge the state rate. I like you. I even like B.J. I bonded him out before. Been talkin' to his family. Maybe you can get him a bail that's reasonable, huh? Besides, it'll be good exposure. This is gonna be a big case, bro."

"Well, if you're willing . . ." I am not sure why I hesitate. As they say, never look a gift horse in the mouth. "Check with Jan and get a copy of what we have. Do some preliminary background stuff and let's meet in the next couple of days. You can also check with his family and prep them for a bail hearing. I'm going to shoot for next Monday. Okay?"

"Gotcha. I'll call." He gives me a mock salute.

"Okay, Bert. Thanks."

"No, thank *you*. This should be interesting." And with that, he backs out of the door and is gone.

I watch the game a couple more minutes and then head for the showers. I stop by the weight room on the way to mention a couple of things to Bert, but he's not there. Nor is he in the locker room. Strange. Must have had a very quick workout, or maybe changed his mind. Oh well, it could wait.

It's a little after 7:00 P.M. when I step out into the parking lot and a good ten degrees cooler than when I arrived an hour and a half ago. The shower has cooled me down a bit, but it's still unusually hot and humid. I turn the car air conditioner on high and head for my home away from home, the Sunset Motor Inn. I pass a couple of familiar bars on my way and congratulate myself that I don't stop. I just told myself that I needed to cut back and, besides, I got too much work to do. I have several files with me to review. As it turns out, however, my forbearance is short-lived. After a sandwich and a beer at home, I put my files aside, watch an old movie on TV, and end up drinking half a bottle of tequila. Olé.

FIVE

Friday—July 12th

I polish off my second beer, look at my watch—7:20 P.M.—pull out the message slip and read it again to be sure. "Mr. Murphy called—Will meet you at Oasis at 7:00." I am irritated that Bert is keeping me waiting, but the beer and the homey atmosphere of the oyster bar are beginning to have a calming effect.

The Oasis is almost a caricature of the north Florida oyster bar, complete with dingy rubber tile floor and obligatory fish netting on the painted concrete block walls. There is absolutely, positively no ventilation. Clouds of cigarette smoke hang in the air above a respectable crowd for a week night, mostly blue collar. Many of them are regulars, judging by the loud and friendly banter between them and the proprietors. Over in the corner a young woman in tight jeans leans over the pool table to make a shot, and I allow myself a brief lustful thought.

The waitress comes over when I catch her eye. She is a hard-looking middle-aged woman wearing a pair of very faded jeans and a royal blue T-shirt which has emblazoned in large letters on the front "I Eat 'Em Raw" with the name of the establishment written below it.

"Another long neck?"

"Yeah. Better give me a dozen oysters too."

The woman grunts her acknowledgment and quickly takes off for another table.

I find myself singing along quietly to the country number that is coming out of the jukebox just a little too loud. I realize that I am beginning to enjoy myself, so lost in my thoughts that I don't even notice Bert until he is right at the table.

"Hey, Teddy Bear. Sorry to keep ya waitin'."

"Don't worry about it. I'm sure the information you've got will make it all worthwhile. Right?"

"Well, it's not bad for a start." He pulls out a chair and sits across from me, placing a file in front of him on the table.

"What have you got?"

He lays a thick legal file on the table in front of me. "Some bedtime readin' for ya. What ya got here are copies of all the police reports and investigative summaries, to date, medical examiner's preliminary reports, some photos, and some notes from my interviews."

"Good. Now, help me read between the lines."

"Okay. As you already know, death was from multiple stab wounds to the neck and chest area—seventeen to be exact. As you might imagine, there was blood everywhere in the kitchen, which is where she was attacked. Looks like her attacker stabbed her first in the back. Also looks like she knew the perp. There were no signs of forced entry or even much of a struggle. She must have known the guy. And it was certainly a guy—the force of the blows was tremendous. This dude was either really pissed-off, real scared, or maybe both—or maybe he's a psycho."

Bert is looking at me as if he expects a response. An image rushes at me like a freight train, but I step aside.

"The probable cause affidavit said they found a knife in the bushes close to the house. Have they matched it as the murder weapon?" I ask, discreetly wiping the beads of sweat off my forehead, willing the heartbeat to slow down.

"The test results aren't back yet, but it's a pretty safe bet. The medical examiner figures it was a knife with a blade eight to ten inches, single edge, probably a butcher knife. It matches a cutlery set from the victim's kitchen. It would be too coincidental to find a knife with blood on it that close to the house and it not be the murder weapon."

"Any prints on the knife?"

"Nothing."

"Good. A jury will wonder why Bobby's prints are not on the murder weapon."

"Looks like she let him in the back door, which is right next to the kitchen. Then, for some reason, she turned away to walk toward the den, and pow!—right in the back. She was probably stabbed at least a couple more times before she could turn around. There were numerous lacerations on her arms, so she was probably trying to defend herself. She was probably too shocked and too weak to put up much resistance—and she had a powerful attacker."

I notice how Bert seems to lose his redneck speech patterns when he wants.

"Any evidence of theft, ransacking the place?"

"It's hard to tell—don't know what was there—but it looks like her purse was emptied, some jewelry, and a camera. There were signs of someone going through the house, but it was not your typical burglary. There was no theft of the TV, VCR, stereo. The theory downtown is that the victim and our boy get into an argument. He loses control, whacks her, and then tries to make it look like a burglary."

"But isn't that consistent with a thwarted attempt—or a rushed or bungled burglary? Wouldn't he be scared enough to try to get out quick, take the easy stuff?"

"You're the lawyer, pal. And I can hear those gears clickin' away all the way from over here. Yeah, Counselor, it could've gone down that way. On the other hand, people usually don't let their burglars in the house, knowingly."

"That's right. Not knowingly. Suppose the guy just asked to use the phone. Maybe it was something to do with a story she was working on. Or maybe there was no forced entry because she left her door unlocked." That would be like Patty, I think. It was not that she was so trusting or naive, just careless, even reckless at times. It was like she enjoyed tempting fate. I think that had been part of the allure for me.

"Yeah, he slips in the unlocked door; she comes into the kitchen, surprising both of them. She turns to run; he panics, grabs the knife off the kitchen counter, and then, boom, he does her. Is this what you had in mind?" Bert looks at me, raises his eyebrows.

"Yeah, that works. Then, see, the guy's in a hurry. He doesn't know if the neighbors have heard her screams, but he takes only a couple of things real quick and runs out the door, dropping the murder weapon along the way. The guy's probably black, similar in build to Jackson, hence the identification, mistakenly, of him running from the house."

Bert takes a cracker, puts one of my oysters on it. "Don't mind if I do."

"Help yourself. So what do you think?"

He puts a dab of hot sauce on it and takes the oyster down in one gulp. "Okay, I'm following you, but tell me, where in this sequence of events does he fuck her?"

"What?"

"Yeah, the medical examiner says the woman had sexual intercourse shortly before her death. Doesn't appear to have been forced either."

"Shit. How much shortly before her death? Twenty minutes, two hours? What?"

"The M.E. can't say for sure, but certainly no more than an hour, two at the most."

I digest these new facts, thinking out loud. "It certainly makes the botched burglary theory a little less plausible. Of course, if her assailant raped her at knifepoint, there would be no physical evidence to prove it had been forced. The man sees her through the window. He tries the door. It's not locked. He sneaks in, surprises Patty, puts a knife to her throat, undresses her. She would not have resisted, trying to keep her attacker calm."

"There's another problem with the stranger-burglary scenario." Bert gulps down another oyster. "The victim very clearly was wearing clothes at the time she was stabbed. That means her attacker sneaks in, puts a knife to her throat, rapes her, lets her get dressed, and then stabs her to death." Bert looks at me with a look that says not a chance.

"Tell me, Bert. What was Patty Stiles wearing when she was killed?" I am looking off now, at the young lady playing pool whom I had admired earlier.

Bert searches through the file, quickly finding what he is looking for. "Yeah, here it is. Shorts, T-shirt, no shoes, no bra. Why? Do you think that's important?"

"Just curious." I look back at Bert, refocus. "Tell me what you found out about our victim. Background stuff."

"Patricia Alicia Stiles. Born and raised in Crestview, Florida. Average middle class family life. Went to college at the University of South Florida in Tampa, majored in journalism. Worked for a couple of years at the *St. Pete Times*, then went back to school to get her master's in journalism from FAMU. She ended up staying on as an instructor part-time, and also began freelancing for the *Tallahassee Times-Union* a few years ago. I haven't had a chance to talk with a lot of people, but from what I can gather, depending on who you do talk to, she was either a queen bitch with no ethics who would do anything she needed to get ahead, or a talented and driven journalist who had to fight unnecessarily for the recognition she deserved. I'll keep digging though, if you want."

"Bert, I need somebody I can point the finger at in this, besides B.J., of course. We need to find out everything we can about Patty Stiles. Her friends, her work, social life, her enemies, anything that might lead us to someone who had a motive, and an opportunity, to have committed this murder. Someone who does not have an alibi."

Bert waves for the waitress, takes another one of my oysters. He doesn't look my way. "Maybe I should start with you then."

"What do you mean?" Maybe I say it too quickly.

"I understand that you were friendly with Ms. Stiles yourself. Maybe you can save me some time."

Bert's half-statement, half-question, sounds both innocent and accusing—I can't tell which is meant. His eyes never leave the oyster. I begin to wonder if having Bert Murphy on this case is such a good idea. "Well, I did represent her in her divorce about a year ago." A slight hesitation. "And I always try to be friendly with my clients if I can. I did get to know her a bit during that time and I have my impressions, but I'd rather not bias your independent investigation and evaluation."

There's no way to tell, looking into Bert's face, how much he really knows. This is how the guilty always end up confessing, I think. But I've played a bit of poker myself. "It might be useful, though, for you to look through our file on that divorce. There's probably a good bit of background information which might save you some time. And, speaking of her divorce case, that might be a good place for you to start looking for suspects. Her ex-husband is a real prick. He was physically abusive to her, and he ignored Judge Cotten's restraining order one time too many. He is a real vindictive S.O.B. I think a jury might believe he could be capable of the kind of cowardly, vicious attack that happened in this case. You should check him out for sure. Maybe he doesn't have an alibi for the night of the murder."

"Okay. Anything else you can tell me about her? What kind of story she was working on at the time, who she might have been seeing—that sort of thing?" He looks at me sideways. Was he still testing me?

"No, I have no idea. I don't think I've seen her since her divorce was final." The lie is instinctive, automatic. What does he know? Bert shrugs at my response, but I still can't read him. Somewhere I hear the faint sounds of warning bells ringing again. "All right, so, Bert, see what you can find out at the college and at the newspaper. As you have already concluded, she was not the type to avoid confrontation, so I suspect you'll find at least a couple of good alternative suspects at one or both of those places."

Bert points an imaginary gun at me and shoots. "You got it. When ya want to get back together?"

"Well, let's do it in two or three days, or sooner if you find out something significant. Also, I'm going to file a request to inspect the murder scene. That'll give us a chance to look through some of her stuff. I'll let you know for sure if and when I go so you can help."

"Okay."

"I'll set the motion same time as the bail hearing."

"Maybe I'll come—see you in action—might even get some bond business."

"I don't think I'd hold my breath. If Rowe does set bond, it's likely to be pretty high."

We stay awhile longer, drinking beer and eating oysters, shoot a few games of pool and talk about more pleasant subjects. Despite my partner's misgivings, I get along pretty well with Bert, who is a few years older. I've known him for several years, when he used to do work with the public defender's office, and we played a couple of seasons of city league flag football together. I realize, though, that I don't know much about Bert Murphy, other than on a superficial level. I also realize that most people would say the same about me. With Bert's encouragement, I have a few more beers than I should. At about 9:30 P.M., we walk out together.

"I see you got that new Vette tonight," I say, nodding toward the early model Corvette roadster parked away from the other cars. It's fire-engine red with a black top and is immaculate. All of Bert's cars are immaculate, as are his clothes, and everything else about him, far as I can tell. "How's it running?"

"Fast as ever, and just as thirsty," he says with a quick grin, obviously pleased that I have taken an interest. "Want that test ride now?"

"Nah, I better get on home."

I remember Bert once told me that perception is reality. He liked the lines from one of Jackson Browne's tunes:

Of all the times that I've been burned,
You'd think by now I'd learned
That it's who you look like not who you are.

Looking the part, to Bert Murphy, was an essential part of his business.

But the image was not just an illusion. Bits and pieces of Bert's story I had gotten from him over a few beers after flag football games, the rest from mutual friends. He had been a rough-and-tumble sort of guy since youth league football, where he delivered punishing tackles as a ninety-pound linebacker, developing a ferocity that made coaches salivate. He excelled in all sports in high school, but it was his reckless abandon as a linebacker that earned him the nickname "Maniac Murphy." It also earned him a football scholarship to FSU.

Everybody had been stunned when Bert, right after graduation from high school, joined the army. I think he had heard some patriotic plug by a recruiter and decided that duty required him to put aside his college education and football for a more important cause. This, of course, was during a time when there was a good bit of antiwar sentiment in town. But even the gung-ho types were a little unsettled by the fact that he would give up a chance to play college football.

Getting drafted was one thing because you were expected do your duty if called. But to volunteer? College football was a dream that should not be denied. Even the flag wavers, I think, knew deep inside that America was not threatened in Vietnam, that we had not made a good decision there. And, by God, priorities need to be fixed.

I suspect that Bert probably came to the same conclusion, had seen his folly, early on in his army career. He would never have admitted it, though, and certainly not intentionally shown it.

On his second tour he took some shrapnel in the leg and was discharged from the service in 1971. Though he still had pretty good mobility, his chance of playing pro ball, or even college, ended. Vietnam changed him, of course, as it did many others. The quick, natural smile was still there, but now it came from somewhere other than his heart.

A career in law enforcement seemed a natural for Bert. He quickly advanced from patrol officer to detective, first in property crimes and then in the crimes against persons division, assaults, batteries, homicides, rapes. In the early 1980s he became an undercover investigator for vice, and made a record number of drug busts in the mid-eighties. Then he had gone out on his own and had done pretty well for himself. I went to his house once for a Christmas party. It is an old English-style stone house located on thirty acres fronting the Wakulla River—not ostentatious, but it speaks loudly enough of prosperity, as do his vintage Corvettes.

I watch now as Bert eases one of those vintage Corvettes into traffic and punches it down the road, acknowledging to myself a bit of envy as I get in behind the wheel of my Honda Accord.

It takes only a short distance down Capital Circle for me to realize that I am really not in a condition to be behind the wheel of any car, not even my drab and dowdy Accord. I can't remember how many beers I've had. Maybe I should go back, call a cab. Maybe just pull into the 7-11, have some coffee, and sit for a while. I don't seriously consider these options, however—too much trouble. I can make it.

Just after I've made my decision I see a reason for having second thoughts. The police car is parked at the BP Station on the corner of Capital Circle and the Apalachee Parkway. It is a sight that makes me instantly nervous, guilty. As a reflex, I let off the gas, look at the speedometer, try to make sure my car is traveling straight in its lane. I look in the rearview mirror as I pass, to make sure I'm not being followed. The police car remains parked. I still watch closely in the rearview mirror, though, until both the car and the station are out of sight. I relax, but only a little, and drive as carefully as I can back to my motel room.

Once there, I am tired but too keyed up to go to bed. I grab another beer from the refrigerator, turn on the TV for some background noise, and pull out the file folder which Bert has given me.

I skim quickly through the paperwork at first, amazed at how much has been generated in such a short time. The investigative report of Detective Randy Powell is very thorough: reports from the first officer on the scene; interviews with neighbors; summaries of efforts taken to obtain samples of blood, hair, semen; fingerprint comparisons; a notation that a small amount of marijuana and cocaine were found. I give the autopsy report a quick glance: several puncture wounds in the chest area, punctured lung, heart; approximate time of death; evidence of sexual intercourse; blood type. I put it aside for later review.

Once I have gone through all of the documents, I begin again, reading more slowly, carefully. Two more empty beer bottles mark the time. Despite the material, I feel myself getting sleepier, ready to nod off. I am looking at one particular photograph, a close-up of Patty's face.

A beautiful face, full of life. She is in a sailboat, my sailboat. The sun gleams off her auburn hair. She is wearing a bikini top and cutoff jeans. I look at her face again. She is smiling, now laughing, a playful laugh at first. Now it is contemptuous, jeering, a mocking smile. And now the face registers apprehension. She hasn't seen him pick up the knife from the kitchen counter but she senses his rage. Apprehension turns to shock, then surprise, then fear as he steps toward her, raising the knife. She is in a blind panic now as she realizes what is going to happen. She turns and begins to run, but it is too late. The man brings the knife down with all his might. There is a dull thud as the blade plunges to the hilt right between her shoulder blades. Stunned, shocked, she tries again to run, but he grabs her by the wrist, plunging the knife again into the top of her shoulder. He flings her around and plunges the knife into her chest. Her initial screams are now muffled. Her lungs begin to fill with blood. Her eyes reflect terror, registering the knowledge that her mind, in its stress, refuses to accept—that she is going to die a violent, cruel, and painful death. She puts up her arm in a futile attempt to block the blows that continue after she has dropped to her knees and now lies on the floor. He plunges the knife in again and again. Helpless now, her strength and will gone, her life quietly ebbing, she can feel the warm, sticky blood spurting from her many wounds. She has a vague, blurred perception of him grabbing her by the hair and pulling her head back, placing the blade of the knife to her throat, and she gurgles her last futile protest. . . .

I wake abruptly, breathing quickly, sweat running down my forehead. I look up at my hand, somehow expecting to see a butcher knife. Then I realize where I am, see the file on the floor next to my chair, see the empty beer bottles on the coffee table. David Letterman is having fun with somebody on the television. I sit there for several seconds, and finally my breathing becomes normal. There is something about the dream that doesn't seem right. I begin searching through the file again. Bert had said nothing about Patty's throat being cut, and I can't remember reading it. I pull out the autopsy report, begin reading quickly. On the third page I find it, a description of a laceration of approximately four centimeters in length and one centimeter in depth directly beneath the chin. That explains it, then, I think. I must have read it earlier and just not made a note of it. "Yeah, that must be it."

I say this last sentence aloud, trying to sound more convincing to myself, perhaps. But as I get up slowly out of the chair, turn out the light, then the TV, a vague sense of unease lingers.

SIX

Tuesday—July 16th

There must be something wrong with the air conditioning. I loosen my tie, roll up my shirt sleeves. My sport coat is already draped across the back of my chair. My face feels flushed, and, feeling the dampness under my arms, I am conscious of the odor there. The air does not seem to be circulating at all.

I look at the others seated around the table in the small, windowless room. They seem unaffected, at ease in this stuffiness. The court reporter sits erect, but comfortably, her fingers poised over the keys of her stenographic instrument. My lawyer, Denise Wilkerson, is dressed casually in black jeans, a black and green plaid long-sleeve shirt, and cowboy boots. She is leaning back in her chair as if it were a La-Z-Boy recliner, feet propped up on another chair. Although I detect concern, annoyance even, in her face, I suspect it has nothing to do with the temperature in the room. It has everything to do with the fact that I was ten minutes late for my deposition—and because she can smell the beer on my breath.

And then there is Don Carey, my wife's attorney. "Dandy Don" has worn a dark blue, expensive-looking, double-breasted suit. His white cotton shirt is accented by a hand-painted silk tie which matches the handkerchief tucked neatly in his coat pocket. He has likewise removed his coat and folded it carefully on the chair beside him, but it is more a gesture of informality, of false congeniality, than an accommodation to the temperature in the room. He has a slight paunch but otherwise is a trim man of about forty-five. The only hair on his head is on the sides and is cut very short, making his nose and his ears appear too large for his face. I see not a trace of perspiration anywhere. He presents an image of unflappable politeness which, once you get to know him, is as transparent as glass.

Beth is not here. As a rule the opposing party is not. Maybe on *L.A. Law*, but not in the real world. Too easy for tempers to flare, for feelings to be hurt, for positions to become polarized. Still, I had hoped she would come.

We have been going now for about fifteen minutes, and Carey has been asking perfunctory, background questions. He is looking in my direction and his lips are moving again, but I cannot quite make out the words. I am thinking of the lawyer joke—"Question: How can you tell when a lawyer is lying? Answer: His lips move." I smile to myself.

"Mr. Stevens?"

"What? Oh, sorry. Would you repeat the question, please?"

Carey gives me an accommodating half-smile. He looks at the court reporter. "Sure. Kathleen, would you read back the last question for Mr. Stevens?"

The court reporter begins to search for the exact spot on her notes. It would have been easier, of course, for Carey just to repeat the question himself, but having the court reporter read it back is so much more formal. That is the way he prefers it. It's part of the game. Denise and I have played this little game too by insisting that the deposition take place in a "neutral" site rather than at Carey's office, which would have been the usual custom and practice.

I have added another dimension by arriving ten minutes late. Fifteen minutes late would have been too much. The deposition would have been canceled and I would be required to pay the costs. But, ten minutes is within the unwritten grace period—late enough to piss off the other side but not late enough to justify canceling the deposition.

The court reporter, having found her place and adjusted herself in her seat, reads back the question. "Mr. Stevens, have you been drinking alcoholic beverages prior to this deposition?"

"I'm not sure how to answer that question. Do you mean have I consumed alcoholic beverages at any time prior to this deposition?"

"I think you know what I mean." Carey smiles that half-smile again, patronizing, like a wise parent dealing with his smart-ass kid. "Let me rephrase the question for you, though. Have you had an alcoholic beverage within the last two hours?"

"No." The lie is instantaneous, amazingly easy. What is strange is I'm not sure why I have not just admitted it. It's really not that big of a deal. But now I am committed.

Carey looks at me in disbelief, looks over at Denise. She is looking up at the ceiling as if thinking of something else. Maybe she is. My wife's lawyer tries again. "Have you had any alcoholic beverage of any kind at any time today?"

"Well, if you mean after midnight, probably so, because I was up late working last night and I might have had a nightcap sometime in the early morning hours, which would be today."

The smile is still there. Patiently, he continues. "Let me ask you then, Mr. Stevens, what time did you go to sleep last night, or this morning?"

I am thinking maybe my lawyer will object to this question, even the whole line of questioning, as being irrelevant. The fact that I may or may not have had something to drink at lunch could not have any real bearing on these proceedings, unless it was suggested that I am now so drunk that I can't give a straight answer. But I look over at Denise, and it appears that she is content to let me dangle out here all by myself on this one. "I'm not sure what time I went to sleep." This is the truth.

"Approximately."

"Like I said, I'm not sure. I wouldn't want to guess. I know you like to be precise."

Carey persists, ignoring the little dig. "Let's not have you guess then. If it's not taxing your memory too much, let's try something a little more recent. It is now approximately 2:00 P.M. We began this deposition approximately fifteen minutes ago. Assuming that you are not sleepwalking, it is safe to assume that sometime prior to this deposition beginning you had a period of sleep or rest. Is that correct?"

"That is correct."

"Then, have you consumed any alcoholic beverages from the time that you awakened or arose from your sleep or rest, and up to the time that this deposition began?" His smug look tells me that he thinks he has me now, no place to go.

But I really cannot allow him to have the satisfaction. "No, I have not."

The half-smile has been replaced by a disapproving frown. "Let the record reflect that Mr. Stevens has the smell of alcohol on his breath, that his eyes are bloodshot, that he seems to have difficulty focusing on questions put to him. Furthermore . . ."

I am about to respond, but my attorney belatedly comes to my rescue. "Now wait a minute, Don. All the record is going to reflect is that you just gave us your own self-righteous, self-serving opinion. And, unless you plan to be a witness in this case, in which event you would, of course, have to withdraw as attorney for Mrs. Stevens, your opinion is irrelevant, immaterial, and certainly inadmissible, and will never become any part of the record in this case."

Carey looks toward the court reporter, who holds her hand up as if to say, don't look at me, I'm staying out of this.

"Furthermore," Denise continues, "in response to your premature, unsubstantiated accusation, I would note that, one, alcohol has no odor, so Mr. Stevens' breath could not possibly smell of alcohol. Two, if you are suggesting that there is a smell of an alcoholic beverage on my client's breath, then certainly you know that there are several varieties of nonalcoholic beer that produce the identical smell or odor of regular beer. Similarly, if you think that Mr. Stevens' eyes appear bloodshot, that could very well be due to the fact that he was up late last night and that he suffers from allergies."

I don't, of course, have allergies, but it sounds good. Denise is in a pretty good swing here now, and I am enjoying it as I watch Dandy Don squirm a little bit. "And finally, as to the suggestion that my client's mental faculties have somehow been impaired by alcohol, the last series of questions and answers, which *is* part of the record, will, to the objective reader, dispel any doubts along those lines in my client's favor. Now, we've wasted enough time on this matter, and I'm directing my client not to answer any further questions along this line."

Denise has been leaning forward on her elbows. She now leans back again in her chair, arms crossed, looking appropriately indignant. The only thing that I could have added would be something like, "yeah, asshole," so I say nothing.

Carey appears relatively unmoved by the rebuff. He says something to the effect that the record will show what the record will show, but he moves on, the half-smile back. For the next hour and a half, my wife's lawyer, with methodical, monotonous precision and detail, goes over every conceivable question that could be even remotely relevant to the case, and many more that are not even close. The rules of discovery in Florida are very liberal, allowing each side to "discover" from the other side, through depositions, written interrogatories, requests for production, any fact or piece of information which might lead to admissible evidence. Thus, lawyers are free to go on a "fishing expedition" that would be highly inappropriate in the actual court proceeding. The intent, which is to avoid trial by ambush, is laudable. However, it has led to abuses which lawyers like Dandy Don have become quite adept at taking advantage of.

One of his favorite tools is time. His unacknowledged motto is: Never do in thirty minutes what you can take three hours to do, and three days would be better still. Ask a lot of questions, ask them again in different ways at different times, try to get an inconsistent answer, lull them into a false sense of security, bore them, then slip in a zinger.

I have made him work, however, for every answer. It has been frustrating for him, I think. Though he tries not to show it, I can tell. The permanent half-smile has become a thin line.

The down side is that we might be here for a long time. I believe this is becoming clear to my lawyer. "Excuse me, Don. How much longer do you think this is gonna take?" Denise is looking bored.

"That depends to a certain degree on your client," he says nonchalantly. "I had planned on perhaps two hours, but,"—here he sighs rather heavily, dramatically, looking at his watch—"I'm afraid I still have quite a few questions, and it may take some time. Would you like to take a break?"

"Let's." Denise rises and immediately heads for the door, motioning for me to follow. I do. She stops to get a soda from the machine, offers me one. I decline. She heads toward the patio area adjacent to the snack bar. I follow, silently, admiring the way her jeans fit. Denise is a few years older than I am, maybe in her early forties, an occasional gray hair standing out here and there in an otherwise thick, jet-black head of hair, layered, and falling just below her shoulders. She's about five foot five, a little overweight, but she carries it well. She walks with authority. She wears no makeup, rarely wears a dress, and makes no real effort to make herself attractive—but she is one of those natural beauties with an earthy sexuality that does not require superficial help. There is a look and sound to her that hints of rural north Florida, though she is originally from Orlando. She also has a certain irreverence that some men find uncomfortable. I like it. It's one of the reasons I have asked her to represent me.

I feel pretty sure that she is somewhat attracted to me as well. But while my control may be suspect, hers is not. She would not act on such feelings—not while I am married—not while I am her client. Still, I can dream.

Denise stops at a table in the corner away from the few others there on the patio. She takes a cigarette from the pack in her shirt pocket, lights it, takes a deep drag, exhales, and looks out over the railing onto the courtyard.

I break the silence. "How's it going, you think?"

Denise shakes her head, slowly. "Ted, Ted, Ted." She is still looking out over the railing.

"What?" I try to sound innocent.

"I'm going to tell you something that I'm afraid you're likely to hear from more people, more often, in the near future." She turns now slowly, to meet me eye to eye, take my full measure. "You are about to fuck up really good."

Somehow, I am expecting more, but I guess that just about says it all. I think I know what she means, but I ask her anyway.

"Either you are too liquored up to know it, or too sorry to care, I don't know which, but I don't want to be around when the shit hits the fan."

"What'd I do, what'd I do?" Of course I knew what I had done, and I thought I didn't care, but now the anger and the disgust that I sense in my lawyer's voice, in her demeanor, is beginning to bring on a panic in me.

"What did you do? Now, let's see. One of the allegations in your wife's petition is that you drink too much. There's a lot of other good stuff, mind you, but there's no question that the premise is that things get worse because you get drunk. You do crazy things. It makes you unfit to have even unsupervised visitation with your child, so your wife alleges. So, what do you do? You show up to your own deposition with beer on your breath." She is shaking her head again. "Then, you lie about it—under oath." She lets the enormity of those words soak in for a minute. "Of course, you are ten minutes late to start with and you look and smell like you haven't had a bath for three days. You look like a damn wino in a suit. Not to mention the fact that you've already intentionally violated an injunction for protection issued in this case by having contact with your wife, probably drunk again."

Any elation, any pride, any satisfaction that I may have gotten from my semantic games with Don Carey has suddenly disappeared. I have clearly misread the situation.

Denise is not through yet. "And this game you're playing with Dandy Don in there. I got to admit it's been mildly amusing so far, but it's getting awfully damn boring. I do not want to be here all day. Besides, you know you're paying double for this time—once for me and once for him—so you're cutting your own throat here. I saved your ass in there, but there better not be a next time or I promise you, you will not have me as your lawyer."

I start to protest, perhaps say something I shouldn't. Remind her that I could get any number of lawyers willing to represent me, that I could represent myself and do as good a job as she's been doing. But, fortunately, I don't say something stupid. I know that she is right, so all I say is "Sorry, it won't happen again."

Denise, noticeably softer, says, "Okay, listen, Ted. I know this isn't any fun for you. But I've also known you long enough to know you're not the kind of guy to lose it all over a divorce." She looks at me intently for several seconds. My face remains impassive.

"Is there something else going on here? Something you're not telling me?" When I don't respond, she continues, "I do want to help you, Teddy, and you don't have to tell me anything you don't want to, but I swear to God, if you pull one more piece of crap trick or do some dumbass thing again, I'm out of it."

I nod. I smile. I think the smile unnerves her a little bit. "Okay, Denise, you're right. I haven't been the best of clients, and I don't blame you for being pissed. All right, I'll follow your direction from now on. You won't have any trouble with me. Listen, I need you to stay on this thing. I don't want to be switching horses in the middle of the stream. I really would like to see if I can't get back together with Beth. But, if not, see if you can't work out some settlement that's within reason. If I can't work it out, then I'd like to get it over with. But, whatever, you won't have any more trouble out of me."

My lawyer seems to be satisfied. Maybe sensing the upperhand, she adds, "Okay, then, the first thing, cut the booze out." She must see the panic, the alarm in my eyes, because she adds, "At least cut back. Don't be seen drinking in public or anywhere that's likely to get back to her or her lawyer. Especially, don't drink anytime when you're about to exercise visitation."

"Sure, no problem." Lying is becoming easier and easier.

She doesn't believe me; I can tell from her eyes—that same look of disgust mixed with pity that I have been noticing more recently in others. Well, the hell with her. The hell with them all. Anyway, I think she'll stay with me. I've given her just enough. In a bit, she'll be too deep into the case to withdraw. It would be too prejudicial to her client. Denise takes the last draw off her cigarette and puts it out in the ashtray on the table, and we head back inside.

When we reach the court reporter's room, she whispers briefly into Carey's ear just outside the doorway. He smiles his easy smile, and I think about changing my mind. I remember the story about how, a few years back, another lawyer, fed up with his antics, had hit Dandy Don right on the head with a large law book. I'm thinking once is not enough. But, I am tired anyway, weary, looking for a reason to get this over with.

Carey, however, is not so inclined. For the next three hours he takes me through every detail of my education, employment history, finances, as well as all of my perceived marital and parental shortcomings.

This is not unfamiliar territory for me, for I have taken countless depositions in divorce cases too, have asked many of the same questions. But the perspective is different as the litigant. Today the whole thing seems so dry, cold, matter-of-fact. Carey is like a pathologist at an autopsy, carefully and meticulously examining the corpse. No checking of vital signs. No diagnosis or evaluation of possible recovery. The only question being how to dispose of the body.

Carey is collecting the details of the marriage, but he is missing the essence, ignoring seven years of tangled emotions. Of course, questions having to do with emotions, with feelings, are never asked. They are "irrelevant." But as the lawyer plods along I ask them of myself.

Opposites attract—they just don't necessarily stay attracted. Beth liked my spontaneity, my impulsiveness, my irreverence for the establishment of which I was an integral part. I was drawn to her warmth, her steadfastness, orderliness, and her naive faith in all things conventional.

Those differences that seem at first so exciting or complementary of our own personalities, often become, over time, annoying characteristics and, sometimes, even a threat to our concepts of who we are. I think maybe I expected that the mixture of those differences would dissolve, or at least soften, into something weighted in my direction rather than Beth's. Could it be as simple as that? That we never come up to our mate's expectations?

If you asked Beth about it—I've tried but she won't sit down and talk things through—she'd probably say that my drinking is one of the main problems. I'd say she looks only at the surface of things, not underneath.

Fact is, I've always liked my booze—been a hard drinker since high school. It's not something I hid from my bride. But it wasn't until after we married that Beth became "concerned" about the amount I consumed.

At first the disapproval had been subtle—a raised eyebrow, a rhetorical question about how many drinks I'd had, a reminder that I was driving. After a while I would get the mini-lecture before we went out; she would insist on driving home, making a point to tell me in front of others that I was in no condition to do so. Often we would argue on the way home about how I had embarrassed her with some obnoxious comment or behavior. She pleaded, she cajoled, with no success.

Eventually, her comments became sarcastic, cruel. Ironically, they usually came after she had been drinking—she never was able to hold her liquor very well. "Maybe Dad was right, Ted." That was one of her frequent opening jabs.

"You're a loser and always will be—'cause you're afraid of success."

Another popular refrain was that I "loved my liquor more than I loved my family." And Beth has always been very big on family—hers anyway. She was on the phone constantly with her mother, insisting that we visit every holiday or other opportunity. She had been disappointed when I refused to consider relocating to her hometown of Panama City.

She had worked obsessively to achieve our own idyllic family setting. We had to have a "nice house in a nice neighborhood." We even had a white picket fence, by God, and the dog in the backyard. Never mind that it was more house than I could afford. "Daddy will loan us the down payment," she had said.

And she had played well the part of the stay-at-home nurturing mother and wife, giving new meaning to the term "domestic engineer." The house was always spotless. Meals were a gourmet treat. She loved to work in the yard, wearing that ridiculous large straw hat, producing some of the most beautiful landscaping in the neighborhood. I think I became very much a frustration for her—did not fit so neatly into the family picture she had painted of herself.

And then there was the disappointment, the concern, when the doctor explained some possible reasons for our inability to conceive a second child. There had been exams, tests, monitored ovulations and scheduled intercourse—but no pregnancy. Beth had suggested the alcohol was lowering my sperm count. She'd leave articles on the subject for me on my dresser. Our sex life became a mechanistic joke.

The more Beth nagged, the more I drank—and the less I cared. I was suffocating in her tidy, orderly world. And my resistance, my "irrational" behavior, was driving her nuts.

She was also extremely jealous, and suspicious. Infidelity, I knew, was unforgivable in her mind. She made that clear.

Of course, for me, one who likes sailing so close to the wind, the affair with Patty was inevitable.

I am thinking of this when Carey decides to broach the subject of marital fidelity. Have I ever been unfaithful to my wife? he asks me. He tries to slip it in toward the end, thinking we are too tired to notice. Denise, who has been lounging back again, suddenly comes to life, objects, instructs me not to answer.

"What objection could you have, Ms. Wilkerson, to that question, unless the answer would be yes?" His eyebrows go up on his forehead a full inch. He looks from me to Denise, to me again. Maybe this is when I should hit him.

"It's irrelevant and you know it. Now move on." Denise moves her hand in a dismissive gesture.

But Carey is not yet dissuaded. "I believe I have a right to inquire into any actions on the part of your client that may have adversely affected the parties' financial standings or dissipated any of their assets."

"Then ask that question, not whether he's had sexual relations with someone."

I look at my attorney, then at Dandy Don. "It's okay, Denise, I'll answer his question," I hear myself say. "I have been faithful to my wife since the day we were married. I have had no extramarital affairs, have engaged in no sexual relations with any woman other than my wife at any time after our marriage." Denise is rolling her eyes, her mouth open. She can't believe I have just volunteered such a statement. I can't either.

The expressions on the faces of both Denise and Carey make it clear that they don't believe this statement. The court reporter's face betrays nothing. Lies are perhaps too commonplace for her. If I were to get caught in a lie, it would be bad. But I won't. I know Beth suspects it. She accused me, but she had admitted she had no proof. I would already know it if she did.

Carey begins several follow-up questions naming specific people, but Denise cuts him off. "Look, he's already said he has had sex relations with no other woman. You don't need to name every woman in the city of Tallahassee. I don't think that's gonna refresh his memory. It ain't something you are likely to forget."

The court reporter stifles a smile. Carey sees the logic of it and smiles himself. "Yes, I suppose you're right. Well, that's all the questions I have for Mr. Stevens. Do you wish to waive the reading and signing of the deposition if it's transcribed?" A person whose deposition is taken has the right to read it and make notes of what he or she believes are errors, though they have no right to change the official transcript. Carey knows that we will not waive the reading and signing of the deposition and Denise says as much. Thankfully, the deposition is concluded.

I walk Denise back out to her car. She seems to have softened some toward me. She is conciliatory, sympathetic, offers to lend an ear. I ask her if she wants to get a beer. She frowns. I tell her I'm just kidding. She hits me on the arm, gets in her car and drives off.

By now it's almost 5:30 P.M. I have an hour before I'm supposed to pick up Annie for a brief visitation. I think that maybe I have time for one drink. God, I deserve it. I need it. What, do you have Alzheimer's, I say to myself? What did Denise just say? With a great deal of reluctance, with difficulty, but with some measure of pride, I put the thought of a trip to the closest bar out of my head. Instead, I go back to the office, freshen up, use the time to get a haircut and a shave, then go to see my daughter.

SEVEN

Thursday—July 18th

"Mr. Stevens, can we speak with you for a moment?"
Nancy Edwards, from Channel Eight News, has cornered
me as I enter the side door of the courthouse. She is standing directly in my path, a microphone in her hand, down
by her hip, like a gunfighter ready to draw. Her cameraman is back a few yards, already filming the encounter. My
first thought is that she looks much better on TV. Up close
she looks like a porcelain china doll, with red cheeks and
bright red lipstick in an otherwise very white face, framed
by jet-black, straight hair, curled under. Large blue eyes
look out from under long mascara-laden eyelashes. There
is no softness in these eyes. They betray the smile that she
offers me.

Paul has already gone in the front entrance of the courthouse, welcoming the opportunity to greet the press. He
had wanted me with him—the defense team he had said,
emphasizing *team*. I could have, I suppose, but, unlike Paul,
I've never liked all the attention, never been particularly
good at dealing with reporters. So I had balked, said I
didn't feel like any bullshit today, told him I might slip up
and say something dumb, shove somebody's microphone
up their ass.

I remember the time in the Faulkner rape case when the reporter quoted me, accurately, but out of context, and thus misleadingly. The headline read: "Defense Attorney: Victim Asked For It."

The newspaper's editorial board took me to task in that edition. The director of the Rape Crisis Center was one of several who ripped in to me in letters to the editor. Paul had come to my defense then with a letter of his own to the paper. I think that incident had come to mind for both of us this morning.

I am thinking about that now, as this woman reporter looks back at her cameraman to make sure that he has a clear view, one that is flattering to her, then turns, thrusts the microphone in my face and begins, "What will you be arguing this morning, Mr. Stevens?"

"I'm sorry. I need to go into the courtroom now. Maybe later."

"Just for a minute."

She is insistent. We are now inches apart. I can see the contact lens move on her left eye when she blinks.

"Sorry," I say again. "No."

She is reluctant to give up the advantage that she has over her colleagues. While everyone else has been waiting by the courtroom or on the front steps, she has guessed correctly that I might try to slip in a side door. But she has apparently picked up on my tone. She steps aside, decides on a different approach, and says, "Will you give me an interview after the hearing then?"

I keep walking, replying over my shoulder as she follows, "We'll see."

As I round the corner, the other reporters, milling around in front of the courtroom, spot us. Seeing Edwards, and believing that they have been scooped, they scramble and surround me like a pack of wild dogs, blocking my path again. They are all shouting questions at once. The mob mentality, the diffusion of responsibility, seems to embolden them. "Does your client have an alibi? Is race an issue in this case, Mr. Stevens? Have you ever handled a capital murder case before? Mr. Stevens, the State Attorney's Office says that your client and the victim were lovers. Is that correct?"

From the back of the crowd I hear one question that gets my attention. "Mr. Stevens, there are reports that you and the victim were quite close. Is that true?"

The tone is accusatory. The questioner has suggested an angle that the others apparently have not considered, as all other questioning stops and the reporters look anxiously at me for my reply. I had recognized the voice immediately, but my eyes now confirm that the questioner is Quentin Martin, hometown boy, reporter for the *Tallahassee Times-Union*. He is cut from the same mold as Patty Stiles, just more obnoxious and less talented. He is also the reporter who had quoted me out of context in the Faulkner case two years ago.

"And what reports are those, Marty?" I look him directly in the eye. My tone is meant to be sarcastic, but it doesn't faze him. He knows the rules. He gets to ask the questions—not me.

"Does it make you uncomfortable representing the man accused of killing someone you were so close to?" he asks, assuming somehow that I have answered his first question in the affirmative.

There are several ways to play this: emphatically deny that Patty Stiles and I had anything more than a professional relationship, which is the obvious implication of the question; acknowledge that we were friends, putting an innocent spin to it, say that I do not feel the least bit uncomfortable representing Bobby Jackson in this case because he is innocent. I reject both of these avenues. I have already given Quentin Martin more than I should have by acknowledging his question and responding. I turn away without saying more. The slight smile on my face is meant to convey to Martin and the others that the question, the subject matter, is too insignificant to justify an effort at reply. The questioning continues as I inch my way forward. It quickly becomes a buzz, with me repeating, "Not now, please," edging my way past them. One of the bailiffs takes pity on me and comes to my rescue, clearing a path for me. I enter the courtroom.

Paul and Tom Haley, the assistant state attorney, are standing inside the rail between the prosecution and defense tables, talking quietly. The volume of the murmuring in the courtroom decreases noticeably as the theatergoers recognize the entrance of one of the leading actors in this melodrama. My entrance has been trumpeted by the babble of the reporters which can be heard as the courtroom doors open and close.

The courtroom is filled to capacity. In addition to the court watchers, there are the reporters, their places reserved on the front rows. There are also lawyers from both the state attorney's office and the public defender's office, hoping to pick up a few pointers, or perhaps do some armchair quarterbacking.

I speak briefly with my partner and Tom. Paul briefs me on some of the stipulations concerning our motions. I then leave the two attorneys and take my seat beside my client. He is dressed in street clothes at my request. Always, at trial, the defense attorneys do not want the jury to see their clients dressed in prison garb and shackles. It is usually not considered important for pretrial hearings, but since this is a high-profile case, I have convinced the judge to allow Bobby to wear his street clothes at all court appearances where he may be photographed. To my surprise, the sheriff has even agreed that, at least while in the courtroom, my client will not have to wear the leg and ankle irons.

Seated at the defense table, Bobby looks like a young college student. I had thought about a business suit and a tie but that would have been overdoing it. Even now, he looks a bit too preppy. He acknowledges my presence with a nod. His posture, his mannerisms, are an appropriate mixture of confidence and anxiety, characteristics of a person who believes that the wrongness of the accusation against him will ultimately be shown. I watch his eyes dart around the courtroom and see that they also evidence the anger and frustration of a newly caged wild animal, tinged with the beginnings of despair. His focus now, his psychic energy, will be spent worrying about bail.

We talked yesterday, prepared for these hearings. I told him then that the state attorney had decided not to seek the death penalty. I was a little pissed that he had not been more happy, more grateful and appreciative of my efforts. I think he knew it had nothing to do with me, and my pretending it did just seemed stupid to him. That's what really pissed me off, I guess.

I follow his gaze around the courtroom where it comes to rest on his mother, sister, and preacher. I make eye contact with Bernice Jackson who gives me a slight nod and a slight smile. From the Reverend I get a slight nod of acknowledgment, but no smile. From the sister I get neither.

I met with them last night. The Reverend L. Lamar Paxton is the pastor of the Mount Zion AME Church, one of the largest black churches in Tallahassee, a major spiritual and political leader in the African-American community and a person who wields significant influence on the politics of this city. He is reputed to be a person who favors confrontational tactics, a "firebrand" as one deputy had described him to me. The man I met last night, however, appeared to be a very thoughtful and reflective individual, sincere in his professed intent to be of help to Bernice

Jackson, her son, and those who were trying to help him, which included me.

He and Bernice Jackson had come to my rescue when Bobby's younger sister, Shirley, had questioned my abilities, my sincerity, in her brother's defense. Not speaking directly to me she had commented, "This white ass ain't gonna do nothin' for Bobby." She had not liked the news, the truth, that it was unlikely that bond would be set for Bobby at this hearing.

Reverend Paxton jumped in her face with an authority that he appeared accustomed to exercising. "Don't you go bringing race into this thing, Shirley. Don't you insult your mother, Bobby, and me, and this lawyer. If you can't act civil, if you can't show some class, then you can stay out of this."

Shirley scowled at the preacher, looked at me with hateful eyes. She looked at her mother who sat quietly, passively, looking away from all of us. Then she got up and left the room in a huff.

Bernice Jackson is a strong woman, optimistic by nature. As she sits here now, in the courtroom, she knows that the chances are slim that Bobby will have bail, or if it is set, that she will be able to raise the money necessary to free him. She is a woman of faith, she told me last night, with Reverend Paxton by her side, nodding. She has faith in me she said.

"Mr. Stevens, I'm not a smart woman. I'm not an educated woman. But I do know people. And I know my son. I know my son is not a murderer. And now, after talking with you, I know that you can make the jury see that. God has chosen you, Mr. Stevens, for this task. He will provide. He always does." The Reverend Paxton had said an "amen" to that. I did not share her optimism, but I knew enough to go along with the program and said "amen" too. But instead of boosting my confidence, her faith has increased the pressure tenfold.

At precisely 10:00 A.M. the bailiff knocks loudly on the rear door of the courtroom. "All rise," the bailiff begins. Judge John Rowe walks briskly through the door and takes a seat on the bench before the bailiff can complete the announcement of his entrance. As usual, Rowe gets immediately down to business.

"State versus Jackson. Mr. Stevens, you have several motions scheduled. Let us begin with your motion to set bail."

"Yes, Your Honor. May it please the court."

I bring up the standard stuff, that my client is presumed to be innocent of the charge against him, that the state is not seeking the death penalty in the case, that the evidence is all circumstantial. Then I point out the facts that suggest that Bobby will not flee.

"Judge, my client has substantial roots in the community. He lives with his mother and sister. He has lived in Tallahassee for all of his twenty-eight years. He has had a steady job for over two years. His life is here. He will not leave while this murder charge is pending. He wants very much to face his accusers and put this behind him, and we need him out to help prepare his defense."

With the foundation laid, I talk money. "His family is of modest means, Judge. His ability, even with the assistance of his family, to post monetary bail is quite limited. If the amount of bail is not reasonable, it will be the same as no bail, and he will be incarcerated for months while the prosecution tries to patch up the holes in its case."

I proffer the testimony of the defendant's mother, Reverend Paxton, and Bobby's employer, but the prosecutor signals that such testimony will not be necessary. The state acknowledges, he says, the facts about Bobby's roots in the community. Rowe gives me a nod to acknowledge my argument, then turns his eyes toward Haley who has risen to his feet in anticipation.

Haley and I go back several years. We were in law school together and started with the state attorney's office at the same time. He started off, though, a better prosecutor than I would ever be.

I think it has something to do with perspective. One of the things I liked about being a prosecutor was the discretion you exercised in whether to prosecute a case. It was the opportunity, I thought, to do justice, however subjectively that term might be defined. Of course, I wanted to practice criminal law and had there not been a position available in the state attorney's office, I would have gladly worked the other side of the street.

Tom Haley, in contrast, would never have considered working with the public defender's office. He is of that breed of prosecutor that could never imagine working for the "dark forces." Some lawyers work for the state attorney because they know they will get a lot of trial experience. They work there for a few years and then move on to more lucrative positions in private practice. There are some, however, like Tom Haley, who are lifers. They come to their job not so much as a lawyer but as a law enforcement officer who happens to be licensed to practice law.

Haley had been, in fact, a former deputy sheriff. He had also been an MP in the Marines. He still has the erect bearing, the crewcut hairstyle of a Marine. There had never been any doubt, either by him or anyone else at law school, that he would end up where he is now. What he lacks in creativity, he makes up in passion and conviction. He is fair and scrupulous. He always plays by the rules. But he is a zealous advocate, a fierce competitor, who will use those rules as best he can to defeat you. I had mixed emotions when I saw that he had been assigned to the Jackson case.

"Your Honor," Haley begins, "the state agrees that Mr.

Jackson has lived in Tallahassee for his entire life, that his family is here, that he has the support of the pastor of the church he attends, and that he is presently employed. The state also acknowledges that it has determined not to seek the death penalty in this case. Notwithstanding that decision by our office, we do not wish in any way to minimize the seriousness of the charge. The state strenuously objects to the setting of any bail in this case.

"Mr. Jackson has been charged with the most serious offense that we have in a civilized society, the premeditated murder of another human being. This murder was particularly brutal. The victim was stabbed with a butcher knife approximately twenty times.

"This man," he says, pointing to Bobby Jackson, "knows that if he is convicted of this heinous crime, he will lose his freedom for the rest of his life. And, contrary to Mr. Stevens' suggestion, the evidence against Mr. Jackson is extremely strong. I submit to you that despite his ties to this community, there is no amount of monetary bail that will assure his presence if he is released.

"Contrary to his attorney's argument, Mr. Jackson does not wish to face his accusers. This fact he has already demonstrated.

"This man," Haley points again at my client, "this man, who his attorney says wants to face his accusers, was hiding in his closet when police officers came to arrest him." Tom looks accusingly at Bobby, pausing long enough for Rowe to consider the import of this fact.

"Your Honor, the law does not give this defendant the right to bail on this charge. It is within your discretion to deny it and we urge you to do so. Thank you."

I stand up, ready to pounce on the argument with more aggressiveness and enthusiasm than I feel. Haley's argument made a lot of sense to me and I thought it probably did to Rowe as well. I start by acknowledging the discretion of the court, implying that denying bail would be the easy ruling, but not the right one. Rowe bristles a bit at this but seems receptive. If he follows Haley's argument, I tell him, then nobody charged with first-degree murder would ever be entitled to bail. I argue a bit more about the weakness of the state's case, then specifically address the fact that Bobby was found hiding in the closet.

"It is true that at the time of Mr. Jackson's arrest, he was found hiding in the closet. We don't deny this. However, he was not hiding because he thought he was to be charged with murder. He was hiding because he knew there was a warrant for violation of probation on a misdemeanor possession of marijuana charge. It seems that Mr. Jackson had not paid the required supervisory fees. He was simply hoping to buy some time in order to raise the necessary funds required by his probation officer. He knew he was guilty of the violation of probation.

"In contrast, he does not admit that he is guilty of this murder charge. He vehemently denies it. He had no idea the police were going to charge him with murder. Now, I know that the state attorney's office is under a lot of pressure from the newspaper to get a conviction in this case where one of their reporters was killed—"

"I object, Your Honor." Haley is on his feet and around the table, looking alternatively at me and then Rowe. "I resent that. The state attorney's office does not prosecute people because of pressure from a newspaper or from anyone else."

Rowe looks over at Haley and says, softly, tiredly, "Mr. Haley, Mr. Stevens is not presenting testimony. There is no jury present. It is not necessary for you to object to statements he makes in his arguments—"

"But I resent the implication, Your Honor." Haley cuts Rowe off—a mistake, and he instantly realizes it as Rowe glares at him. "Sorry, Your Honor." Haley sits back down.

Rowe looks at me and inquires, "What figure did you have in mind, Mr. Stevens?"

I can hardly believe my ears. It is probably just for show but I am struggling to contain the excitement I feel. I recover quickly, though, and suggest fifty thousand dollars. Suggesting a specific amount is always a difficult call. Obviously, you don't want to suggest an amount that's too high or else your client will never make bail. On the other hand, an amount that is too low will cost you credibility with the judge and maybe your chances of any bail at all.

Haley is up like a shot, straining at the bit and anxious to respond, but cautious not to rile Rowe any further. I suspect that Rowe kind of likes sparring with Haley a bit. He appreciates a good advocate, and Haley rarely crosses the line. He nods to Haley to go ahead.

"Your Honor, the state certainly feels and has argued here that the defendant should be held without bond. However, if the court is considering bail, the amount of fifty thousand dollars would be ludicrous. If you were to set a bail I would suggest that it should be a minimum of one million. And, Your Honor, unless it is posted in cash or property, the defendant would have no real incentive to appear in court because he would have paid the bondsmen the premium and it would be the bondsmen, not the defendant, who would have the incentive."

"But, Judge," I respond, "that's true in all cases. That's why we have bail bondsmen. And a million-dollar bail for my client would be tantamount to no bail at all."

Rowe waves me off. "Mr. Stevens, I'm going to grant your motion for bail in the amount of two hundred fifty thousand, cash or surety. Okay, what is your next motion?"

In the courtroom there is a spontaneous, collective gasp, followed by a low buzz. I look over at Haley who is holding onto the table as if he would slide out of his chair otherwise. Several reporters dart out of the courtroom. Rowe does not bang his gavel. Instead, he holds his hand up to me to wait a moment and then glares out over the courtroom. In a matter of seconds it is like a funeral again. "Proceed, Mr. Stevens."

I try my best to act as if I am not the least surprised at Rowe's ruling. "The other two motions we have scheduled today, Your Honor, are not, I believe, opposed by the state." I look over at Haley briefly and then back to the judge. "First, I have asked the court to appoint an investigator to assist in the defense."

"No objection," says Haley, still a little dazed.

"All right, Mr. Stevens, you can have your investigator, as long as he, or she," he corrects himself quickly, "is willing to work at the state rate. Do you have anybody in particular in mind?"

"As a matter of fact, Judge, Bert Murphy has agreed to work on the case." I look over in the direction of Bert who is seated next to Reverend Paxton. Rowe follows my eyes over to Bert, then says to me, still looking at Bert, his face impassive, impossible to read, "Very well. What else you got?"

"Judge, I would like to view the crime scene."

"Your Honor," Haley begins, "the state has no objection to Mr. Stevens, Mr. Morganstein, and/or Mr. Murphy viewing the crime scene, on two conditions. First, that there be a law enforcement officer present, and, second, that Mr. Stevens limit the viewing to the area of the house in which the murder was actually committed. There is no reason for the victim's privacy to be invaded by rummaging through her entire house."

Rowe looks back to me. "Is that agreeable, Mr. Stevens?"

"No, it is not agreeable, Judge. With all due respect, the victim is dead. Her privacy is not an issue because she has none. If Mr. Haley can stand here and tell you that the police have not had access to the entire home of the victim, that the police have not been through every room, looked in every drawer and searched every nook and cranny of that house for something that might be relevant to their case, then he may have a point, but I don't believe that is the case."

Rowe looks at Haley. "Sounds fair to me, Mr. State Attorney. I am assuming that the police searched the entire house?"

Tom knew when to quit. "Yes, Your Honor. Very well, the state has no objection to the defense's request."

"When do you want to do this, Mr. Stevens?"

"The sooner the better, Judge."

Haley shrugs. "We can make arrangements for someone to be there tomorrow or the next day." He then looks directly at me. "Just call my office, Ted. Talk to Linda, and she'll set up whenever is convenient for you."

"Fine."

"Anything else?" Rowe looks at me, then at Haley, and then back to me.

"No, Your Honor."

"State?"

"No, Judge."

"Very well. Next case. State versus Andrew Weiss."

Both the state and defense tables scramble to make room for the next set of attorneys. As Bobby is led back to the holding cell I tell him that I will be out to see him later in the day. I tell him I will talk to his mother and to Bert about making bail. He is noticeably buoyed by the crumb that has been given him, though it's still unlikely that Bobby's friends and family can raise the ten percent, or twenty-five thousand dollars, needed for the bond. But given the slim chance of any bond being set, it is a victory. There will be time later to speculate on Rowe's motivation.

Paul and I motion Bert, Bernice, Shirley, and the Reverend into a small vacant room off of the courtroom where we discuss briefly the effect of the rulings, the status of the case. Paul does a good job of patting the defense team on the back. The Reverend and Bernice appear to be cautiously optimistic. Shirley is still pouting. I leave Bert to hold hands with the family and work on the bail situation. I leave my partner to deal with the press, and I seek out the same bailiff who had come to my rescue earlier. He takes me back to the holding cell area and down the back elevator, to a side entrance that nobody in the press has thought of.

It was overcast when I had walked over from my office. Now a light rain is falling. Not a cleansing rain, but a melancholy, uncertain drizzle. Somehow, it seems perfect. I step out and walk unhurriedly back to my office.

EIGHT

The shudder is involuntary, like a spasm. It has nothing to do with the cold air blowing through the air-conditioning vents, but rather it's a signal of the foreboding I feel as I turn my car off South Meridian onto the side street that ends up on Golf Terrace. I am a short distance from the house where Patty Stiles lived. With effort, I shake the feeling and ready myself to meet whatever ghosts I might find.

Patty had rented the house when she was a grad student and had continued to live in it after graduation. When the owner died in the late eighties, Patty managed to purchase it from the estate. She had added a deck with a hot tub, as well as a privacy fence, but the house looked much the same as it had a decade before.

The area had once been an exclusive neighborhood, showcasing some of Tallahassee's finest homes, all of which were only minutes away from the Capital City Country Club, home of the city's first golf course. The club and surrounding residential area had been the refuge of white segregationists in the late fifties. Back then, to avoid the integration of a public facility, the city had leased the land on which the country club sat to private citizens at one dollar a year for ninety-nine years. Though the stately homes remain, encroachment by lower income housing and higher crime rates have taken away some of the luster.

Patty's is one of the second-tier houses, away from the golf course frontage. These are not so grand, but still well-made, attractive, and architecturally interesting—California bungalow style. Few of the houses have garages or carports, their owners long ago having converted them to dens and extra bedrooms. As a result, there are cars parked all along the street, in driveways, and into yards. Patty's 1975 MGB is still parked in the driveway.

Seeing it reminds me of Patty's divorce. The car had always been unreliable, a mechanic's dream. But Patty had been attached to it and appreciated its idiosyncrasies. Also, she reminded me, it was paid for. So, she let her husband take the BMW, together with its payments, and a generous portion of joint possessions, in return for the house and the MGB, and her freedom—freedom, she had told me, from his dependency, both financially and psychologically, freedom from his insane jealousies, and freedom from his physical abuse. It was not that Patty was magnanimous by nature. No, she had a mean streak of her own, a cold, calculating, vindictive side to her, which I would find out later. But money and material possessions did not mean so much to her. Nor was it that she was intimidated. She had grown tired of Peter, more than afraid of him.

I park along the side of the road in front of the house, get out, and start walking up the sidewalk. The yard, which was never what one might call finely manicured, is now looking seriously neglected. I note that Bert has not yet arrived. A TPD officer is waiting just by the front door, as promised. There is yellow tape across the door frame. A sign, still posted on the door, advises that this is a crime scene, threatening all sorts of awful things for anyone who tampers with it in any way or intrudes past its flimsy barrier.

"Counselor." He speaks as though he knows me.

I look at his face. It doesn't seem familiar. I look at the name tag. Charlie Foster. Still no bells. I decide to wing it. "How have you been?"

"Not bad. Not bad."

"I appreciate you coming out. I'm not sure how long I'll be. I guess your orders are to stay with me?"

"Yes, sir. Maintain the integrity of the scene, so to speak." He smiles. "But you take your time. I was told to stay as long as you wanted. I got nothing else to do. Come on in." He turns and opens the front door which he had apparently already unlocked. I slip under the yellow tape and follow him inside. I feel another cold shiver.

"By the way, I turned on the a.c. in the house a bit ago, but it's still pretty warm in there."

"Thanks. It can't be any worse than out here though," I say as I wipe a roll of sweat from my forehead. A wave of nausea rolls over me. I put my hand out against the door frame for support, gain control and walk on in. "I'm expecting somebody else to join me. My investigator, Bert Murphy."

"Yeah, I know Bert. He gets around, don't you know," he says, giving me a wink. "He's stepped on a few toes over at the department, I suppose, but I ain't never had no trouble with him. I think he gets the job done, and that's what counts, ain't it?" He looks at me for confirmation, almost like a coconspirator. I nod and that seems to satisfy him.

I think back to Paul's reaction when I told him Bert had agreed to work on the case. It was not real positive. It had to do with questionable tactics Bert had used when he worked for the public defender. Bert's good, real good, he had said. But, he had warned, I'd better keep a tight rein on him.

I follow Officer Foster through the dining room back to the kitchen where he stops just outside the door, like a tour guide waving his hand toward the next item of interest. "I figured you'd want to see this area first." But he does not go inside the room. I walk in cautiously, my sense of foreboding returning, stronger now.

I stand a long while just inside the doorway, absorbing the surroundings. Black and white tile, white cabinets and countertops. There are glasses and dishes on counters and in the sink. There are a couple of dishes on the kitchen table. On the floor broken glass and a plate. Suddenly, I have a vision of Patty being thrown onto the table, dishes and glasses being knocked off onto the floor. The vision comes and goes quickly like the flash from a camera.

On the refrigerator there are post-it notes, coupons, a first-aid instruction sheet. On the counter a coffeemaker, coffee can, mail unopened. All in all it looks as though the police have not altered things much. They certainly have not cleaned up.

On the floor I notice the obligatory white outline of the body, where she had come to rest, face down, one arm clutching her throat, the other out to the side. I see the outline of her fingers where the blood had oozed and settled, where she had placed her hand in a futile effort to push herself up.

There are a couple of large bloodstains on the tile floor near where her head had rested. There are smaller spots splattered all on the walls, the countertops, as well as on the stove and refrigerator, the result, the expert will say, of blood being slung from the knife as her attacker brought the knife back and forth, back and forth. Some of it is from where Patty reached with bloody hands for support, on the sink, on a chair, on a wall. I look over at the kitchen counter, imagine the wooden block with its knives sticking out, the one slot empty.

Another involuntary shudder. I am beginning to feel nauseous again, but worse now. Beads of sweat pop out on my forehead. I glance around to see if Foster notices, but he has wandered somewhere else.

I look back at the cutlery block, to the chalk outline, the bloodstains on the floor, the cabinets.

Blood is dripping down the walls and the cabinets. I lean against the wall with my hand for support and feel a wet stickiness. I look at my hand, and it is covered with blood. I wipe my hand on my pants leg. I feel drops on my head and I look up. Blood is dripping from the ceiling, on my forehead, into my eye. I wipe it with my shirt sleeve and look back again at the chalk outline. She is there. The blood flowing from her mouth, forming a puddle, pulsating still. I stare in horror, unable to look away.

There is a movement, a twitch maybe, of her lips. Her hands stretch out beside her, palms down. She is trying to push herself up, pull herself to her knees. She turns her head slightly toward me, her lips part into a half-smile—a smirk. She beckons me with her eyes. Her lips move. Is she trying to say something? I cannot control my actions. Compelled to lean closer, I am down on one knee now, my ear to her face so I can hear her words—

"Ted. Ted."

I look up from my squatted position on the floor to acknowledge Bert Murphy, standing in the kitchen doorway, Foster just behind him, a look of concern, alarm on both their faces. I look at my shirt sleeves and pants leg to see if the bloodstain is noticeable, but I see only wetness. I put my hand to my head but I feel only sweat, not blood.

"Whoa, Teddy Bear," Bert says. "You don't look so hot. You sick?"

No, I think, not sick. I've just been hallucinating, that's all. "Yeah, I think I must be coming down with the flu or something."

The room is back to normal now for me but the nausea remains, and I feel weak. What I really need is a drink. I remember where Patty keeps her booze and tremble with anticipation.

He talks of possibilities, logistics, keeping his voice low so that Foster cannot hear. I am trying to listen but his voice is far away, in a tunnel. After a while, I suggest that we go over the rest of the house, independently, and then compare notes.

Bert heads toward the den/office while I go in the direction of the bedrooms. Foster, not quite sure what to do, and unable to stay with both of us, gives up and goes out onto the front porch to smoke a cigarette. When I am sure they are both out of sight, I go to the kitchen again, open the cabinet above the microwave, remove a bottle of Wild Turkey, and take two large swigs. The effect is immediate, if only psychological. Now, I say to myself, let's get on with it.

As I walk down the hallway there is a feeling of déjà vu that is both comforting and disturbing. I had forgotten how many photographs are on the walls. Not so much on the tables and shelves, but on the walls. They are all black and whites—dark, somber shots of people, places. The overall effect is one of melancholy.

The centerpiece of the master bedroom is an antique mahogany four-poster bed. There is a photo of her parents on the nightstand, a clock radio, and a paperback, *Russia House*, with a Garfield bookmark halfway through. There are several articles of clothing hung over the bedposts and on every other piece of furniture in the room, several pairs of shoes on the floor. The bed is unmade.

Slowly, carefully, I survey the room, go through the closet, and then through the dresser drawers in detail. I glance over my shoulder from time to time, a little embarrassed, thinking that Foster or Bert might come in and wonder why I am examining her underwear so closely.

Other than more evidence of her taste in clothes, though, I find nothing of real interest in the bedroom.

Similarly, my search of the bathroom proves unenlightening. The second bedroom is relatively tidy, probably because of disuse. There is a twin-size bed up against one wall. Up against the other is a small dresser with a mirror, and on either side several boxes stacked on top of each other. In the closet there are some additional clothes and more boxes. Some of the boxes, I find, are sealed with tape, apparently having never been opened since Patty's move here several years before and apparently not an item of the police search. I am relieved to know that the police were not so comprehensive in their search.

Inside the boxes I find some old clothes, kitchen appliances and utensils, the kind of serving platters and the like that look nice, were nice gifts, but are never really used. There is a scrapbook of some of her work, stuff from high school. Nothing really current and nothing that I expect to find relative to the case. I am fascinated by these personal items of Patty Stiles though. How strange that you can be intimate with a person and yet not know them very well at all—not the first time I've had this thought.

I pick up a high school yearbook. On the outside it reads "The Talon" in large letters, then in slightly smaller script "William P. Foster High School." It occurs to me that I have forgotten where Patty grew up. The advertisements of the sponsors confirm that it is Crestview, in northwest Florida. Inside, I quickly find her senior class picture. She looks amazingly just like she would thirteen years later, a little thinner, perhaps a little more innocence in the eyes. Her dark auburn hair contrasts with the blue eyes and the pale white skin. There is just a hint of a smile on her face.

Her senior résumé is impressive: vice president of the student body, editor-in-chief of both the school newspaper and the yearbook, the Debate Club. Her senior thought:

> "The great masses of the people will
> more easily fall victims to a big lie
> than to a small one."
>> Adolph Hitler, *Mein Kampf* 1923.

Interesting choice, I think, for a future journalist.

I move on to the living room. On one wall are makeshift shelves made from varnished lumber and decorative blocks. There are lots of books on them, hardback and paperback, stacked vertically and horizontally on the shelves and crammed into every nook and cranny available, in no particular order. There is great variety here, contradictions: conservative and liberal political commentaries, fiction that runs the gamut from trashy romance to spy novels, mysteries, and science fiction.

Her collection of CDs is also haphazardly arranged in and about the stereo stand. There are probably well over two hundred of them, some in their wooden slots as intended, others stacked on top of the CD player and on the table on which it sits. Like her books, her musical tastes paint a picture of a woman not afraid to try new things. There is classical music, jazz and hard rock, country and western.

Police found the marijuana, crack cocaine, and a crack pipe in the drawer of this table, all inside a cigar box. Another crack pipe, recently used, had been on the ashtray on the coffee table. The fingerprint expert will testify that Bobby Jackson's prints were on the pipe and the glass coffee table.

Foster has wandered into the living room area and taken a seat in a bentwood rocker. I curse silently to myself. I have not yet found the one thing that I am specifically looking for, a packet of photos that would connect me to the murder victim in a way that would be compromising. I have gambled that it is not in the area of the house where

I have sent Bert, and I don't want to have someone looking over my shoulder when, and if, I find it.

In the dining room buffet, in the top drawer, there are several shoe boxes filled with photographs. They are personal photographs, not work-related. My pulse quickens. I quickly find the box containing the more current photographs and begin to go through them.

Bert's booming voice startles me and I immediately remove my hands from the box of photographs. I turn around to face him, trying to act nonchalant. It doesn't work.

"Boy, you look like the kid who got caught with his hand in the cookie jar."

Very close, I think, but I have regained my composure now. "You startled the shit out of me. You know, you feel a little strange looking through all of these personal items of this dead woman. You through in the den area?"

"Yeah, I've gone through the kitchen real good and the den, which obviously was her office. There's a lot of interesting stuff there, but we'll talk about it after you've had a chance to look through it—compare notes so to speak. What about you?"

"Nothing to speak of." It's probably obvious that I want to get back to my search. Bert, unnecessarily, tells me he's going to go back to the bedroom area and then disappears down the hallway. I notice that the officer has stepped out onto the deck to have another cigarette. I turn back to the photos.

They seem to cover probably the last five or six years. Photos from vacations, ski trips in the Rockies, various beaches. There are shots that look like family get-togethers—Thanksgiving, Christmas. There are quite a few with the ex-hubby. Finally, I come across the group of photos I have been looking for.

The affair with Patty had been a stupid, reckless thing

to do. I know that now. I knew it then really. My little voice had screamed at me, "Dumb! Dumb! Dumb!" Of course I had responded, "Shut up. I know what I'm doing."

If the decision to become involved with my client had been reckless, though, I had resolved to conceal it from everyone, especially my wife. And, I had been careful. Very careful. Speculation, suspicion might be unavoidable. Proof was another thing.

But then, there were the photos, the ones she had taken using a timer. Both of us in various stages of undress, suggestive poses, naked in the hot tub. Some real pornographic, frontal nudity stuff. I should've said no. "Oh, Teddy Bear," she had said. "Don't worry. Nobody will ever see them—just me. Souvenirs. I'll develop the film myself." We had both been drunk on champagne. I had been blinded by my lust, the excitement of taking from the forbidden fruit. I gave in.

I had not known then that she and I saw our affair from different perspectives. Neither of us, I thought, wanted any long-term relationship. I was wrong. When I told her it was getting too risky, that it was time to go back to our real worlds, she had been furious. Threatened to send those photos to Beth.

How ironic, I think. I had been so concerned that those photos, the revelations of my indiscretions, would reach my wife. Beth would surely have left me if she had seen those photos. She never did see them though and she had no proof to confirm her suspicions. But she left me anyway.

Now, for different reasons, I still can't afford to have these photos turn up. I look around to make sure Bert and Foster are not close by. I consider my options. Have the police seen them? Probably not, or I would already have been asked questions that I would not want to answer. I could leave them. Chances are Patty's family wouldn't find them for a long time, wouldn't recognize me in them.

Bert might see them. He's pretty thorough. What if the police had discovered these photographs but were seeing what I would do—setting me up. It would look suspicious, wouldn't it, if they go missing? I hear Bert and Foster talking as they head back down the hall. I make my decision, and put the packet of photographs in my back pocket just as they walk in.

"Anything of interest?" Bert asks.

"Yeah, plenty of interest, but nothing that's probably going to help on the case. See what you think though."

I leave Bert and Foster in the room and walk toward the den/office, consciously avoiding the kitchen on my way. I feel as if those dizzying, nauseating visions are waiting for me around a corner, under the next photograph, in each mirror that I pass—a jumble of images that I struggle to keep locked inside.

The feeling is stronger as I enter the den. Though I don't remember ever being in this room before, it seems somehow familiar. I take a quick look around this room. It feels almost as if I have entered into a completely different house. While the rest of the house paints the picture of a slob, this room speaks of an organized, even fastidious person. In the corner is a large rolltop desk, its front open, with the writing surface clean and bare. Though the cubbies are full, the contents are neat and look as if they belong. Four old wooden filing cabinets are against the wall next to the rolltop desk. On one side wall there is an old wing chair with a magazine table and holder beside it, an antique brass lamp on the narrow surface. Here, in contrast to the living room, all the magazines are neatly arranged on the table or in the canvas holder alongside. On the wall opposite the rolltop desk, looking a little out of place, is Patty's computer and laser printer. The walls, again, are a collection of photographs, obviously mementos of different news stories.

In the file cabinet drawers I find what looks like a file on every story she has written over the past several years. A quick review indicates that they are filed chronologically. Each file label has a title for the story and a date. I look to see if there is a file on drug use, which is what Bobby had told me she had been working on. The last file, however, is the story on a local white supremacist group which she had done last year. I remember the story. Its target, a building contractor and county commissioner, had suffered a nose-dive in his business and his political career after Patty had exposed him as a secret member. I note that this might make him an attractive alternative suspect, but it is not the file I am looking for.

There is a file on battered spouses, the jail construction fiasco, indigent medical care, a sex scandal involving a local minister and an underage girl working for an escort service, but no drug use file. I notice that in each file the contents are similar. Each has the newspaper article or a copy of it. There are photos, computer-typed outlines, and pocket-sized spiral notes. Most have letters to the editor about the articles, and miscellaneous materials, such as copies of applicable Florida statutes, other newspaper or magazine articles, excerpts from books or other publications relative to the subject matter.

Nowhere in the file drawers, nor anywhere else in the office, however, do I find even a temporary file folder with preliminary notes on a story involving drug use in the black community. It is a Patty Stiles-type story, but perhaps she was not far enough along with her story, or maybe she kept her notes at work, or at school. Maybe my client lied to me. It would not be the first time. Maybe there is something on her computer, I think. I glance over at the unfriendly-looking conglomeration of equipment. I am what can be generously be called computer illiterate. I'll need help getting into that thing.

The antique wing chair looks inviting so I sit down and casually look through some of the magazines in the canvas rack next to it. For some reason unknown to me I lift the magazines up out of the holder. In the bottom is a small spiral notebook. I pick it up and thumb through it. Some of the pages have been torn out, about half, I judge. The first few pages have some writing on them, notes. It appears to be some sort of shorthand. On the first page: "6-9 A.M. Meeting SS—photos—SB tag—$$$" are the only terms that are recognizable to me. The 6-9 is most likely the date the notes are taken. The A.M. I think probably refers to the morning. Perhaps she was meeting someone with the initials of SS, maybe about some photos, or maybe she wants to have photos of the meeting. "SB tag"—I have no idea. And money apparently has something to do with all of this. If only I could interpret some of the squiggly stuff. The next page does not have a date but again there is another "A.M.", the morning I guess, "Miami," and then underneath that "—cars, house, $$$." The line underneath that has a "P.M."—a reference to the afternoon or evening? "Deeds," "CHs." There is another reference to "A.M." And then *"Big deal!!!"* Just as I start to call out for Bert, he walks into the room.

"Hey, look at this."

"Whatcha got?"

"I'm not sure, but it might be some notes on our victim's last story she was working on."

"Where did you find it?"

"It was underneath the magazines in the rack. It probably just fell down there, or perhaps Patty Stiles hid it there. I don't know. Do you know how to read shorthand?" I ask him as I hand him the notebook. He shakes his head no as he looks it over.

"Bobby told me that Stiles was supposed to be working on a story on dope dealing, crack in the inner city, something like that. These may be some quick notes that she planned to flesh out later. Maybe there's something else on the computer. I don't think the police have checked this out."

"Could be nothing more than her little notes to remind her to do something, Teddy. Did you find anything else— files, photos, research material?"

"No, but like I say, maybe there's more on the computer."

Bert looks at me skeptically. "Pick up milk, prescription, get some cash." Bert is looking through the notebook, giving a more innocent interpretation. "I wouldn't put a whole lot of stock in it." He hands the notebook back to me.

"Maybe you're right, but think about it. If she was working on such a story . . ." I look up at Bert.

"Yeah, I see, she gets a little too close . . ."

"Right, and that's bad for business. And if she's gone high enough up the chain, we're talking very big business. The kind of money people sometimes kill for. He, or maybe they, wait for an opportune time. Patty is too stubborn, or too stupid to be afraid. She lets her killer in. He kills her, takes a few things to hide the fact that what he is really after is her notes on the story—so that it dies with her."

"But what about this notebook. Why is it left behind?"

"Well, like I said, it probably fell down and got lodged underneath these magazines where I found it. Obviously the killer didn't know about it. It's only got a few pages. I suspect she transferred her notes daily or fairly regularly to the computer. Anyway, I want you to verify her work assignment at the paper. Her editors, other reporters, somebody will know what she was working on, I'm sure. She had to have been working on something, Bert. Find out what it is. You got your eyes and ears out in the community too. See if you can come up with some corroboration. See if any of our small-time dopers out there on the street might have been interviewed by this lady reporter."

Bert is rubbing his chin. "Okay. No problem." He shrugs his shoulders and it appears as if he wants to say more but doesn't.

"In the meantime, I'm going to leave the notebook here on the table and make a request for discovery to get copies of it. I'll get Janice or somebody to decipher this shorthand stuff for me. Also, Bert, do you know anything about computers?" I point over to Patty's computer. "Think you can get into hers—see what's in there?"

"I know just enough about computers to be dangerous," he says. "I don't think it's such a good idea that we try to do this now. I could mess it up."

"Yeah, you're probably right. I don't want the state to complain that we've tampered with any evidence." I think of the packet of photographs in my back pocket. "I'll get Janice in here with a state attorney representative and we'll see what we can find on Ms. Stiles' computer. I'll wager that somewhere in there she's got some notes on her story that are going to prove helpful. And you know what else, Bert? I looked around here but I don't see any floppy disks. None. Isn't that kind of unusual? Wouldn't you expect a writer to store a lot of stuff on floppy disks?"

"Maybe. I guess everybody is different." Bert is noncommittal. "Maybe it's on the hard drive."

"Maybe it is. But if our theory is correct . . ."

"*Your* theory," Bert corrects me.

"Okay, for now, *my* theory, but you'll come on board, I'm sure. If my theory is correct, then the killer would probably take any floppy disk he could find, assuming there might be notes on one of them that match the printed notes in the file. But maybe he didn't think of the fact that they may be in the hard drive memory, or maybe he couldn't find it and thought no one else would look."

"You better sit under this fan, son, and cool off that brain of yours. It's goin' too fast."

While I am thinking about it, I pull the cell phone from my jacket pocket and call the office. I look at my watch. Since it's after 6:30, I'm not surprised when I get the disembodied voice of the recorder. What the hell, it'll save me the trouble of dictating it later, and I have to be in court first thing in the morning.

"Jan, listen, it's me. I'm at Patty Stiles' now. I need to do a supplemental discovery request in the Jackson case. Use our standard form, and in the body of it put two things. One, the original or copies of a two-by-three notebook that will be found on the magazine rack next to the wing chair in the den/office of the victim's house. Two, authorization for a search of the victim's computer in that same room. I'll be going straight to case management in the morning and I want to get this done asap. You can get Paul to review it. I'll see you at about eleven. Thanks." I hang up the phone.

Bert and I take one last look around the house, comparing notes. We go out the back door and down the path that the killer supposedly took, see the location where the knife was found. Finally we make our way back to the front door. It's 7:35 P.M.

"Officer Foster, I appreciate your patience."

Foster is standing on the front porch, smoking another cigarette. "No problem, Counselor. If you were my lawyer, I'd want you to take as much time as you needed. If you want to get back in again, just call the captain."

"Stay out of trouble now, Charlie." Bert gives him a big grin as we walk past him down the sidewalk to our cars.

"Back at ya, Bert."

Bert has parked his El Camino in the driveway just behind Patty's MGB. He stops as he opens the door. "You want to leave your car here and go get something to eat?"

"Thanks, Bert, but I think I'm just going to grab something quick and get on home. I'm pretty whipped." Only a small lie. In fact, I have an urge to be around some people, just not people that I know, and certainly no one connected to the Jackson case. I also have a strong urge to get very drunk. "Maybe next time."

"Okay, buddy. I'll get back with you as soon as I have something to report."

"Good. See you later."

Inside my car, the heat is stifling. New rivers of sweat flow from my body almost instantaneously. I roll down a couple of windows and turn the a.c. on high. I take a used paper napkin from the console area and mop my brow with it. Finally, the inside temperature stabilizes and I can roll the windows up, feel the cool air flowing through the vents. I realize that I am exhausted, more mentally than physically, and I have a great sense of relief having left the crime scene. I have a second thought about going any place public now. Maybe I should go on home. But then I think of my not so exquisite accommodations at the Sunset Motor Inn, and I decide to stop by on my way at the Rajun Cajun Bar and Grill. I lift up the lid on the console, take out a pint of vodka, take off the top, and take a huge swig. "Whooah," I say aloud. This stuff's pretty nasty, I admit to myself, but it's too much trouble to keep a cooler with beer, not to mention too obvious. Also, vodka is not so noticeable on the breath.

The parking lot is full when I reach the Rajun Cajun so I park at the clothing store next door. I pull out the packet of photographs from my back pocket. My earlier conflicting thoughts come back in a flash. I rationalize my decision to take them. They were, after all, partly mine. They were an invasion of my privacy anyway. If they came out now, there would be a lot of explaining to do. "And where were you, Mr. Stevens, on the evening of June twelfth, the night

Ms. Stiles was murdered?" I was at St. George Island, I would say. Yes, how could I forget. There had been the anonymous call to my home. It had resulted in a big fight between Beth and me and I ended up driving down to the island. I was at Harry A's part of the night. Some possible alibi witnesses maybe—but not completely.

"And when did you leave that establishment, Mr. Stevens, what time?"

What would I answer?—that I'm not sure, that I was too drunk, that I woke up in my car in Eastpoint the next morning?

"How exactly did you say you got those scratches on your arm? And what about these photographs, sir. Would you care to explain these?"

No, I don't think I want to go down this road. I look around the parking lot. Empty. I take the photos out of the packet, tear each of them into several pieces and throw them in the Dumpster, then walk through the doors of the bar.

NINE

There it is again. Some kind of bell, ringing in the distance. Now, it's stopped. There it is again. The sound is closer now. Is it the school bell? I can't afford to be late to class again. No, it's not a school bell. It's a phone, my phone. There it goes again, annoyingly loud now. I look over at the alarm clock on the nightstand. It reads 8:40 A.M. I fumble with the phone and pick it up but say nothing. As soon as I hear Jan's voice calling my name on the other end, I realize my situation.

"Yeah, I know, I overslept. My alarm didn't go off."

A brief pause. "I got your message on the recorder about the Jackson case this morning. Typed up that motion and asked Paul to take a look at it. He tried to reach you over at the courthouse before docket sounding, but Eva said you hadn't arrived yet. He told me to see if I could get you at home. I thought you'd be heading out."

"Yeah, I am," I lie. "Never mind about the motion. I'll see it when I get back to the office. It's not that big of a rush. Better go. Talk to you later." I quickly hang up the phone before Jan can respond, get up and hit the floor running. I am not yet fully awake. Only adrenaline and anxiety are getting me going at all.

My head feels twenty pounds heavier and off balance on top of my neck. It hurts with each step that I take to the bathroom. I run cold water and splash it on my face. It helps, but not much. My stomach is a simmering volcano, putrid gas escaping up my esophagus—the hint of a pending eruption. I brush my teeth and stare in the mirror at the puffy eyelids, the matted hair, the day-old beard. Not much I can do about the eyes, or the hair, but I can use the electric razor on my way in. I take three Advil from the medicine cabinet, cup some water in my hand from the faucet, and swallow them.

I get dressed quickly and then search for my keys. They are not on the dresser with my wallet. I look in the bed, on the floor near the dresser. No keys. I look on the kitchen table and on the counter near the phone. Maybe I left them in the car. Pretty stupid, but it wouldn't be the first time. To my horror, I realize when I step out the front door that my car's not in front of the room or anywhere else in the parking lot that I can see. Somebody has stolen my car.

Well, maybe not.

Where are those keys? The sickening realization dawns on me that I have no idea what happened last night. I don't remember driving home, or even coming home for that matter. I do remember the Rajun Cajun, the poker game in the back room until the wee hours. I remember consuming vast quantities of alcoholic beverages. Perhaps I should not jump to any conclusions.

"Yes, sir. And where was your car when it was stolen? Was it locked? Do you have the keys? Who drove it last?" No, I think I'd better not call the police yet.

First things first, I think. I go back inside and call a cab. Then I call Jan back. "Listen," I tell her. "Call Rowe's office for me, will you? Tell Eva I've got car trouble." Well, in a way, I definitely have car trouble. "I may be a few minutes late."

"You okay?" I can hear concern in her voice. "You want me to come get you?"

"Nah, that'd take too long. I'll get there. Just run a little interference for me."

"Okay."

After I hang up, though, I have second thoughts about that cab. They're not always so prompt. I go to the front office. Ami is behind the desk. Though he does not strike me as being overly charitable, he is a shrewd business man—a fact on which I now depend.

"Mr. Majeed, good morning."

He looks up from his paperwork, smiling politely. "Yes, good morning, Mr. Stevens. May I help you?"

"Well, actually, yes. I'm afraid that I loaned my car to a friend last night and I need to get a ride up to the court-house this morning. I'd take a cab but I don't want to have to wait that long. It would be worth twenty dollars to me if I could get a ride right now." I hold a twenty-dollar bill in the air.

The man's smile widens a bit. He sticks his head into the back room and calls for his teenage son who is there almost instantaneously. He speaks to the boy quickly, then turns to me. "My son, Sanji, will take you, Mr. Stevens." He hands the boy the keys and I follow him out the door.

"Mr. Stevens." I turn to see Mr. Majeed with his hand out. "You said twenty dollars?"

I smile, walk over and place the bill in his hand.

"Thank you very much. Have a nice day."

Sanji is a cautious driver. Too slow and cautious for my taste. I keep looking at my watch, but I say nothing. By the time I am at the courthouse, it's 9:15. Docket sounding began fifteen minutes ago. Not too bad, though, consider-ing. Depending on where I am on the docket, Rowe might not have gotten to my cases yet, might not even notice that I'm late.

He does.

I try to slip in unobtrusively to the prosecutor's table to see where I am on the docket, but just as I approach the table I hear my name being called. "Yes sir, Your Honor," I speak up.

Judge Rowe fixes his icy stare on me, gives me the once-over. I don't think he likes what he sees. "So nice of you to join us this morning, Mr. Stevens."

"Sorry, Your Honor. I had car trouble this morning." Not too terribly original, I know, but the truth would sound a lot worse.

Rowe does not, obviously, think much of my excuse, but after only a brief pause he says, "The state attorney indicated that you wish to set Mr. Jerome Nellum for a plea on the third. Is that correct?"

"Yes, sir."

"And what about Mr. Tony Proctor, then?"

"Judge, I still haven't received discovery in this case."

"When did you file your demand for discovery?" Rowe looks at me then at Mike Abrams, the assistant state attorney.

"Two weeks ago, I think." A guess. I realize that I have left my files in my car, which is somewhere. "I don't have my file with me."

"Mr. Abrams?"

"Your Honor, the state hasn't received a request."

"Judge, there is no demand for discovery in the court file either." Van Johnson, the deputy clerk volunteers this information. I give him a dirty look, which he returns.

"I don't know what the problem is, Judge. I'll get another copy to the state attorney today."

"You do that. All right, pass Mr. Proctor's case for two weeks. Thank you, Mr. Stevens. I hope you get your car trouble taken care of." With that he is off to the next case.

My whole body relaxes, thankful for the reprieve. I had

expected to be told to report to chambers after docket sounding. I have been late only once before to Judge Rowe's courtroom. I had been with the state attorney's office about six months then, was on the phone with a witness in the office, and had not realized the time. Rowe had not made a big deal about it publicly, but in his chambers afterwards he had glared at me hard and told me that I had better not ever be late to his courtroom again. Unless I had a hell of a lot better excuse, I'd get him "real pissed off," is how he put it, "and you don't want to do that, do you?" he had asked. "No," I had quickly responded. Today, perhaps he believed my excuse. One thing is sure, though, my credibility is being used up at an alarming rate.

By the time I get back to the office, the pounding in my head has turned into a dull throb. And I feel like maybe I can eat something without throwing up. Ah, the marvel of modern medicine.

"Good morning, Adrienne."

"Good morning, Mr. Stevens," she replies with a big smile on her face. She obviously either does not recognize the sarcasm, or chooses to ignore it, as she does my somewhat disheveled appearance.

Upstairs, Janice is not as diplomatic. "Whoa. Tell me you didn't go to court like that?"

"Thanks."

She follows me into my office, standing at my desk. "Seriously, you don't look too good. Do you feel sick?" She knows what the problem is, so I just confirm it.

"What I feel, honestly, is hung over."

"Coffee?"

"Yeah, thanks, black."

"Of course."

Jan returns with the cup of coffee. "By the way," she says a little sheepishly, "Paul knows you were a little late to court. He told me to ask you to pop in when you get a chance."

"Yeah, I'll do that." After I take a trip to the little boys' room.

In the bathroom, I shave with a razor I keep in the office, then I change my old shirt for a new one. My decision to start keeping clean shirts at the office is beginning to pay off. The hair is still dirty, and the bags under the eyes are still there, but I look a little more presentable. I make my way back toward Paul's office. His secretary, Cathy, looks up from her work, smiles slightly, and nods. I respond in kind.

Cathy is a very competent legal secretary. Paul hired her when he first opened his office. She is always pleasant, hard-working, and willing to stay late when necessary, without a grumble. But she is an extremely shy person, uncomfortable in most settings, and I find I usually have to drag any conversation out of her. I long ago tired of this task, so a smile and a nod is our most common form of communication.

"Paul in?" I ask.

"I think he's just doing some dictating," Cathy responds, looking back toward Paul's office as if to reassure herself that he's still there.

Paul puts his dictaphone down when I walk in. I feel a little bit like a school kid who's been called to the principal's office. Technically, Paul is not my boss. He is my partner. But he is five years my senior, clearly the rainmaker of the firm, and a natural leader. Though we almost always agree on what is the best policy on firm business, both of us know that it is Paul who calls the shots.

Paul is more like a big brother or mentor to me. He had been an experienced attorney in the P.D.'s office when I first started with the state attorney's office. Though we were on opposite sides, he was always willing to share his knowledge and expertise. He has an uncanny knack of being able to disagree without being disagreeable—a trait that had allowed him to be the de facto head of the public defender's office. He has a way of getting the most out of people by expecting it. I notice that I'm already feeling defensive and guilty and Paul has not yet spoken.

"Okay," I begin. "I overslept this morning. My alarm didn't go off." This wasn't going to cut it. I fidget in the silence.

"Okay, I had a little too much to drink last night. It's been a heavy week. Hell, I wasn't too late. My luck that I happened to be early on the docket."

Silence.

"Okay. I got a little drunk."

Paul still says nothing. Just looks at me expectantly.

"Okay fine, real drunk. My head is killing me. I feel like death warmed over. Hell, Paul, I don't even know how I got home last night. Or where my car is."

More silence.

"You're right. I acted irresponsibly, unprofessionally. It makes you look bad when I look bad. I'm sorry, really. It won't happen again."

More silence. I am just about to continue when Paul finally speaks.

"I'm glad we could have this chat." Paul seems to be about to elaborate, but decides against it. There's a long pause. Thinking the conversation is over, I turn to leave.

"By the way," Paul adds as I turn back to him, "how about joining Anna and me for dinner Friday night, at our house. And no last-minute cancellation on us, like last time."

"Uh, that'd be real nice. Have you checked with Anna though?"

"It was her suggestion. You didn't think it'd be my idea, do you?" He smiles.

"Okay. What can I bring?"

"A good appetite. About sevenish."

I start to leave again but realize Paul still isn't finished.

"Incidentally, Red called me from the Rajun Cajun. He was checking to make sure you were okay and to remind you that you're parked in front of that woman's dress shop next door and you need to move it 'like real soon' I think were his words. He's got your keys, by the way."

"Well, I'm glad I didn't file that stolen vehicle report," I answer sheepishly.

"Why don't you get one of the secretaries to give you a ride?"

"Nah, I think I should handle this myself."

Paul nods his approval. "Check you later then, Ted."

The taxi ride from the office to the Rajun Cajun gives me time to think about what Paul had said, without saying it. Though I've always liked my booze, I have to admit I have been hitting it pretty hard lately. If I were talking about someone else, I could point to early signs of alcoholism, the increased amounts, drinking myself to sleep at night, the bottle in the car console, and scariest of all, the blackouts. Today is not the first time I've waked up in the morning with no memory of the night before.

Scary. Actually, though, I've done pretty well, I think. This is the first time that I could say that drinking has affected my work. Besides, this is only temporary, just until this thing with Beth is worked out and this case is behind me. They say that time heals all wounds, and I believe it. If the booze helps me in the healing process, some adverse effects will have to be tolerated, for a while anyway.

I've just got to make sure that it doesn't get out of hand. I've got to cut back, sure, but not quit cold turkey. That would be stupid. Just maybe put a limit on how much I can have. A little self-regulation. Let's say no more than two drinks at a time. No, don't be unrealistic. Let's say four, or six if it's on a weekend, maybe. Yeah, that ought to do it, I think. I can handle that, I think, as the cab pulls into the parking lot of the Rajun Cajun.

Red gives me the keys without much comment and with the understanding look of someone who's been there before, and has seen many others there too. I thank him for keeping me out of my car last night, even though I don't exactly remember him doing it.

On my way back to the office, I stop at the Sing Store, get a honey bun and another cup of black coffee. By the time I get back, the sugar and caffeine have kicked in and I am almost back to normal. I look through my messages on Jan's desk. There is one from Denise Wilkerson, my divorce lawyer. Something tells me it's not good so I put off returning the call. At lunch, I'm proud of myself as I take a quick workout at the gym, sweating out some of that poison, then have a lean roast beef sandwich, no beer.

It's 2:00 P.M. when I return Denise's call. She is not happy. "Tell me, Ted, what is it with you? Do you have some kind of death wish? Do you just like to piss everybody off? Is that your idea of fun?"

"What are you talking about? What did I do?"

"What do you mean what did you do? Don't you remember that little talk we had at your deposition? How many times do you think you can violate that no-contact provision before your ass ends up in jail? Now I warned you—"

"Whoa, just a minute, now. I haven't violated the no-contact provision."

"Well, I got a call from Dandy Don this morning. As a courtesy, he tells me, he wants to let me know that he'll be filing a motion for an order to show cause why you shouldn't be held in contempt of court, says you called his client about three o'clock in the morning, obviously drunk."

I ponder for a few moments my response. "She's lying, Denise. I may be stupid, but I'm not crazy."

There is a pause while she tries to make up her mind
whether to believe me or not. Of course, I have no idea
whether I actually called her or not, but I can't admit it to
Denise. I am counting on the fact that my wife will have
no corroboration. Just her word against mine. "Don't you
think I'd remember if I called my wife?"

Denise has apparently decided to give me the benefit of
the doubt. "Well, I just wanted you to know what was up,
what they're going to say. There'll probably be a hearing
scheduled pretty quickly. I'll let you know."

"Okay. Thanks for calling." I hang up the phone and
sit, in a trance, considering my situation. I can't deal with
this right now though. With a great deal of effort I push
these thoughts back into that little locked cabinet. Later I
will deal with them. Not now.

The rest of the afternoon and into the night I work on
an appellate brief that is due next Wednesday. This office
work is interrupted briefly by an interview with a new client
who is being sued for, what else, a divorce. I leave the office
at about 5:30 P.M. I pass by a couple of my usual watering
holes on the way home, proud of myself for not stopping.
It is a full two hours later, after my pizza is delivered to the
motel and I have the Jackson files spread out on the table,
reading, that I decide to reward myself with a cold beer.

I am reviewing Bert's investigative notes, recalling his
comments when he gave them to me.

"Depending on who you talk to," Bert had said, "Patty
Stiles was either a talented, conscientious reporter, a popular adjunct professor of journalism, or, a scheming, back-
stabbing, amoral, lying bitch. The folks down at the paper
were pretty high on her. Said she was an independent
thinker, creative and persistent in her approach to a story.
Said she had good credibility. Always backed up her statements with good sources. Not everybody at the paper liked
her, but, bottom line, I didn't see or hear anything that

pointed to a likely alternative suspect for her murder. On the other hand, some of the subjects of her articles over the last few years, including our neo-Nazi ex-commissioner, have a somewhat lower opinion of her."

"But why wait so long?" I asked. "The white supremacist story is her most recent and that was several months ago.

"The guy may be an asshole, but that doesn't mean he's a stupid asshole. You know the old saying, revenge is a dish best served cold. And, if you wait long enough people will ask the same question you just did."

I had thought about that for a second. Eugene Johnson had been a county commissioner for three and a half years until his defeat in the special election last year. He was a law-and-order candidate who rode the waves of fear and hatred into office. There had been some rumors or accusations of his membership in a secret society. It was a charge he had resolutely denied.

Patty Stiles had proved him a liar, however, in a series of articles, complete with pictures of Johnson in the company of his white-robed brethren during a meeting at an out-of-the-way fishing camp off Highway 20. When Johnson could no longer deny the truth, he had come out front with his racist views and ran a tough and dirty campaign against his challenger. Johnson lost badly and skulked away into oblivion, at least that's what most people thought.

"I wonder if Mr. Johnson has an alibi for the night of the murder?" I had asked. Bert had pointed me to the file and suggested that I decide for myself. In the file, under "Johnson," I read the notes from his interview. It was short, if not sweet, as Mr. Johnson was rather hostile to Bert's inquiry. There is a quote: "Ms. Patty Stiles' death has been so depressing to me that I don't wish to talk about it." What an asshole, I think. He said he had an alibi, though, and gave Bert the names of his buddies with whom he was supposedly playing poker until the early morning hours on the date of the murder. Bert's notes show that he contacted two of the three people, who had confirmed River's story. His file note, however, suggested that it could very easily be a conspiracy, or at least a jury might believe it, in which event they were all in on it together. Weak, though, I think.

I pick up the file marked FAMU. Bert had not given me much to work on there either. Some of the folks at the university didn't think much of Patty Stiles. As Bert had said, "Some of the folks there think she was pretty much of a slut, that she slept her way into her job, so to speak. And, you gotta remember, some of these black professors didn't like the fact that this white bitch, my words not theirs, was given the position to start with. I didn't find any murderous intent though, just some resentment. She wasn't such a muckety-muck that somebody could have been passed over for some big promotion because of her. Just your usual petty jealousies, like at the paper. There may have even been a couple of dejected lovers along the way but nothing real recent, nothing that I would count on."

Nothing in my review of the file makes me think otherwise either. The one suspect that looks somewhat appealing is the ex-husband, Peter Stiles. A lot of the information in the file I already know since Bert had gotten much of it from our divorce file on Patty. It appears that he is still in town, playing with a local band.

The good news, for our case, is that he has no firm alibi. He was supposed to play that night but was sick with the flu, so he says. Bert checked out the story and could confirm that he, Stiles, had in fact told his fellow musicians that he had the flu, but nobody had called him at his home that night. He could have lied, planning to go over to Patty's and murder her. Unfortunately, Bert had not yet found any evidence of contact between Patty and Peter since their divorce. I think maybe I could show the jury that the man was capable of a brutal, callous, and vindictive violent act, but he was more the type to act impulsively, in the heat of the moment. It would be hard to sell him as a person who would wait several months to get even with his ex-wife, who had in fact been fairly generous to him in the divorce settlement. There would have to be some evidence of his continued stalking or harassing of her. Well, maybe something would turn up.

A little after 11:30 I realize that my reward of one beer has turned into a twelve-pack. I am just about to turn in when the phone rings. I answer it.

"Hey, nigger lover, listen up." The voice, though obviously disguised, sounds vaguely familiar but I can't place it. The words have stunned me into silence.

"You'd better call off your dog, asshole."

"Who is this?" And, just as importantly, I say to myself, how did he get this phone number, but I don't ask.

"The whore bitch got what she deserved and the little nigger's gonna fry for it. There is a God after all." I could hear laughter in the background but the voice on the phone did not sound amused. "Don't fuck with us, man, or we'll fuck you up good."

"You must have the wrong number," I say as nonchalantly as I can and hang up the phone. I immediately regret it. I should have kept him talking, try to identify the voice, find out some useful information that might nail him. But I don't want him to think I am intimidated. Though my caller did not identify himself, I don't have much doubt about the source. Well, I think to myself, it looks like ole bird-dog Bert has been scaring up some birds.

TEN

Friday—July 26th

The Morganstein home is a stately Southern colonial in Killearn Estates, an upscale housing development in northeast Tallahassee that opened in the late 1960s. Though it has long since been eclipsed by more exclusive neighborhoods, Killearn Estates still remains a stable enclave of mostly middle-aged professionals with good incomes. The folks that live here thrive on the country club life, manicured lawns, swimming pools, good schools—an updated suburban Norman Rockwell painting.

When Paul and Anna purchased the house a few years ago, I had been a little surprised. Paul had been living then, and for several years before, in Los Robles, an eclectic, older downtown neighborhood, which seemed to fit him well, I had always thought. But, actually, Paul Morganstein is not the same person he was a few years ago at the public defender's office. Whether as a concession to his new clientele, or as a result of simple social and cultural evolution, he seems to enjoy swimming in the mainstream a little more these days. I guess, upon reflection, he doesn't seem so out of place here. For Anna, it is a natural.

I pull into their driveway and turn off the engine, sit for a minute, but only a minute, because the effects of the cool air conditioning dissipate quickly. Outside, the heat and humidity are oppressive, as usual. But in my short-sleeve shirt and shorts it's a little more bearable.

The door opens after my first knock. I almost expect to see Scarlett O'Hara, but it is Anna. She gives me a huge smile and a hug. Anna is a counselor by training and temperament. She has an office on Park Avenue and specializes in marital and family counseling, which I find ironic just now. She invariably knows when to be empathetic, when to cut to the heart of the matter and force the issue. She is both intuitive and logical. I remember one evening when Paul and I had suggested to her that she would make a good lawyer. She had made it clear that she found our chosen profession rather odious, for the most part, but had lessened the sting by assuring us that we were "special" and were the exceptions that proved the rule. She is a classic Italian beauty with dark hair, eyes, and skin, all highlighted by her bright and frequent smile.

"Teddy Bear. So nice to see you. How have you been?" Anna's eyes looked searchingly into mine. I am both appreciative and a little embarrassed by her concern. A divorce always makes it awkward for friends. They don't know whether to be supportive of one, the other, or both, or how to do it. I wonder now whether Anna has been keeping in touch with Beth. I want to ask her if they talk about me. I want to ask her if she thinks Beth and I have a chance. Maybe she could counsel us both. That is what she does, after all, and I know she does her job well. I want to tell her that I have been living a nightmare and that I need her help. Instead, I say in as sincere a tone as I can muster,

"I'm doing fine, Anna. Thanks. How about you?" I give her a kiss on the cheek and follow her into the living room.

"Great! I hope you're hungry." I can tell she doesn't believe me, but she doesn't contradict. "Paul's made a ton of lasagna."

"Oh, just a minute. I forgot something." I walk quickly back to the car, come back and hand her two bottles of wine, one white and one red. "I hope you can use these." I have already had three or four beers before coming over, careful to hide the odor on my breath by a heavy dose of breath spray. I don't want Paul and Anna to think I'm drinking too much, but I needed just a few to get me on a functioning level.

Anna takes the bottles with a smile, turns around again and heads back toward the kitchen, saying over her shoulder, "Everybody's in the family room, or thereabouts. Come see the kids."

"Everybody" includes Paul and his two children. Andrew, not Andy, is the oldest at thirteen. He is the spitting image of his dad with dark curly hair and dark intense eyes recessed behind John Lennon-style glasses. He is good-looking and quite intelligent, but he has a tinge of cynicism that hides his brightness and a sarcasm that does not endear him to many adults. I am the exception. We seem to get along quite well. He shakes my hand limply and makes some crack about my taste in clothes.

Then there is Jeffrey, not Jeff, age ten. He has the same dark features, but where Andrew is quiet, Jeffrey is ebullient. He is wearing a tank top, soccer shorts and shoes. He gives me a big smile and shakes my hand enthusiastically. After getting the latest news from these two, pulling the barest information from Andrew and simply opening and turning off the spigot for Jeffrey, I turn my attention to Paul.

He is putting the finishing touches on a tossed salad, looking rather frumpy in his baggy shorts and Hawaiian shirt. He is wearing an apron which reads "Paulo's Ristorante." It was a gift from Anna and the kids on Father's Day a couple of years ago. I always find it extremely ironic that it is Paul, the Jewish husband, rather than Anna, the

Italian wife, who loves to prepare, and eat, Italian food. He seems to be having fun tonight. He smiles at me and says, "Thanks for bringing the wine, bud. You want a beer?"

He acts as though Tuesday's fiasco is forgotten. Good.

"Don't mind if I do," I reply, opening the refrigerator door without further invitation and pulling a Bud Dry from the shelf.

"How's the Jackson case coming?" Paul asks, looking up briefly from his salad.

"Well . . ."

"Oh no you don't." Anna steps between us like a referee in a boxing match, shaking her head. "I told you, no shop talk." She gives Paul a stern look.

"Aw, come on, Anna," Paul pleads. "I hardly get to see the guy anyway to talk business during business hours. This is juicy stuff, anyway. I'm sure you'll be interested."

Anna throws up her hands and mutters, "Lawyers," then goes back to arranging garlic bread sticks on a tray and slips them into the oven.

Having been given the green light, or at least a caution light, to proceed, I look back to Paul and continue. "Anyway, I've got Bert looking at a couple of things, some alternative suspects. We've just got to give the jury something to hang their hats on besides Bobby Jackson."

Paul nods his approval. "What kind of angles?" He turns off the burner on the pot of fettuccini, opens the lid on the sauce pot and stirs it a bit.

I tell Paul about the ex-husband and our ex-county commissioner. I relate to him my theory about the supposed drug story. He seems intrigued, thinking about it for a second, scratching his chin. "Mmmm, interesting. Has Bert come up with anything else?"

"I don't know. I haven't talked to him since we were at the crime scene."

"Have you gotten any plea offers from the state attorney?"

"No. I guess Tom feels like he's done enough by not going for the death penalty without any concession from us."

"Yeah," Paul agrees. "Tom Haley's a good man, a straight shooter. I suspect, though, that somebody up top is pulling his reins in a little tighter than he would prefer on this case. I can imagine the strategy sessions going on. The good news for us is that the more control the top brass tries to exercise, the less effective Tom's going to be."

Anna, who had been checking on the kids, comes in to announce that dinner is ready. At this, we head for the table, heed Anna's warning and shift the subject of conversation, forgetting about work for a while.

Dinner is a long, but pleasurable experience. Paul and Anna are both good conversationalists. They can talk intelligently and with much animation on just about any topic. Politics, though, is always a favorite of Paul's. He is one of those people who seem to be able to find out all of the juicy information first. I rarely can repeat some rumor to Paul that he has not already heard. He is not a total pragmatist, however. There is still a good bit of idealism in him. He likes to talk policy, sincerely believes in the efficacy of good government. I suspect that one day he will take some high-level government position, maybe run for office.

After the kids have been put to bed, we are still at the dinner table, and Paul pours the last of a third bottle of Chianti into our glasses. It is how you often spend an evening at the Morgansteins'. Paul and I lapse again into a discussion/strategy session of the Jackson case. Anna, out of polite curiosity, aided by the wine no doubt, does not object and, indeed, listens intently. She occasionally joins in with a probing question or comment.

As Paul talks on, I find myself stealing glances at his wife, mesmerized by her beauty. Anna is wearing a summer dress of light fabric which fits snugly around the breasts and loose around the hips complementing her dark, smooth skin and her full figure. I imagine her now standing in front of me. Slowly, I unbutton her dress, then lift her up onto the dining table, knocking a wineglass out of the way. . . .

The sound of breaking glass brings me back to reality. I looked sheepishly at the floor where the remnants of my wineglass lay at my feet.

"God, I'm sorry. Mr. Klutz strikes again." I bend down to pick up the pieces of glass, assuring myself that they could not read my thoughts. Paul and Anna quickly recover from their initial shock.

"Okay, Stevens. No more for you," says Paul, with a grin.

"Well, at least the glass was empty," I say. "Sorry, Anna."

"Don't be silly," she says. "Here, I'll get that." Anna makes her way over toward me while Paul gets up and says he will get the broom.

Anna's closeness now to me as we pick up the glass makes me anxious. I grab one of the pieces of glass just as our hands accidentally touch. I grab the glass too hard and too quickly. I feel the jagged edge cut into my finger and see the bright red blood spurt quickly from the wound.

"Damn!" I drop the glass. "I'm not much use at all, am I? You got a Band-Aid?"

"Jesus, Ted." Paul is back carrying a broom and a dustpan. "It's not that big a deal. You don't have to slit your wrists. We'll get another wineglass. Here, move out of the way."

I do as I am told, holding a napkin on my finger to stem the flow of blood. Anna returns quickly with an antiseptic ointment and a Band-Aid. She makes me rinse off the cut, stops the bleeding again and I stand there, guiltily, with my finger out, as she places the Band-Aid around my finger.

The shattered glass has also shattered the alcohol-induced, hazy, feel-good aura that had enveloped the three of us for a while. When I declare that it is time for me to leave, Paul and Anna seem relieved.

Paul and Anna are, in fact, the best friends that I have ever had, and I tell them so as I leave. I tell them that I know I have been a little out of control lately and how much I appreciate them standing by me. I am getting back on firm ground, I assure them. A little dramatic perhaps, certainly unconvincing, but they both nod, a little embarrassed, but pleased. We say our good nights and I shuffle off to my car feeling better for some reason. As I drive back along Thomasville Road, however, I can't help but wonder why I could not talk to Anna, of all people, tonight about Beth and the divorce. She had given me several openings, but I had steered the conversation away each time. Now, I cannot stop the images, the memories.

The camping trips, weekends at the beach. Her beautiful, smooth skin, long, dark hair, the lovemaking, not hot and heavy, but gentle, warm. Sundays on the couch together, watching old movies. And my Annie. Beautiful, sweet baby, irascible toddler, precocious little girl. It had been too good, better than I deserved.

I shake my head as if to physically shake the memories out, dislodge the images. Then there is a familiar cold shudder, an overwhelming feeling of dread as I notice that I am now about two blocks away from Patty Stiles' house. Lost in thought, I have apparently been on autopilot. But why have I ended up here? Karma, I think.

ELEVEN

Thursday—August 8th

The package stands out in the stack of mail on my desk. Wrapped in plain brown paper, the size of a box of stationery, it has my name on the front but no address. There is no return address, nor postmark. My suspicion that this is not a box of stationery deepens when I pick it up and it is cool to the touch. I place the package immediately back on my desk.

"Jan, would you come in here a minute."

She pokes her head in the doorway, one hand on the door frame. "Yes?"

"Where'd this come from?" I ask, pointing to the package.

She shrugs. "It was sitting on your desk this morning when I came in."

"It's weird, feels cold—like it's been refrigerated or something. Let's have a look." With a strange sense of foreboding, I carefully remove the outer wrapping which has been rather crudely taped on both ends. Surprisingly enough, I see that it is indeed a stationery box underneath. Then I remove the lid.

"Oh my God!" Jan holds her hands to her mouth as if to stop herself from saying anything else, but she continues to stare at the contents, as do I. A small cat, a kitten really, obviously dead, apparently frozen, lies in the box.

"What is it?"

"It appears to be a cat, a dead one," I say.

"I know it's a cat. I mean what is it doing here, on your desk?"

"That's what I'd like to know."

Just then I notice part of a piece of paper that is sticking up on one side inside the box. I carefully remove and unfold the single sheet of plain white typing paper, containing one short paragraph:

> Curiosity is generally considered to be a good thing, Mr. Stevens. But too much of even a good thing is not wise. Remember what they say about curiosity and the cat.

I show the note to Jan. She reads it over and looks up at me. We both look suspiciously at the package.

"Is there anything else in there?" she asks.

"I don't see anything, and I don't particularly want to pick up the cat and look underneath."

Jan puts her hands to her mouth again. "This is sick. Who would do such a thing?"

We both look at each other knowing that we suspect the same thing. I state the obvious. "This Jackson case sure seems to generate a lot of fan mail. It's hard to tell who it's from though, 'cause these folks don't show the courtesy of signing their correspondence." I pick up the phone and buzz Paul's secretary. "Cathy, is Paul in?"

"Yes, Ted. But he's on the phone right now. Should I interrupt him?" She probably senses the anxiety in my voice.

"No, that's okay. I'll come over in a minute."

I put the lid back on our package. Then I call the police

and briefly describe the situation. A few seconds later I am talking to Detective Randy Powell. He seems to be more amused than concerned, but he says he'll be over in about twenty minutes. I hang up the phone, contemplating the bizarre correspondence I have just received.

It is the third such warning in as many weeks. The first letter had come inside a plain white envelope a little over two weeks ago, just a few days after the "nigger lover" phone call, as Janice had dubbed it. It had been similar to the phone message: a stream of epithets and racial slurs, warning me to keep my nose out of other people's business, and ending with the proclamation, "Death to nigger lovers." The letter was composed completely of words and letters clipped from magazines. It was like something out of a cheap B movie.

I felt sure our friends in the Brotherhood were responsible for this first correspondence and phone call. I had told Bert at the time that it didn't mean Johnson and his cohorts were murderers. Maybe they just didn't appreciate the attention. Bert had said it didn't matter. It had to help in the defense. I had agreed. Bert's got good instincts about this kind of thing.

Detective Powell also took my first report. He had pointed out what I already knew, that there wasn't a whole lot the police could do. Calling someone ugly names and even threatening them is not against the law unless the person making the threat appears to have the intent and present ability to carry out the threat. His matter-of-fact manner had annoyed me, though, like he thought I was making a big deal out of nothing.

"It doesn't really bother me," I had said as nonchalantly as I could muster. "I just thought I should report it—so there would be a record, that's all."

"You did the right thing." He nodded as if to reassure, but his arrogant smirk gave him away. "Now, if the phone calls continue, the person can be charged with making harassing phone calls, though it's gonna be tough to prove without a recording." His look and his tone echoed his earlier lament that I had not had the presence of mind to use the star tracer which would have revealed the source of the call.

As it was, I explained that I had to decline the offer to have my phone calls recorded. It would be inconsistent with attorney/client confidentiality. He had promised, at any rate, to have a little talk with our suspects. Somehow, I had the feeling that Detective Powell might have been more sympathetic to them than to me and probably would be a little more diplomatic in his approach than I would prefer. He called later to tell me that Johnson and the others had denied any involvement. Surprise! He also said he felt sure I wouldn't have any more problems. Right!

The second letter came about a week later. It also had been preceded by a phone call a few days before. But there the similarity ended. The second letter was more sophisticated in style, tone, and format. Rather than cut-out words or letters, it had been typed. The writer suggested: "Look deep within your heart, consider your own personal problems, your own close ties to the victim, and do your client a favor, get off the case."

The phone call that preceded that second letter came at the office one evening when I was working late—and after I had managed to down about a half a fifth of bourbon.

"Hello?"

"Is this Attorney Ted Stevens?" The caller's voice was obviously disguised. It sounded like a black male, perhaps, but it was too hard to tell.

"Yes. Who is this?"

"This is a friend."

"Most of my friends don't disguise their voices. As a matter of fact, they usually come right out and identify themselves. Even perfect strangers do that, those who have manners do anyway." I was tired, a little drunk, and in no mood for games. "What can I do for you."

"Well, Teddy Bear, let's just say I want to give you some friendly advice," a pause and then, "about the Jackson case."

The use of my nickname was unsettling. The group of people who knew it was not large, and even fewer actually used it. The caller either knew me or had made the effort to find out about me. The man had my attention now, but I still could not place the voice. "I'm listening. Who is this?"

"It doesn't matter. Let's just say that you are annoying some people who can, and will, make your life very uncomfortable and, if necessary, much shorter."

"You have a very polite way of threatening to kill someone," I remarked. I tried to keep the casual sarcasm in my voice, but I could hear it shaking. I tried to stay calm, remembering Powell's recommendation and made a mental note to try to trace the call. The voice on the other end continued.

"These people know the truth about you and Patty Stiles, Counselor. You were a damn fool to take this case. Now, as I see it, you have two choices."

I knew this was supposed to be the time when I say something sarcastic, but I couldn't think of anything smart and, truthfully, I didn't dare interrupt, anxious to hear my two choices. I could feel my world coming down around me.

"Your first choice, and personally, I think the best one, is to get off this case before it blows up in your face. It shouldn't be too hard. Everybody knows you've had some personal problems that you need to work through. Plus you've been getting some threatening mail . . ."

"How'd you know about that?" I ask, cutting him off,

and immediately upset with myself for confirming what might have been just speculation. He didn't respond, though, to my question. "Anyway, you shouldn't have any trouble getting off the case. I am sure if you file a motion to withdraw, Judge Rowe will grant it."

This person seemed to know quite a bit, too much about me personally and had a very good grasp of legal procedure. A lawyer? "And my other choice?"—a little false bravado.

"Let justice take its course. Go ahead and continue on the case. Just don't go making trouble for people when you don't need to. Nobody expects you to be Perry Mason and expose the real killer. That only happens in the movies. Besides, we both know you don't really want to do that. You're too smart for that. Look, nobody's saying you have to roll over on this thing. But you've got enough right now to be able to argue reasonable doubt to a jury. If you can get him off, it's a feather in your cap but, if you lose, no one's going to blame you. Hell, everybody thinks he's guilty anyway."

"Sounds a lot like you want me to throw the fight." It was hard now to disguise the sarcasm.

"No, just don't swing blindly and hit the wrong person."

"Thanks for calling, Mr. . . . ." There was no response from my caller. "How can I get back in touch with you?"

There was a short sneering laugh on the other end. "Good night, Counselor, and good luck." And he hung up.

The call had unnerved me. I sat there for several minutes. The only light was from the table lamp. The a.c. fan was not running, the windows shut out the outside noise, and it was eerily silent inside my office. Clearly, Bert or I had hit a raw nerve with somebody. The caller assumed I knew for whom he was speaking. If he knew so much about the case, though, he would know that there were several persons who might be annoyed with our investigation of this case. My neo-Nazi friends? Perhaps, but I didn't think so. Whoever made the first call and sent the first letter had a completely different style of communication from the more recent caller. The ex-husband? Again, a possibility, but Peter was the more direct type, not likely to be so subtle. It could be one of the folks at school, or at the paper. Although we had nothing we could use on anyone at either of those places, they had no way of knowing that. People with something to hide often tend toward paranoia if you get close to discovering their secret, especially if it is a dark one. Again, even if I were to identify these people who were "annoyed," it didn't mean I could show they were guilty of murder. But it might help me establish reasonable doubt. I had also realized something else. I had forgotten to trace the call.

I had not shown the second letter to Detective Powell nor told him about the phone call preceding it. It had hit too close to home. I had not wanted to have to explain what the author had meant about my "close ties to the victim" and my "personal problems." Besides, given the ambiguous language, the detective would not have seen it as a threat.

I walk downstairs to Paul's office. His door is open and, as usual, he is on the phone, standing and looking out his window as he talks. He motions me in as he hangs up.

"What's wrong?" He has detected my anxiety.

"You got a second? I got something you probably ought to see."

"Sure."

He follows me back to my office where I show him the package and the note, explain to him what happened and what I know about it. Had I called the police? Yes. Did I have any idea who might have sent it? Some, but not conclusive. We talk about my theories.

"Whoever delivered this package," I observe, "was pretty bold because they could easily have been seen."

"Not really. You walk by here late at night on the sidewalk. You look to see if anybody's in the office or on the street. If not, you stick the package in the slot and keep on walking. If there's somebody around you don't do it."

"You've got a pretty devious mind, Morganstein. So tell me then, what is this criminal thinking?"

Paul goes through an analysis similar to what I have done, except that he is unaware of the second letter and call. He says that Bert or I had obviously stepped on somebody's toes, that the person had somehow gotten close enough to know some things that the general public would not. He says it's someone who knows something about criminal proceedings, someone who is desperate, because to make contact with me at all is a risk, certain to raise my suspicions. "One thing is clear," Paul says. "Whoever it is obviously has something to hide. Find out who it is and you'll have considerable power over them. People with something to hide are very vulnerable."

Was he talking about me? I return his look, nod my head in agreement. Perhaps, I think to myself, the person is more arrogant than desperate, confident that his knowledge has given him power over me.

Paul puts the note back on my desk, turns and looks out the window, his hands clasped behind his back. "Teddy, you will be careful won't you? I can't afford to break in a new partner." He turns and smiles briefly at me, then gives me a concerned look. "Seriously, though, maybe you ought to get Bert on this a little tighter if our friends at the police department don't want to give it the attention it deserves."

"Hell, Bert's the one stirring up this pot, I think. He's managed to piss off just about everybody he's interviewed.

Mr. Tact he is not. But I will see what he can do about finding out who my pen pals are. It just might prove very helpful.''

"Good. So, what else is new on this case?"

I give him the good news first, a modified blow by blow as best as I can remember from Bert's written reports to me. Some of it Paul already knows about and he nods impatiently for me to keep going. He is surprised and intrigued though, when I give him the bad news. The state has a new witness, one Curtis Warner. "Mr. Warner, it seems, is a clerk at a Mini Mart on Adams Street near FAMU," I say. He told police investigators that Bobby Jackson came into his store the night of the murder, some time between eleven and eleven thirty.''

"That's not necessarily bad is it? Doesn't it support Jackson's story in the sense that it is on his way home."

"Yes. To some degree it does, except for one significant point. The time. Bobby first told me he went straight home. When I told him about the clerk, he said yeah, he did stop in to get a beer. He says it was about eleven forty-five."

"So, what's the problem?"

"I'm getting there. Now, B.J. says he made it home a little after twelve. His mother backs him up, says it wasn't too long after she heard the clock in her living room chime twelve that she heard her son come in the door. Of course, mama may be lying, though I doubt it. She might fudge a little, or maybe she's mistaken, but let's assume for the minute that it's true."

"The victim was killed somewhere around midnight, right?" Paul has now seated himself in my chair and is rocking gently back and forth, his elbows resting on the arms.

"That's right. This is based upon the medical examiner's report as well as the fact that one of Patty's neighbors heard, or thought they heard, a scream right around that time."

"So, as I was saying, if Bobby got home a little after twelve, then it took him an hour to walk home."

I look at Paul and pause to make sure I have his attention. "An hour is a long time, Paul. Bert and I walked it off ourselves. It took us thirty-five minutes at a leisurely pace to walk from the restaurant to Bobby's house. It took us twenty minutes to get to the Mini Mart. If Bobby's mother had said he came home around eleven thirty, the clerk would be our alibi witness. As it is, he places our client three blocks away from the victim's home forty-five minutes before her death with no reasonable explanation of where he was, or what took him so long to get home."

"Maybe the clerk is mistaken as to the time," Paul suggests.

"Interestingly enough, that is also the theory of our client. It's going to be a hard one to float, though. The clerk says that Bobby purchased a beer and a pack of cigarettes, Winstons to be exact. The man has an eye for detail. And he says no, it was not eleven forty-five, it was certainly before eleven thirty. He remembers because the eleven o'clock news was still running. Apparently they have a small TV they keep behind the counter for when things are slow."

"And here's the best part," I add. "Guess what kind of cigarettes they found in the ashtray in Patty Stiles' living room?"

"Winstons?"

"You got it."

"And a beer can?"

"No, thank God. But, the state will argue he drank it on the way and got rid of it before he got to the victim's house. Haley will say that B.J. got off work at about ten forty-five P.M., then went to the victim's home, stopping first for cigarettes and a beer. Patty Stiles' home is a short three-block walk from the Mini Mart. He arrives sometime between eleven fifteen and eleven thirty. Jackson is a regular visitor there. They're lovers. He comes in, they waste no time. They're like dogs in heat—right on the living room couch. That's consistent with the physical evidence including semen spots on the sofa. Maybe they smoke a little crack first, maybe after. At any rate, he's there long enough to smoke a couple of cigarettes. For some reason, they turn from lovemaking to quarreling, to a physical fight. Maybe she even grabs the knife first, but he gets it away from her. He loses control and begins to stab her over and over again."

"Boy, you can tell you used to be a prosecutor," Paul shakes his head. Both of us know it sounds very plausible. I feel obligated to point out some positive points. The physical evidence, though damaging, is not conclusive and the only eyewitness who perhaps saw the killer running from the house isn't sure of his identification. It could have been Bobby Jackson. But the neighbor, to his credit, has not let the investigators bully him into a positive ID. We are hanging by a thread, a thin one no doubt, but we are still hanging, I point out. Shaking up the Mini Mart clerk's testimony, though, will be a high priority at trial.

Paul nods his agreement. "I've got a ten o'clock appointment," he says. "Let me know how I can help. If you want, I'll help you on some other cases while you concentrate on this one." He rises, looking at his watch, the signal that our conference is over.

"I'll let you know. Thanks." I say to his back as he walks out the door.

I concluded after my first contact with Detective Randy Powell that he was an arrogant asshole. Nothing in our second encounter so far has changed my opinion. I get the impression that he looks upon the crime victim as causing him unnecessary work.

Powell is a short, thick man, with large muscles that are on the verge of turning to fat, his suit one size too small. He looks about forty and wears his sandy blond hair midway over the ears and sports long sideburns, a modified Beatles look. The overall effect is of a person who is always a little behind the times. A redneck nerd. I also get the impression that he is hindered in his job by the fact that he already knows it all. Though this is a learning disability usually associated with teenagers, some people never outgrow it.

Powell looks at the dead cat in the box on my desk with curious detachment. The cat is still frozen stiff. He is able to pick it up by its tail to look at its underside. He puts the cat down and circles my desk looking at the cat from different angles as if he were a golfer preparing to make a putt. His questions are, surprisingly, relevant and direct. Who was the last to leave the evening before? I was. Who was the first in the office? My secretary, Janice. Who first came in contact with the package? Again, Janice. How did it get in the office? Most likely through the after-hours delivery slot. Adrienne had delivered the other mail but didn't remember seeing the package. Any ideas about who might have sent it? A few. I don't think it is from the same person that sent my first letter. I do not tell him of the second one.

Before I know it, the conversation has turned to my relationship with Patty Stiles. When had I represented her? Is that when I first met her? When did my representation of Patty Stiles end? When was the last time I had seen her professionally or personally?

When I question the relevance of these questions, he assures me that he is only looking at possible connections between the threatening mail and the phone calls I have received in the Jackson case. Maybe, he suggests, the person sending me these letters has something very personal against me. He suggests that even if there was nothing to it, someone might get the impression that Stiles and I might have had something going. People sometimes tend to think that about divorce lawyers. He smirks. When he says this I want to slap him, but he is too close to the truth. Is this hick Columbo act for real? Is he setting me up? Maybe it's the ex-husband, he suggests. I agree that the ex-husband is a distinct possibility.

"We got to look at all the angles, you know." Then he wants to know a little more about how the package got on my desk. Am I sure it came in the after-hours delivery slot? We call Janice back into the office, ask her. She checks with the other folks in the office. Adrienne comes back with her. Says she brought the overnight packages and mail to my office. She is sorry but she doesn't remember whether the package was there or not. No one else in the office, Janice says, knows how it got on my desk.

Powell looks at me with raised eyebrows. He asks me if there are any signs of forced entry. No. He asks me who all has a key. I tell him only the people who are here now. He doesn't say but I am sure he is considering the possibility that someone here planted the package. He thanks me for my cooperation, tells me someone is just trying to shake me up a bit probably. He leaves, promising to follow up, requesting again that I consider a tracer on my phone. Again I refuse.

About 4:30 P.M., Tom Haley calls me. It has been almost two weeks now since I filed the motion for additional discovery regarding the notebook and the computer. I expect he is calling to let me know he has my copies and to arrange for access to the computer.

"Hey Ted, how's it going," he says when I get on the line.

"It hasn't been a great day." I tell him about the cat.

"Yes, very interesting," he says. "So the threats continue. This is serious, Ted. Anybody who would go to this length just to try to scare you off a case has got some serious problems."

"Have you got my notebook ready for me yet?" There is a long pause before he responds. "That's really the main reason I called you. Well, you see, we have a bit of a problem. The TPD guys tell me they can't find the little notebook. Not on the magazine table, not on the desk, not anywhere in that area. Are you sure that's where you left it?"

"What do you mean? Of course I'm sure." I almost shout into the telephone. "What the hell's going on here, Tom?"

"I don't know, Ted. I don't know. I will tell you, though, that there's a group of people up here that think you might be sending hate mail, and now dead cats, to yourself, think maybe you might also be making up this thing about the notebook." He senses that I am about to explode again and cuts me off. "Now I know that's not true, Ted, but you ought to know what is going around."

"That would mean that both Bert and I are liars, then, because he saw it too. Who are these people?" I say, my voice rising in volume.

"That wouldn't be wise for me or you, Ted. Suffice it to say, I don't work in a vacuum here and I can't control what some people think, or what they do about it. You might just want to watch yourself. Don't give anybody an opening. If one assumes that notebook existed, either somebody has intentionally or unintentionally misplaced it. Consequences or ramifications of that scenario do not fly well over here, as you can imagine."

"What about the computer?"

"You're welcome to check it out anytime. My written response is going out today, but," another long pause, "you probably won't find anything. We've already checked it out. There's nothing, absolutely nothing, on the computer. Must have been some kind of short in the electrical wiring or something."

I calm myself as best I can. Finally I say, "In the immortal words of Bugs Bunny, you realize that this means war."

"Yes, I know you'll file your motion to dismiss and you know I'll vigorously oppose it and wait and see what happens. But whatever happens, you can rest assured that I've got my own people working on this. I do intend to find out what happened to that notebook."

"Thanks for the call, Tom. I'll talk to you later."

Without hesitation, I dial Bert Murphy's number. He isn't at his office, but I reached him on his mobile phone.

"Bert, this is Ted. How's it going?"

"Can't complain. What's happening?"

"New development in the Jackson case. You know the small pocket notebook we found at the victim's house? The one that might have been notes about that drug story she was working on?"

"Yeah."

"The state attorney says they've lost it."

"What do you mean they lost it?"

"My sentiments exactly. I need you to find it."

"I don't get it, pal. If they've lost it, isn't that kinda good for you? I mean can't you get the case dismissed, 'cause they've lost, or destroyed, evidence?"

"Well, I'm going to damn sure try, but it's no guarantee. I still think this is a lead that's real promising and we need to follow it up. The fact that it's missing confirms it to me. We just need to put some meat on this somehow."

"Okay, boss. Whatever you say. But I still think you'll get more mileage out of the fact that it's missin' than if you find it. After all, it didn't seem like it had a whole lot in it."

"Maybe not, but something tells me to follow up on it. Humor me, okay? Oh, and by the way, that's not all. I got an interesting package today."

"What kind of package?"

TWELVE

Thursday—August 8th

I notice the blue flashing light in my rearview mirror right away, or so it seems. But I've been lost in thought and I can't be sure how long the police car has been behind me. What does he want? My speedometer reads thirty-five miles per hour, well within the speed limit. Must be something, though. He doesn't go around. My heart races wildly. The sweat, a result of nerves as much as climate, makes large wet spots underneath my arms.

The first available place to pull over is, ironically, the parking lot of an ABC Liquor Store. The patrol car stops directly behind me, blocking my exit. Next to the building there is a group of college kids loitering around the back of a pickup truck. They all lower their beers, look our way. I roll down my window and watch in my side mirror. The officer seems to be in no hurry to get out of his car. He is talking on his radio. Finally, he gets out and walks slowly, cautiously toward me. He stops about three feet from the driver's side and bends down slightly. I have taken my license out of my wallet and have it ready for him.

"What's the problem, Officer?" I ask, handing him my license.

He looks at the license for what seems like a very long

time, without responding to my question. Finally, he says "Mr. Stevens, I stopped you because you were going unusually slow—thirty miles per hour in a forty-five mile per hour zone—and you were weaving a bit in your lane. Would you step out of the vehicle, please?" His tone is polite but it is a directive, not a question.

Wiping the sweat from my forehead, I consider my options, regretting now the half pint of Jim Beam that I had consumed at the office. It had been a long day though, starting with a dead cat on my desk. I had been working late and needed a little bit to keep me going. There is no question in my mind that I am over the legal limit. In truth, there has hardly been a time lately when I have not been. I know that I cannot risk giving him any more evidence on which to charge me with a DUI, which is clearly what he has in mind. On the other hand, refusing the "request" of a law enforcement officer is usually a losing proposition. I look at the man standing outside of my car a little more closely, reading his name tag—Gilbert King. He is a young man, well built, clean-cut looking. Too bad, I think. I know a lot of officers, but not this one. No matter, I have decided on a course.

"Officer King," I say, trying to sound polite but resolute, assured. "You have my license. If you intend to give me a ticket for something, you can do so without me getting out of the car. From what you have just said, however, it doesn't appear that you have a basis to issue me a citation."

If Officer King is surprised or taken aback by my response, he doesn't show it. The look in his eyes, though, tells me that I will probably not be driving away from this encounter. I start to question my decision but I also realize that I cannot undo it. The die, as they say, is cast.

"Mr. Stevens," he says, "something tells me that you might be a lawyer." A trace of a smile has replaced the brief flash of anger I had seen a moment before in his eyes.

Well, at least the guy has a sense of humor. Maybe this can be salvaged after all, I think.

"Good assumption. Actually I used to be with the state attorney's office and did several months in traffic court. I'm in private practice now. As a matter of fact I have represented plenty of the guys on the force." I smile, more nervously than I had wanted.

"Must have been before my time," he deadpans. "At any rate, Mr. Stevens, given your experience, I am sure you can understand why I have stopped you. And you are right. I have no basis to issue you a civil traffic citation. However, as I am sure you are aware, the facts I have outlined give me reasonable suspicion to stop your car. Having done so, I noted that it took you longer than normal to stop your car. Also, having approached your car, I now smell the odor of alcohol upon your breath, and I note further that your eyes appear watery and bloodshot. All in all, I'd say I have probable cause to believe you are driving under the influence of alcoholic beverages. I therefore feel that I have sufficient reason to request that you perform some field sobriety exercises which will either confirm or allay my suspicions. I am sure that you can appreciate the situation, so I ask you again, Mr. Stevens, to please step out of your vehicle."

Damn. Of all the patrol officers who could have stopped me, I draw Robo Cop. He's much too young to be such a pro. I had hoped to rattle him a bit, maybe goad him into making a mistake, even perhaps intimidating him into letting me go. Not a good move, I see now. I slowly open the car door and get out, making sure that I don't lean on the car or appear unsteady on my feet. I decide to give it one more try.

"Officer King, I appreciate your concern and I can see your perspective. However, let me point out a few things. I've been working late in my office, which would account for red or watery eyes. Nonalcoholic beer smells the same as regular beer, which would account for the odor of an alcoholic beverage. You will no doubt have to agree that I do not appear to be unsteady on my feet, my speech is not slurred, my thought process appears to be rational and appropriate under the circumstances. Since I don't believe you have justification to require it, I do not intend to perform any field sobriety exercises or submit to a breath test. If you plan to arrest me for DUI, this is all you are going to get."

"Very well," he says, not missing a beat. "You will please then turn around and put your hands behind your back." It is now painfully clear that my gamble has not paid off. The officer's words are said with such cold detachment that I struggle to contain an involuntary shiver. He places the handcuffs on me and puts me in the back seat of his cruiser.

The implications of my situation are serious. I probably would not be disbarred, but I could be suspended from the practice of law, receive a public reprimand, at the very least. There will be whispered gossip, people shaking their heads. Bunch of hypocrites! I can drive better drunk than most of them can sober! Dandy Don's going to like this. He'll go running to Judge Miller, trying to cut off my visitation. "See, I told you, Judge. He's an alcoholic. He can't be trusted with a young child's safety." Damn! Damn! Damn!

I am so angry I want to scream. Angry at this young upstart of a cop who has to realize that he doesn't have much of a case. Angry at the humiliation of being handcuffed and arrested on the street. Angry that I have not thought of something to say, to do, to avoid this. Angry at the timing, which couldn't be worse. I want to kick the back seat of the car. I want to cuss this little asshole for everything he's worth. But I do not. I am angry but I do not show it. My anger gives me focus. I will give him nothing.

The DUI testing and observation room appears just as cold and detached as Officer King. It is approximately twelve by twelve, and, except for the small wooden bench on which I sit, a telephone on one wall and a video camera mounted on the other, it is devoid of any furniture or equipment. We have been here now about thirty minutes.

Down the center of the room for approximately ten to twelve feet is a red line that connects to a small red box. This is the proverbial straight line which drunks are required to walk. I wonder how I would have done. Since I have refused to do any field sobriety exercises, as King called them, I will never know—and neither will a jury.

Officer King had, for the benefit of the video camera, again requested that I perform the field sobriety tests and submit to a breath test to determine the amount of alcohol in my blood. He had read to me the implied consent law which basically says that anyone arrested for a DUI who does not submit to a breath test will lose their license for a year for the first refusal and eighteen months for a subsequent refusal. King had taken my refusal to do the exercises, the breath test, or to give anything other than my basic name, rank and serial number, without any visible sign of annoyance. He had just marked on his little clipboard, said "Very well," and walked off.

Through the glass window I notice him now speaking with another officer, whose back is to me. When the other officer turns around and gives me a nod, I realize it is a former client. Bart Milligan and his wife had saved their money for years to invest in a nice home, only to discover serious structural damage from termite infestation soon after they moved in. They had retained me, and we had sued both the seller and the termite inspection company. The jury, having been convinced that there was fraud and collusion, had awarded enough punitive damages to take care of all of the Milligan's repair bills and their legal expenses, with a significant amount left over. The facts had been good and it had not taken a lot of talent to win it, but you could not have convinced Bart of that. For a moment, my hopes rise. Maybe Bart will intercede on my behalf.

Bart walks over to me, a serious look on his face, with Officer King in tow. I rise to shake his hand.

"Officer Milligan," I say with mock formality. "Fancy seeing you here."

"Ted." His tone is noncommittal. He turns around and looks at King, who bows slightly, taking his cue, saying he'll be in the next room if he is needed. Bart motions me into a side room, a small cubicle actually, in which there are two chairs and a desk in between. He takes one seat and I take the other. I slouch a little bit in the chair, leaning back, not quite knowing what to expect but looking at my former client for some clue. He leans forward in his chair putting his arms on the desk, looking at me very intensely for a moment, and then looking at my arrest paperwork. He shakes his head slowly from side to side. "I don't know, Teddy. This doesn't look too good."

"Well, this is not my idea of a fun evening either." I decide to broach the subject. "What do you think, Bart? Can you help me out on this one? Can you convince Officer Gung Ho there that he doesn't have a case?"

"Ted, this may not be the best case in the world, but a good prosecutor will burn your ass on it. Even if you beat the DUI, you'll lose your license under implied consent. Anyway you look at it, it ain't good. Listen, buddy, I wish I could help you. But once you're brought in, the ball starts rolling and there ain't no way to stop it until it gets to the end."

I nod, watching my last hope shake his head and walk out of the room.

I have been to this jail hundreds of times, but the sights and sounds here are a little different when you're on the inside looking out. I am thinking about this as I am told to undress, exchanging my clothes for the olive-green uniform of the Leon County Detention Center, my street shoes for the standard-issue sandals. The attending officer has, thankfully, foregone the further humiliation of shower and delousing. Since I am here only on a misdemeanor and likely to be released soon, they do not bother. Fingerprints have already been taken.

The pretrial release officer has interviewed me, explaining what I already know. A person charged with DUI cannot be released after arrest either on bond or otherwise, unless either his blood alcohol level is below .05 percent or eight hours have elapsed since his arrest. Because I have declined to submit to the breath test, I am to be held over for first appearance in the morning.

The large holding cell is surprisingly clean and my other cell mates reasonably quiet and nonthreatening. The lecherous looks that I somehow expect are not forthcoming. There is a small old homeless-looking guy who smells of booze and sweat and other unpleasant but indistinguishable odors. He tries to make small talk but I am in no mood and he senses it, leaving me alone. I try to sleep, but barely doze. My dreams are fitful, visions of Beth—the painful, hurtful goodbye. In one dream Beth is pointing an accusing finger at me but her face suddenly turns into Patty Stiles. Patty is blood-drenched, pointing her finger at me and shouting "Murderer! Murderer!"

"No," I shout back at Patty Stiles, then suddenly bolt upright, realizing where I am. None of the others seems to have noticed. My jail-issue shirt is soaked and sweat is dripping down my forehead and the sides of my face. I cannot sleep anymore. I need a drink, bad. I try to push thoughts of Beth and Patty Stiles out of my mind. I try to think of pleasant thoughts, but I cannot. I think how surprised some of my clients might be to see me in their cell pod. "Hi, how you doing—I'm your lawyer. That's the bad news. The good news is we'll have time to chat." I smile involuntarily.

It is 8:15 A.M. I declined the breakfast offered at 5:30 A.M., but now I'm having second thoughts. I do not know when I have last eaten. There are ten to twelve similarly dressed men in the small room with me. The correctional officer wheels over a TV monitor with a VCR, plugs it in, tells us to listen up, and then plays a tape of Judge Raymond Smith. Judge Smith advises us via video of what is about to happen.

"The purpose of this first appearance proceeding is to allow a judge an opportunity to review the arrest affidavit in your case and determine if there is probable cause to charge you, inform you of the charges against you, and set reasonable conditions for your release from jail pending the disposition of your case. You are entitled to a lawyer and if you are unable to hire your own, one may be appointed for you. . . ."

He tells us that the judge will be glad to listen to whatever we want to tell him or her but cautions us that everything we are saying is being recorded and could be used against us in court later.

One by one we are led to a small room. There is another small monitor and a camera there which I am told to look into. On the split screen in front of me I can see the state attorney, the public defender, and the judge. The judge is Carlotta Moore, a petite African-American woman of about forty. She is a recent appointee but conducts her court with the authority of a long-termer. I possibly could have done worse in picking a first-appearance judge for my case, but I don't think so. Moore is a teetotaler and she strikes me as the motherly type who would not hesitate to slap her kid in the face if he gave her any backtalk, even if she had to climb a stepladder to do it. But mostly, she disciplines with her disapproval. It seems to work on adults as well as children.

I do my best not to show the embarrassment I feel, but I can see it in the eyes and hear it in the words and tones of the judge, the clerk, and the state attorney. Painfully, personally, I understand the myth of the presumption of innocence.

"Mr. Stevens, good morning."

"Good morning, Your Honor."

"You are charged with DUI. I am sure you are not in need of court-appointed counsel. You are to be released without the posting of a monetary bond on the condition that you consume no alcoholic beverages, that condition to be monitored by the pretrial release office via random alco checks. Also, that you submit to an alcohol abuse screening and participate in whatever counseling, if any, is recommended as a result of that screening. Any questions?"

"Well, Your Honor, I don't have any questions, but I would like to be heard."

"Yes?" Her face registers surprise that I would want to say any thing at all.

"With all due respect, Your Honor, I don't believe that you have the authority to require that I engage in counseling as part of pretrial release conditions. And, although the no-alcohol condition is certainly within your discretion, I respectfully submit that a complete ban on alcohol whatsoever is unreasonable and unnecessary. As you can see, the probable cause in this case is very weak at best and to impose these conditions on me before I'm convicted makes a mockery of the presumption of innocence. I have no prior criminal history. I have significant ties to the community. A simple ROR with no conditions is more than sufficient in my case to protect the community and to ensure my attendance at all court proceedings."

Out of the corner of my eye, I can see the prosecutor covering his eyes. Moore looks at me as if I am in fact drunk right now, or perhaps crazy.

"Mr. Stevens, those are the least restrictive conditions with which I feel comfortable. Your comments have served to confirm in my mind the correctness of my decision. If you believe I have exceeded my authority, you may seek a writ of habeas corpus, or you may seek a modification of these conditions from the trial judge."

"Oh well, no harm in trying," I say with a smile, though the look she gives me suggests that there may very well be real harm in trying.

"Mr. Stevens, I am dead serious about the no-alcohol condition. Don't make the mistake of testing me on it. Do we understand each other?"

"Yes, Your Honor. You'll have no problem with me," I say as sincerely as possible.

THIRTEEN

Wednesday—August 14th

"Mr. Stevens?" Judge John Rowe looks at me expectantly.

I rise slowly from my seat at the defense table. Rowe's words to me are like a spotlight, and I can feel all eyes shift to me. The room is packed, as it has been for all the proceedings in the Jackson case. The excitement and attention, however, are at a new level. Paul has played the story with the press well. Destruction of evidence? A cover-up? He has been planting the seeds of reasonable doubt before the trial begins. Reverend Paxton has gotten into the swing of things, as well, having been quoted as suggesting the possibility of some conspiracy and that race may be playing a part in the motivation of the unnamed conspirators. I had hoped the press coverage might bring out a witness who knows about the drug story, but it has not happened.

Unfortunately, the press lost no time in pouncing on the story of my DUI arrest. I have taken my usual "no comment" approach. Paul is still pissed at me, but he did his usual snow job with the press, words to the effect that the young officer had made a mistake and that we expect the charges to be dropped. Thankfully, after several days the story has grown a little stale and things have quieted down a bit. Bobby's family and Reverend Paxton will need a little more massaging, however. Paul has promised to work on them.

"We are asking the court to dismiss all charges against my client because the state has either intentionally destroyed or negligently misplaced certain crucial evidence—specifically, a small pocket-sized notebook in which the victim made notes concerning a news story that she was working on. This evidence is crucial because it could lead to suspects other than the defendant. Without this evidence, the defendant cannot receive a fair trial and due process requires that this case be dismissed. I am ready to proceed with witnesses."

Tom Haley rises quickly from his chair, speaking as he does so. "May the state be heard, Your Honor?"

"Briefly," Rowe replies.

"The state's position as to this motion is quite simple. There is no evidence that the state either intentionally destroyed this notebook nor negligently misplaced it, because it was never in the state's possession. Although the victim's home is still closed to the public because it is a crime scene, there is not a guard there. Secondly, and probably most importantly, any relevance of this notebook to the case exists only in the mind of Mr. Stevens. Its disappearance by whatever means, does not justify a dismissal. Thank you." He sits down.

"Mr. Stevens, call your first witness."

"Yes, sir, my first witness will be me. I will be questioned by Mr. Morganstein." The clerk administers the oath and I take the stand. Rowe nods to Paul. My partner's questions are short and to the point, as are the answers. I explain how I came to find the notebook, and by use of an exhibit I testify as to what I remember had been written there. I explain how I had filed my motion for additional discovery and how, two weeks later, Tom Haley had called to tell me that the item could not be produced.

"What about the other discovery request, concerning the computer," Paul asks.

"Objection. The motion deals only with the notebook, Your Honor. Questions about the computer are irrelevant."

"Overruled."

"Yes, Mr. Haley also informed me that their investigators had already examined the computer and could find no files. He suggested that there must have been an electrical short, that all of the specific computer files of the victim were no longer on the computer."

"And, did you examine the computer anyway?"

"Yes, my secretary and I accessed the computer and tried to locate any work or personal files of the victim on the computer."

"And were you successful?"

"No, we were not. We could find no files whatsoever."

"And do you find that particularly unusual?" Paul asks.

"Objection, Your Honor." Haley is on his feet again. "That calls for speculation, and besides, what Mr. Stevens thinks is unusual is irrelevant."

"Sustained."

"All right, Mr. Stevens, let's get back to the notebook, then," Paul continues. "You have suggested in your motion that this notebook was important evidence in this case. Why, from the defense's perspective, is this notebook important?"

"Objection. Again, this is speculation and irrelevant."

"I'm going to overrule it for now."

"Do you recall the question, Mr. Stevens?"

"Yes. This notebook is significant because it is corroboration that the victim was working on a news story at the time of her death involving drug usage and transactions in the African-American community. The finding of this small notebook, together with the fact that I could find no other notes, files, or other computer record of the story, points in the direction of the killer being somehow connected with this ongoing story."

Haley is on his feet again with a pained expression on his face. "Your Honor, I fail to see how Mr. Stevens' fantasies can be relevant to this motion at all. If he has information, other than hearsay, about this alleged story, then he should produce it."

"Well, Mr. Prosecutor, I think I can separate the wheat from the chaff here. Everybody's got a right to dream, I guess. I'm going to overrule the objection, but I do note that there has been no evidence so far to substantiate this theory." Rowe looks at me, then at Paul.

After a few more questions from Paul, it is Haley's turn. His first line of questioning I expect: an attempt to shake me on some details, try to show that I could have been mistaken about what I remembered being in the notebook. He points out that I have no particular expertise in terms used in the drug trade. He gets me to admit that I have no personal knowledge of the victim's work habits, that I have no personal knowledge that the victim was working on a story involving drug dealing, or any other story for that matter. How long had it been, he asked, after discovering the notebook, had I made my notations as to what was in it? About two weeks. Had I shown the notebook to the officer? No, I had not. He asks me if my investigator had been with me. Yes, he had. I know the implication of the question. Would Bert confirm my memory of what was in the notebook. I had already asked him and he said it looked familiar but he couldn't be sure, so I had ruled him out as a witness. The failure to call Bert won't be lost on Rowe either, I am sure.

"How long were you at the victim's residence?"

"About three hours."

"Did you look through the area of the house that was apparently set up for work or as her office?"

"Yes."

"Did you look through her file cabinet, her files?"

"Yes."

"Her desk?"

"Yes."

"It would be safe to assume, would it not, Mr. Stevens, that you went over this area with a fine-toothed comb, in fact, searched the entire house thoroughly, specifically looking for any evidence that would support your theory about a drug dealing story?"

"I was looking for anything that might help me in my defense, including the theory that you mentioned."

"Did you find anything else, anything at all, in your extensive examination of this work area and materials, and in the search of the entire house, that would suggest or corroborate your theory that the victim was working on some story about drug dealing?"

I pause for several seconds. "It was more what I didn't find."

"Yes or no, Counselor. Did you find anything else to corroborate this fantasy about some drug dealing story?"

Paul is on his feet. "Your Honor, I object to Mr. Haley's characterization of the defense's very legitimate theory of defense."

"Sustained."

Haley nods deferentially toward Rowe, but presses on. "The question, Mr. Stevens, is whether, after your extensive and exhaustive search and examination of the victim's house, did you find anything at all, other than some scribbling in a pocket-sized notebook, that would support or corroborate your . . . theory." Haley pauses and looks at Paul, letting his choice of words make his point.

Having thought of nothing better, I answer, "No."

"And do you have any other corroboration of this theory?"

Since I cannot divulge that my client is the source of my information, I answer, "No."

"So,"—Haley was relentless—"you did not find a file on this drug dealing story?"

"No, I did not."

"No rough draft, no notes, no photographs?"

"Mr. Haley," Rowe interrupts, "I think you've beaten this dead horse enough. Move on."

"Yes, Your Honor. That's all I have." Haley strides confidently back to his table and sits down.

"Mr. Stevens," Paul begins as he pushes his chair back from the table and eases himself to a standing position with an ease that belies his large size, "you were asked by Mr. Haley whether you *found* anything at Ms. Stiles' home which tended to support or corroborate your . . . *theory.*" He looks again at Haley, clearly enjoying himself. He pauses, looking expectantly at the judge. Even with no jury he has an inherent dramatic flair, and he knows how to keep his audience in suspense, eager for what is next. "Was there anything that you did not find that struck you as unusual?"

"Objection, Your Honor. Mr. Morganstein is again trying to get into evidence what Mr. Stevens thinks is unusual. It was irrelevant when he did it earlier, and it's irrelevant now."

"Sustained."

"Yes, well, Mr. Stevens, let me ask you this. Did you find anything, anything at all, that would show or suggest that the victim was working on any other story at the time of her death?"

"No, I did not."

"No notes, no files, no photos?"

"No."

"Were you looking for such evidence?"

"Yes, I looked for cassette tapes, computer disks. I didn't find anything at all. There weren't even any blank disks. It was like someone had erased the computer files and taken the floppy . . ."

"Objection." Haley is on his feet once again. "This is pure speculation."

"Sustained. Mr. Morganstein, you need to move on to something else," Rowe says with finality.

"Very well. Thank you, Mr. Stevens. No further questions, Your Honor."

"Call your next witness."

Lawrence Haden, an assistant editor at the *Tallahassee Times-Union*, is a small, thin man. With his out-of-date clothes, his large, black-rimmed glasses, scraggly beard and stooped shoulders, his physical presence as he takes the witness stand is not terribly impressive. He speaks, however, with a booming voice that is inconsistent with his nerdy appearance. His answers are concise, his manner confident.

Yes, he confirms, he is employed at the local newspaper, the *Tallahassee Times-Union*, and has been for seventeen years, the last seven of which he has been the assistant editor in charge of the local and state sections of the newspaper. Yes, he knew Patty Stiles, had been her editor since she became a freelance reporter associated with the paper. He had conferred with and consulted often with her regarding her stories and felt he was familiar with her methods of work. It was her habit, he testified, to carry with her at all times a small pocket-sized notebook which she used in the formative stages of a story. She would then, generally, flesh out those notes on computer. The finished product was printed out and kept in a file, along with photographs, background information, and other written materials, miscellaneous memorabilia associated with a story.

She had been, he observes, a little careless in her work, even reckless sometimes, regarding her personal safety. That was why, he says, she needed a good strong editor. But, he says emphatically, when it came to business, she was extremely organized and methodical.

No, he answers, she had not told him about any story she was working on. But that, he says, was not unusual. She rarely came to him anymore until she was fairly well along with a story. She liked to work alone, and in secret, as much as possible, until she could dump the whole thing at once in his lap. She operated, he muses, under the axiom that it was easier to apologize than to ask permission.

On cross, Haley brings out the obvious, that Haden was not, in fact, aware of any drug story that Patty Stiles may have been working on. No, he did not assign any such story to her. No, they had not discussed any such story in the past. Yes, he had checked, at defense counsel's request, with other staff to see if anyone else knew something about such a story, and no, no one did. He shows Haden the cryptic notes from the exhibit that I have produced. Haden admits that he would have to guess about its meaning.

Our next witness is Detective David Ash, a narcotics and vice officer with the Leon County Sheriff's office.

"Are you on duty today?"

Ash smirks a bit. "Oh, you mean these?" pointing to his clothes, "and this?" pulling on a small gold earring in his right ear. "Yeah, this is how I dress for work. It makes it a lot easier to get information, to blend in, if I'm not wearing a uniform or a business suit out there on the street." Ash looks at Haley, and then at Rowe for acknowledgment as to his wit. Neither smiles. He shifts in his seat and then turns his attention back to me.

In answer to my questions, Ash acknowledges that he comes into contact regularly with people who sell or use drugs, that he is familiar with the various terms used by drug dealers and drug users, and yes, some of the terms I show him on my exhibit are consistent with the vernacular street language of that culture.

"Okay, thank you," I say. "Now, let me ask you this, Detective Ash. Do you consider your work dangerous?"

"Sure." Ash seems to be enjoying himself, not aware of where I am heading.

"Why is that?"

"Objection, Your Honor." Tom Haley does not like the way things are going and wants to alert his witness not to be so cooperative. "Mr. Ash is a police officer. Of course he faces danger every day. There is no relevance to this motion hearing, however, in that fact."

Rowe overrules the objection, and Ash, a little more hesitantly, not sure what he's supposed to do but still impressed with his own importance, states that people who are high on drugs or desperate for drugs sometimes do crazy things, that there are often guns involved in drug deals. He also adds, voluntarily, that a significant percentage of the murders in Leon County are, in his opinion, drug-related. With this last answer, Ash looks over to Haley and seems surprised at the expression of disgust that is clearly visible on Haley's face.

"No further questions."

Haley seems to be considering his options, then plows ahead. "These terms that Mr. Stevens asked you about, Detective Ash, you did say that such language was consistent with what a user of drugs might employ?" There is an emphasis on the word user.

"That's right."

"Would it surprise you then to learn that drugs were found in the victim's house?"

"Objection. Irrelevant as to what would surprise the witness. And further, the question assumes facts not in evidence."

"I ask, then Your Honor, that the court take judicial notice of the supplemental investigative report in this case, containing an inventory of items seized from the crime scene. Specifically, Exhibit A, attached to that report, about one-half of the page down, listing a 'bag of marijuana, one roach, one crack pipe.' "

"No objection to judicial notice of the report, Your Honor," I counter, "but I object to the judicial notice that the item was, in fact, illegal drugs or paraphernalia, unless Mr. Haley can produce test results."

"Well, we'll just call it suspected marijuana—sort of like suspected drug story." Haley's sarcasm is a little too obvious and Rowe shoots him a look that wilts him quickly.

"All right, Mr. Stevens, your objection is sustained, but I will take judicial notice as requested—mindful that the items have not been conclusively shown to be marijuana or cocaine."

"Thank you, Your Honor, that's all I have." Haley sits back down.

I announce that we have nothing further to present and Rowe looks at Haley.

"The state calls the defendant, Bobby Jackson."

There is an instant buzz in the courtroom at this announcement. Haley has taken everyone, including Paul and me, by surprise. But I recover quickly.

"We object, Your Honor. That's ridiculous. My client doesn't have any information relative to this motion."

"We won't know that, Judge, until I am allowed to ask him a couple of questions. I'd like to ask Mr. Jackson if he is the source of Mr. Stevens' idea about some drug story. Also, I'd like to ask him if the victim ever gave him a key to her house, and if so, where that key is."

Rowe waves the attorneys up to the bench with his hand. I renew my objection and we argue the issue in detail. I remind Rowe that I will most certainly direct my client to exercise his Fifth Amendment rights and refuse to answer any questions along the lines suggested by Haley. Rowe rules in my favor and sends Haley packing with a look mixed of both disgust and admiration. Haley is not surprised. It's a cheap trick and he knows it. But, I am afraid, it will be an effective one.

We both make our arguments, but Haley's last tactic has sealed my fate. He points out again in argument the lack of any corroborating evidence, the ambiguous nature of the notes I have recounted, and the fact that any number of people could have had a key to the victim's apartment and entered without being detected. He reminds the judge, unnecessarily, that Bobby had been released on bond the day after Bert and I had toured Patty Stiles' home. Finally, he points out correctly, that, in all the cases in which the destruction of evidence had resulted in a dismissal of charges, it had been found that the destruction was intentional and that the evidence was clearly exculpatory. Everyone, including me, knows that we have not shown that here.

Rowe takes no time in making his decision. "I will deny the motion to dismiss. Let us now set a trial date." We agree on October the sixth, about six weeks away. The trial is expected to last four, maybe five days, so Rowe sets aside the entire week.

Though his ruling is expected, I can't help but feel deflated anyway. Like any good lawyer, I have conditioned my client and his family to expect the worst. But still, I see my mood reflected in Bobby. He and I stand silent in the hallway, somber, as Paul does his thing in front of the news cameras, reporters shouting questions. Paul is suggesting, subtly, that we will, in fact, find a hole in this cover-up. I steal a glance over at Bernice Jackson standing next to her son. Strangely, it is she who tries to comfort me. My guilt level rises another notch.

Back at the office I get my stuff and leave early. I don't

feel like doing any work, and I certainly don't feel like talking strategy with Paul. I stop by for happy hour at the Rajun Cajun. Having just had an alco check yesterday, I think my chances are good that I won't have another one for a few days. They are supposed to be random, but they have so many to monitor that they usually only do it once a week. Otherwise they couldn't keep up. If I do get a call earlier than expected, I'll figure out an excuse to delay going in.

At about eight thirty I decide to go back to my office rather than my luxury accommodations at the Sunset Inn. I need to go ahead and get myself an apartment, I tell myself. There is no one at the office—the way I like it. I listen to the messages on my recorder. It has been awhile since I have gotten any nasty or threatening telephone calls. Maybe tonight, I think. I am almost disappointed that there are none. The last message on my recorder, however, gets my attention.

"Hello." The voice is a little shaky, the natural uneasiness of talking to a recorder, I suspect. "This is Shawn Wolfe, W-O-L-F-E," the caller spells it out, "calling for Mr. Ted Stevens, concerning the Patty Stiles murder case." My ears prick up immediately. I don't recognize the name but the voice sounds authentic to me. "I saw you on the news tonight." A long pause. "Well, I've got some photographs you might want to take a look at."

FOURTEEN

Wednesday—August 14th

At 9:30 P.M. exactly I pull up in front of Bert's office. I had called him right after my conversation with Shawn Wolfe and arranged to pick him up on my way to Wolfe's house. Bert is standing on the porch smoking a cigar, talking to another man when I arrive. He sees me, shakes hands with the man, then comes over to my car and gets in.

"Teddy Bear, how's it goin' ?"

"Hey, Bert. Glad I caught you in. I figured you might want to come along."

"Wouldn't miss it. So, tell me, what'd this guy say, exactly?"

"Okay. Wolfe is a freelance photographer—does most of his work for magazines and has assignments all over the world. However, on occasion, he does do some work for the local mullet wrapper. And, he has worked with Patty Stiles. Wolfe said Patty was a fairly good photographer and did most of her shots herself. The problem is she didn't have a darkroom, and she didn't like using the darkroom at the newspaper—too many prying eyes, or something like that. He used to develop her film for her.

"She gives him some film to develop. She gets killed a couple of days later and then he goes on a six-week shoot in Europe somewhere. Never gets around to developing the film."

"Wasn't he just a little bit curious?" Bert asks.

"My sentiments exactly. As a matter of fact, I asked him that. He told me he was a bit curious—his words, exactly—a bit curious. The guy is Australian, I think. Got a weird accent. But anyway, he says he was busy with his preparations for his assignment and that he had no reason to think there might be a connection to Patty's murder. That is, until he saw me and Paul on the evening news tonight. So, he decides to go ahead and develop the film."

"Well, what's on the film?"

"All he said was that he thought it might be consistent with our theory that Patty was working on some story involving drugs and drug dealing in the African-American community. I didn't ask for any more details—that's all I needed. I arranged to meet him, and then called you, and here we are." I found that I could barely contain my excitement. Wolfe's words had brought me a rush of adrenaline that I was still riding thirty minutes later. One thing bothered me, one nagging thought. How was it that Mr. Thorough, Bert Murphy, had not contacted someone who worked directly with the victim, sometimes developing her film?

"So, Bert, you must be getting a little sloppy in your old age."

"What do you mean?"

"How come you didn't know about Shawn Wolfe?"

Bert is looking straight ahead now. "I knew about Shawn Wolfe. But, as you say, the man's been out of the country. There had been no indication that he was working with Patty Stiles at the time. He's on my list of folks to talk to. I made a note to follow up when he returned. I just didn't think it was important enough to put in any of my reports." Bert sounds a bit defensive.

"Well, better to be lucky than good anyway," I joke. Judging by his expression, though, Bert does not think the subject a joking matter, and he suddenly becomes very quiet. After about thirty seconds of silence I decide to change the subject.

"Guess who I got a call from yesterday?"

Bert looks in my direction but does not respond.

"Peter Stiles."

"No shit," Bert finally says. "You didn't say nothing about this at the motion to dismiss today."

"No, I didn't really get the chance."

"Well, what'd he say? Tell me the details."

Deciding what details Bert should know, I replay the conversation in my mind, word for word:

"Hello."

"Ted. This is Peter Stiles."

"Hello, Peter, nice to hear from you."

"Listen, asshole. You'd better leave me out of this shit with Patty. That's old news and you know it."

"Well, from what I hear, Peter, you don't have an alibi for the night of her murder. You got a history of physical abuse on her, and everybody knows that you are a vindictive sonofabitch. You've got to admit that you make a pretty appealing alternative suspect for this case." I smiled to myself at the thought of him on the other end of the line fuming, squirming.

"Fuck you, Ted. I think the same thing can be said about you, lover boy."

Silence.

"Yeah, don't you think for one second that I didn't know you were fucking my wife. I knew it, and I've got proof, too. You try to get me involved in this case and two things are going to happen. First, I'm going to tell the world about your dirty little affair with my former wife and, number two, I'm gonna kick your ass."

"Peter, I appreciate you calling me and giving me this information. Now let me give you some information. Fuck you."

Then I'd hung up the phone. I wasn't so worried about the threat of physical violence. At least not if I saw him coming. It was the suggestion that he had proof of my affair with Patty that gave me concern. Was he bluffing? What kind of proof could he have? The only concrete evidence I knew about had been retrieved and thrown away. Yeah, he was probably just bluffing. But even without proof, he could cause some problems. I give Bert the gist of the conversation sans the allusion to my affair with Patty.

Bert is quick with his assessment.

"The little shit," he says. "All you gotta do to this guy is raise your hand up in the air and he'll run like a scared dog. He'd be funny if he wasn't so pathetic. Speaking of annoying phone calls, you heard from our neo-Nazi friends lately?"

"No. Actually, it's been kind of quiet for a while now. I suspect it may pick up, though, closer to trial when those subpoenas go out. I know this guy is your favorite, Bert. Have you had any luck in shaking his alibi?"

"Maybe," he says, still looking straight ahead. "I think one of his alibi chumps, Jimmy Bob Boyd, may fold. He might have miscued with the wife because she told me he was at home all night. I'm going to try to get a statement from her recorded, then pin him down a little more. I was going to go out there tomorrow afternoon. You want to go?"

"No, I'd like to, but I got a divorce hearing tomorrow afternoon." The words "divorce hearing" suggest a new topic—my own divorce. There is a brief awkward silence as we acknowledge our thoughts. Fortunately, we have now arrived at 427 East Randolph Circle, the address Shawn Wolfe had given me.

Wolfe's house is a small Southern colonial sitting on a half acre of manicured lawn. A brick walkway leads from the roadway to the front door where the owner stands, door open, ready to greet us, before we can ring the doorbell. "I happened to be passing through the living room and saw you get out of your car," he explains. "You are Mr. Stevens," he says looking at me. "I recognize you from the telly." He extends his hand to me and I take it.

"Ted," I respond. "Let me introduce my investigator. Mr. Wolfe, this is Albert Murphy."

"And everybody calls me Bert." The two men exchange handshakes.

"Everyone calls me Mr. Wolfe." The man raises his eyebrows at us, and then gives us a brief smile. "Just kidding. My name is Shawn. Please, gentlemen, come right in."

We step inside the foyer area which opens onto a modest-sized living room. At the far end are sliding glass doors which lead to a pool beyond. The room is tastefully furnished. A small Indian-looking rug centers the oak floor and separates a wicker couch and matching chair. Next to the fireplace is a massive lounge chair that appears to be carved from a cypress tree. Next to it is an antique lamp. There are a couple of abstract sculptures, strange, exotic-looking. There are several framed photographs on the walls and on top of the fireplace mantel.

"This is your work?" I ask.

"The photos you mean?" The Australian accent still seems out of place, but intriguing. In the light, I can see that Wolfe is a tall, thin man, about forty. He has black wavy hair and a beard, both of which are specked with gray. His serious dark eyes are contrasted by an easy smile. "Mostly," he says. "I'm a big fan, you see. Probably the biggest." He gives us a wink.

He is obviously pleased at my interest and begins to identify some of the photographs, giving a background story or two, clearly enjoying himself. Though I'm interested, I am also anxious to get on to what we came here for. Thankfully, Bert finally breaks in.

"Mr. Wolfe, Ted here says you told him you got some other photos we might be interested in—you know, the ones Patty Stiles asked you to develop?"

"What? Of course. So sorry. I've been rambling on here, haven't I? Come. They're in the study." He leads us down a long hallway into a room that I suspect was a former master bedroom and bath, now converted to a study/office and darkroom combination.

Wolfe tells us again of his working relationship with Patty, her request that he develop some film for her, his explanation of why he had not thought that there might be a connection with Patty's murder. Then he opens a large envelope and pulls out a stack of black-and-white photos, spreading them on the table like a dealer with a deck of cards.

"When you said that evidence had gone missing, I thought maybe I'd better bypass the police for the time being and show you what I've got. I made three copies. One for you, one for the police, and one for me."

Before he can finish his sentence, Bert and I are poring over the photos, spreading them out more in order to get a better look. We are like a newlywed couple with wedding photos. Wolfe explains that Patty used color film but requested that he develop them in black and white—something he said was fairly common with her, a personal preference. He could make them color if we wanted.

The photographer rambles on, but he is talking to himself. Bert and I ignore him, concentrating on the photographs before us. It doesn't take long for us to communicate silently to each other—these photos were definitely related to some story about drugs. There are shots of young kids hawking their wares, obvious drug transactions on the streets, close-ups of what looks like crack cocaine in the palm of a hand. Some of the photos were obviously taken with a telescopic lens, some were close-ups. There were young people, clowning for the camera, and old people, worn and weathered-looking, their eyes hollow and hopeless. Some look back at the camera with defiance, anger in their eyes. Black and white had been a good choice. These shots were extraordinarily revealing. Very little prose would be necessary to complete the story. I am also thinking that Haley will now have a hard time arguing that the notebook is irrelevant, that my theory is simply speculation. Rowe may take a closer look at a renewed motion to dismiss.

"Recognize any of these characters?" I ask Bert.

"Sure, several of them. I see two guys who told me they didn't know anything about no lady reporter."

"What about this one?" I pull out one photo and toss it toward Bert. It is a shot apparently taken from a distance, with a telescopic lens. There are four men in the photo, two of whom are centered in the photo and obviously having some discussion. One of the men is facing the camera. He is a short African-American, dressed conservatively in a pair of black jeans and a striped polo shirt. I don't recognize him, but it's obvious that Bert does.

"The guy looking at the camera is Sammy Smith."

"Is he into drugs?"

"Well, let's just say I've bonded him out a couple of times in the past on drug charges. That was a few years back. Now, I do business with him, but it's when he puts up the bail for associates. That means he's a little higher up on the feeding chain. Old Sammy's smart, very businesslike, and mean as hell. The other two guys off to the side, they're a part of his entourage—bodyguards in part, I'd say." The two men Bert refers to look like bodybuilders with an attitude. Both are wearing sunglasses, though the photograph was obviously taken at night. Both look to be a good foot taller than their employer.

"What about the guy with his back to the camera?" I ask. There are three or four photographs of this same scene, but in none of them is there even so much as a profile shot of this man. There are a couple of photos taken as he was walking up, and away, but in all of these, there is something blocking him from the view of the camera. The man is wearing a black hat, black pants, and a black long-sleeved shirt. He has longish black hair which sticks out from behind the hat. From the little I can see of his hand and wrist, I think he is Caucasian, but it's hard to tell.

"I have no idea, Teddy Bear," Bert says as he looks through all of the photos depicting the same scene. "Too bad Miss Patty didn't get a frontal shot on this dude, right?" Bert looks at me.

"Yes, isn't it," I respond. "Wouldn't you say, Mr. Murphy, that our mystery man is a fairly big dealer—I mean, assuming Sammy Smith is a big dealer. The guy with his back to us doesn't strike me as being in the employ of Sammy Smith, maybe vice versa."

"Could be," Bert says noncommittally.

"I think we need to talk to this Sammy Smith."

"Whoa, now. Better let me do that. That's what you pay me for anyway. Like I say, Sammy can be a mean son-ofabitch."

"Maybe, Bert, but I want to be in on this. He'll talk—either to us on his turf, or to a lot of people, very publicly. I'll subpoena his ass in a heartbeat. Probably will anyway, but he doesn't know that. These photos give us a grip on his balls, and we're gonna squeeze real hard until he tells us who Mr. X is. Think you can arrange a meeting?"

Bert gives a big sigh, shrugs his shoulders. "You're the boss, Teddy Bear. I'm sure I can arrange something in a few days. But," he gives me a quick smile, "you might want to be wearing your steel jock strap. You start squeezing Sammy's balls, I got a feeling he's gonna start squeezing back."

FIFTEEN

The lobby of the Tallahassee Addiction Recovery Center has an antiseptic, institutional look about it. It reminds me of the lobby at the jail, just with more plants. The receptionist gives me the once-over as I approach her.

"May I help you?" She shows me a mouthful of teeth. Yes, you can help me. You can wipe that knowing, condescending look off your face, I think. But I say, "Yes, I'm Ted Stevens. I have an appointment with Christine Carter at four thirty."

"Yes, Mr. Stevens, have a seat. She'll be right with you." She shows me some more teeth and points in the direction of several straight-back chairs spaced along two walls. I sit in one.

There are some magazines on the end table but I am not interested, so I study the room a bit. There are three other persons in the room, presumably waiting for similar services. One is a pimply-faced kid with long hair, baggy jeans and T-shirt, and high-top Converses. Next to him is a woman I presume to be his mother, though I would never have made the connection had they not been sitting next to each other. She, in contrast, is dressed elegantly and

carries herself in a manner that speaks of money and breed-
ing.

Several seats over from them is an emaciated-looking
woman of about twenty-five. She is reading a *People* magazine. We all steal side glances at each other but carefully
avoid eye contact. I am embarrassed that anyone would
associate me with this place and imagine they feel the same.

There are three or four motel paintings on the wall and
several potted plants scattered about. I notice the grease
spots on the wall behind the chairs, a sign of a clientele
with poor hygiene habits who are, habitually, required to
wait. I sit, slouched in my chair, looking at my watch, hoping that I will not be here long. I lean back in my chair
and close my eyes.

"Jimmy." I open my eyes and sit up. A man with a big
beard and a big smile peeks around the corner, looking in
the direction of the pimply-faced kid and his mother. The
kid gets up, shakes his mother's hold on him, and follows
the man down the hallway. The mother looks around, embarrassed, but then goes back to her magazine. I lean back
in my chair and close my eyes again.

It has been two weeks now since my DUI arrest. The call
to schedule my assessment had come this morning. There
had been a cancellation, I was told. Could I come in today
at four thirty? I thought about making some excuse, some
reason why I couldn't make it, but then I thought, what
the hell, get it over with. As the day wore on, I began to
feel nervous and anxious. I had taken the edge off during
the afternoon by sipping a few bourbon and Cokes while
I worked, careful not to let anyone else in the office notice.
I had just done an alco check yesterday, so I was pretty sure
I was safe for a couple of days anyway. And, I thought, I
can hide the odor. The irony of loosening up with booze
for an alcohol screening was not totally lost on me.

Breaking the news to Paul about the DUI had not been

easy. His reaction had been expected: shock, disappointment, but, in the end, support. We had both agreed that he would not represent me, for a lot of reasons, not the least of which was that he and Anna were potential witnesses as to how much booze I had consumed that evening.

Denise had been a possibility since she was already representing me in the divorce. But criminal law wasn't her strong suit, and besides, she was pretty much fed up with me as it was. I had finally settled on Gary Cooper. No, not the movie star. He's dead. This Gary Cooper is a former public defender who is very sharp, experienced—and on good terms with the prosecutor in traffic court. He had agreed to get right on the case and file a motion to dismiss and also to try to get my pretrial release conditions modified. He had looked at me hard, though, told me that I *would* abide by those pretrial conditions unless he could get them changed. I had sincerely assured him that I would.

I try to imagine what a counselor named Christine Carter would look like. I picture a post-hippie type, long straight blond hair, exceedingly thin, no makeup. When a large black woman with short hair calls out my name, introduces herself as Chris Carter, and asks me to follow her down the hallway, I am sure that it is a mistake. But, I follow her anyway, trying to keep up. I notice that she moves quickly for such a large woman. Her snug-fitting purple dress accentuates a large rear end that gives the effect of two beach balls side by side going up and down as she walks. Her ankles—well, she has no ankles really. Her legs just extend below the dress and pour into and over the sides of white sandal-like shoes with low heels.

Her office is very small—just enough room for a desk, three chairs, a bookcase, and not much else. There are books and magazines everywhere. Her desk is somewhat cluttered. There are several family photos on the desk and on the bookcase. On the wall there are a couple of certificates which I cannot read from my position, though I can make out an M.A. degree from FSU in something.

My interviewer appears to be in her early thirties. She wears a short Afro hairstyle; her skin color is a very deep dark brown, which accents the beautiful, perfectly straight, white teeth she is showing me now. I think to myself that this must be how they tell the staff from the patients. The ones with the large smiles are the staff. Those with no smiles are the patients. Her smile does not look fake to me, though. It seems to spring naturally to her face from deep inside her. For the first time since walking in the door, I don't feel completely like a leper.

"Mr. Stevens, my name is Christine Carter. Most people call me Chris, though."

"My name is Theodore A. Stevens," I say in return, rather formally, "but most people call me Ted. Some folks call me Teddy Bear." I don't know why I have shared this information with her right off; it just came out.

She smiles bigger, pondering this new information. "Teddy Bear, huh? I like that. You look like a Teddy Bear." There is a soft, warm-hearted chuckle as she says this and a hint of north Florida accent beneath the formal speech. I know that I will lie to her in this interview. That was a given from the beginning. I think, however, that I may regret it.

She reviews quickly the rules and procedures for alco checks. I am subject to being called anytime. I must report within eight hours of the call. The alco check is simple, easy, and free. I simply blow into a short glass instrument that will give an approximate reading of the alcohol in my blood. If I blow positive for alcohol, it will be grounds to revoke bail.

Carter notes with approval the negative results of my first two alco checks.

Then she tells me what to expect from the screening

and evaluation today. The interview will be a series of questions designed to see whether I might benefit from some sort of alcohol counseling.

I've seen many diagnostic summary/screening assessments, and I have a good idea of what to expect. She starts out with some general background questions about my family and childhood history. I give her straight answers, mostly. I grew up in Miami, I tell her. My dad was a firefighter, also did some construction work on the side. My mother worked a little bit as a waitress, but mostly she was an occasional secretary at a real estate company. I am the oldest of two brothers. Charlie is two years my junior. He dropped out of Dade Community College several years ago to follow his girlfriend out to California. He eventually ended up in Tucson, Arizona, where he is a real estate broker. He makes tons of money. No, I don't resent the fact that he makes tons of money. I'm happy for him. Yes, we get along well. We're just a little different, that's all.

She asks me how Charlie and I are different. A collage of scenes quickly runs through my mind: Dad and I loading up the boat to go fishing, Charlie saying he's going to the beach with friends; a picture of Charlie about to go to a high school dance, a sharp dresser even then; Charlie daring me to shoplift with him, getting caught, and me getting the blame; me covering for Charlie when he lies to my parents about where he was all night; an image of me threatening my dad with a butcher knife after one of our parents' drunken brawls, mother crying hysterically in the corner, frozen, as if in a trance. Dad is egging me on, opening his hands wide. He slaps the knife from my hand, grabs it, pulls me to him, then takes the knife and puts it to my throat. He cuts me just enough for the blood to run. I think he might kill me. Charlie talks him down, calms him, gets him to put the knife down. My dad leaves in a huff.

"We just have different tastes, in music, sports, women.

We don't see each other that much anymore, except during holidays. He flies down to Miami once in a while to visit my mother, and I get down when I can," I say.

"Did either of your parents ever abuse alcohol when you were growing up?" Her question triggers memories I have successfully suppressed for many years. "No," I tell her. "Maybe once in a while at Christmas or some other holiday they might have had a bit too much."

Like watching an old movie, I can see my father and my mother, his two brothers and their families. It's a madhouse. There is lots of food, lots of booze, lots of alcohol-induced laughter, false joviality. My parents at their worst, putting on a show for everyone. The kids, all of us a bit schizophrenic, waiting, knowing that at any second the season's cheer could explode into fierce, mean-spirited hostility as the mild ribbing and the jokes at the other's expense become more and more sarcastic, the tension eventually so thick it covers the gathering like a blanket. Later after everyone else is gone, there are escalating shouts and screams. Things are thrown; there are the sounds of fist against flesh, doors slamming, sobbing, the motor starting up in the carport, the car driving away. I can hear Charlie talking quietly, my mother crying.

"No, nothing out of the ordinary," I say. I shuffle the memories to the bottom of the deck and focus on her next question.

"My relationship with my father? I'd say we had a good relationship."

My interviewer pauses but when I don't continue she says, "What do you mean *had*?"

"He's dead."

"Sorry. Recently?"

"Nah. Long time ago. I was in high school. I tell her about our fishing and hunting trips, the Boy Scouts, him teaching me to work on cars, how to build things—all of which later came in handy when I was working my way through four years of college and three years of law school. I don't tell her about the beatings. My father was a hard man. He worked hard, he played hard. And he could be mean, especially when he was drinking.

"How did he die?"

Maybe I should tell her the truth, just for the shock value. No, I think, better not. "It was an accident. A hunting accident." Well, I think to myself, it was kind of a hunting accident. He was hunting for something, maybe some meaning in his life, when he accidentally placed a twelve-gauge shotgun in his mouth and pulled the trigger. "I'd rather not talk about this further, if that's all right."

Chris Carter tactfully accedes to my wishes and asks me about my mother. I tell her that she's alive and well and living in Miami. She remarried after my father died. Too soon after, I've always thought, but I've never said so and don't now. I tell her that my stepfather is okay, I guess. In fact, my stepfather is a decent fellow, but I hate him nonetheless. I hate him for getting all of the love and attention that my mother never seemed to have for me, Charlie, or my father. I hate him because I don't have the courage to hate my mother.

"My first experience with alcohol? Well, let me think. I was about thirteen," I tell her. "A friend and I had lifted a couple of tall-boy Budweisers from the Seven-Eleven. I didn't like the taste at first—but who does?"

She wanted to know my drinking habits in high school. I explained that I drank mostly on the weekends. I usually drank about a six-pack a night, I tell her. Yes, I have experimented with other drugs. Some marijuana, cocaine. But not to any extent. Alcohol has always been my poison of choice I say, grinning. She does not grin back.

"What would you say your average daily consumption of alcoholic beverage is now?"

"Now, now, Ms. Carter—not fair. That's a trick question. My average consumption of alcoholic beverages now is zero, thanks to Judge Moore's harsh pretrial conditions."

Chris smiles and then chuckles. "You too quick, Teddy Bear. Okay, before you were harassed and jumped on by that policeman, how much booze were you putting away in a day, usually?" She throws wide her hands. Her affectation of north Florida black dialect is amusing, disarming.

Be careful with this woman, I remind myself, or you'll end up spilling your guts. "I'd say, maybe one to two."

"Uh huh," she says in obvious disbelief.

"Sometimes more if I'm at a party or some social gathering." Of course I consider a trip to the local bar a social gathering.

Do I ever have a few drinks before a party to lower the anxiety? I think of my last dinner at Paul and Anna's, the drinks I had before going over. "No."

Have I ever drunk more than I intended. "Maybe a few times," I tell her.

Have I ever tried to stop or cut down? "Not really," I say, "except this forced reduction."

"Have you ever felt like you experience problems due to your alcohol drinking?"

"Not really."

"What do you mean, not really?"

"Well, what do you mean by problems?"

"I mean, for example, have you ever had any physical problems, family problems, social problems, psychological problems, that you would attribute to your use of alcohol?"

Of course, the answer is yes. I think of Beth's allegations in her petition for divorce, which is a family and a legal problem. I remember the times I've regretted my slip of the tongue in social situations. I am not sure how much to tell her. If she checks further and I lie about it I am cooked. On the other hand, she is not likely to go further than this interview, and if I tell her the whole truth, I'm doomed anyway to some serious alcohol counseling.

"Well, there have been a few occasions when I have had too much to drink and suffered the physical effects the day after. You know, headaches, upset stomach. And some people would say that being charged with a DUI is a legal problem caused by drinking. I, of course, being innocent, don't think that is the case." My interviewer gives me another smile and another "uh huh."

"Have you ever experienced blackouts from drinking?"

For some reason, this is the question I have most anticipated, and most dreaded, since I knew this interview would take place. The answer, of course, is yes—a few times. But there is one time in particular that concerns me at this juncture. One unaccounted-for span of time which has haunted me since I woke up in my car that morning, shirtless, scratches on my arm and blood on my pants and no recollection of how I got there.

"No," I lie once more.

"Has anyone close to you, a family member, friend, business associate, ever expressed worry or concern over your use of alcohol?"

"No." What's one more lie?

There are questions about my psychiatric history and my current relationships. No, I tell her, I've never been institutionalized, nor treated for any mental illness, never attempted suicide, nor seriously thought about it. Have I ever experienced violent tendencies or homicidal thoughts? Only during alcohol screening and counseling assessments, I answer, with a straight face. This brings another soft chuckle from the woman.

She asks about my marital status. I describe our current problems as a result of simply "growing apart." What a cliché! I tell her it is a relatively amicable split, that I still love my wife but respect her decision to end the marriage.

No, there are no real problems about child custody and visitation; we just have to iron out some details, mostly the financial matters. I lean over confidentially, to tell her that the real problem is lawyers—she knows how they can be. I give her a wink. She nods her head. "I know that's right," she says.

What about my leisure and recreational activities? Sports, fishing, sailing. Religion? Raised Catholic but nonpracticing. I prefer small groups to large ones. I think that I have a good reputation, am respected in my peer group. I have a few close friends, but not many.

Finally, it's over. Throughout the interview, Chris Carter has presented a posture of nonjudgmental understanding, nodding her head repeatedly, issuing a few "uh huh's" to show her empathy. I've been here about two hours. I ask her what she thinks, anxious to see how I've done. She explains that she'll have to summarize her notes, make an assessment, and discuss my case with other professionals before making a decision. Still, I press her.

She hesitates a moment, trying to decide, then, "Ted, let's be honest here." She's looking at me like the mother of a child who's been caught red-handed with cookie crumbs on his mouth, claiming that he didn't do it. "I've been doing this now for almost ten years. I've seen a lot of people who are addicted to alcohol—and all kind of other things too, for that matter. People come in here on these interviews and lie like crazy. They think they're being smart, sly. They try to be evasive. They're manipulative." I start to protest, but she raises her hand and continues. "Unless I'm mistaken, you've been drinking today. Bourbon and Coke, would be my guess, though it's hard to tell after all the mouthwash and breath mints you done stuck in your mouth. I thought about having you do an alco check here today . . ." She pauses and I feel a bit of panic coursing through my body. "But I want us to start off on the right foot. I want us to try and see if we can have a relationship based on trust.

"You say that you don't need any alcohol counseling, and you may be right. But if you've got the kind of problem I think you have, you're going to be having a positive alco check result before too long if you don't get serious about this problem and get some help with it. If you want my opinion, you ought to get into AA or something, quick. You're a grown man, Teddy Bear, and I suspect you know your situation. I'm one of those folks who believes that the first step towards recovery starts with the individual. I'm gonna give you some rope now, either enough rope to haul yourself up with, or enough rope to hang yourself with. It's up to you. You let me know when you're ready to get serious."

I can feel the color draining from my face, the strength flowing from my knees.

"In the meantime, you'll need to come in tomorrow morning at 7:00 A.M., either here or over at the pretrial release office to blow in that alco check instrument again. And, until I say otherwise, you are to do that every morning."

"Now, wait a minute." The reality of this new information has jump-started me back to life. "The judge didn't say anything about daily alco checks, just random. You can't make me come in every day."

"Ted," she gives me a smile, "you don't want to fight me on this. You'll get the results of the assessment in about a week. Then we'll talk. Come on, I'll walk you out."

"Don't bother. I can find my own way." I start to leave, thinking to slam the door in indignation, but I stop myself. Never lose control, I tell myself. I compose myself, turn around, and smile at Chris Carter who looks at me expectantly. "Though I disagree with your assessment, Chris, I appreciate your frankness. I think maybe you tend to get a little jaded in this job. I know the feeling. But I'm going to prove you wrong on this one. You won't be getting any positive alco check results from me."

"I hope not, Ted. I surely hope not," she says with a hearty chuckle that moves the whole upper half of her body. "You take care of yourself now."

I close the door gently and walk quickly down the hallway and out of the building. Only when the suffocating heat hits me outside do I realize that I have already been sweating profusely. The idea of a few more bourbon and Cokes is very appealing but I am thinking of my appointment for an alco check tomorrow morning. I quickly do some calculations based upon my limited knowledge of the dissipation rate of alcohol in the body once consumed. Well, I tell myself, a couple more now won't hurt anything.

SIXTEEN

Shortly after the American Revolution the leaders of the new country, grateful for the enthusiastic assistance of the French General Lafayette, granted him title to an extremely large tract of land, part of which later became known as Leon County, the site of the first capital of Florida. Some of the general's distant family settled in the area and brought with them many French workers to establish vineyards. The area that the workers settled in came to be known as "French Town."

Gradually, Florida became a state and Tallahassee its capital. The vineyards withered, the general's family and the workers eventually left, and their settlement gradually became populated by former slaves. Though all signs of the French origin have long since disappeared, the name has stuck.

As I turn off Tennessee Street onto Macomb, I enter the heart of French Town. I roll up my windows and lock the door instinctively. Whatever other attributes French Town may have, it also has one of the highest crime rates in the city.

Stopped at a traffic light, I suddenly feel very self-conscious. Men and women are crowded onto the sidewalks, liquor or beer bottles in the hands of many. I notice a couple of folks around the side of a building, obviously smoking crack cocaine, oblivious to passersby. A man in the group looks over in my direction, and I quickly look away. When I steal a glance again, I am sure that he is looking directly at me. He pushes one of his friends in the arm, pointing me out. Others share in the joke, smiling, smirking, laughing.

The light changes and I turn left onto Brevard Street, travel down the two blocks to Bert's office which is just beyond a furniture store. Bert's office is a shotgun house, similar in appearance to the several that extend to the west of his, all built in the years just after World War II. It looks like just another house in the neighborhood, complete with security bars over the windows. The only difference is the sign in front: Murphy's Investigations, Bail Bonds.

Though not fancy, it looks well kept. The parking lot is small, though, and there is no room for me. I park my Accord on the street, making sure to lock it, and then take the brick walkway to the entrance. I notice, as I am getting out of my car, a man with expensive-looking clothes and gold jewelry coming out of Bert's office building. He gets into the black Lexus that was taking up two parking spots. I notice, as he drives off, the Dade County license plate. As I cross the brick walkway to the entrance, I can see a young black woman sitting just inside, working furiously at a computer monitor. The door is open.

"Hello," I call out.

The woman, probably in her early thirties, swivels around in her chair and rises and walks over to greet me as I cross the threshold. She has a sure smile, confidence in her stride.

"Mr. Stevens." She says it as a statement, not an inquiry. "Bert has been expecting you. I'm Angie." The voice, the clothes, the accent, all speak of education, sophistication.

"Nice to meet you, Angie." I am speaking to her back because she has already turned and started walking briskly toward the rear of the building. "Bert always keep you here so late?"

"Sometimes, but I don't complain," she says with a smile, looking over her shoulder.

Looking around, I am surprised that such a nondescript exterior can hold such an impressive-looking interior. The furnishings are tasteful, but not expensive. There is a casual professionalism that exudes from everything, including Angie. As she leads me down the hallway to Bert's office I notice the same symmetry in the other rooms. The door to Bert's office is open and I can hear the murmur of voices within as we approach. Through the doorway I can see Bert and two other men sitting at a round table in the corner. All have playing cards cupped in their hands. Bert motions me into the room.

"Teddy Bear, come on in. Have a seat." He points with his chin toward an armchair. I take a quick look around Bert's office as I walk toward the chair. There are some unusual small sculpture pieces on bookshelves and on Bert's desk. They look African in origin. The desk is a beautiful antique mahogany piece, which matches a secretary sitting along one wall and the table where the men are sitting. There are also plenty of sports memorabilia: trophies and photographs of Bert's early days, and some adult city league mementos as well. The photographs on the wall show Bert with various persons, including politicians and a few celebrities. Though there is much to look at, it doesn't have a cluttered feel.

"Let me finish this last hand, Ted. These boys need to be relieved of the last of their money. How's it goin' ?"

"Not bad." In fact, I'm feeling a bit anxious about our planned meeting with Sammy Smith. Bert's easy manner and quick smile do not have the expected effect. The fact that Bert has chosen this time to play poker with these two unknown men for some reason annoys me, makes me even more uncomfortable.

As if reading my mind, Bert adds, "Oh, sorry. Where are my manners. Ted Stevens, this is Jimmy Tolliver and Sherman Hutchinson. Jimmy and Hutch are two of our operatives, Ted." Each man turns in my direction and nods a greeting. "They are also two of the unluckiest sonsabitches on the face of this earth."

The two men smile, but only slightly. Both of them appear young, in their twenties, and both are very dark-skinned. The one to Bert's left is large, at least six feet five inches and I'd guess about 250 pounds. His nose looks like it has been broken—more than once. The other, Tolliver, is much smaller, with delicate features, but seems more threatening in some vague way.

The larger man, Hutch, responds to Bert: "We'll just have to see about that, now won't we." He places two chips on a pile in the middle of the table. "I'll see your ten and raise you another ten," he says as he leans back in his chair, then turns toward Tolliver.

The smaller man looks at his cards for a long time. Finally, he puts them face down on the table. "I'm out," he says.

Bert gives a brief smile and shrugs. "Well, Hutch, looks like it's just you and me."

Hutch gives Bert a predatory grin. "Yep. The bet's to you, chief. I raised you ten."

"Yes, you did, didn't you," Bert says, taking a chip from his pile and placing it in the middle of the table. "I'll see your ten . . ." He hesitates now, looks at his cards, his remaining chips, and then fixes his gaze on his opponent for several seconds. "And I'll raise you—well, let's see . . ." He counts out five chips. "I'll raise you fifty," he says.

Hutch smiles briefly, meets Bert's stare head-on, but I

can almost feel his anxiety from across the room. I can sympathize with him. I've been in his position before—the last remaining player opposite Bert, high stakes. We often ended up in a poker game after flag football. The money was never a lot—like here, maybe five- or ten-dollar chips. You might lose a couple of hundred total in a night. But that didn't mean the stakes were not high. With Bert Murphy, you played for respect. Bert always said that you could tell a lot about a person by the way they played sports and the way they played poker—especially when the game was on the line. If you choked on the big play, you'd probably choke in life too.

One night we ended up with a large pot, one last hand, and it was down to Bert and me. I had a pretty decent hand. I started with two kings and had drawn a third. I felt sure Bert, who had taken four cards, was bluffing. He had done so successfully on several hands. I watched for signs, studying carefully his facial features, his movements, his tone of voice, anything that might give me a clue, but had come up with nothing. I could only rely on my gut.

The pot had been close to five hundred dollars when I called. A wave of relief washed over me when Bert laid down his cards, smiled at me, and said, "Pair of jacks." I thought then that he was smiling because he thought he had the winning hand. Later, though, I would conclude that he smiled because he knew that he didn't. Though he never admitted it, I think he was trying to give the team's new quarterback some confidence, some practice at risk taking. Bert never let anything so arbitrary as scores, touchdowns, or money define winning for him.

Hutch's deep voice brings me back to the present. "I'll see your fifty and raise you another fifty."

At this point, folding is out of the question. Both players have reached the point of no return. Bert, without hesitation, puts his chips onto the pile. "Call. Let's see what you got."

Hutch puts his cards down, fanning them out. "Three kings," he says, looking defiantly into Bert's face. Both Jimmy and I also have fixed our complete attention on Bert.

"That's a good hand, Hutch, damn good," he says, looking over at me, smiling. Maybe he is remembering our game. "But not, I'm afraid, good enough." I say the words silently as Bert says them aloud, placing his cards on the table in front of him. "Three aces." Bert begins raking the chips toward him.

"Damn," says Hutch, but he is smiling. So is Jimmy. So am I. "Damn," Hutch repeats, "I thought sure you was bluffing."

"Hutch," Bert says with mock severity, "I don't bluff. I just sometimes overestimate the strength of my hand."

After Bert has put away the poker paraphernalia and ushered the two men out, he turns his attention to me.

"What can I getcha? You want a beer?"

I look at him. Is he kidding, being sarcastic? I can't get a read. I think of possible responses, most of which concentrate on my firm belief that he has a warped sense of humor, but instead I say, "Sure." The surprise on his face is the payback. "Nah," I say, "just kidding. Actually, I've been weaning myself off. I will have a Coke though."

Bert tells me to help myself and points to the mahogany secretary. I open the doors to find a variety of bottles of liquor. On the bottom is a small refrigerator, from which I take a Coke. "Anything for you?" I ask.

"Well, since you're havin' a Coke, I will too—just fill the glass halfway with bourbon 'fore you put the Coke in." He grins at me.

I don't think it's funny, but I smile back. I find the bottle and pour. The aroma of the bourbon fills my nostrils and

I find myself salivating like one of Pavlov's dogs. With supreme effort, I put the lid back on and the bottle in the cabinet, pour the Coke for both of us, sans bourbon for me, hand Bert his glass, and sit down in a large overstuffed chair in the corner.

"Yeah, this lady, the counselor, is a real pain in the ass," I volunteer. "She's got me on daily alco checks. What's it been now? Eight days, I think." I don't tell him that I missed one of those alco checks—got loaded the night before and called in sick. Even stayed away from work, just to cover my tracks in case she checked. But mostly, I've just had to scale back, make sure I don't drink more than will dissipate by the next morning. There is also a margin of error with those instruments, and they're going to give you the benefit of the doubt if you've got a little bit of a reading.

"That must be pretty tough," Bert says.

"Nah, not really. I mean, I can do it. It's just I don't think I ought to have to."

"I know what you mean. I'd hate to have to give it up too," he says as he takes a large gulp from his drink. I can still smell it from where I am, feel myself weakening.

"Well, what's the drill?" I say.

"We're supposed to meet him at a place called Terry's. B.J. coming?"

"No, I convinced him to let us go it alone."

"Good," Bert says. "It's best that he keep a low profile. If anything happens, he doesn't need to be in the middle of it, that's for sure."

Middle of *what?*, I'm about to shout, but I swallow hard and nod in agreement. "I haven't been able to keep a real tight rein on him though. He's talked to a couple of those folks in the photos, people he knows. They will confirm the drug story, in court. That's not going to be a problem, anyway."

"That's great. Now if we can just get Mr. Smith to help you out."

We spend the next ten minutes shooting the breeze until Bert looks at his watch and announces, "Let's go." On the way out he and the young secretary exchange looks, an unspoken message, and then, "Come on, Angie, we'll walk you out."

She quickly puts away what she is working on and grabs her purse. She gets into a late model BMW, waves goodbye, and pulls away from the curb. Bert must pay her pretty well, I think to myself. "Okay, Counselor, are you ready?"

"Sure, we walking or driving?"

Bert smiled, "Let's just walk. It's not far."

"Yeah, I think I passed it on the way in here—Terry's. Looks like a real popular place—on Macomb, right?"

"Yeah" is all he says.

We walk together, both of us hunched over, our hands in our pockets. Though the temperature has dropped a bit, it is still hot and humid. I had changed out of my suit and tie, mostly to avoid looking more out of place than I already would be, but also to be a little cooler. Still, my shirt is sticking to me in a matter of seconds. As we walk, Bert speaks to at least a half a dozen people along the way. Their responses are friendly, or at least respectful. I feel a little more secure and a little more at ease. On a couple of occasions he stops to chat. An obviously intoxicated man almost stumbles in his enthusiasm to greet Bert.

"My man!" the drunk bellows. Bert returns his high five with just enough enthusiasm not to embarrass the man, calls him by name, and keeps moving. He is like a politician on the campaign trail.

"Clients, I presume?"

"Most of these folks I've either bonded out, or I've bonded out somebody in their family, or maybe a friend."

"Doesn't it ever make you nervous, having your business

in this part of town, I mean, being one of only a few white people?"

"Sure I'm nervous, Teddy Bear, but color's only the smallest part of it. Folks are folks. Some are good, some ain't. A lot of white folks are afraid of big crowds of black people. They're thinkin' these people are judging them by their color, afraid they will automatically hate them 'cause they're white. I think that's 'cause a lot of white people judge black people by their color. It's sort of like the liar who can never believe anybody 'cause he thinks everybody else is a liar too. In truth, there are some black people who hate you if you're white, but I've found that most are willing to give you the benefit of the doubt.

"I've got a reputation down here, a well-deserved one, for treating people right. Now, I don't put up with no bullshit and I'm a good businessman. But I ain't heartless neither. A little bit of charity is usually good for business. And I'll tell ya, I feel a helluva lot safer being a white man walking down Macomb Street in the middle of French Town, than if I was a black man walking into some juke joint on Highway Twenty. A lot of those sons of bitches are just plain mean."

"What about Sammy Smith. Is he one of your clients too?"

"Yeah, he has been, but not in a long time. He's moved up the chain a bit, got himself insulated, so he doesn't get popped anymore. What he does is front the bail money for other people."

"Well, if this is common knowledge—"

"And it is," Bert interrupted.

"Well, if it's common knowledge, why don't the police arrest him?"

"As you know, Counselor, proof and truth are two different things." I suddenly have a strong feeling of déjà vu, but I shake it off as Bert continues. "The big ones insulate themselves from the law. They got people working for them who are loyal because of money or fear, or both. They make good money, and if they have to take a short break in the slammer, that's part of the business. It's a lot better than having no money and being dead, which is what happens if you mess with some of these people." Bert looks over to me to see if I am getting the message. I am.

"Let me tell you, Teddy, this Sammy Smith ain't no different. Don't be fooled by his polite manner. The guy is smart and smooth. He was a junior at Florida A & M when he got popped last time. Good student, good family background, somewhere from Daytona Beach I think. Now he's an agent for a few local musical groups. He books them into the joints on the weekends. That's his front, though. Also he don't show how much money he makes. He don't walk around with a bunch of gold, driving limousines, all that shit. Like I say, he's careful, he smart, and he's ruthless as hell." Bert is looking straight ahead. He pauses, then continues. "I'm gonna tell you a secret about Sammy, though. Underneath it all, he's scared. I'm sure of it. But, listen, now. We're gonna play the game by his rules tonight. Don't give this guy any flak. Don't do something that makes it look like he's being treated with disrespect, 'cause he's gonna have to save face. He's big into this Eastern bullshit stuff, martial arts and all that goes with it. Anyway, whatever happens, don't react, just be cool. We'll get whatever information we can, and then plan on what to do another day." I nod in acknowledgment.

We approach the entrance of the bar that Bert had spoken of and slow down. Bert has not said whether we were supposed to meet this guy inside or what—and it appears that Bert is not sure either. Our hesitation, though, is only temporary.

"Yo." We all look in the direction of a large man standing alone at the corner of the building. Some of the other people standing around look briefly and then go back to their conversations, seeing that he is not calling for them. The man motions us to come over.

"You looking for Sammy," he says, without looking at us, as if there were something across the street more interesting. "He be back on the side." He turns and walks, struts rather, around the corner and down into a narrow alley. Red flags immediately jump up all around me. I lean over and whisper into Bert's ear. "Why don't we just meet him inside?" I ask reasonably. Bert ignores me, starts after the man. I follow. Maybe I've been watching too many movies, but I envision some seedy character stepping out behind us halfway down the alley, surrounding us.

Strangely enough, that's just what happens. We get about halfway down the alley. I look over my shoulder and notice that there are three large men standing at the entrance, obviously more than just casual observers. I nudge Bert, who looks around, and then mouths to me, "Stay cool."

From the shadows of a side doorway another man echoes these words as he steps out into the alleyway and places a gun to my head. The man who had been leading us down the alley now turns and does likewise to Bert. "Okay," he says, pointing with his chin toward the end of the alley where a small, thin man steps out from behind a Dumpster.

The man walks slowly, casually, up to greet us. I whisper to Bert, "Sammy Smith, I presume?" He nods slightly. As the man gets closer, I recognize his face from the photograph. He has short-cropped hair and a pencil-thin mustache. He looks to be about five foot nine and 150 pounds. Sammy is wearing a denim work shirt, rolled up at the sleeves, blue jeans, and white Reeboks, no jewelry, no hat. Not the stereotypical drug dealer, I think.

Perhaps he is reading my mind because his first words are, "You were expecting Super Fly, maybe?" It's a rhetorical question, thank God, since I don't know how I would respond. He continues, while the guys with the guns pat us down. "Sorry about the inconvenience, gentlemen, but you've got to be careful these days. There's a lot of crime and violence on these streets."

I look over at Bert who seems to be unconcerned, so I fake calmness as well.

Smith looks at Bert, a small smile on his face. "Ah, Mr. Murphy." He makes a slight bow and Bert does the same. Then Smith looks at me. "This must be the famous lawyer, Mr. Ted Stevens. The one who wants to talk with me." He is looking at me closely. "Yes, Mr. Stevens," he says with a slight bow, which I return by reflex. "How can I help you?"

"You can start by having your men put their guns away. We're no threat to you."

"That remains to be seen," he says, but he nods to the men and they put their guns away.

Bert gives me a look and then speaks up. "Sammy, Mr. Stevens, as you know, is Bobby Jackson's lawyer."

"Yes, I know Bobby well, and his family."

"Well, we think that maybe this Patty Stiles lady was getting a little too close to some people who have a drugstore down here in French Town." He pauses for what seems to be a long time, but when nobody fills the void, he continues. "Well, no sense in beating around the bush. We think maybe you might know something that might help us on that angle." Bert reaches in his jacket slowly, and as he does, all of the other men reach for their guns again. Bert raises his hand as if to show that he means no harm, then slowly pulls out of his pocket a photograph.

"This is one of the photographs Stiles took a few days before she was murdered. We know who the guy facing the camera is, Sammy. That's you. What we don't know is who the other guy is."

"Yeah, and you ain't gonna find out from me either, Bert," Smith says, taking only a cursory glance at the photo.

"I don't recognize the dude. I talk to a lot of people. I can't remember everybody."

"Mr. Smith," I break in. Both he and Bert look surprised, like they have forgotten I am here at all. "Look, we've already talked to some of the people in other photos from this same batch and they confirm that Patty Stiles was working on a story about drug dealing in the black community. They put her on to you." I am bluffing, but I figure Bert will back me up, and Smith won't know otherwise. Smith does not, however, looked surprised, or concerned. "I've also got her notes of the interview with you," I lie.

This time, though, I have Smith's attention, and Bert's too. It seems as though Smith exchanges a glance with Bert, but I can't read it. He quickly regains his poker face, and I go on. "Look, I'm not looking to give you any exposure you don't need, but it's no use denying you weren't part of the story. All I'm interested in is the mystery man." I lie again because I know that if I get nothing else, I will point my finger at Sammy Smith.

Smith's face gets a little harder, and I can see a nerve twitch beneath his chin. His eyes have gotten quite large now, and I think I can detect a faint wisp of steam beginning to come out of his nostrils. He grabs my shirt, pulls me to him with more strength than I could have imagined for such a small man.

"That sounds sort of like a threat, Mr. Lawyer," he says with contempt. "I don't like threats." Sammy Smith is now about six inches from my face and his eyes are like stones.

Bert tries to come to my rescue. "What he's saying, Sammy, is that he's not looking to give you a hard time, that's all. He's just hoping maybe you can steer him to someone who might be, ahh, shall we say, a little more appealing as a suspect than his man B.J. Maybe this guy in the photo."

Just like that the malice is gone from the man's face. He

releases me from his grip, smiles, and, still looking straight at me, answers Bert. "Ain't gonna happen, Bert my man."

I want to tell him that my name is not Bert, that Bert's over there, but I don't think he is confused.

"Yeah, man, I talked to the bitch." His tone and his speech pattern have changed dramatically. He sounds like a streetwise drug dealer. "She said she wasn't gonna use no names, no photos. I told her not to take no pictures. I told her some stories, some bullshit stories, you know, pulling her chain, but I don't know nothing about her getting whacked. She didn't know jack shit. She talked to some street users, some useless losers who she probably paid just enough so they could get a bit of crack. They'd tell her anything just to get the money so they could buy their crack.

"I'm not saying I've never seen any illegal drugs in my life." The upper middle class, educated man is back. He winks at Bert. "But, I do not sell or use drugs. Not anymore. Maybe this Stiles lady thought she had something with that photograph, but I swear I don't know who that guy is." He is looking at the photo again. "I don't know when the picture was taken, don't know what it was about. Probably somebody asking directions, maybe from out of town, who knows. You can't tell nothing from this angle anyway. What I do know, Mr. Lawyer," now his attention is directed back at me, "what I do know, is that I don't plan to be part of some wild-haired scheme to get your client off. If you try to drag me into this and defame my character, I will seek a remedy . . . and I don't mean a lawsuit." He gives us his best victim pout.

"Now that sounds like a threat, Mr. Smith. And I don't like threats either." I try to give him the same stone-cold stare that he had given me, but I don't think it's working. I notice Bert put his hand over his face. Smith simply looks at me hard for a moment, and then gives me another smile.

"I don't threaten, motherfucker." Mr. Hyde is back. "If I'm gonna do something, you won't know it until it's too late. Now, in case I wasn't clear, what I mean to say is—stay the fuck out of my business."

With that, Smith takes the photograph that Bert had given him and tears it up into several pieces, drops it on the pavement, turns, and slowly, casually walks off. His cohorts follow right behind, the last one giving Bert his gun back as he walks by. With nothing else apparently left to do or say, Bert and I turn around and head out back into the street. I notice that I am sweating. I wipe a roll of it from my forehead and wipe my hands on my pants leg. I look over at Bert. He is staring straight ahead, eyes narrow and jaw set. I wait until we round the corner and are heading down the sidewalk to his office before I speak.

"Did I blow it, Bert?"

"Well, chief, I told you not to get too aggressive with the man. I'm afraid he may have clammed up for good." Then Bert smiles a little bit. "You're a crazy fucker, Teddy."

"I don't know if this guy's so cool and so smart as you think, Bert. I think I can make him come undone on the witness stand. And Bert, did you notice anything familiar about Sammy Smith, physically?"

"What do you mean?"

"I mean he looks like Bobby Jackson, doesn't he? Same height, weight, build, easily mistaken for one another, wouldn't you say, at night, seen running from someone's house?" Bert looks at me for a moment, but he does not respond. I guess he knows it is a rhetorical question.

"And one other thing, Bert."

"What's that?"

"I think I'll have that drink now."

SEVENTEEN

Monday—August 26th

"I swear to God, Ted!" There is disgust and a touch of sadness in Denise Wilkerson's voice as she looks directly into my eyes, her right hand holding onto my left elbow.

"What?" I say, knowing what it is, instinctively backing up a step.

"Tell me you haven't been drinking."

"I haven't," I protest, but I cannot hold her gaze.

"Shit!" She throws up her hands and starts walking down the hallway toward Judge Miller's office. I scramble to catch up. "Just don't get close to anybody, sport," she says over her shoulder. "Soon as this hearing is over, I'm out of here. You can get yourself a new lawyer."

"Aw, come on, Denise. You're wrong about the booze." We are now walking side by side. She stops, rolls her eyes at me, then continues walking.

"I warned you, Ted," she says. "Did you think I was bluffing?" I start to respond but she waves me off. "It's bad enough that you won't, or can't, lay off the liquor. But worse, you wouldn't know the truth if it bit you on the ass. Don't bullshit me, pal. I've been there."

I am trying to think of something to say, put her down perhaps, maybe play the sympathy card, appeal to her fi-

duciary duty as a lawyer. But just then we round the corner
and there, fifty feet away, I see my wife sitting in a chair
just outside the entrance to Judge Miller's office. Next to
her is my father-in-law. Don Carey is in a chair across from
them. Denise continues her quick stride, but I instinctively
slow down as if I were driving and suddenly came upon a
school zone with a flashing yellow light. Beth's father puts
his hand over hers as they both look up and see me ap-
proaching, then look away. Beth looks back in my direction
again as I come closer. It has been almost two months since
I have seen her. I am struck by the thought that she looks
very much as she did seven years ago when we first met.

She had been working at the Silver Slipper, tending bar
at the dinner meeting of the Tallahassee Bar Association.
She was short enough that only a small portion of her was
visible above the bar. But what you could see was captivat-
ing. She wore a low-cut black dress which complemented
her dark Panama City tan and her brown eyes. She wore
her long, dark brown hair in a French braid. She had the
pouting lips of an only child. I was immediately under her
spell, and I pursued her with every persuasive skill I could
muster until she, likewise, fell under mine.

She had been a senior at FSU then, majoring in hotel
and restaurant management. Beth's parents had not ap-
proved of the romance. I was significantly older, and even
though I was a lawyer, I worked for the state and therefore
had no ambition. Worse, I was not willing to relocate to
Panama City. They had dreamed that Beth would join them
in the family business, a large, popular seafood restaurant
called Captain Turner's.

There were other early warning signs. Beth came from
a wealthy family. It wasn't so much that she was spoiled,
just that she had been raised to expect the advantages that
material wealth brought. Her parents had provided her
with all of the creature comforts, and she had taken it for

granted that her husband would do likewise. The subsequent pressure for me to "live up to my potential" would eventually drive a wedge between us.

Love and reason do not always go hand in hand, however. We were too much in love to give these red flags the significance they deserved. Though her parents put on their best face in adapting to the situation, I would never feel welcome in their family. When Beth got pregnant and dropped out of school in her last semester, and we had to move the wedding date up three months, the rift between her parents and me became too wide and deep to ever be bridged.

As if on cue, Beth's father reaches over and pats her hand once again, looking briefly in my direction, as if to say to both of us, "See, I told you so. Father knows best." Dressed impeccably in a dark blue suit, he has a refined look that is a million miles away from the hardworking Greek fisherman who worked eighty-hour weeks to build up a business that now grossed over a million dollars a year.

Beth looks pale, despite her usual tan. She has always struggled to control her weight, and it seems that she has been losing the battle recently. Still, she is very attractive. She is wearing a conservative gray outfit but I can make out her full breasts outlined underneath the fabric. Involuntarily, I think of her other soft lines, our soft, intimate lovemaking. I think of Patty Stiles—hard, thin, freckled, white-skinned, and with auburn hair, lovemaking so fierce it was like a war dance. Two women so different, but both able to make me feel out of control. I push back my hair, then wipe my greasy, sweaty hand on my pants, suddenly feeling self-conscious.

I stop, standing in front of Beth. Carey looks a little nervous, as does my father-in-law, but nobody shoos me away.

"Hello, Ted," she says, looking up. "How are you?"

The inanity of the question almost makes me laugh. I

want to say something witty and sarcastic, but all I can manage is "Fine, Beth, and you?"

I can almost feel the knives coming out of my father-in-law's eyes, and I avoid looking directly at him. Beth is about to say something when my lawyer, perhaps sensing trouble, calls out and motions me over. "See you," I say to Beth as I head toward Denise. When I am by her side, Denise whispers in my ear.

"Not that it wouldn't serve you right, Ted, but, as your attorney, I suggest that you keep your distance from those folks. I don't think you want them close enough to be smelling your breath. Now, let's talk about what we're going to do in there." She moves her head in the direction of Miller's office. We huddle for a couple of minutes, talking strategy. I can tell that she is still pissed, but the professional in Denise Wilkerson has taken over. Now and then I steal a glance over at Beth, who I notice is doing likewise. After a few minutes, Judge Miller's secretary calls out through her open doorway.

"Mr. Carey, Ms. Wilkerson, the judge will see you now."

Judge Charles Miller is a white-haired, kindly-looking man in his mid-sixties. He is seated at the head of a tiger oak table, which is long enough to accommodate eight matching chairs. The room is appropriately furnished, legal-themed prints on the walls, bookcases filled with law books. But there is nothing personal in the room, nothing that speaks of the man or the judge who presides here. I have never had a case with this judge before and know little of him, only that he was in private practice before his appointment to the bench twelve years ago, doing mostly insurance defense work.

He is reading through a file in front of him as we enter. He looks up at us with pale blue eyes. "Come in, come in," he says, motioning us to have a seat. Once we have all settled in, he continues. "I see that we're here today on competing motions, but both concern visitation with the parties' minor child. Presently, by agreement of the parties and a stipulated order for temporary relief, the child primarily resides with the wife. The husband has visitation with the child on Saturdays from nine A.M. until six P.M. and every other Wednesday evening from six to eight P.M." Both lawyers nod in agreement. "Now, the husband wants to make this every weekend from Friday at six P.M. until Sunday at six P.M., and for every Wednesday evening from six to eight P.M." At this he looks over at Denise Wilkerson who again nods in agreement.

"The wife, on the other hand," the judge continues, "feels that any visitation should be supervised only and with strict alcohol conditions imposed." With this, the judge looks over at Dandy Don who also nods in agreement. "Who would like to go first?"

"If it please the court," Carey begins in his best ass-kissing style, "since Ms. Wilkerson's motion was filed in response to ours, we should probably go first." Carey's implication is that our motion is a knee-jerk reaction, not made in good faith. He looks at the judge to see if his point has hit home, but Miller's expression does not change. Before Denise can suggest otherwise, Carey continues. "I'd like to call my client, Beth Stevens." After several useless preliminary questions, Carey finally gets down to the heart of the matter, asking her why she is asking for the prohibition of alcohol as a condition of visitation.

"I have lived with this man for almost seven years. I know what happens when he drinks, and I know that he cannot control it. It has already affected the visitation."

"How could you know this, Ms. Stevens?" Dandy Don looks over at the judge, arching his eyebrows.

Beth relates, tearfully, how our six-year-old daughter, Annie, has told her that I often drink when she is with me and that sometimes it makes her frightened. Denise objects, rightfully, to the hearsay, but Miller lets it in.

Beth looks at me, her eyes are moist, and her voice trembles as she continues. "It's hard to explain. I love him, but I don't trust him. He is a skilled manipulator, and he doesn't understand the control his drinking has over him or what he does when he gets drunk."

Her words, uttered with such apparent sincerity, cut into me like a knife and I look away, unable to hold her gaze. An overwhelming sense of sadness washes over me, and I find that I am unable to summon the anger, the bitterness, and the feelings of betrayal that have thus far shielded me from the truth. I start to say something but Carey cuts in with another question.

"Is that often?"

"Objection." Denise tries to break up the rhythm.

"Overruled."

Beth is sobbing softly now, fighting to maintain control. Her father pats her on the hand again. The judge gives her a tissue. Out of the corner of my eye I see my attorney putting her hands over her eyes, averting them from this disaster scene. My wife continues.

"Whatever conditions you impose, whatever rules you give him, he will find a way to get around them." She is looking directly at Judge Miller now and I note that he does not hold her gaze either. I'm not sure whether that's a good or bad sign.

Beth continues in this vein for a few more minutes, giving some details, burying me deeper, it seems. She concludes with a profession of her love for me and her desire that my relationship with my daughter flourish. But, Beth insists, she must protect her daughter. She tearfully asks the judge for his help.

I have to admit to myself that she has made a good case

for herself. Some coaching from Carey for sure, but still, she's a natural.

"Ms. Wilkerson?" Miller looks at Denise.

Denise offers to take a brief recess so Beth can "compose herself," but my wife says she's okay. Then she asks Beth about the circumstances under which Annie talked of my drinking.

"It was right after one of her visits with Ted. She was very tearful, very upset about the drinking."

"Are you sure the tears were not because of the fact that she had to leave her father?"

"Yes, I am sure of it."

"Well, what brought the subject up?"

"I don't remember exactly."

"Isn't it true, Ms. Stevens, that your daughter's statements were made in response to your questions?"

"I, I'm not sure. Probably." Beth is looking over at her lawyer and her father, not sure of what the right answer might be, but apparently sure that she does not like where this is going.

"You're not sure whether these alleged statements about my client's drinking were made in answer to your questions?"

"Objection, Judge," Dandy Don interjects. "This has been asked and answered. Counsel is badgering the witness."

"Judge, I'm just trying to get her to say something for sure. Statements of impressionable young children are very easily misinterpreted. It's important to know the context in which these alleged statements were supposedly made."

"I beg your pardon. There is nothing alleged about his drinking." The annoyance is evident in Beth's voice now, and both her father and her lawyer put their hands on hers, trying to calm her down.

"Overruled. Answer the question if you can, Ms. Stevens."

Beth steadies herself. "It might have been in answer to my questions. I don't remember. I've got a right to ask my daughter questions, don't I? I am anxious every minute she's with her father. It's natural that I want to know how things went. I don't see that it matters that I ask her a question." She is looking over to Carey and her father. My father-in-law has turned his dagger eyes from me to my lawyer. Denise has made her point, though, and wisely decides to plow different ground.

She asks some questions about my drinking problem. How severe was it? How long had it been a problem?

"It has been going on since the day we got married, and before, obviously," Beth says.

"When did it become severe, as you describe it?" Denise feigns sympathy, concern. It works.

"It's always been bad, but it's gotten really bad in the last year, year and a half." Beth is trying to regain her composure and play the innocent victim.

"Well, then, I guess over the last year and a half or so you've never left your child with your husband without someone supervising their interaction?"

Beth looks like a deer caught in headlights. "I did, but it often made me nervous. Besides, he was always at the office."

"Providing for you and Annie?"

"Or elsewhere," Beth ignores the last question.

Denise then addresses the allegation that I have been trying to manipulate my daughter, poison her mind against Beth. She testified earlier that Annie had asked her why she made daddy leave, why she wouldn't let daddy come home. Beth acknowledges that she had been the one who filed for divorce, who got the injunction to force me from the family home.

"Don't you think it is entirely natural and normal for a six-year-old child in this situation to ask those kind of questions, to want her father to return, to blame the person who has sent him away?"

"No, she knows her daddy had to leave because he drinks too much and gets angry and frightens both of us. I explained all that to her. . . ." Beth realizes her mistake and quickly stops, but it's too late.

"What was that you said, Mrs. Stevens? You talked to your daughter about why her father left?"

"That's not what I meant to say."

"I'm sure," Denise says.

"Objection, Your Honor." Carey is almost out of his seat. Denise waves her hand in concession but she lets Beth's last statement hang in the air for several seconds. Although Beth never loses control again, by the time the questioning is done, it is obvious that she has lost some credibility with Judge Miller.

Next on the stand is my father-in-law. He explains in a matter-of-fact voice that he has seen me drink heavily and become very intoxicated on several occasions. He says that he has refused to allow me to drive in such a state, even though I would try to get in the car and leave with his daughter and granddaughter. He testifies that he has witnessed verbal abuse of Beth.

He acknowledges on cross that he has never seen any evidence of physical abuse, nor has his daughter reported any—only that I had smashed a few items of personal property. If he had heard of any physical abuse, he assures the judge, he would have beat the tar out of me. He, like his daughter, proclaims his only motivation is concern for his granddaughter, that all he wants is for his wayward son-in-law to get his act together, to get sober, and get responsible.

On cross, Denise is able to throw some doubt on the sincerity of his professed affection for me, and she gets him to acknowledge that he is not exactly a light drinker either, but in general, Beth's father handles himself much better than she did.

Now it is my turn. Prompted by my attorney's questions, I tell the judge that my daughter is the light of my life, that I miss her. I tell him that I used to read to her almost every night. When I was served with the divorce papers, I say, I was too shocked, too stunned, to think rationally. I had hoped for a reconciliation with my wife. That is why I took up temporary residence at a motel. I have recently, however, put down a deposit on a two-bedroom apartment and will be moving in the first of next month.

"What do you do when you and Annie are together?" Denise asks.

"I take her to gymnastics on Saturday. Sometimes we watch TV, we talk, play games. Sometimes we go shopping, catch a movie. There is an elementary school close to where I am staying and sometimes I take her there and let her play on the slides and swings and stuff."

"Since your separation from your wife, and your visitation arrangements with Annie, do you drink alcoholic beverages when you exercise visitation?"

"Absolutely, positively not." Beth, her father and the lawyer look at each other as if shocked to be hearing such a lie. "What about the DUI arrest?" Denise has invoked a common strategy. Get the bad stuff out early, deal with it. It takes the wind out of the sails of the opposition. And, if they harp on it in cross-examination, it will seem repetitious and unfair.

"An unfortunate mistake by an overzealous young officer," I answer.

"You are innocent then?"

"Yes."

"Oh, and by the way, Mr. Stevens. When you were ar-

rested on this DUI charge had you been exercising visitation that day?"

"No."

"Were you set to exercise visitation later?"

"No, not for a couple of days."

"Now as part of your pretrial release conditions on the
DUI charge, you are prohibited from consuming any alcoholic beverages, is that correct?"

"That is correct."

"And how is that monitored, if at all?"

"They have what are called alco checks. It's a small glass
tube device about the size of a flute. It operates similar to
a Breathalyzer instrument, though not as accurate. I am
required to give a breath sample into an alco check instrument on a random basis."

"And how often have you been required to do this, on
a random basis?"

"Up until recently, I was required to do this daily."

"And have you had any positive readings. Have any of
your tests indicated that you had been consuming alcoholic
beverages?"

"Well, let me put it this way. My pretrial release officer
told me that if I had any positive readings, I would be revoked from bail immediately. And, I'm still out on bail." I
do not mention the two times that I have feigned sickness
in order to avoid an alco check. "In fact the alco checks
have been cut back to once a week now." I see Miller nodding approvingly.

What I don't say is that this has nothing to do with the
results of my testing. If Chris Carter had her way I'd still
be doing daily alco checks. But my lawyer found a sympathetic ear in Judge John McDonald, who had been assigned
the case. He had bought Gary's argument that, tradition-
ally, an order for random alco checks meant no more than
once a week, unless the pretrial judge specified a different

schedule. McDonald also agreed that there was nothing in the facts of the case to justify more stringent monitoring. Finally, as a bonus, the judge had decided that requiring someone to attend counseling before they had been convicted of anything was not legal. The man is, after all, innocent until proven guilty, he had said.

I had been ecstatic when I got the news but did feel a little guilty when I talked to Chris Carter later. She had chuckled good-naturedly and congratulated me on my determination. She said when I wanted to put that same determination to work where it would do some good, she would be ready.

As Denise finishes and Carey begins his cross-examination, I am wondering whether he has talked to Chris Carter in preparation for this hearing. I would have. But, even if he has, there is little he can use as I see that he has not brought Chris as a witness. There is little in my testimony that he will be able to contradict. He has, however, done his homework. He produces my alco check log and forces me to acknowledge that I missed two alco checks, and that there were a couple of positive alco check readings on the log. I explained that because of the margin of error of the alco check instrument, such low readings are not considered to be a positive result. He makes a few more dents in the armor with his next several questions but is unable to do any real damage. Then:

"Have you been drinking today?" Carey is grinning like the Cheshire cat, sure that he has caught me now.

"I'm getting a feeling of déjà vu with that question, Don."

"Would the court direct the witness to answer the question please, Your Honor."

Judge Miller, with a bored look on his face, says, "Can you just answer his question, Mr. Stevens?"

"Sorry, Your Honor." I look back at Carey. "No."

"No?!" He looks at me in disbelief, then arches his eyebrows at Miller. "Your Honor, I ask the court to require Mr. Stevens to come close enough so the court can smell his breath. I believe the court will detect the very noticeable odor of an alcoholic beverage." Carey is now clearly excited. I detect what looks like concern in Denise's eyes, mixed with resignation. She gives a slight shrug of her shoulders, but does not object. Surprisingly, Miller puts the kibosh on the idea himself.

"I'm not going to be smelling anybody's breath, Mr. Carey. That's not within my job description. Now move on."

"As you wish, Your Honor." He gives a fake smile, then goes through the motions, asking a few more questions. It is obvious, however, that the unexpected thwarting of his coup de grâce has zapped his enthusiasm.

Noting that we are already five minutes over the allotted time for the hearing, Miller declines to hear closing arguments from either attorney and quickly tells us his ruling. He is going to leave things just the way they are, for the time being. He has insufficient evidence, he says, as of yet to justify the restrictions requested by the wife. He will reconsider my request when my living arrangements are more settled. While quickly disclaiming that he is pointing the finger at anyone, he cautions both of us to be very cautious and careful about what we say around our child concerning our partner or these proceedings. Then it is over.

Beth and her father quickly leave the chambers, with Carey leading the way. Denise and I linger a few moments in the hallway to make sure we do not have to ride the same elevator down. I am relieved, pleased with the outcome. I tell Denise how impressed I am with her skills, hoping that the flattery and the thrill of challenge will be enough to keep her on the case.

It appears that it is not. There is plenty of time, she says, before the final hearing for me to retain other counsel. I ask her to reconsider, make all kind of promises I know I won't keep. She shakes her head. I ask her to wait a couple of days before deciding, at least to sleep on it. She finally agrees.

One of the first things I do when I get back to the office is to call Gary Cooper.

"Hello."

"Gary, this is Ted Stevens."

"Yeah, Ted, how's it going?"

"Well, things are looking up in my divorce case. You know I told you I had that hearing today."

"Yeah. So it went okay—you got the visitation?"

"Not yet, but it's looking good. Thanks in large part to the good job you did in getting my pretrial release conditions changed. I think it made an impact on the judge."

"Good."

"But Gary, listen. I'm thinking maybe you should handle my divorce from now on. You know, it'd be less complicated, just one lawyer for both cases."

There is a pause, then, "What about Denise?"

"Well, I like Denise and she's a good lawyer. I just think maybe she's not aggressive enough. I need a real ball-breaker on this thing with Dandy Don. I wasn't real impressed with the way she conducted the hearing today. She's good, but she's just not nearly as good as you are. Look, I don't want to put you on the spot. Just thought I'd bring it up, something for you to think about. Maybe I'll end up staying with Denise. You know the old saying about switching horses in mid-stream. Plus I wanted to tell you what a good job you're doing. Speaking of which, you got that motion to dismiss ready to file yet?"

"As we speak. My secretary is typing the final draft. It'll

be filed tomorrow. Probably have a hearing in two to three weeks."

"Okay, Gary, thanks a lot. I'll talk to you later."

I attack my office work with renewed vigor and enthusiasm and have a very productive afternoon. I am headed out the door at about 6:00 P.M., having decided to have a decent sit-down meal for a change, when the phone rings.

"Morganstein and Stevens."

"Ted, this is Beth. We need to talk."

I fight to control the surprise at hearing her voice. Play it cool, I tell myself.

"No can do, Beth. In case you have forgotten, you've got a restraining order keeping me from having any contact with you. And, as I recall, your well-dressed lawyer has threatened to hang me by my thumbs if I so much as breathe in your direction."

I am feeling a little smug after today's hearing. Maybe she is finally realizing she may not hold all the cards after all. Well, I certainly was not going to make it easy for her. "I don't think it's such a good idea for us to be talking anyway just now," I say.

There is a long pause, then, "It's about Patty Stiles, Ted."

EIGHTEEN

I pull into the parking lot of the Publix Supermarket a little before 8:00 P.M. I am nervous, anxious. This meeting with my estranged wife has all the earmarks of a setup. Things did not go so well for her at the hearing today. Maybe she's hoping to regain her advantage. She'd thrown out the name of Patty Stiles, then told me she couldn't talk about it on the phone but to meet her in front of the Publix on Mahan Drive at eight. Then she'd hung up.

If this is a setup she will have told her parents she's received another harassing phone call from me, maybe even called the police, tell them I've been driving by her house, something like that. She will have arranged to have a witness, someone who can testify that her estranged husband approached her in the parking lot, obviously stalking her. Suddenly things would be looking up for her again and there'd be another nail in my coffin. I cannot, however, refuse the bait. "It's about Patty Stiles," she had said.

Maybe I'm being paranoid. Perhaps she has important information about the murder case, completely unconnected to me. And I've known Beth long enough to know that, whatever her faults, she's not sneaky. I also know that I have to find out what she knows.

I get out of my car, walk over to the supermarket and sit on a bench off to the side. I try to relax, focusing on watching the people coming in and out of the store. But I'm too self-conscious, hoping that I see no one I recognize. I don't want to explain what I'm doing here, don't want to engage in any chitchat. This doesn't feel right; I feel too exposed. I decide to get back into my car.

Twenty minutes pass. I am about to give up and leave when I spot a familiar-looking gray Volvo driving slowly through the parking lot. Beth parks in a spot a few cars down. I look quickly around for any spies waiting for me to make a wrong move. I can't tell, so I decide to play it safe and stay where I am. She has spotted me, and after a moment she motions me to come over to her car. I shake my head and motion for her to come over to mine instead. If someone is going to say they saw us together it will be her walking over to my car, not vice versa.

"When did you start smoking again?" she says after she slides into the passenger side.

I look over at the pack of Winstons on the dash, then at the one in my hand and suddenly realize that I've chain-smoked almost half a pack waiting for her. "I haven't, really—just once in a while." I suddenly feel very anxious and have to fight to control it. "You doing okay?"

"Yes, I guess." She looks over her shoulder as if she wants to make sure no one is watching. She hesitates a few moments and then says, "Ted, listen, I never wanted to hurt you. There've been so many people telling me what to do. I, I just don't know anymore. All I ever really wanted was to stop the drinking. You become a different person when you drink. It's scary—to me and to Annie." A tear forms in the corner of her left eye and runs down the side of her face and she gives a short sniff.

I start to clap my hands and congratulate her on a fine performance, but her words have the ring of truth to them.

Not knowing how to respond, I look away, then change the subject. "You said you wanted to talk to me about Patty Stiles."

Beth's face shifts quickly from sad to angry—a shift I've seen a few times before in our married lives. I know I may not like what comes next. "I thought you might want to see this." She takes an envelope from her purse, opens it, and removes a photograph, which she drops in my lap. I recognize it immediately. I fight to control the panic which is spreading through my body like a fire out of control. Stay calm, collect your thoughts, I tell myself. Analyze the situation. What are the implications? Had someone dug the photos out of the Rajun Cajun Dumpster? No, I had torn the photos up. Had there been copies made before I took them from Patty's house? What about the negatives? Yes, of course, I had destroyed the photos themselves, but not the negatives. Was it an inadvertent discovery and someone somehow recognized them for what they were? Not likely. Was Beth having me followed? Had she been waiting to play this trump card? I look at her, trying to decide who this woman is.

"Where did you get this?" I ask.

"Excuse me, Mr. Cheat, Mr. Lying, Sonofabitch Stevens. You don't get to ask questions here." Her face is flushed now, from anger and embarrassment. "You don't have the right." The truth of her statement and the frankness of its delivery shocks me into silence. She relaxes a little, then answers my question anyway.

"It came to the house this afternoon, hand-delivered by some teenager. He asked me my name, I told him, and he handed me this package. When I opened it up, I found this lovely eight-by-ten glossy."

I look at her. Is she telling me the truth?

"There was no stamp, no return address on the outside." She pauses, then, "There was a note though."

"What?"

She hands me a folded, letter-sized piece of typing paper. I open it up and read the short paragraph: "Of the seven deadly sins, lust is one of the cruelest. Don't you agree? I trust that you will find some use for the enclosed." The wording and the look of the note is familiar.

"I recognized Patty Stiles from her picture in the paper, even without her clothes on. You I'd recognize even without seeing the face." I'm surprised to see a slight upturn of her mouth, not quite a smile.

"Look, Beth, I know this looks bad, but somebody is obviously trying to set me up here. I think they've doctored this photograph somehow."

"Oh please, Ted. That's pathetic. Don't insult me with more of your lies. It was Patty Stiles who called me that night, wasn't it."

I don't know what to say, so I say nothing.

"This must be one of the photographs she told me she'd be sending me. It's crazy. I don't know why I didn't know this before. I knew you were seeing someone; I just didn't know who. My father even hired a private detective to follow you, but he came up with nothing."

A private detective! I try to stay calm. "You hired a private detective to follow me?"

"Not me, my father. You know how he is. I told him that I thought you might be running around . . . and he just took it from there. And I don't think you need to be acting indignant, not with that thing sitting in your lap."

"Who did he hire?" I say it as nonchalantly as I can.

"What does it matter? Obviously he wasn't any good."

"It could be very important. I'm thinking it might have something to do with that note."

She shrugs. "I don't know. Some guy from Panama City, I think. I never met him. Dad doesn't always tell me what he's doing on my behalf. Doesn't want to worry me with

the details, he says. Some ways, I think it's better that way."
She seems momentarily lost in thought, then refocuses.
"So, how long was this thing going on? I want to know the
details."

"Listen, Beth, I don't want to talk about it, okay? You've
got your photograph. I assume you want to use it as some
leverage. So, what's it going to be?"

"Well, maybe this is what it's going to be. Maybe, for
once, you'll tell me the truth. All of it. I think I deserve
that."

I start to tell her what I think she deserves but decide to
keep it to myself. Actually, she's probably right, and, besides, I don't see a good way to get out of it. So I tell her
the truth. Some of it, anyway. Well, actually, only the bare
minimum, explaining that it was a one-time thing only, that
we got drunk. The typical bullshit—and she wasn't buying
it. She has me by the short hairs now and we both know
it. She pauses for what seems a long time, then: "I probably
should turn this over to my lawyer, and maybe the authorities, but I'm not planning on it."

The words almost knock me over. "I don't get it," I finally
say.

"Have you ever heard the expression, Ted, 'don't look
a gift horse in the mouth'? The fact is, I don't need to
make this photograph public to get what I want, do I? We
both know the answer. And, I don't like to be manipulated.
It occurs to me that whoever sent this wanted to get you
into a hell of a lot of trouble, and is probably figuring that
I'm just the vindictive bitch to do it."

I bite my tongue.

She puts the photo and the note back in her purse. "I
despise people who don't have the guts to tell you something to your face," she says, looking at me, "and I'll tell
you what else: I don't like people thinking I'm so damn
predictable." There is an air of finality to her last state-

ment. She looks sideways at me. I can detect not a trace of the conciliatory tone, the remorsefulness with which she had begun this conversation. "I assume, of course," she continues, "that you will be reasonable."

I take a drag on my cigarette but say nothing. I don't have to. There is a long pause during which we both stare straight ahead. An ally, with a price. I will give her what she wants in the divorce case. I even agree to alcohol treatment—after the Stiles case is over. She agrees to keep the photo and note to herself—for now. Basic contract law. Also I am wondering if there are more recipients of these photos. I am imagining what would happen if Tom Haley, or Judge Rowe, or Marty the news hound, were to receive a similar package. I have a sudden chill as I realize that similar photos may already have been delivered. I force my focus back on Beth, and we sit and talk for several minutes more. By the time she leaves, I actually see some glimmer of hope for us—providing, of course, there's any hope for me.

The feelings of marital goodwill, however, are fleeting. As I drive west down Mahan Drive toward my motel, the reality of my precarious position starts to eat away at my confidence. Maybe whoever sent Beth that photo is the same person who's been sending me the ominous correspondence. That approach has worked so far so I think he's upping the ante. It's weird. I think he wants me on the case, but just to go through the motions. He doesn't tell me who, of our alternative suspects I'm supposed to stay away from. Right now, he's just messing with my mind.

And his strategy is working. Everything is coming unraveled. When I got rid of those photographs, my anxiety level went down significantly, and I felt myself gaining control. The visions, the nightmares, began to ease up. But now, ironically, those photographs have come back to haunt me. I have ignored my little voice one too many times, and now,

I'm afraid, I'm going to pay for it. Guilt and remorse are powerful weapons, especially when coupled with fear and uncertainty. And sometimes the truth is too illusory to be an effective defense.

As I stop at the traffic light at the corner of Tennessee Street and Woodward Avenue, I notice the lighted sign in front of St. Thomas More Cathedral: IT'S NEVER TOO LATE. On impulse I cut my wheels to the right and pull into the parking lot. Though it's almost nine, the doors are open. The portable sign, just inside the door, tells me that reconciliation is offered Friday nights seven to nine. I make my way over to a confessional as a young woman exits. I walk in and sit down. The unseen priest slides back the partition, and I begin. "Bless me, Father, for I have sinned."

NINETEEN

Saturday—September 20th

The heat and humidity had been oppressive when I left Tallahassee, but now the sun feels more warm than hot and the sea breeze along Highway 98 has made things comfortable enough that I have turned off the a.c. and rolled down the windows. The familiar smell of salt and sea life is both invigorating and calming at the same time. The sun sits balanced on the top of the pines preparing for its inevitable descent as I approach the bridge that connects St. George Island to the mainland.

When I reach the highest point of the bridge I have a good view of the central part of the island. Homes peek in and out of the trees along the bayside, the modest and the not-so-modest. Above it all is the water tower which looks like a giant lime-colored golf ball sitting on its tee. Straight ahead is the quaint, somewhat tacky cluster of stores and gas stations that greets the visitor immediately upon arriving on the island.

The symbolic crossing of the bridge has always allowed me an escape, a psychological release from the pressures of the city. It has been over two months since my last trip here and though my sketchy memories of that visit are more haunting than reassuring, I find that I still feel the familiar magic calm as I traverse the last segment of the bridge. I have come to relax, to escape the distractions of the office, but also to concentrate. A lot has happened since the meeting with Beth three weeks ago and the Jackson trial is coming up soon. I need time by myself to prepare before I get caught up in the inevitable frenzied whirlwind of the trial.

I stop at the small grocery on Pine Street and quickly fill my basket with some provisions for the weekend. I pause by the beer cooler for a moment and then grab a twelve-pack of beer. Ironically, even though I no longer have to do the daily alco checks, I find that I am drinking less these days. Maybe those weeks of daily alco checks jump-started me back to reality. Maybe the revelation that someone out there knows too much about my involvement with Patty Stiles has sobered me up. Maybe confession is really good for the soul. I don't know for sure, but, whatever the reason, I feel more in control than I have in quite some time. I understand the grip that the alcohol has on me, but, for the first time in a long time, it doesn't feel like a death grip.

After my meeting with Beth I did some serious soul searching, even had a couple of sessions with Chris Carter. Once I got past my skepticism, those sessions proved helpful. I did not bare my soul—it was like pulling teeth, Chris had said, to get me to say anything—but I was able to look inside it, see the ugliness there, and not blink. I had cursed the alcohol-induced voids in my memory. In the end I had decided that the past cannot be changed. The future was another question, however, and I was determined that Bobby Jackson would have one. There would be time later to redeem, to reclaim my soul for good. Full recovery, however, would have to wait. For now, professional pride and sheer willpower would have to keep the demons at bay, a temporary truce.

I have brought my complete files with me and intend to use my time effectively. The secret to success as a trial lawyer is not flamboyance and dramatic presentations, nor saber-like cross examination. In the end, style without substance is useless. Nothing takes the place of good, solid, thorough preparation. You have to consider every angle, anticipate the state's theory, its evidence, its objections, and its arguments; then everything else will fall into place. A weekend of solitude, with no deadline pressures, will be invaluable.

The Turners' beach house is a relatively modest one-story, three-bedroom, two-bath place, but it sits on three acres of prime beach-front property on the east end of the island. My father-in-law purchased the property more than twenty-five years ago, before the bridge that would bring thousands of people and higher prices for land. While developers were selling off large chunks of property in the exclusive, gated community on the west end, Captain Turner had purchased almost twenty acres on the east end. He sold half of the acreage several years later for a huge profit but retained the beach-front acreage, plus approximately seven acres on the bayside across the road. He had built the house mostly for rental.

When Beth and I were married, my father-in-law made a big show of giving me a key to the beach house. But with Captain Turner, you never get something for nothing, so the deal was that Beth and I would look after the property, make all arrangements with the property manager, see that maintenance and repairs were done, and keep all the paperwork current. He was too busy, he said, to fool with it. In exchange, we would have the use of the house any time it wasn't rented, except of course, when Mom and Dad preempted us.

When Beth filed for divorce I was relieved of my responsibilities as the liaison with the property manager in a letter from my father-in-law. He had not, however, specifically told me to stay away from the beach house and no one had thought to demand that I return the key. It probably never occurred to them that I would even consider using their house under the circumstances.

That's what makes it so satisfying. I had called the management company, found that the house was not rented this weekend, and made arrangements to come. Captain Turner will eventually discover this oversight when he receives the paperwork from the property management company. The thought of his reaction makes me smile as I turn the key in the lock and open the door.

There's not a lot about my father-in-law that causes me to smile. I think back to when Beth told me he had had me followed. It was like someone had stuck a tap in my leg and started draining the energy and confidence from me. That same night I'd called Bert at his home.

"What's up, Teddy Bear?"

"Bert, do you know any private detectives in Panama City?"

"Sure, I know a couple. Why?"

"I talked to my wife tonight."

"Teddy, Teddy, Teddy, are you asking for trouble, or what?"

"No, Bert, it was her idea. She wanted to talk to me. She told me that she has irrefutable evidence that I was running around on her while we were married."

"Were you?"

"That's beside the point. Let's just say there may be certain evidence she could produce that might be misconstrued or misinterpreted."

"Yeah, sure."

"Anyway, she says she thinks her father hired a private detective out of Panama City to follow me. I need to know who it was, and I need to know what they know. Think you could help me on this?"

"Gosh, I don't know, Ted. I'll try. If your father-in-law went to the best P.I.s in Panama City, then I know who they are. But getting them to talk will be another thing. It's not likely they would acknowledge it—you know, confidentiality."

"Yeah, I understand. Let me know how much money it will cost me."

"Teddy Bear, you stab me through the heart. You have such low esteem of my profession?"

"No, not really, I just have a high estimation of financial gain as an incentive. As a lawyer, I am well familiar with the paradoxical technique of divulging information without betraying a confidence, technically. This is important to me, Bert. It may be connected to the hate mail I've been getting."

"You got some more?"

"No, and that makes me more nervous. I need to know, and the sooner the better."

"Okay, chief, I'll see what I can do. I'll get on it first thing in the morning."

"Thanks. Let me know as soon as you have something."

Denise Wilkerson had been a much harder sell. I had started off by acknowledging that she had been right, that I had lied to her, that I did have a problem controlling my drinking. This had noticeably softened her. It may have been all she wanted to hear, but then I told her about my meeting with Beth and added the clincher.

"Beth told me her father hired a private detective who followed me around before she filed for her divorce. She says that her lawyer has a photograph, a compromising photograph of me with another woman, and now they're planning on using it."

"They can't do that, Ted. Florida is a no-fault divorce state. Unless they can show that you were spending your marital assets on another woman, infidelity, no matter how distasteful or low-life it might be, is not relevant evidence in a divorce proceeding."

"Thanks for that encouragement, Denise."

"Well, sorry. I tell it like I see it." She continued, "On the other hand, they might be able to argue that it's relevant to show that you're a liar. Seems that I recall that you emphatically denied any such extramarital activity at your deposition—even when I objected and you didn't have to answer the question." I could hear the frustration in her voice.

"I know, I know. I was a fool."

"No argument here." I could hear her smile on the other end and thought maybe she was hooked. "It wasn't relevant at the deposition and it's not relevant now. An impeachment on irrelevant matters is not something that Judge Miller is likely to entertain."

"Dandy Don's probably going to be filing a motion for reconsideration and is going to dredge this stuff up."

"The twerp."

"So, you'll stay on the case then?"

A long pause, then, "I guess I shouldn't walk away when the house is ablaze. And I'm thinking maybe you might have turned some kind of corner here, Ted, so, yes, I'll stay on—for now. See if you can follow through. And . . ."

"Yeah?"

"No more lies, right?"

"No more lies, Denise."

Denise had then agreed to schedule my father-in-law for a deposition. It's set for a couple of weeks from now. She subpoenaed his financial records and specifically asked for any documentation, correspondence, reports, etc., relative to the hiring of any private detective within the past year. We had decided that there was no sense in hiding what our intent was and we wanted to make sure that there could be no evasiveness or protestations of miscommunication about what was going to be asked and what documentation was required.

Bert's report had come quickly but was not very satisfying. Despite offers of money and some cajoling by Bert, neither of the two private detectives he had talked to in Panama City had admitted to being hired by Captain Turner. Bert had said he believed them, so we decided to let these two follow up where Bert had begun, asking questions and talking to other private detectives in the area, so far with no luck. Either the ethics of the private detectives were stronger than I thought, or Captain Turner has outpriced me. The good news, I guess, is that I have not received a call from Tom Haley, or some police detective or newspaper reporter, wanting to ask me about some photographs.

I get settled in, boil some shrimp, open a beer, and set my files out on the dining room table. Three hours and six beers later I decide to quit for the night. I turn on the TV, flip through the channels quickly but, finding nothing I like, turn it off. It's midnight, but I don't feel sleepy. I decide to go out, maybe listen to some music, watch some people. I end up at the Oasis. On the screened-in upper deck a woman is singing country blues. It's crowded and there's the smell of marijuana, sweat, and beer in the air. They are having a two-for-one special on beer and oysters. I spend the next two hours taking full advantage of that special.

As if in a cocoon, I peer out at the other customers from my seat at the corner of the bar. I concentrate on the singer. She is dressed in jeans and an Indian-patterned shirt, both of which fit loosely around a somewhat obese body. Her tan is dark and her hair a sun-bleached brown that looks as dry as straw. It hangs straight and limp down to her shoulders. Some of the tunes I recognize, but others seem original. She has a raspy, unique voice that seems well suited to her choice of songs. After a few more beers, and a few more songs, she is looking more and more attractive to me. On one of the breaks she heads directly to me, stops beside me, and then calls to the bartender. "Hey, Ray, can I get a beer from you."

"Sure, Maggie."

I remember seeing the sign on the way in: LIVE MUSIC—COUNTRY/ROCK, BLUES—MAGGIE MAY WATERS—10:00 TILL . . . —2 FOR 1 SPECIALS ON LONGNECKS & OYSTERS.

"How's it going?" She's looking at me now.

"Pretty good," I respond lamely.

"You like the music?"

"Very much."

"So how come I never see you clapping?"

The question surprises me. "I was too mesmerized, too entranced," I manage.

She seems to like my answer and for the next five minutes engages me in small talk. I learn that she is originally from Louisiana, that she lives in Apalachicola, where she has a small antique shop. She ends the conversation with a surprising question.

The sun is peeking over the horizon. I have awakened and judge by the unfamiliar furnishings that the answer to her question had been her place, not mine. I quietly get my clothes together and leave a message telling her that I will call later; then I slip out the door.

Back at the house, I change into shorts and take a quick jog along the beach. At first it is torture, my head pounding and my stomach tightening. I silently chastise myself. Broken promises! After a while, though, the quiet solitude of the beach, the cool sand beneath my feet, the sound of the surf crashing and the birds calling helps me establish a rhythm as I pound out the poisons, clear the cobwebs, and get the blood flowing for another day of work.

The day goes by quickly but productively. I work some inside but mostly out on the covered deck. The day is beautiful, sunny, and cloudless with a hint of fall in the air. The breeze off the water and the rhythmic sound of the surf are soothing. Around noon, I have a sandwich and a coke, take a short nap in one of the beach chairs, then attack my work with renewed vigor. By late afternoon I have organized my files and my notes about as well as I can expect and decide to reward myself with a sunset sail on the Hobie Cat.

Out on the water the wind is a little stronger and the craft clips along at a good pace away from the shore. The warm sun together with the sea breeze and the occasional spray of water are a pleasant combination. I turn to the west and face the sun, a large orange ball of wax that melts into the gulf, sending colored streamers across the water in all directions. Once it sinks beyond the horizon, its color reflects upward, mixing with the blue of the sky to paint with broad strokes a canvas of pink and purple clouds. The light is filtered through a strange yellowish color that seems artificial as it reaches me. Several times the images come, unbidden, unwelcome. They come quickly. With practiced skill and renewed willpower, I push them back each time. I can feel the control returning, becoming stronger.

For about an hour I enjoy the solitude, the meditative rhythm of the surf and the wind as I sail quickly and smoothly, expertly across the water. Reluctantly, I make my way back to the beach under the dim reflected light of the sun, which has long since passed out of sight. It is a perfect ending to the day. But there is a queasy feeling in my stomach as I pull onto shore. I sense a vague but familiar premonition, hear the little voice, like a distant radio signal I can't quite tune out, a voice that will not allow me the peace that I seek.

I consider packing up and heading back to town, but decide against it. What's done is done. A good poker player must know how to make the most out of the hand he is dealt. Besides I need to check something out. After another sandwich and my first and only beer of the day, I head down to Harry A's. The place is relatively quiet for a Saturday evening. Mike Andrews, the son-in-law of the owner, is at the bar.

"Hey, Ted. How's it going?"

Though Harry A's is mostly a local hangout, a few of us weekenders, those who show that we can drink with the best of them, are sometimes accepted into the fold. I am sure I passed the test with room to spare.

"Not bad, Mike. How 'bout a margarita?"

"Sure. Long time no see. What's it been, a couple of months?"

"Yeah, I've been kind of busy. Haven't had a chance to get down to the island recently." I decide that Mike does not need to know the details, but then realize that he'll probably know after a few more drinks anyway, so I add, "I'm working on a big murder case that's going to trial soon, plus as you may have heard, I'm in the middle of a not-so-friendly divorce."

"Yeah, I remember you telling me about it the last time you were here." He pauses and looks to me for confirmation. He is right, of course. The last time I was here was the night Beth left with Annie. Also the night Patty Stiles was killed.

"That's right. By the way, Mike. Do you remember when that was? The date, I mean?"

He looks at me sort of quizzically and says, "Sure I do. They were having the finals of the NBA playoffs. We had a big crowd. And you got drunk as hell," he adds.

"Yeah, I'm trying to piece together exactly what happened that night, you know, part of the divorce. My wife's thinking that maybe I was shacking up with somebody. I didn't leave with any woman that night, did I? Do you remember?"

"Not that night." He gives me a wink then continues. "I don't think you were in the mood for anything that night. You were kind of crying in your beer, feeling a little bit sorry for yourself. A bit of a pain in the ass really, but hell, what are bartenders for anyway," he laughs.

"Do you by any chance remember how long I was here? Did I stay till closing?"

"I can't say exactly when you left, Ted. It was well before closing though. Like I told your associate, I'm sure it was before the end of the game, probably about ten thirty or eleven."

"My associate?" The sweat pops out on my forehead instantaneously while my heart goes down to my stomach and back up again with a jolt. "Somebody else was in here asking about my whereabouts?"

"Yeah," Mike looks at me a little sheepishly. "He said he worked for you. I hope I didn't mess you up, Ted."

"Who was it?"

"I didn't know him. Small, wiry-looking black guy. He said your wife's lawyer accused you of being out all night, was trying to prove that you couldn't have been home in Tallahassee at twelve like you said you were. The wife was claiming that she heard that you had closed this place down. I set him straight, though. I told him you left about ten thirty." Mike looks fairly pleased with himself. "Did I do okay?"

"You did fine, Mike." The sickening feeling makes me almost numb. "The problem is, I don't have a black associate. Now, what exactly did this guy look like? What did he say? I want the details."

* * *

I'm on the couch in the living room of the beach house,
though I don't remember how I got here. The light outside
prompts me to look at my watch, which reads 9:45 A.M. I
slide my legs off the sofa and sit up straight. The pounding
in my head reminds me of why I cannot remember. Except
for my shoes, which are on the floor next to the couch, I
am wearing the same thing that I had on the night before.
I feel clammy and my clothes are sticking to me. I slowly
make my way into the bathroom, take off my clothes and
surrender, mercifully, to the shower.

Feeling somewhat refreshed, but wanting to get something in my stomach, I hop in the car and head down to
the Paradise Cafe for some breakfast. I'm sitting at a booth
sipping my coffee and waiting for my order when the couple in the booth next to me gets up to leave. The man asks
if I'd like his paper, as he is done with it. I say I do and
thank him as he heads for the cash register. I unfold the
paper to the front-page headline: THREE SLAIN IN EXE-
CUTION-STYLE MURDERS. Underneath the headline
the subtitle reads: Police Suspect Deaths Are Result of Drug
Deal Gone Sour. I read on quickly.

> The bodies of three men, identified as Samuel L.
> Smith, Alphonzo Olds, and Jeffrey M. Walker, were
> found in a small wooded area of Myers Park early
> this morning by TPD officers who had responded to
> a report of gunshots. Although authorities are with-
> holding details pending their investigation, TPD
> spokesman Bret Meadows indicated that all three
> men had been shot and killed in what was described
> as an execution-style slaying, and that all three men
> had histories of drug use and drug dealing. . . .

Suddenly, I have lost my appetite.

Back at the house I call Bert's office and leave a message on the recorder. I try his mobile number but it's out of range. While I'm waiting, I pack my stuff and load up the car. Just as I'm leaving, the phone rings. It's Bert.

"Hey, Ted."

"Bert. Have you seen the morning paper?"

"No, but I know what's in it. Guess I won't be serving Sammy with that subpoena after all."

"What do you think—what does it mean?"

"I don't know yet. But there'll be another twist in to-morrow's edition."

"What do you mean?"

"The police want to question our client."

"What?"

"Yeah, I got a call about two hours ago. Bobby's bond is being revoked. He apparently violated his curfew last night. Cops want to know where he was about three A.M."

"But that doesn't make any sense. He'd have no moti-vation. Sammy Smith was going to help the defense."

"Unless perhaps B.J. is the mystery guy in the Stiles' photo."

My mind races to plug the known facts into this theory. Possible maybe, but not likely, I conclude.

"But there's more, Ted."

"What is it?"

"Sammy Smith had a piece of paper in his pocket. Know what it said?"

TWENTY

The smell of pan-fried bacon greets me as I enter the door of the small restaurant. For over forty years Terry's Cafe has been an early morning gathering place for loyal customers, from construction workers to cabinet officials, all of whom share an appreciation for good, down-home Southern cooking.

The physical appointments of the restaurant are as unpretentious as the menu. You can see the entire restaurant from the entryway. Just inside the door to the left is the cash register. To the right, toward the rear, is the cooking area, which is enclosed by a lunch counter. White Formica tables dot the floor space. The tables are serviced by sturdy metal chairs with dark red vinyl cushions and backs. Booths with matching red vinyl seat cushions and backs line the remaining wall space.

Even when the place is only half full, the acoustics are such that you can barely hear the person sitting across from you, much less at the next table. This out-in-the-open privacy is a large part of its appeal to government and business power brokers who meet here regularly. I come because of the food and because it's only a block from the office. Bert waves to me from a corner booth. I walk over, slip in across from him and, without preliminaries, get right to it.

"What you got?"

"Maybe a little more than you read in the paper yesterday," Bert replies, "but not much. The boys were executed, plain and simple. Sammy took one in the throat, one in the head. His buddies, you met them, took two shots each to the head. They're still running ballistics on the slugs they removed, but it looks like it was a thirty-eight caliber. The same gun fired all six shots."

"You mean the same guy shot all three?" I ask, unconvinced.

Bert has read my thoughts, my tone. "Yeah, just what I thought too," he says. "Either someone else held a gun on our friends while the killer did his thing, or it was one guy with a lot of balls who was quick and knew how to use the element of surprise. Their guns never came out of their respective hiding places.

"The person who reported the shots," Bert continues, "said he heard three of 'em right in a row, real quick—bam, bam, bam. Then a pause of several seconds and three more shots two or three seconds apart. The theory is that this was some kind of drug deal gone bad. The police didn't find any sums of large cash or drugs on the victims, but they did have their wallets intact and all of their jewelry on them."

"But what do you think, Bert?"

"I think they're probably right. I think maybe Sammy got a little too big for his britches. Maybe he was playing out of his league."

The hard edge in Bert's voice is a little disconcerting, but I remember the look in Bert's eye when Sammy's men had disarmed him. It was there for only an instant but I could not mistake the anger that flashed in that brief moment. His look now reminds me of that as he continues.

"Sammy had been running his mouth, talking to Patty Stiles, playing the big man with me and you. Folks on up the food chain probably thought he got to be a bit of a security risk. They would have set up a meeting, maybe to transfer drugs. Normal business."

"This happened at Myers Park, right?" I say. "That's not your usual place for a drug deal, is it?"

"You'd be surprised, Teddy Bear. You'd be surprised." Bert explains that the spot is a popular hangout because it's wooded, away from regular parking, and you can see the cops coming in time to ditch anything you have on you.

"So, was it one guy or more?"

"Oh, probably two or three there, but only one shooter. The way I see it, Sammy and his boys are standing at the rear of his El Dorado. That's where the bodies were found. Sammy's smoking a cigarette, playing it cool. Then the other car comes up slow, with the lights off, stops twenty feet away. The other guys get out of the car and walk over to Sammy like there's nothing unusual going on. When they get within arms reach, they pull out their guns before Sammy and his goons know what's going on. Then, one of the guys, probably the head honcho—yeah, he'd want to make a point—he puts a bullet into the head of the man on the right, then the left, real quick. They go down right away.

"There's a moment's hesitation as Sammy, who's shittin' in his pants now, watches the gun barrel turn toward him. He puts his hands up, a useless gesture because there's no doubt what the guy has in mind. He fires a shot into Sammy's throat. Sammy puts his hand up to this gaping hole, but he can't stop the blood gushing out of him like a fountain. It would probably take several seconds for Sammy to realize what was happening. Then, just as Sammy is on his knees and about to pass out, the guy puts a bullet in his head at close range. For good measure, he goes over to the other two and puts another bullet in each of them as well."

Bert has been suggesting this scenario matter-of-factly, while looking at his menu. I suddenly realize that there are goose bumps on my forearms.

"Shit," Bert says, looking up from his menu and grinning. "I gotta quit reading them true detective magazines." Bert's eyes are friendly again and his voice has lost the edge, but I think I'll be looking at Bert a little differently now.

"You think it might have had anything to do with our case?" The answer is obvious to me, but I want to see Bert's reaction.

"You mean, could it be the guy in the photograph? I don't know. It could be. Do you really want to find out?" Bert is looking at me intently, and I at him, trying to figure out if there is a hidden meaning in this question. I realize, that the chill I felt moments before was born of fear, the same fear that now makes the sweat pour from my forehead.

"I don't know," I answer truthfully.

"Look at the bright side, Teddy. You can still point the finger at Sammy. An empty witness chair in this case might be a lot better than a live witness."

"So, the killer, or killers, did us a favor here? Is that what you're saying?"

"Maybe not on purpose, Teddy, but, hey, you got to admit, it might work out for the best."

In fact, the thought had occurred to me, but I had not wanted to admit it. "I don't know that Sammy and his friends would agree."

Bert shrugs his shoulders in acknowledgment of the obvious.

"Maybe," I say, "my pen pal might give it a rest too."

"Maybe."

"All right, what about Bobby? Have they got anything really?"

"They ain't got shit, boss. Leastways, not that I can find out. Like I said yesterday, he was unaccounted for at the time of the murders, and Sammy had a piece of paper in his pocket with the initials B.J. on it, and Myers Park. But that ain't proof of nothing." Bert says it with authority, but I'm not so sure. Bert continues. "Now, who knows, maybe they can match some of the footprints, or tire tracks, or some other physical evidence at the scene, but I doubt it. This is not B.J.'s style."

"That's what you said about the Stiles' murder charge too."

"Still say it."

After a moment's pause, "I agree."

"What can I get you fellows?" The waitress is suddenly standing beside the table, pad and pen in hand. She looks about fifty, tall, thin, with bleached blond hair. She is smiling, but it is clear that she is in a hurry and we oblige. Bert smiles back at her, orders the country breakfast. I do the same and she disappears quickly back toward the kitchen. Bert then leans over the table toward me.

"I've got a couple more leads we ought to talk about," he says, looking at me intently again. "One of my operatives reinterviewed one of Patty Stiles' neighbors. Not the one who supposedly saw B.J. running from her place, but another one. We like to reinterview witnesses sometimes after they've had time to let the dust settle, so to speak. You never know what you're gonna turn up."

I nod in approval as Bert continues. "Anyway, he asks this neighbor again about Patty's friends, visitors, that sort of thing. The neighbor gives him a description. Let me see now, I've got that report here somewhere." Bert pulls out a folder from his briefcase, opens it, and then turns to the page he is looking for. "Yes, here it is. A white male, maybe mid to late thirties, longish sandy blond hair, tall." Bert looks up at me from the file. "The neighbor says she didn't get a real good look at the guy. He mostly came at night. But she did see him occasionally. What was strange was he always walked up to the house. Never saw him in a car."

I don't respond.

"So, what do you think, Counselor? Got any ideas who that might be?" Bert is looking directly at me now.

Still I don't respond.

I am remembering when my sixth-grade teacher, Mrs. Bassett, asked me a similar question about some fairly graphic graffiti she had found on the cloakroom wall. I had been sure then that my inquisitor had known the answer to her question. The dilemma was unavoidable. Fold your cards, own up to your involvement, and take a certain punishment, even though it might be a bluff? Or, call her bluff, deny any involvement, but risk a harsher penalty for lying about it as well, if she, in fact, had all the cards and knew the truth?

Each hand is different. There may be different odds, different risks, different players. I hesitate for several moments now, considering my options, finally deciding I have nothing to gain from continuing the farce.

"Okay. You're right. The details aren't important. Suffice it to say that my relationship with Patty Stiles passed beyond the purely professional stage. The important thing, however, is that it was brief. And it was over long before Patty Stiles was murdered." I look into his eyes, trying to get a read, but can't.

"Yeah." Bert takes a long breath and pauses. "I remember you saying that you hadn't even seen Patty Stiles for at least a couple of months before her death." Another long pause. "You should know, however, that the neighbor says she saw you at least a couple of times within the two weeks before Stiles was murdered."

I look directly at Bert. "She must be mistaken then." Bert doesn't look convinced, but I return his stare. "Trust me on this, Bert. Somebody out there may be trying to tie me to this case, but it is a red herring. I suggest that you could spend your time more productively on other matters." I have summoned all of my poker-playing skills to these last few words and to the look I now give Bert.

Bert shrugs his shoulders, gives me a smile. "Well, it's your money. You point, I'll follow."

I am feeling sick to my stomach.

"But, you gotta think, if I found out, there's a chance that even those dimwits at TPD might find out too. It could be," he hesitates, "embarrassing." The implications of this remote possibility hang in the air long after the words are uttered.

"You hot, Teddy Bear? You're sweating like a pig."

I can feel the little beads of sweat popping out on my forehead, the expanding circles of wetness under my arms. I take a napkin from the holder on the table and wipe my forehead. "Yeah, they need a little better ventilation in here."

The waitress suddenly appears again with our food. Though I find that I have lost my appetite, I am thankful for the brief pause as we eat in silence for a few minutes. I quickly reassess my situation and conclude that nothing has really changed. If my relationship with Patty Stiles were to come out, it would be very embarrassing. No question that I would be off the case. That, of course, is the least of my worries. I am walking a tightrope, and I'm not sure how long I can keep my balance. What if Bert were to share this information with Paul, or Bobby Jackson? What if he already has? I am beginning to think that I have no safe harbors anymore, no one that I can truly trust, even myself.

I am still considering my options when Bert breaks the silence and drops another bombshell.

"Got a description of another visitor to the Stiles house," Bert says nonchalantly as he shovels his breakfast into his mouth. "This one's a heavy-set guy, with glasses and short dark hair. Businessman type, maybe a lawyer." Bert looks up at me again. "Drives a white Volvo station wagon."

I try to hide my surprise. "That sounds kind of like Paul Morganstein," I say matter-of-factly, though my mind, and my heart, are racing wildly.

"So he was having a thing with her too?" Bert's voice is incredulous.

"Not that I know of. I'm sure it was business-related. I was the main lawyer on the case, but Paul and I sometimes work together, you know." I know that this was not the situation, however—at least to my knowledge. Paul never did anything in Patty's divorce case. He had, in fact, referred her to me. I knew that they knew each other, but he had very deliberately stayed away from it after that. Could it be some other legal matter that I was not aware of and, for some reason, Paul has not told me about? The other alternative is just too weird for me to accept. "When was it that the neighbor said they saw this visitor?"

"This is the same lady, by the way, who saw you," Bert says. "She wasn't sure. Maybe only a couple of times, maybe only once. But she did say that it was fairly close in time to the date of the murder. Maybe within a week or ten days."

"Was the guy carrying a briefcase?"

"She couldn't remember."

"Well, that's probably what it was, some situation where he was running something by her house."

"Do y'all usually make house calls?" Bert asks.

"Not usually," I concede. "But it wouldn't be that uncommon. You don't have anything connecting Paul up to the night of the murder do you?"

"No, but I can follow it up if you want."

There was certainly no love lost between my partner and my private detective. Part of me wants very much to give Bert the green light, but my little voice is pointing me in a different direction. "Nah, listen, I'll talk to Paul. I think we got enough suspects without pointing the finger at my own partner." I try a smile and Bert gives me one back, nodding in agreement, but I am not sure that he is completely convinced. I wonder to myself why I have tried to put Bert off his scent.

We finish our meal, which Bert insists on paying for, and part company. If Bert had seen through any of my hidden agenda, I could not tell from his words or demeanor. Bert Murphy always knows more than he will tell. I have never liked playing poker with him. Why, I wonder to myself, in this cosmic world of chance, have we been thrown together at this particular time in this particular situation. I cannot shake a vague feeling that this will not end well.

The rest of the day is like a fog. Try as I might, I find it too difficult to concentrate on my other cases. I go through the motions, dictating some letters, drafting a complaint in a breach of contract case, and doing an initial interview of a client. But the uneasiness from breakfast follows me like a shadow.

Several times during the day I start toward Paul's office, going over in my mind what I will say, then I stop, return to my office. The fact that I have not gone right up to him, confronted him with the information I have been supplied, speaks volumes of my suspicions and fears, and my cowardice. It makes me miserable, almost physically sick, but I avoid him, nonetheless, all day. The confusion about my own secrets has colored the processing of the information and clouded my judgment. I rationalize my inaction, telling myself that I should try to get a little more information, be sure of my facts, before I talk to Paul.

In the late afternoon, I pull out the Jackson file. It has grown such that it fills up three expando file folders. Then I get Janice to pull up our computer files on Patty Stiles. I ask her to check and see if there are any entries of time spent on the divorce case by Paul Morganstein. She checks and tells me what I already knew. Just entries by me. Are there any other files that were opened for Patty Stiles on some other legal matter? No, she tells me. I mull this over a couple of minutes. Noting that Paul has left for the day, I head down to his office. His secretary stops her typing when I approach and looks at me expectantly.

"Cathy, I was wondering. I've been looking over the records of Patty Stiles' divorce case, which I handled. I seem to remember that Paul told me that he did some work for Patty as well, on something, but I can't seem to locate those on the computer. Would you have any files someplace else, not on the computer, or do you remember whether Paul was doing any work for Patty Stiles?"

"Ted," she says, looking through a three-by-five index card file, "I don't see anything here under Patty Stiles. Would it be under another name?"

"I don't think so. You don't remember anything?"

"Well, now that you mention it, I do remember a couple of phone calls from Ms. Stiles to Paul. I remember the name because she was a client of yours. I think she even made an appointment one time, but canceled it."

"When was this, do you remember?"

"Oh, it's been a few months ago. It was after her divorce case, though, I believe."

"Would it be on your appointment calendar?" I ask.

"No, because she canceled it. I always write in pencil."

"And Paul never mentioned anything about it to you?"

Cathy is unsure of what the significance of all this is, but senses the urgency somehow. "No, Ted, I'm sorry, not that I recall. Sometimes he just makes a temporary file and, unless he dictates a letter or something, or bills the client, he may not even give me any information about it. It's possible that Paul just gave her some advice over the phone and didn't charge her. That wouldn't be unusual. He does that often. Of course, you could ask him."

I smile. "Yeah, thanks, Cathy. That's just what I'll do. It's not that important. Just tying up some loose ends." I try to dispel any alarm that may have begun ringing in her mind. I turn around and head back to my office.

An hour later I am in the office alone sipping on my second bourbon and Coke. I am looking through the Jackson file, making notes. I pull out the file folder which contains my notes about Patty's unfinished news story. I look back over the notes I had made from memory of what was in the pocket notebook I found in Patty's house. "Cars, house, $$$, A.M., P.M.," followed by "Deeds, C H's."

I had thought that the P.M. referred to the time, that Patty was to meet somebody at night. But now, another interpretation seems so obvious to me that I wonder why I have not thought of it before. What if the P.M. were someone's initials, I think? What if, for example, P.M. stands for Paul Morganstein?

TWENTY-ONE

Monday—October 6th

I look in the mirror, adjust my tie, admire the fresh hair-cut, clean shave and new suit. I turn from side to side, checking out the profile. Not too shabby, I think to myself. Then I lean in closer, studying the red nose, the puffiness around the dull eyes that stare back at me. Must be the lighting in here, I think.

Trial in the Jackson case is set to begin in a few minutes and I have slipped into the rest room in the back hall of the courthouse to take just a few moments to compose myself. I take a paper towel and wipe the perspiration from my forehead. Looking around quickly to make sure no one else is around, I take the bottle of vodka from my coat pocket. I look around once again, and then turn the bottle up, taking a long swig. The vodka burns as it goes down, but it's a calming, reassuring burn, a controlled burn I tell myself. I pause a couple of seconds more, and then turn the bottle up one more time and drain it.

I had renewed the motion to dismiss yesterday concerning the missing notebook, and it looked as though Rowe was sorely tempted to grant it. In the end though, he said he didn't see any real prejudice and denied the motion.

As I toss the empty bottle into the trash I hear the door

open behind me. I quickly remove another paper towel from the dispenser and begin wiping my hands, pretending to have just finished washing them, self-conscious about the preening. In the mirror I can see the face of Quentin Martin as he rounds the corner into the rest room. His face registers surprise, followed by amusement as he recognizes me.

"There you are," he says with false joviality. "I didn't know you were so shy, Teddy."

I had hoped to avoid the press, and everyone else for that matter, by coming in the side door and using the employees' rest room. Quentin Martin is the last person I want to see now. It bothers me beyond description that this sleazebag excuse for a news reporter calls me by my first name, but he will never know it from me. "That's Mr. Teddy to you, Marty."

Most of the coverage of the Stiles murder case has been relatively low key, considering the circumstances. Martin's pieces have stood out though. From the first he has latched onto the fact that the victim had been a former client, hinting strongly at more, and making it sound as sinister as possible. I had wanted to complain but I didn't want to look like a real fool in the event that my pen pal decided to send Quentin a photo or two. Thank God he hadn't. At least, I felt sure he hadn't. Otherwise, Martin would not have been able to help himself. He would have had to print it.

Then there was the DUI. None of the articles on this slant had been particularly kind to me, but Martin had gone out of his way to hound me every chance he got. He had an annoying way, not uncommon to his species, of making my repeated no comments look like admissions of guilt.

* * *

Reverend Paxton had been holding one of Martin's articles in his hand when he confronted me. Bernice Jackson and B.J.'s sister were sitting on either side of him in my office. It had been right after B.J. had been picked up on the bond revocation. The anger and the disgust had been under control but evident underneath the surface as he spoke.

The family, he had said, knew about the DUI and had heard rumors about me and the victim. They had tried to be understanding at first, considering I was going through a divorce, but things seemed to be getting worse. Friends had told stories, given warnings. Words like "betrayal," "conflict of interest," "asleep" or "drunk at the wheel" were used.

It was obvious to me that someone had been feeding them information. I didn't ask who. It was enough that it was accurate. B.J.'s sister had been uncharacteristically quiet, nodding approval in the background, the "I told you so" look on her face. She clearly enjoyed the skewering. Bernice, for her part, looked sad, disappointed. She did not make eye contact.

I was not in much of a position to complain or to act righteously indignant, but I bluffed it anyway. I told them that I would withdraw from the case if Bobby and his family had lost faith and confidence in my abilities. My divorce, I admitted, had been rough but I was handling it, and it was not interfering with my representation of Bobby. The DUI charge, I reminded them, was just that—a charge. I suggested that they give me the same presumption of innocence that they want the jury to give Bobby on his charge. Somebody, I suggested, wanted me off the case and was trying to do whatever they could to bring that about. That would, I told them, be a mistake because no one else knew this case like I did, no one else could be as prepared as I was, and no one else had a better chance of getting a favorable verdict for Bobby than I did.

They had met with Mr. Morganstein, the Reverend said. Maybe there could be a compromise, he suggested. Maybe I could assist Mr. Morganstein, instead of vice versa. No, I had said, taking a gamble. Paul could do a good job, but not as good. The trial was too close. I did not want to tell them the real reason, my lingering doubts about my partner. If I even hinted of my concerns, I would appear paranoid, defensive. All the time, though, I was wondering whether Paul had not somehow confirmed or validated the family's fears, led them ever so subtly towards this meeting, towards this suggestion of a compromise. I was also beginning to wonder if I had been outmaneuvered. In the end, I had told them that it was Bobby's decision. If he wanted me off the case, I would get off, plain and simple.

The preacher had called me back later that same day. Bobby, it seemed, had insisted that I stay on as lead counsel. He liked me, trusted me, and didn't want to switch lawyers at this late date. The Reverend, I could tell from his voice, was not so sure, wondering whether this was a good decision, but had resigned himself to it. The news had, quite frankly, surprised me as well. It wasn't until I met with Bobby that night at the jail that I understood.

Bobby had seemed strangely calm, unconcerned, when he was led into the interview room and took his seat opposite me. I had let myself believe that my client really did have faith in my abilities. It had restored some self-confidence, put me in a better mood. But as I shook hands with my client I had the feeling that the aura of goodwill was illusory. I was right.

"How are you doing, Bobby?"

"Been better."

"Looks like you blew it, fella."

"I blew it?" He gave a derisive half-laugh, looked away, then back at me. "I'd say it looks like you blew it, man."

"How do you figure? I wasn't the one who violated the conditions of pretrial release." Actually, I had violated my conditions of pretrial release, but that wasn't the point, I told myself. "You were the one unaccounted for when Sammy Smith was murdered." The parallels were becoming too obvious each time I opened my mouth. My little voice was screaming at me, and something in Bobby's eyes disturbed me.

"I had nothing to do with that, Ted. I think you know that."

"I don't know whether anything you've told me is the truth, Bobby."

"Likewise, Counselor."

"What do you mean by that?"

"Come on, man. Remember that first time you came to see me? You made a big point of telling me you represented Patty Stiles. Wanted to make sure I understood the possible conflict of interest and that I didn't have a problem with it."

I nod my head, agreeing. He continues. "You didn't tell me, though, that you were fucking her too, did you?" I bring all my willpower to control my poker face as he lets down the other shoe. "Remember when I told you I had heard the name? Well, Patty told me all about you, man. She may have let me in her pants, but she was in love with you. Obsessed. It was a little weird when she talked to me about it, but it didn't bother me too much. She was just a piece of ass to me."

The words washed over me like a storm surge, knocking the confidence out of me. My mind worked frantically to find some way up to the surface.

"You didn't say anything about this when we first met." My tone was accusatory.

"Thought it might serve my purposes better not to," he had responded.

Good point, I thought. Who was I to act indignant. I quickly evaluated my options. It had never occurred to me that my own client knew, not only that I had been having an affair with Patty Stiles, but that it had continued right up to the time she was murdered. Forget the photographs. They could have been taken anytime, possibly explained away, even if embarrassing. The neighbor could be mistaken about when, and even if, she saw me at Patty Stiles' home. Together though, they could corroborate the testimony of the man seated across from me. Testimony that normally would be taken with a large grain of salt. As bad as it was, though, Bobby was not through.

"You remember that first day too, when you came to the jail to see me? I noticed those scratches on your wrist."

Self-consciously, I looked at the scars, faint but still visible on my right forearm.

"You told me you got them playing basketball." He paused, searching my face for some acknowledgment. I tried to remain expressionless, neither denying nor confirming his statement. "Well, in truth, you hadn't played any ball for several weeks before that."

It was true, but how did he know this? Had he checked the gym? Already I was thinking of how to get out of this. A reasonable explanation, a defense attorney's stock in trade. Clearly though, I did not like the direction of the conversation. When I didn't respond, Bobby continued. "You speak of me being unaccounted for when Sammy Smith was killed, talk about holes in my alibi for the night Patty Stiles was killed. What about you, Ted?"

"You haven't been down to Harry A's recently, by any chance, asking questions, have you?" I remember the bartender's description of the small, wiry black man who had inquired as to my whereabouts on the night of Patty Stiles' murder.

Bobby just smiled. "I wonder whether your gas card receipts will show if you bought enough gas for an extra trip to Tallahassee?"

The thoughts came to me like rapid fire. Was he bluffing? Did Bobby Jackson find all of this information out on his own, think it up by himself? Had he been in contact with my pen pal? I tried to lure Bobby into revealing who his collaborator might be, but all he would say was that he had his sources. The bottom line, he had said, was this: I had better make sure that he was acquitted. If not, then everything he had just told me—and more that he hinted he still had not revealed—would go as public as he could make it. He would be certain, he figured, to get a new trial when the information turned up.

He was right, I realized. There was a good chance that the police might turn their attention toward me as a possible suspect. But, at the very least, there would be enough to show a conflict of interest on my part and likely give Bobby grounds for a new trial.

It appeared that he and I were on separate horns of the same dilemma. If he revealed the information now, I'd be off the case in a heartbeat and a new attorney appointed. If the conflict of interest was resolved before the trial, Bobby might still have a good chance of acquittal, but this way, with me as counsel, he might get two bites at the apple. I had to admire his logic and his ruthlessness. Still, what if he got convicted, and then no one believed him?

From my perspective, my choices were not good. Going to the authorities now was not appealing. Oh yes, I'd say, I forgot to mention that I was having an extramarital affair with the victim in this case. She had threatened to ruin my marriage when I broke it off. She had some rather embarrassing photographs, which, incidentally, I stole from her house. She had made this threat on the night she was murdered.

Yes, actually, I might have killed the lady, but I seemed to have forgotten. Well, you see, it's this problem I have when I drink too much. I black out. On the other hand, it might be several other persons, including a neo-Nazi, a former husband, my own law partner, or the private detective I've hired on the case, all of whom may be taking advantage of my confusion and setting me up. Yes, I realize the fact that I may be paranoid does not mean that I'm not a murderer.

No, spilling my guts now to the police did not seem prudent. On the other hand, if I hold off going to the authorities, go through trial, and Bobby Jackson is convicted, then all of these suspicious circumstances will come out anyway, and I will look all the more guilty for it. Of course, if I try too hard in defense of my client, my anonymous pen pal may just blow the cover. The words from one of Leon Russell's songs comes to mind: "I'm up on a tightwire, one side's ice and one is fire."

I wipe my face with the paper towel. Still looking in the mirror at Martin, I nod an acknowledgment but don't speak, determined not to give him any ammunition. Silently, I sing along with Leon—"I'm up on a tightrope. One side's hate and one is hope." I turn toward the door, but Martin moves to block my path.

"So, you're content to let Morganstein run the show, huh?" Quentin Martin's voice breaks my train of thought, and brings me back to the present. "The man does like the spotlight, doesn't he. Listen, Ted, why don't you get your two cents in. You're the real lawyer on this case, aren't you, or do you have to have Morganstein hold your hand all the time?"

He is looking closely at me, his words and his tone taunting, trying to find some break in the armor. "Would you like to answer a few questions, Counselor? Clear up some of those nagging questions the public has about you?" I've got some nagging questions myself, I think, but I'm not about to share them with the public.

"Hey, I hear the state is about to revoke your bond on your DUI case, something about some positive alco checks? Would you like to verify that, Ted? Is it true? What's going to happen if you get pulled off to jail in the middle of the Jackson murder trial? Is Morganstein up to speed?"

The questions are like the rapid fire of a machine gun. The bastard. How did he find out so quickly about the bond revocation hearing? It had just been filed yesterday and everyone involved had agreed to keep it sealed. The hearing was set for this afternoon at four thirty in chambers. I wonder if Martin knows that information as well. I had tried to push the matter to the back of my mind.

Why did I have to run into this jerk now? How he could keep going with no response from me was fascinating. I am wondering if he will be looking in the trashcan when I leave, finding the spent bottle of vodka. Ah, too many questions, too little mind.

"See you later, Marty. Nice talking to you," I say throwing the paper towel in the trash and walking out the door. My little voice is saying, "I tried to tell you, didn't I, but you wouldn't listen." Shut up, I tell it, but I can't seem to keep my stomach from churning.

TWENTY-TWO

I nod to the bailiff as he opens the side door to Courtroom 3A. Strangely enough, the excited murmuring of anonymous voices is calming to me, like the constant whirring of an overhead fan at night. I scan the courtroom quickly, exchange nods with B.J.'s mother and the Reverend. The sister's not there. The potential jurors are all on one side of the courtroom. I note the usual covey of reporters sitting just behind the rail. I see some new faces, some from the larger regional papers, some television news coverage. I notice a few of the regular theatergoers as well.

Paul, Bert, and B.J. are all looking over the notebook which contains the questionnaires completed by the potential jurors. At the prosecution table, Tom Haley and his assistant, Lyle Russell, are doing likewise. I have already studied the questionnaires, receiving a copy earlier from the clerk's office. I still have a few friends left in this building.

What may appear like nonchalance in my manner is, in fact, confidence. A lot of booze-filled nights without sufficient sleep have taken their toll, no doubt, but I have prepared for this trial better than anybody sitting at these tables. It is this confidence which comes from thorough preparation that will keep me calm and focused as nothing else could.

As I sit down, Paul is filling me in, explaining his notes on the questionnaire forms and the jury seating chart. We have previously discussed in general terms the types of jurors that we want and the types that we do not want. In short, we want young black males who could identify with our client, followed by older black females, who might identify with Bernice and see B.J. as a son. Younger black females are likely to be a mixed bag—attracted to our handsome client with his charming smile, but likely to resent his "thing" with a white woman.

By the same token, white folks are to generally be avoided if possible. Since the population makeup is seventy percent Caucasian, however, that is unlikely. So, the strategy would be to seek out jurors who may be outraged at the victim's "loose morals," or flaming liberals more likely to believe that the system was out to get this young black male, more likely to believe that the police might intentionally destroy evidence helpful to the defense. In the final analysis, though, this stereotyping could only be a guideline. Questioning would confirm our basic assumptions or prove them wrong.

At exactly 9:00 A.M. Judge John Rowe comes through the side door and quickly takes his seat behind the bench. He calls our case, asking if both sides are ready to proceed. We both say we are.

"Mr. Reed, if you please."

Jimmy Reed, the trial clerk, calls the first fourteen names on the jury list, instructing them to take their places in the jury box. Rowe, who has been looking through some papers on his desk, now turns his attention to the fourteen persons seated in the jury box, and to those in the courtroom.

"Ladies and gentlemen, good morning." Gator grins. The jurors give tentative good mornings in return.

"Welcome to the Circuit Court for Leon County, Felony Division. You have been summoned here this morning as potential jurors in the case of the State of Florida versus Robert Lee Jackson. Mr. Jackson is charged with the offense of first-degree murder. Specifically, the indictment charges that on the twenty-first day of June, Robert Lee Jackson did intentionally, with premeditation, and with malice afore-thought, take the life of Patricia Alexandra Stiles, by stabbing the said victim, Patricia Alexandra Stiles, to death, and further that . . ."

As Rowe continues matter-of-factly in reading the indict-ment, I study the faces of the potential jurors. From the moment the words "first-degree murder" were uttered, there was a noticeable change in the looks and the de-meanor of the persons seated in the box, as well as in the courtroom. The gravity of the situation is etched in their faces. Some of them steal glances over at my client. Some of them have already leaned toward the prosecution. They will nod their heads when asked if they can follow the law, but some of them will not be able to help themselves. It will be my job to determine who they are and find some way to keep them off the jury.

"This portion of the trial is called voir dire," Rowe says. He is all warmth and smiles. "It is a French term which means to speak the truth. I will be asking you a few basic questions and then the attorneys will have an opportunity to inquire. All that I ask is that you answer their questions as frankly and as honestly as you can. Also, this is the only time during the trial in which jurors are allowed to ask questions of the attorneys or the judge. If you have a ques-tion, please do not hesitate to ask."

Rowe inquires into the background of each juror: how long they have lived in Leon County; what they do for a living; if married, what their spouse does; the ages of their children, and if grown, their occupations. Have they ever been on a jury before and if so was it a civil or criminal case? Did they deliberate and reach a verdict, and were they the foreperson of the jury? Rowe explains the different roles of the jury and the judge. They determine what the facts are, he determines what the law is. He tells them that even if they disagree with the law that must be applied, it will be their duty to apply the law to the facts, as they find them. All jurors nod yes when he asks if they can agree to do that. Judge Rowe, even when he is trying to look kind, which isn't often, is a person that you just want to agree with. The jurors are no exception.

Rowe then tells the jury that the trial is scheduled to last the entire week. Do any of the jurors have any conflicts, pressing matters that would keep them from being able to give their undivided attention to the evidence presented? One man in the back tentatively expresses his concern over an important government report his company must file by Friday.

"Mr. Hampton," Rowe looks at his jury sheet to find the name. "Will the demands of your business keep you from fulfilling your duty as a juror in this case?" The tone of his voice and the look that Rowe gives the juror prompts the man to meekly allow that there may be others in the business who can carry the load for him.

"Excellent," Rowe says. "Anyone else?" No hands go up.

"Are there any persons with physical problems, presently taking medications, who may have difficulty sitting through a one-week trial?"

One juror, an elderly man in the front row, volunteers that he uses a hearing aid, but quickly adds that he is able to hear the judge fine, and if the lawyers will speak up, feels that he will have no problem hearing everything that

goes on. Rowe thanks him for his candor and his willing-
ness to serve. He gets him to promise that he will hold his
hand up any time during the trial if he is unable to hear
a question from an attorney or an answer of a witness.

After a few more minutes of questioning, the judge then
asks Tom Haley if he wishes to inquire of the panel. Haley
gives the perfunctory, "Yes, Your Honor," and strides
quickly to the podium, legal pad in hand. Rowe has turned
down requests from both the state and the defense to interview jurors separately. The advantages of individual voir
dire are that the questioning tends to be more focused and
thorough, jurors are more likely to be interactive with the
attorneys, and decisions about the jurors are considered
to be more accurate. Also, there is less risk that the answer
of one juror might taint the rest of the panel. On the other
hand, individual questioning of jurors tends to be much
longer and less efficient, which has generally been a primary concern for Judge Rowe.

Tom Haley looks neat and trim, wearing a conservative
dark blue suit. Everything is in place. His short hair and
boyish features make him look younger than his forty years.
He has a look and a manner that instills confidence in
men, romantic thoughts in younger women, and in older
women vague undefined desires to mother him. It is a won-
derful combination for a trial lawyer. He always manages
to slip into the jury selection process the fact that he is a
military man and former college football player, which only
adds to his appeal. Suddenly, I am feeling old and sleazy-
looking.

"Good morning, ladies and gentlemen." The jurors respond in unison back to him. Damn, I think. Instant rapport.

Haley starts with some follow-up questions on the jurors'
backgrounds, designed to develop and strengthen that instant rapport. He does a good job of finding things that

he and the jurors have in common. He smiles often, but not too much. He appears to have a genuine interest in who they are. He asks questions about their families, their work, the clubs and organizations they belong to. For the most part, he is content with questioning around the edges, then making assumptions based upon the information he gathers. He knows that I, like many defense lawyers, will do the dirty work, will ask the pointed questions that run the risk of offending. This way, he remains unsullied.

Exclaiming that the state gladly accepts the burden of proof beyond a reasonable doubt, Haley then asks the panel, "Do you all understand that proof beyond a reasonable doubt is not proof beyond all doubt, is not proof beyond a shadow of a doubt, or all possible doubt?" They nod, a little uncertain, wanting to accept what he says, but looking at the judge for guidance. There is none. "If I show you that this defendant," he says, pointing at Bobby, "is guilty beyond a reasonable doubt," he emphasizes the word reasonable, "will you return a verdict of guilty?" Again the collective nods. Haley calls each juror by name and gets each one to agree verbally.

Generally speaking, any question of a potential juror that begins with "do you understand" or "will you promise me that," is objectionable, because it does not elicit information from the jurors relative to their ability to be fair and impartial. Rather the intended purpose is to educate the jurors on some legal theory or to condition them to what the attorney will be arguing later. Since both sides want desperately to do this, neither usually objects to these types of questions. Thus, I have not objected yet to Haley's. I have a few of my own.

The Gator, however, has other ideas. "Mr. Haley, the jurors have already promised that they will follow the law. A clear understanding of that law is not necessary at this point. Please move on."

"May we approach the bench, Your Honor?" Haley moves toward the bench, assuming his request is granted, but is stopped in his tracks as Rowe says, "No, you may not. You may move on to another area of inquiry or you may sit down."

Chastised, Haley tries to appear unfazed, but the implication is clear. The judge has suggested that the prosecutor has tried to do something wrong, tried to get the jurors to do something improper. It will do much to destroy the good relationship Haley has been building so far. Rowe could have cut him off earlier. By waiting to interject himself now, the impact is stronger. I wonder if it is coincidental.

Haley moves on to less controversial topics. He spends a little bit more time, perhaps more than he normally would, with what I call conversational questions—very little information gathered, but tons of good feelings. When he finally tells the judge he has no further questions, it is ten-thirty and I sense that Haley has regained the ground lost earlier. Rowe calls for a recess.

During the recess I take the elevator down to the underground parking garage, slip over to my car, and steal a couple of large swigs from the bottle I keep in the console. I pop a couple of breath mints and make it to the courtroom just before Rowe reenters.

Where Haley's style of jury selection is conservative, not too many probing questions, my style is more confrontational, the questions more pointed. My approach is more risky perhaps, but if I am successful, I will have a jury that is firmly behind me, who share an intense and firm readiness to make the state prove its accusations. After a few safe questions, I plunge right in.

"You may have noticed that my client is African-American, a black man." I sense some unease immediately from several members and key in on them as I continue.

"How do you feel about that, Mr. Jones?" I single out an older white man in the back row, a retired insurance agent.

"What do you mean?" He shifts in his seat.

"Well, do you think because he is a black man, it is more likely than not that he is guilty?"

"No, of course not," he says indignantly.

"I don't mean to offend you by that question, Mr. Jones, but there are many people, wouldn't you agree, who may make that assumption. They read newspapers, they see TV news, see all of those black faces when they show persons charged?" Mr. Jones is nodding in agreement. I continue. "I'm not here to debate the rightness or the wrongness of that perception. The question is," and here I look at all the jurors, "whether your personal feelings might interfere, even a little bit, with your ability to judge this man by what the evidence shows or doesn't show." I can sense Mr. Jones beginning to lean over backwards, figuratively speaking. I make a mental positive checkmark by his name.

"How do you feel about black men who date white women?" I pause a second and then look at another white man, middle-aged, a supervisor in the city utility department. "Mr. Stinson?"

"I don't think about it." His look is challenging to me.

"It doesn't bother you?"

"No, it doesn't bother me." The man's tone now is openly hostile. I make another mental note and then move on. "What about you, Ms. Johnson?" I direct my attention to a young black woman on the front row, next to Stinson. She is a secretary at the Department of Transportation.

"That's his business, I guess," she says.

"Yes, but what do *you* think about it? Do you think, do you believe in your heart, a black man who dates a white woman is somehow insulting black women, that he is saying he can't find an attractive woman of his own race?"

The woman thinks for a few seconds then, "Some people

feel that way. I'm aware of that," she says, no trace of malice in her voice or in her features, no unfriendly body language. "But I'm not one of them."

Two other black women give me similar responses, but I had noticed the disapproving looks on their faces when I had questioned Ms. Johnson earlier, as well as their conflicting body language when I questioned them. Another mental checkmark.

I ask questions about drugs and sexual habits of people. I ask about reporters and their tactics at getting information, including having sex with potential sources. I tread on thin ice here because too much of an attack on the victim will backfire.

Some of the jurors have indicated prior jury service. I attempt to use questions of these jurors to educate the panel about the difference of the burden of proof in a civil and a criminal case. Haley, smarting from his earlier chewing out, objects and Rowe sustains it.

Next I ask the panel if anyone has ever been accused of anything they haven't done. After a pause three hands go up. I choose one, a young college student who explains how she had been accused of taking money from a cash register where she worked as a clerk part-time in high school. After she explains the circumstances, I continue.

"Ms. Phillips, from your description of this incident, you would agree, wouldn't you, that your employer did have some reason to suspect you?"

She thinks a moment, then, "Yes, I guess so, but it wasn't true."

"I understand. Let me ask you, Ms. Phillips, how did it make you feel to be falsely accused of something, have people assume that you were guilty, and be unable to prove your innocence?"

There is a pause of a couple of seconds as the obvious

answer sinks into the minds of all the jurors on the panel. "I was frustrated, and I was angry."

"Ms. Phillips, if you are selected on this jury, will you give my client the benefit of the doubt that your employer was not willing to give to you?"

"Yes," she says, nodding her head.

As I move from subject to subject and juror to juror, I begin to feel that I am getting an accurate read on each, but I also sense that I am risking alienating the positive ones that I have latched onto by dragging out the voir dire longer. At a little bit before noon I am through. After both sides have approached the bench and exercised challenges for cause and peremptory challenges, eight of the fourteen jurors in the box still remain. Since we will require twelve jurors, we begin the process again after lunch with the additional jurors.

Finally, a little bit before four, both the state and the defense have exercised all available peremptory challenges and our jury has been selected. Rowe has the clerk administer the oath and then he gives the jury preliminary instructions: Avoid any news reports about the case; do not discuss the case or form any fixed opinions about the case until you have heard all of the evidence. After informing both the jury and the lawyers that he will begin promptly at nine the following day, Rowe leaves the bench.

After a quick few words with my client and his mother, I follow Paul and Bert out the side door. Once outside, we stop in the hallway.

"Well, what do you think?" I say.

"You mean the jury?" Paul responds. "I think we did pretty good."

"Yeah, I'm thinking the school teacher's going to be the foreperson."

"Maybe," says Paul. "I kind of like the hairdresser. You know, the heavy-set black lady. The main thing is we got rid of a few that were really bad. You did a good job, Ted, of figuring out those ringers."

"You had them eating out of your hand," Bert joins in.

There is an uncomfortable silence as we all recognize what is to happen next. Finally I say what is probably on everyone's mind.

"Well, I guess we better go find out if I'm going to be able to finish this case as lead counsel, or be assisting Paul from a jail cell."

TWENTY-THREE

Monday—October 6th

God, but I need a drink. There is a nervousness, an anxiety rising in me that is almost like electric shock impulses. I can hardly keep my arms and my hands still. It feels as though my body has a thin film of moisture encasing it, pinning in the nervous energy that is in stark contrast to the exhaustion that I feel. I look at my watch again—4:25 P.M. Not enough time to go down to my car and back. Hell, I'll just have to make it till after the hearing.

Judge McDonald will not be happy. He had given me a break before, the benefit of the doubt. He would feel betrayed, embarrassed. In short, I have made him look bad. Intellectually I have accepted the possibility that he might revoke my bail and have made contingency plans, but emotionally I refuse to accept it. I look around the room quickly to see if my reactions have been noticed, but everyone else is busy reading files or magazines.

Strange, I think, that earlier in the heat of the battle with the pressure of a murder trial and the uncertainties about me and those around me, I had felt calm, relaxed, enjoying the contest and caught up in the choreography. I have rehearsed my lines well for this little play as well, but it's harder to pretend when you are the defendant.

When Paul, Bert, and I arrived a few minutes ago, Blake Edwards, the assistant state attorney on the case was already here, as was my attorney, Gary Cooper. To my surprise, Tom Haley and Randy Powell, one of the detectives on the Jackson case, had also come. We murmured our hellos. "Long time no see," I said to Tom with a half-smile. "Yeah," was all he said. He didn't look at me. No smile.

Detective Powell is wearing the same suit he wore several weeks ago when he came to investigate the case of the frozen feline in my office. The suit looks like it has shrunk even more and I doubt he could button the coat. His hair is plastered to his head and combed down. His face is solemn, unsmiling, but all in all he looks slightly ridiculous. I can't seem to stifle a snort as he takes a seat across from me, his pants legs going up instantly, revealing one blue and one black sock.

"What's so funny?" It's as if Powell has been reading my thoughts. His look is challenging, threatening.

"Nothing," I say. My stomach is churning, like a cement truck, heavy sloshing. My thoughts go again to the bottle of vodka I have in my car. Before the silence becomes too awkward, the judge's secretary motions for us to go into the office.

John McDonald is one of the older county judges, probably in his early sixties. He is a tall, thin man with crinkles around his eyes and no hair on his head. He has been a county judge for almost twenty-five years and is well suited for the job, amiable and with a good sense of humor. His office is cluttered, in disarray. His desk is piled high with several stacks of files, correspondence, newsletters, and magazines. Behind the desk and to the right is a computer stand, surrounded again by overflow from the desk. Likewise for a bookcase in the corner and a credenza directly behind his desk. The piles are neat, though, and I imagine he knows where everything is. On the walls there are several fish stuffed and mounted. There are also a couple of *Field and Stream*-type paintings—macho men hooking rainbow trout in mountain streams, posing with grizzly bears. Somehow, they don't seem to match the man, but, in fact, there are photos on the wall with the judge in similar poses.

Actually, I was a prosecutor in front of Judge McDonald many years ago when I was first with the state attorney's office. We got along well then. I found him to be fair, if perhaps a little defense-oriented, and always able to make the day go a little easier, finding some humor in even the worst of situations. He does not appear to be in a joking mood, however, this afternoon. Suddenly, I have the feeling that the man has already decided what he is going to do. He has read the affidavit, assumed it is true, and decided on a course of action. Everything in between is just a dog and pony show. Entertaining perhaps, mildly interesting, but of no particular significance. Oh well, I think, the show must go on.

Haley and Edwards take their seats on one side of the table that extends from Judge McDonald's desk. Gary, Paul and I take our seats on the other. Bert takes a seat over in the corner in a wing-backed chair. I take a moment to study Paul. After all the years as partners, and friends, I can't shake my lingering doubts. The information from Bert has continued to eat at me.

When I realized that the P.M. in Patty's notes might refer to Paul, I had decided to see if I could find some file on Patty Stiles in Paul's office. I searched everywhere, with no luck. I was looking in his desk drawers when I heard my partner's voice.

"Looking for something?"

I tried to act unsurprised, told him that I was looking for some booze. Paul didn't believe it, I'm sure, but he didn't push it either. He just looked puzzled. I agonized over it for several seconds and then decided to confront him with the information I had. I told him what Bert told me, what I found out from Cathy, and what I was doing in his office. He looked hurt. There was a long, uncomfortable silence, and Paul walked over and looked out his window into the courtyard. Then, still not looking at me, he said, "Well, I suppose under the circumstances, Ted, I don't blame you for being concerned, maybe suspicious. I am disappointed, however, that you didn't come straight to me. We can start over though," he said, turning around and looking at me. "What would you like to know?"

I told him I wanted to know exactly what his relationship was with Patty Stiles, professionally and otherwise. He told me that Patty had called him on a couple of occasions. She was thinking of doing a will, setting up a trust for her niece. She said she also had a real estate question of some kind. She wasn't specific. She did set up an appointment about three or four weeks before her death, but she never showed. "Frankly, I didn't see any connection, didn't see it as relevant information," he said. "In fact, I had really forgotten about it, until you just mentioned it."

I didn't know whether to believe him or not. A real estate question? I thought back to the entry in the small notebook I had seen in Patty's house. It seemed like there had been addresses there, or numbers: "727 BVD." Boulevard? Brevard Street? "C H" Crack houses? There had been the word "Deeds," I remembered.

"So what were you doing at her place?" I ask.

"I wasn't."

"But what about the neighbor?"

"Your witness must be mistaken." It was a common theme, Bert would say. "I've never been to Patty Stiles' house—ever."

I didn't know then, and I still don't know whether he had.

McDonald brings me back to the present. "Gentlemen, let's get started. Mr. Haley, I didn't know you had been reassigned to traffic."

"Just sitting in, Judge."

"Humph," he says. "Mr. Edwards, your motion."

Blake Edwards is a young lawyer, no older than mid-twenties, a recent FSU grad. I have met him before, but I do not really know him. From what I can tell he is a pretty good lawyer, though. This is not, however, a routine motion in a routine DUI case. It's obvious that he is feeling the pressure. He is tentative at first, almost apologetic.

"Mr. Stevens is a respected and capable attorney," he says, "and I take no pleasure in this. He is not, however, above the law. It seems pretty clear that he has not abided by the conditions of pretrial release. The state would leave it in the court's discretion as to a proper remedy."

Edwards then offers the affidavit of Chris Parker as we have stipulated that live testimony will not be necessary. In fact, I know that it would be worse to have her here live. She is too credible and can rebut my explanations. Ah, youth and naiveté.

Edwards tries to make some further argument, but McDonald cuts him off and takes Gary's job over, as well. "Let's hear from the defense. Mr. Stevens, let's cut to the chase," he says. "What about these allegations? Let's take them one at a time. It says here that you tested positive on two occasions in the last three weeks for alcohol. Do you dispute this?"

"There may have been alcohol in my system, Your Honor, but it was not from drinking."

"Could you explain?"

"Yes, well you see, I've had a cold and a cough, and I've been drinking cough medicine like it was going out of style. I didn't think that I had drunk that much, but that's the only explanation I can see—unless the instrument was misreading, which I understand happens on occasion."

"You have not been drinking alcoholic beverages?" McDonald looks directly at me.

"No, I have not."

Disbelief hangs in the air like a dark cloud. I can feel perspiration forming in my armpits.

"And, what about the allegation that you failed and refused to provide breath samples, perform alco checks, on two separate occasions?" McDonald continues.

"There were two occasions when I was sick and not able to get to the alco check. But, as my partner can verify, I was sick those days. Like I said before, I had had a bad cold and cough. I didn't even make it into the office on those days." I can see Paul out of the corner of my eye nodding his head. "I offered to come in the next day on both of those occasions but was told never mind. On one of those occasions I was not told personally that I was supposed to come in for a check. They apparently called and left a message with my secretary at work, but I didn't get the message until the next day." Not great, maybe, but plausible I think.

McDonald listens to brief arguments from both attorneys, then looks to me as he speaks.

"Mr. Stevens, I'm not buying this. I gave you one chance. I think you've got some real problems on your hands. Alcohol abuse is one, perjury may be another." I am too stunned to speak. Gary starts to object, but McDonald holds his hand up to cut him off. He is picking up the phone on his desk. "I'm going to have a bailiff come on up to take you into custody." I can feel the energy drain down to my feet and puddle out from my shoes onto the floor. I am literally paralyzed and cannot move. I can see

McDonald's lips begin to move again but the sound seems delayed, as in a bad movie. "I understand you have just started a trial, but I guess Mr. Morganstein will have to take over for you."

Both Gary and Paul seem to be speaking at once, protesting, pleading, asking that he stay his ruling to allow a quick review in circuit court by a writ of habeas corpus. But McDonald seems unconvinced.

Relief comes, surprisingly, from the other side of the table. "May I be heard?" Tom Haley folds his hands together and looks to Judge McDonald, who nods for him to speak. "I haven't had a chance to confer with my colleague, Mr. Edwards, on this, but I have a little different interest here which I hope the court will consider."

"Yes."

"While I agree that Mr. Stevens does not deserve another chance or favorable consideration from this court, the fact of the matter is that I'm afraid his withdrawal from the murder case might jeopardize the conviction I feel sure we will get. I wouldn't want Mr. Jackson to be able to argue that he was denied the attorney of his choice. I believe in this particular situation, both the state and defense might be well served by some form of strict release that would allow Mr. Stevens to continue on the case."

A silent tension has taken over the space we share as McDonald ponders this request for several seconds, looking alternatively at Haley and me. I cannot return his gaze.

"Okay, here's what I'm going to do. Your bond's going to go up to five thousand dollars. Your alco checks are going to be daily and you're going to turn over your keys to me.

"Let's get something straight here, Mr. Stevens. I'm not revoking your bond at this time only because I don't want to prejudice your client's rights. But don't misunderstand me, Mr. Stevens. You mess up, you even breathe in the wrong direction, and your ass will be in jail until your DUI case is over. Do you understand?"

"Yes, Your Honor. Thank you. I swear to you you will have no problem."

TWENTY-FOUR

Tuesday—October 7th

The image is blurred around the edges, shifting, distorted, like a kaleidoscope. Patty is sitting cross-legged on the couch, smoking a joint. The smoke swirls, folds into itself, then reappears in different contours. I can hear Jim Morrison in the background: This is the end—Beautiful friend. . . .

Now she is leaning back stretching, arching her back, her auburn hair spreading out over the back of the couch, her arms reaching toward the ceiling. I can see the outline of her nipples hard against the brown T-shirt, see that she is wearing only panties underneath.

My emotions seem separated from me, as if they are tied together in a bundle that I keep at my side. Hatred, rage, sadness, loneliness, lust, fear, excitement. Within reach, but too jumbled, too confused to draw out any particular one and isolate it. I have no idea what will come out next, nor do I care.

The image shifts again. A man in front, blocking my view so that I see only her arms which are still stretched out over her head, and her legs which are wrapped around the man. He holds her up to him and they move as one, in rhythm. I can hear their moans, increasing in volume, becoming more urgent.

I shake the tube, twist it to get another image. Her face, turned to the side, the lips opening slightly, now smiling with pleasure. She is looking directly at me now as the man quickens his pace.

She seems suspended, aloof. The smile turns into a sneer, her eyes staring right through me.

The light reflects off the knife blade shimmering and shooting in several different directions, changing colors. Another shift. Patty's face. Defiance replaced by horror. Now only colors, patterns, blending into each other and becoming one color—red. Dark, rich red. Blood, like the smoke earlier, swirling and folding into itself. I shake the container again, trying to catch a glimpse of the pictures underneath. I can see the knife again, then a man's face. But it is too fuzzy for me to tell who it is.

The Doors are beginning a new tune and the images are changing quickly now, in rhythm with the jungle beat of the drum. I can see a black shirt, blood splattering, arms flailing, a body twisting, turning. I struggle to see the entire scene.

I give the lens another shake, looking intently into the center. The film begins to subside toward the bottom and I see that I'm looking at the face, the form, of Tom Haley. He is looking directly at me and he is speaking.

A juror coughs loudly and brings me back to reality. I realize that I have been looking at Tom through the bottom of my upturned water glass, entranced by his words to the jury. I put my glass down, wipe the sweat from my forehead, glance around self-consciously. My partner and my client sit beside me at the defense table, stone-faced, their full attention on the prosecutor. As Haley speaks, he continues to look in my direction, and the jury is following his gaze. The words begin to register again.

"And then, after stabbing her seventeen times in the chest and the back, as she lies helpless on her kitchen floor, attempting to crawl away, he grabs her by the hair, pulls her head back, exposing her throat." He pauses. Jurors and spectators alike lean forward in anticipation, even though they know what is coming. "Then he takes the knife and slits her throat." Haley makes a motion with his finger underneath his own chin.

There is a collective gasp from the jurors. I take another sip of water, watching my adversary work his magic in his opening statement. He started by painting a picture of Patty Stiles. Not a false picture, but selective. She was, he said, a person who had a lot to live for. She was young, ambitious; she loved her work and had a zest for life, a bit unconventional, not afraid to take risks.

Patty's risk taking, he said, had, sadly, led her to a relationship with a dangerous, unpredictable man. "She let this man into her house on the night of her death. They had sex." You could see some of the jurors shifting in their seats, stealing glances at Bobby while Haley explained what, in his version, had happened. An argument turns violent, the man grabs a knife from the cutlery block and, in a fit of rage, begins stabbing Patty.

Haley has not pointed a finger at Bobby Jackson nor called him by name yet. Instead, at the appropriate moments, he has looked in the direction of the defense table. Haley's method is less dramatic perhaps, but more effective. By the end the jurors themselves will be pointing an imaginary finger at Bobby for him.

Haley has described in detail what his investigators, lab technicians, and the medical examiner will tell them about when and how the murder occurred, finishing with the dramatic slitting of the throat so well received by the jurors. Now he points them toward the next obvious question. "Who could have committed this cowardly, brutal, horrible act?" He looks again at the defense table, pauses. "You will learn from the witnesses exactly what investigators did in order to find the answer to that question.

"Unfortunately, as is often the case in a murder, there were only two witnesses to the act itself, and one of them is dead." Another look in the direction of Bobby. "There is a witness, a neighbor of Patty Stiles, who will testify that he saw a man, dressed in black pants and shirt, fleeing from Patty's house shortly after another neighbor heard screams. He recognized this person because he had seen him before at Patty Stiles' home, had actually met him. Will he tell you that he is absolutely sure of the identity. No, he will not. It was at night. It was dark. And he saw the man only briefly in the light of his headlights as he pulled into his driveway that night. But as much as is humanly possible under those circumstances, he will tell you who he thought he saw. Who he later picked out of a lineup.

"The physical evidence in this case will corroborate this identification, showing that this person was, in fact, there at Patty Stiles' house, that he had sex with her and then killed her." Another look our way. "This person left his fingerprints all over the house, in the kitchen where the murder occurred, on the counter, on the kitchen cutlery board, on the back door which was left ajar when he fled the house. His pubic hair was found intertwined with that of the victim. His semen was inside her. His saliva was on the filters of two cigarettes, recovered from an ashtray in the living room—the same brand of cigarettes he had purchased less than an hour before. You will hear from the convenience store clerk who sold them to him at a little after eleven P.M.

"This was about fifteen to twenty minutes after this person got off from his job at a downtown restaurant where coworkers will testify that he was wearing . . . you guessed it, a black shirt and black pants. You will learn that this man lives less than four miles from his work. Yet his own mother will testify that he did not arrive home until some time after midnight." Another look toward the defense table.

"Investigators will tell you how they obtained a warrant for the person the neighbor identified, the person who left his calling card with all of the physical evidence he left behind. You will learn that when they came to arrest this person they found him hiding in a bedroom closet." Haley lets this last statement hang in the air for several moments, looking again directly at Bobby before continuing.

"Officers also found, when they made the arrest, a pair of tennis shoes in his closet. Shoes that had apparently been washed but still showed slight traces of blood on them—the same blood type as the victim, Patty Stiles. Something that the officers did not find, however, though they searched high and low in this person's home, was a pair of black jeans and a black T-shirt.

"When all of the evidence has been presented to you, you will have the answer to the question of who committed this heinous crime. The evidence will lead inescapably to one person and one person only—the same person who stands before you today, charged with the premeditated murder of Patty Stiles." Haley has been looking at Bobby while he delivers this last sentence moving closer and closer toward the defense table as he speaks, until now he is less than six feet away and staring directly at Bobby. My client returns the stare with such cold detachment that I feel an involuntary shiver. I am wondering if the jurors feel it too as I watch Haley walk crisply back to the prosecution table. The only sound in the courtroom is his heels clicking on the wood floor.

"Mr. Stevens." Rowe is leaning back in his chair his arms folded in front of him, looking at the ceiling.

"Thank you, Your Honor." I can see my anxiety reflected back at me in the faces of my partner, my client, and Bert, seated directly behind our table. I rise from my seat and move slowly, deliberately, toward the podium, trying to gather my thoughts, aware that I must somehow derail the train that Haley has just put into motion. I look at the jurors and wonder if their hearts have hardened like their faces have. I steal a glance out into the audience. Familiar faces. Bernice Jackson and Shirley and Reverend Paxton.

Several of the reporters that have been on the case. There, in the back, to my surprise, is Beth. I do a double take and realize that her dad is sitting next to her. My stomach churns a little more. What are they doing here?

I am thinking that maybe I should have had some food for breakfast, rather than the half pint of vodka I put away just before court. Last night had been tough, but I managed to keep off the booze and had a negative alco check this morning. I will have to be very careful, I realize, but I've got it down to a science now. Figuring on a very slow dissipation of alcohol from my body, I have calculated how much I can drink and when I must stop in order to be alcohol-free by my 7:00 A.M. alco checks.

At the podium I pause several seconds more. I open up my notebook, glance at it and then back to the jury. I can sense some equilibrium returning, the looks of disgust melting slowly into expectation. Some are just curious. What ludicrous fiction will he concoct? Some, though, are waiting to hear something, anything, to make them think that the handsome, clean-looking man at the defense table did not do this awful thing. I concentrate on the young black woman from the Department of Transportation. She looks the most receptive to me. I look at my notes, my carefully outlined argument. This is no time to panic, I tell myself. So the opposing team has scored a touchdown on its opening drive. Well, you've got the ball now, let's see what you can do.

"May it please the court," —a slight nod of acknowledgment from Rowe. "Ladies and gentlemen of the jury. I listened closely, as I know you did, to Mr. Haley's opening statement, and, I have to admit, he is good. He is very good. Some of you have to be saying to yourself—boy, it sure sounds bad for Bobby Jackson." I note two or three involuntary nods from the jurors.

"I know that it must be tempting for you to say to yourselves after listening to that opening statement that my client must be guilty. But all of you told me when you were selected for this jury that you would keep an open mind, and I'm sure that you will. You might be saying to yourself that there is probably more to this story than what you have just heard from Mr. Haley—and you are right."

Vindicate their trust, their faith. A small step, but an important one. I can almost feel the prosecution's engine slow down a notch. "Judge Rowe told you before Mr. Haley started that the opening statement is sort of like the preview or a coming attraction at the movie theater. But how many of you have ever seen a preview and thought to yourself, hey, this looks pretty good. But when you saw the whole movie you were disappointed. You found out that the only good scenes were in the preview." A few of the jurors nod in agreement. "Well, what you have just heard from Mr. Haley is a very well done preview. But when you have seen the whole thing, after you have sat through the entire trial and listened to all of the evidence, you won't be too impressed.

"Mr. Haley talked about a witness, a neighbor, who saw a person running from Patty Stiles' house. Listen closely to his testimony. This witness will not, I repeat, will not be able to say with any certainty that the man he saw that night from twenty-five to thirty yards away, in the dark, for only a few seconds, is my client. He will not, he cannot, identify Bobby Jackson as even being there on that night.

"That is not to say that Bobby has never been to Patty Stiles' house. There will not be much question that he has, on several occasions in the past, been there. Which will, of course, explain why his fingerprints were found there. The state's fingerprint expert will not be able to tell you when Bobby Jackson's fingerprints were left in Patty Stiles' home. It could have been several days before, a week, maybe even several weeks before her murder. You just can't tell. Likewise, no witness will be able to tell you for sure when those cigarette butts in the ashtray had been left there."

I am getting into a rhythm now, and I can feel the confidence in my voice. I move from behind the podium and pace in front of the jury box, pausing to give an accusing look toward the prosecution table. If Haley's opening statement had a weakness, it was that he has promised more than he can deliver. Speaking in absolutes can come back to kick you in the butt if you're not careful. For example, Haley has told the jury that the semen and the pubic hair are a match with Bobby. In truth, analysis of this evidence shows that Bobby is in a very, very small percentage of the adult black male population consistent with that DNA. But Haley has said it is a match, and that is different in the minds of some jurors.

So I tell them that the evidence will not show that the semen and pubic hairs are a certain match with my client. I also tell them that the state's expert witness will not be able to tell them with certainty—always use the qualifying term, "with certainty," because almost nothing ever is— that the blood found on the defendant's shoe, in his closet, is that of the victim, Patty Stiles.

Next I hit on the state's theory concerning the time line. The key here is the testimony of the 7-11 clerk, and I feel that I may have an ace in the hole here, but I keep it vague, not to tip off the prosecution. I talk again in terms of certainty, the inability of the witnesses to be absolutely sure. At the very best, I tell them, the evidence could only make out a possibility that the defendant was at Patty Stiles' house that night—not a certainty. A possibility, I remind them, is not consistent with proof beyond a reasonable doubt. Then I hit upon probably the weakest link in the state's chain of evidence.

"There is something else that you will not hear evidence of in this case. Motive. The state will not, and cannot, answer the question of why. The question can't be answered of course because there was no reason for Bobby Jackson to kill Patty Stiles."

"Objection, Your Honor, argumentative."

"Sustained."

"As I was saying, listen closely, because you will hear no evidence of any motive on the part of Bobby Jackson to want to see Patty Stiles dead."

Motive is not an essential element to be proved by the state. But most jurors, having been weaned on numerous television and movie courtroom dramas, are always looking for it. They want some explanation for the crime and some will not return a verdict of guilty if they are not comfortable with this aspect of the case.

"I expect, however, that the evidence will show you that there were plenty of other persons who did have a motive to kill Patty Stiles." Without getting into too many specifics—it sounds more mysterious that way—I go through our alternate suspects, saving the best for last.

"But perhaps the most promising lead in this case that was never followed concerns a story Ms. Stiles was working on at the time that she was killed, a story involving drug abuse and dealing in the African-American community.

"You will see photos taken by the victim shortly before her death which depict several people using and selling drugs, especially crack cocaine on the streets of our city. You will see a photo of a man named Sammy Smith, known to have a history of drug use and dealing. A man, who less than two weeks ago, was found murdered with two other men in what authorities suspect was a drug-related killing. Sammy Smith, you will see, looks remarkably similar to Bobby Jackson."

The jurors are clearly intrigued by this information and become even more so as I lay out the suspicious circumstances of the missing computer disks, lack of files found, and the missing notebook. I decide to stop while I'm ahead.

"When all of the evidence has been presented to you in this trial, you will wonder why these other suspects were not actively investigated. You will wonder why the prosecution has chosen instead to point the finger at this young man who had no reason to harm Patty Stiles. And, I am confident, you will return the only verdict appropriate in this case—not guilty."

Rowe waits until I am at the table, seems to hesitate, and then looks at the jury. "Ladies and gentlemen, this looks like a good time to take a break. It's now approximately ten forty. Let's take twenty minutes." With this he is up and out the side door before anyone else can stir.

Even as I accept the pats on the back from the defense table, my confidence already is ebbing. I make my excuses and then sneak down to my car for a quick couple of swigs—a confidence boost. The relief is almost instantaneous. I know, intellectually, that I need to cut down on the booze, but at the same time, I am desperate for the comfort it gives me, the tension release. Whether it's physical or psychological, I am sure that I perform better with a certain amount of alcohol in my system. It will be tough, but I am determined to limit myself to no more than sixteen ounces of booze per day.

I sit for several minutes in the car, smoking a cigarette, trying to let the tension drain out. I look at my watch again. 10:53 A.M. I stub out my cigarette, don't want to cut it too close. I decide to take the stairs. The first thing I see when I go through the stairwell door on the third floor is my wife. She is sitting on a bench along the side of the hallway. I look around but her father is nowhere in sight. She sees me and motions me over. I hesitate and then walk over quickly. She stands when I get close. I think to myself that she is looking good, a lot more confident and relaxed than when I last saw her. I'm still not sure about her, don't trust her, cannot afford to. But yet I am inextricably drawn to her, despite the warning bells.

"Hello, Ted."

"Beth."

I back away a bit, self-conscious now, remembering the vodka, but she doesn't seem to notice. I ask how she's doing and about Annie, feeling awkward. She tells me she wanted to watch some of the trial. Her dad insisted on coming too. She says she's impressed, watching me in the courtroom. She used to come and watch some of my trials when I was a prosecutor, but that was a long time ago. I would perhaps be flattered if I did not have a nagging feeling that she was not revealing her true motives.

"Well, I'd better get on back in," I say, looking at my watch.

"Yeah, sure. But listen, and this may not be the best time, right in the middle of your trial, but I thought I should let you know that I might have found out who it was that Daddy hired to follow you—if you're still interested. Which I don't know why you should be, since he apparently never found anything anyway."

"Yes, I'm still interested," I say, containing my excitement. "What have you found out?"

"Well, I was working at the restaurant on some accounts, and I was going over some canceled checks. I saw one that looked a little out of the ordinary."

"Oh, there you are." My father-in-law's voice stops Beth in mid-sentence. I turn to see Captain Turner walking toward us. I look back to Beth, hoping that she'll whisper the answer to me, but she is turning, speaking to her father.

"Hey there." Her smile is big, but fake. "I just happened to run into Ted."

Her father's look says he has sized up the situation and does not approve. He does not speak to me or acknowledge my presence in any way. "We need to be going, Beth. I told mother we'd be home for lunch."

"Okay," she says, looking down. "I'll talk to you later, Ted."

"Sure," I say to her as she turns to walk away. My father-in-law gives me a look over his shoulder that says—don't count on it.

TWENTY-FIVE

Tuesday—October 7th

Detective Randy Powell swaggers up to the witness stand, his suit tight against his thick body. My first thought is that he will be less than impressive as a witness, that the jury will not warm up to this guy. I am wrong. It doesn't take long to see that he is truly in his element on the witness stand. He has the attention of the jury and, I am afraid, their trust as well. As I watch and listen to Haley lead him step by step through his testimony, I notice that the afternoon sun, filtered through the half-drawn blinds, has the effect of creating a soft yellow light on the witness stand—almost like a muted spotlight.

He describes in detail the initial steps of the investigation. He made sure that the ID technicians had been called, placed surgical gloves on, then made a cursory examination of the body. He noted the pooling of blood, which was still damp, only a little air-dried around the edges, indicating recent death. He explains how he had directed the photos of the scene, starting with a few from outside the house, the various rooms, showing distances, triangulations, having photos taken of anything that appeared out of the ordinary. There were many photos marked as exhibits and introduced as evidence, some over my objection as being too gory, "likely to inflame the passion of the jury," an argument which always sounds good but is rarely successful.

Powell tells the jury how he directed the taking of several samples of blood from different places. He identifies the cigarette butts, the ashtray, the cutlery block from the kitchen, the suspected marijuana cigarette, and the crack pipe.

He sent officers out to every residence within a two-block radius, had them search every trashcan within the vicinity as well, including Dumpsters of apartments as far as a half mile away. Then he describes how he came to determine what the murder weapon was and where it was found.

"I was just sitting quietly, studying the body and the room. If you listen, the body, the room, will talk to you."

"Talk to you, Detective?" Haley feigns surprise at this question. It's obvious he has planned it this way.

"Well, not literally, of course." Detective Powell turns toward the jurors, gives them a sage smile. "It's just that there are often subtle clues that you can miss in all the hubbub of activity. Sometimes it helps to just take some time, and some quiet, to absorb the scene. So, anyway, I'm sitting there, and I notice the cutlery board on her kitchen counter. There's one knife missing and I'm thinking, maybe it's the murder weapon. So I look all in the kitchen drawers and all over the place to see if I can find it."

Powell then tells the jury how the knife was found. He identifies the cutlery board and the other knives. The exhibits are introduced into evidence, and Powell points out to the jurors that the larger knife fits neatly into the remaining slot and is the same brand name. The bloodstains are still quite noticeable.

On cross-examination, I ask Powell about the evidence of burglary.

"Well, that was, of course, a theory, based upon some of the things we found, at least at first."

"Forgive me, Detective, but I'm not really interested in your theories, at this point, only what you observed. Isn't it true that you found drawers that had been pulled open and clothes tossed out?"

"Yes. That's true."

"And isn't it true that contents of the victim's purse had been emptied out on an end table in the living room?"

"Yes."

"And there was no money found in the purse, was there?"

"That's correct."

"And isn't it also true that you noticed that the victim's camera had been stolen?"

"Well, what we noticed was that there was some film canisters, and a lens, some other camera accessories, suggesting that the person may have owned a camera, and we didn't find a camera in the house."

"Well, didn't you later discover that the victim did in fact own a camera and took photographs as part of her job as a reporter?"

"Objection, Your Honor. Calls for hearsay."

"Sustained."

I move on, the point having been made. One by one I open the door on some alternate suspects. Powell attempts to close the door with his responses but is not entirely successful. He frankly acknowledges the motivation of the ex-husband but, he adds, there was no evidence showing that he'd had any contact with the deceased for several months. Similarly, former Commissioner Jones had threatened to get even with the victim, but he had an alibi. There was no question that the deceased made some enemies he says, but he found no compelling evidence to connect anyone else to the scene. He has a little more difficulty with the Sammy Smith angle.

"Did you check to see what kind of news story Ms. Stiles was working on at the time of her death?"

"Yes, we did try to ascertain what she had been working on. We checked with her editor, her coworkers. Nobody seemed to know." And no, he says, they had found no active files or stories in her office at her home, no floppy disks by her computer, and nothing in her main computer files.

"When you were talking to her coworkers, did you talk to a photographer named Shawn Wolfe?"

"Not until recently. He was out of the country at the time, I believe."

"Having talked with him now, let me ask you if you have seen these photographs, marked as defense composite exhibit three."

"Yes."

"Are these the photographs you received from Shawn Wolfe?"

"Yes, that's correct." Powell shows no signs of frustration, no defensiveness. He goes on to acknowledge that the photos seem to be shots of drug use and sale in the Frenchtown area. He identifies Sammy Smith in the photographs, agrees that he has a drug history.

"Sammy Smith was murdered recently wasn't he, along with two other men?"

"That's true."

"And the police suspect a connection to the drug trade, isn't that also true?"

"We're looking at all the leads," he says. "I can't say it was drug-related."

"But that is one of the main theories you're working on isn't it, Detective? Would you like to look at this offense report?"

"Well, that's just preliminary stuff, Mr. Stevens." A little annoyance now in his voice. "We're still investigating the case." He shifts a little in the silence as I look at him, then at the jury, as if to say—what do we have to do to get him to answer a simple, straightforward question. Finally, he adds, "That still is one of our main theories. But there are other theories as well," he says, looking over at Bobby. "Would you like me to tell you about them too?" He knows he has me because one of those theories involves my client.

"Thank you, Detective, but I'm really only interested in this theory for now." I pause only briefly. "And, while we're at it, looking at that report, can you tell me how big Sammy Smith was?"

"Five ten, a hundred and fifty-five pounds."

"And would you say, looking at my client, compared with Sammy Smith, that they have similar hairstyles and skin complexion?"

"Yes."

"And, Detective Powell, do you know what blood type Sammy Smith was?"

"Not right offhand."

"Thank you." I head back to the defense table.

"Detective Powell." Haley is standing but does not move toward the podium. "You just told Mr. Stevens that you didn't know what Sammy Smith's blood type is."

"That's right."

"Did you, however, yesterday, and at my request, ask FDLE to perform some tests on some blood samples from Mr. Smith?"

"Yes, I did."

"Objection, Your Honor. Request to approach." Judge Rowe motions us to the bench, where I continue. "This is a discovery violation, Judge. The prosecution has not disclosed any such test results to us." I try to keep the anxiety out of my voice.

"Your Honor," Haley begins, "we haven't provided Mr.

Stevens with these test results because we haven't gotten them either. When Mr. Stevens pointed the finger at Sammy Smith in opening statement, I thought we'd better check it out."

"That's trial by ambush, Judge. If they were going to do these tests, they should have done it before trial. He waits until I commit myself, then springs this crap on me. It'll change my whole defense."

"Well, Counselor." Rowe is looking at me hard. "You shouldn't ask about something if you don't want to know about it." He now looks to the prosecutor. "Of course, the state takes a big risk by bringing it up without knowing what the results will be."

"Judge, we're after the truth. If there's a Sammy Smith connection, we want to know." His smile and his argument are flawless. I have been outmaneuvered big time and my stomach turns over again as Rowe slams it home.

"Objection overruled."

As I sit stewing at my table, Haley goes through a few more questions, exposing the weaknesses in the burglary theory. The jewelry box was opened but some of the most valuable pieces were left. Drawers were pulled out and clothes strewn around, but there were still clothes in the bottom of drawers, untouched. Several expensive accessories for a camera were not taken. A camcorder was left behind.

"Another thing," Powell adds, "was the fact that there was no forced entry. The way she was, shall we say, casually dressed, and the items we found in the living room, suggested that whoever had been in the house had been invited in.

"Then there's the fact that she was killed in the kitchen. If she had surprised a burglar, or if the burglar had come in with the intent of committing an assault and/or a theft, it would be unlikely that he would not be armed prior to his entry into the house. And, finally, the way the victim was killed. The multiple stab wounds, the throat being slit, suggests that the killer wasn't just a burglar who panicked. The type and the extent of the wounds inflicted suggest a person who was in a rage."

"How would you explain, then, the missing items, the pulled out drawers, and the clothes in disarray?"

"Objection, Your Honor."

"Overruled."

"I'd say the killer tried to make it look like a burglary."

"Thank you, Detective."

I sit, mesmerized by the smoke which drifts lazily up from my cigarette, curling and twisting slightly in the still air of our office conference room. I take another drag, inhaling deeply, then release the smoke in a long, steady stream.

In this interior room with no windows and with the door closed, there are no outside noises to distract. But I am beginning to find the quietness very distracting. From the corner of the room, I can hear the click of the radio clock as it marks the passing of another minute. I glance over, noting the time: 9:48 P.M.

For at least an hour now, I have been pacing, smoking, thinking. Finally, frustrated and exhausted, I have returned to my chair, feet propped up on the table surrounded by all my files in the Jackson case. It has been over three hours since my last drink. But I know that I dare not have another. I have consumed more than I wanted to today.

Paul had wanted, maybe even planned, to stay later, his image of the partners, sleeves rolled up, side by side with me, working on the case. I told him never mind. Too little too late. I said some other things that were unkind, but I'm not feeling repentant. Paul is so good at professing to be tolerant, understanding, while cutting you off at the knees.

It really had not been my fault. I had told Quentin Martin, at least three times, to get out of my way. But there he'd been, standing right in front of me, inches from my face, taunting me with his questions. The truth may be a defense to slander, but it's no defense to a strong right hook.

Fortunately, we had been alone at the time. Marty had cornered me in the back hall, before anyone else had discovered my way of exit. He was already picking himself off the floor, and I was walking away, when the other news hounds rounded the corner.

The six o'clock news aired Marty's version. There he was, holding his face, outraged, pointing in my direction, telling the camera I had just physically assaulted him, punched him in the face. When one of the reporters finally caught up with me and stuck a microphone in my face, confronting me with what Marty had said, my response had not been ambiguous. "He's a lying scumbag."

"I think maybe you could have handled the situation a little better," Paul had said in his understated way when he had heard about it. Didn't I have enough troubles, without punching out a reporter? He had quickly assessed the situation and concentrated on damage control. Perhaps self defense, he had intimated. Maybe Martin had grabbed me by the arm and I had slung my arm free, accidentally hitting him in the head. I said that's pretty close to the way it probably happened. Paul assured me that the sympathies would probably be more on my side than on Martin's. Nobody really liked the guy. They only tolerated him because of the power of his pen. Paul arranged to make a statement to the press on my behalf. Our "discussion" later had not, however, been pretty.

As I sit here in the eerie silence of the conference room, I am reminded of Randy Powell's testimony earlier. The body will speak to you, he had said, if you will just listen.

Well, here I am, I thought, with the corpse—the Bobby Jackson murder defense—laid out on the table.

For all of my puffing in the opening statement, I am not at all confident. I was spending way too much energy pumping myself up. Too many variables, too many forces pulling me in different directions. I have the feeling that I am missing something, maybe on purpose.

I am thinking this while looking at the photos that Shawn Wolfe had given us when something catches my eye. I look closer. It's probably nothing. I am reminded of the little boy who was asked why he was looking for his key several yards away from the place where he had dropped it. He explained, "But the light is much better here." Was I doing the same thing? Perhaps I have a suppressed the little voice inside me because I am afraid of the truth. But this time I listen. I pick up the phone, recheck the number from my notes, and dial. He answers on the third ring.

"Hello."

"Mr. Wolfe, this is Ted Stevens. Sorry to call you so late."

"Yes, Mr. Stevens, no problem. I am, what I believe is called, a night owl. How are you? Saw you on the telly tonight. Nasty business."

"Yeah, never a dull moment. But, listen, could you do something for me?"

"If I can," he says.

"Those photos. Can you enlarge a couple of them a little more?"

TWENTY-SIX

"What, in your opinion, Dr. Simmons, was the cause of death?"

"Several of the puncture wounds I have mentioned could have caused death. Both lungs were punctured. And, of course, the severing of the carotid artery was also fatal. These wounds would cause her to bleed to death in only a few minutes. However, when the carotid artery was cut, so was the trachea, causing her to literally drown in her own blood."

Dr. Bruce Simmons is in his mid-fifties. Except for the salt and pepper in his hair, however, he looks to be a good fifteen years younger. He is a little over six feet tall and is a trim one hundred and eighty pounds. Very experienced and very competent, he has that unusual ability to act and speak with confidence without seeming immodest. He has been on the stand now for over an hour and much of the testimony has dealt with rather technical medical terminology, but he has managed to put it in layman's terms and thus keep the jurors alert and attentive. He has described in detail his physical examination of the body, the tests performed pursuant to the autopsy, and his careful study of the photographs and other physical evidence taken at the scene.

Thus far in his testimony he has surmised the following: Judging by the angle of the stab wounds and the force of the blows, some of which went right through ribs and the sternum, the killer was most likely tall, maybe five ten or more, strong, right-handed, and male. The degree and location of blood spatters throughout the kitchen area and the amount of blood inside the body suggest that the puncture wounds to the chest, back, and shoulder area came prior to the laceration across the neck. The victim was in a prone position on her stomach, or in a semi-kneeling position on hands and knees when this last wound was inflicted. The butcher knife found some distance from the house is most likely the murder weapon. The victim had sexual intercourse within a few hours of her death with a black man who was either sterile or had had a vasectomy. The victim had also ingested cannabis, cocaine, and alcohol within a few hours of her death. She had been dead only a few minutes, no more than thirty, when the police arrived on the scene. His opinion as to the cause of death is given with the same matter of fact directness that has characterized the rest of his testimony.

"Thank you, Doctor, no more questions."

I glance over at the jury, then at Rowe. Maybe he'll decide to give them a short break. He gives no indication of such, however, so I rise quickly, bringing my notes with me to the podium. "Counselor," I say to Haley as we pass.

"Dr. Simmons, you testified that in your opinion the victim had sex within a few hours of her death."

"Yes."

"Did you discover any medical evidence during your examination or your tests by which you could conclude one way or the other that the sexual intercourse was consensual?"

"I could not say for sure." A pause, then, "Would you like me to explain?"

"Please do."

"There were no signs of force being used, such as tears or trauma of the tissues in the vagina area, nor were there signs of bruising or redness around the wrist, forearms, or legs, to indicate that she had been held against her will. However, the victim could have been forced to have sex at the point of a knife. In such a case it would be the threat of force, rather than force itself, used to obtain the submission of the victim."

"And thus there would be no physical signs of the use of force?"

"Correct."

"You also said that it was your opinion that the person she had sex with was a black male." Simmons is nodding in agreement as I continue. "And this was based in part on the fact that you combed several hairs out of the pubic region of the victim, sent samples to the FDLE lab for analysis, and that such analysis confirmed that the hairs belonged to a black male. Is that correct?"

"Yes."

"Is it possible, Doctor, that those pubic hairs could have been left there as a result of some contact with a black male, not on the night of her murder, but the day before?"

"It is possible, I suppose," the doctor says, as if he had not previously considered the possibility, "assuming the victim had not taken a shower or otherwise cleaned herself for that period of time." He pauses again, and then adds, "But the semen I found inside the vagina of the victim was only a few hours old."

"But isn't it possible, Doctor, that the semen you found might have been from some other person, perhaps a white male?"

"Again, it's possible, but not likely, given the fact that I found no pubic hairs from any other source."

"Well, let me ask you this, Dr. Simmons. If I understand this correctly, the pubic hairs from the male are found there because of the contact of his sexual organ to hers, and the, shall we say, friction of the two meeting together time after time."

"Yes, the act of sexual intercourse, I think you mean." There are a couple of suppressed giggles in the courtroom.

"Yes, I'm a little clumsy, I suppose. But what if, instead of full skin-to-skin contact, pubic hair to pubic hair, the male does not remove his outer garments. Suppose he opens his pants only enough so that his penis may make penetration. Would that make it more likely that he would leave no pubic hair?"

"Yes," he says reasonably. "In that situation, the likelihood of pubic hairs being left behind would be less, although I still think you would find at least a couple."

"And, Doctor," I say, "from your examination of those pubic hairs, could you make a match to anyone in particular?"

"There are tests that can be performed to determine that. However, that is beyond my expertise, and I did not perform any such tests. I did send the samples, however, as I've mentioned, to the Florida Department of Law Enforcement lab."

"But all you can tell this jury today is that those pubic hairs belong to a black male."

"That is correct."

I ask the doctor a few more questions and point out the fact that, despite his very detailed and vivid account of how Patty Stiles died, he cannot identify her killer. After a short redirect by Haley, Rowe calls a fifteen-minute recess. I look around the courtroom, trying to see if Beth is here again, but I do not see her. I had hoped to get a chance to talk to Beth again today. My attempts to reach her by phone last night had been fruitless, with mama or daddy screening the calls. I thought maybe she might call me, but she hadn't.

I make another trip to my car, finish up the pint bottle of vodka, smoke a cigarette, contemplate the likely order of the remaining witnesses, and analyze the case so far. There has been some punching and counterpunching, but I don't think there has been any knockout by either side. The state's case should take the rest of the day and most of the next. The defense should take at least a day and a half, probably two.

I stop by the rest room on my way back, splash some water on my face, straighten my tie. I can feel the dampness underneath my arms but it's not too bad yet. "Oh well," I say to myself in the mirror. "Back to work."

The rest of the morning is taken up with the testimony of Bobby's coworker, his mother, and Patty's neighbors. Nothing unexpected with any of these witnesses.

From the coworker the jury hears that Bobby left work at about 10:45 P.M. on the night of Patty Stiles' murder wearing a black shirt and pants. When Haley asks him if Bobby had said what his plans were, the worker looks embarrassed, but says, "Bobby said he needed a beer and some pussy, and not necessarily in that order." On cross he acknowledges that a lot of times the guys just talk trash, kidding around, but I'm not sure the jury is satisfied. He also remembers that Bobby cut himself that night on the hand, shucking oysters. This is important because the serologist will testify that Bobby's blood is the same type as Patty's, thus possibly explaining the blood on his shoe.

Bernice testifies that Bobby came home shortly after midnight. She remembers because he came home after she heard the grandfather's clock in the living room strike twelve. She also tells the jury that Bobby had been married two years and that, to her knowledge, he has no children.

One of Patty's neighbors, a woman named Alma Bradford, says she heard screams, called 911, and watched the house until police arrived. No, she says, she didn't see anyone go in or out of the front door during this time.

Alonzo Johnson, one of Patty Stiles' neighbors, is a graduate student in the FSU/FAMU School of Engineering. His house backs up to Patty's. He says that he met Bobby once, shaking hands across the fence, and has seen him from a distance on other occasions.

He tells the jury that on the night of Patty's murder, he had been working, studying at the library until late. He got home right around midnight. As he was pulling into the driveway, he saw a man walking very quickly from the direction of Patty's house, actually along the side of her back fence.

"When I pulled into my driveway and my headlight hit him, he broke off into a run, past my yard and on toward Monroe Street."

"Could you tell what he was wearing?" Haley asks.

"He had on a black T-shirt and black pants."

"Could you describe him?"

"He wasn't a big fella, a slight frame, maybe about five ten. It was kind of hard to tell."

Haley questions Johnson about his identification of that person from a lineup. Johnson says yes, he did pick out a person who he said was the one he saw running from Patty Stiles' house. Haley will later have the detective testify that it was the defendant who Johnson had picked out of the lineup. Then Haley asks the big question.

"Do you see in this courtroom today the man you saw that night?"

Johnson looks in our direction for what seems to be a very long time. It's as if he's trying to pick Bobby out of a lineup again, although there are no other black males sitting at the defense table. Then he says, "Yes, that's him—the man in the middle there at the table."

"Can you describe what he is wearing?"

"Dark blue blazer, white shirt."

"Your Honor, will the record reflect that the witness has identified the defendant, Bobby Jackson?"

"The record will so reflect," Rowe responds.

"Are you sure, Mr. Johnson, that this was the man you saw running from the house?"

"Yes."

"Thank you. Your witness."

My gut tells me that Alonzo Johnson's sureness is a frail animal indeed, and it doesn't take long on cross to show it. In my questioning I bring out the fact that, at most, he saw this person for a few seconds, at night, from a distance of twenty-five or thirty yards. I point out that he had seen Bobby at Patty Stiles' house on other occasions in the past. Isn't it possible, I ask, that you thought you saw Bobby Jackson, because you had seen him before and associated him with Patty? It's possible he says, but he doesn't think so.

"Now, Mr. Johnson, when you picked my client out of the lineup, did you tell the detectives then that you were sure that my client was the man you saw that night?"

"Well, no, not exactly."

"Didn't you say, Mr. Johnson, that you *thought* that was the man, but you couldn't be sure?"

"I said something like that."

"Because you weren't sure then, were you, Mr. Johnson?"

"Not completely."

"And that lineup was a lot closer in time to the night of the murder, than we are now, at this trial, correct?"

"Yes."

"Thank you, Mr. Johnson."

On redirect, Haley tries to rehabilitate him, but the certainty he had displayed on direct examination never returns.

During lunch I avoid the rest of the defense team by telling them I need to get back to the office and attend to a couple of matters—which is actually true. I pick up a sandwich along the way. When I get there, I see that Janice has already left for lunch. She has, however, left plenty of messages for me as well as a stack of mail. I hang my suit coat on the rack, take off my tie, and then exchange my damp dress shirt for a clean, dry one from the drawer where I've been keeping them. I also pour myself a little bourbon into the Coke I take from the refrigerator and settle down behind my desk for a bit of a working lunch.

The Jackson trial has been consuming almost all of my waking time, and some of my sleeping time too for that matter. As a result, I have had to put my other cases pretty much on hold, doing what I can during lunches or after hours, reviewing mail, pleadings, signing off on correspondence.

As I quickly go through my mail, I see with satisfaction an envelope from Shawn Wolfe. I quickly open the envelope and take out the photos inside. Looking closely at them, I suddenly have a large weight in the pit of my stomach as I realize that I had been right.

At just that moment, Janice comes through the door, carrying her own sack lunch.

"Sorry I missed you. I had to run get something to eat."

"Give them an inch they take a mile," I say, giving her a quick smile. "Anything I need to know about?"

"Nothing that can't wait, I don't think. There were a couple of things though. Oh, I see you have already got the photographs from Mr. Wolfe. He dropped them by this morning. Is it what you wanted?"

"No, Janice, it's not what I wanted, but it is what it is," I say as I slip the photographs back into the envelope.

"There's also something in there from your wife."

I shuffle quickly through the stack until I see the familiar stationery. I open the envelope quickly and take out the contents—a canceled check, written on the business account of Captain Turner's restaurant. It's made out to Capital Hill Properties in the amount of six hundred and fifty dollars and dated May fifteenth, roughly one month before Patty Stiles was killed. In the bottom left corner in the memo section, it reads simply "Beth." There is also a handwritten note: "Found this the other day—not a usual business expense. I suspect this may be the P.I.—Beth."

I pick up the phone and in less than a minute I am speaking with Michelle Thompson, a clerk in the property appraiser's office.

"Michelle, how you doing?"

"Doing pretty good, Teddy. I've been seeing your picture in the paper a lot recently." I can't tell from the tone of her voice whether that's good or bad from her perspective. "What can the property appraiser's office do for you today?"

"I need you to check on the record owner of some property, and also give me a list of properties owned by a particular company." I give the name of the company, Capital Hill Properties, Inc.

There is a long pause, then, "That's interesting."

"What's interesting?" I ask.

"Oh, it's just that someone else asked for this exact same information a few months back. 'Cept she came into the office."

"Patty Stiles?"

"You got it. This got something to do with that case, Ted?"

"Could be, Michelle. Sure could be. I won't know though

till I get the information," I say. She says she'll call me back in a few moments.

I spend the next twenty minutes finishing my sandwich, having another bourbon and Coke, and returning as many messages as I can. One message seems particularly intriguing.

"Jan," I call out. In a moment her head is sticking through the entry with a questioning look on her face. "This message from Alonzo Johnson, did he say what he wanted?"

"No, just asked you to return the message. Who is he?"

"He's a neighbor of Patty Stiles. The only eyewitness in the state's case. I wonder why he would be calling me," I say as I lift up the phone and dial the number written on the message. Busy. I try two more times. Busy.

As I sip on the bourbon and Coke, I review some of the newspaper articles about my run-in with Quentin Martin. Jan has been conscientious enough, or sadistic enough, to collect every regional paper that had run the story. Most accounts are relatively low key, mildly interesting slants on the murder trial itself. The *Tallahassee Times-Union*, however, has seen fit to run a front-page story. They have gotten another reporter to do the story, a display of objectivity supposedly. But in fact, most of the information is either direct quotes from Marty or attributable to him: an in-depth portrayal of me as a man on the edge. There's stuff about my divorce, the allegations of alcohol abuse, the DUI, and the positive alco checks. "The man is wound up extremely tight," Martin is quoted as saying. "He has threatened me before, but there was something in his eyes yesterday, just before he hit me—really scary. I sure don't want to be around when that rubber band really breaks." The state attorney's office says that it is still investigating the case, the article reports.

Some of this stuff is, of course, old news. Unfortunately,

all of it is true and it sounds pretty bad. I am beginning to wish now that I hadn't even read it. Twice more I try to get through to Alonzo Johnson and twice more I get a busy signal. Just before I am ready to leave for the courthouse, though, Michelle Thompson calls back.

"Sorry to take so long. I got tied up with something else."

"No problem. What did you find out?"

"Coincidentally, the company you gave me, this Capital Hill Properties, Inc., is the owner of the property at the address you gave me on Brevard Street. The company owns several other properties, some houses in the French Town area, some over near FAMU, a couple in the north and northeast sections. Also two or three acreage parcels outside the city limits. Not a major property owner in Leon County, but not insignificant either. Who are the principals?"

"I was hoping you might know," I say in return.

"No, sorry. Can't help you there."

"That's all right, Michelle. You've been a lot of help. Listen, would you mind making a copy of the printout of those properties and faxing them over here?"

"Sure."

"Thanks. Talk to you later." I hang up the phone and stare off into space for several seconds, trying to place this piece into the puzzle.

"Jan."

"Yeah," she calls from her office.

I pick up my coat, briefcase, and the slip of paper on which I have written down Capital Hill Properties, Inc., and walk out to her desk. "I need you to do something for me this afternoon. Michelle Thompson's going to fax a computer printout of some properties owned by this company. Call the secretary of state. Find out who the officers and directors are of this corporation." I hand her the slip of paper.

"Important?"

"Could be. We'll see."

The bulk of the afternoon is devoted to more expert witnesses, the folks who have tested and compared blood, semen, prints, and saliva. No real surprises here. Bobby's prints were found all over the house, but the witness admits that the prints could have been left sometime other than the night of the murder. He also acknowledges that there were no prints of the defendant found on the murder weapon—a point that I will hit hard on in closing argument.

The witness from the Florida Department of Law Enforcement lab, who testifies concerning blood, semen, saliva, and DNA match ups, is effective. She confirms that the blood on the knife is that of the victim. She gives her opinion that the defendant was the person who had smoked the cigarettes and had sex with the victim shortly before she was killed. This is based in large part, she says, on an analysis of the semen found in the vagina of the victim, the pubic hairs found on her, and the saliva from the cigarette butts in the ashtray found in the living room. The samples were sufficient, she says, to show that the same person who had intercourse with the victim had smoked the cigarettes. She tells the jury that only three percent of the adult black male population have a blood type consistent with the samples she tested. Bobby Jackson, she says, is in that three percent. Although she concedes on cross that the tests can only exclude people, not identify them, and thus the match with Bobby is not certain, the jury a now has a good basis on which to conclude that Bobby was the source.

After Rowe recesses for the evening, Paul and I sit down with Bobby to discuss the status of the case and the relative strength of our defense theory. Bobby has thus far, throughout my defense of him, insisted that he never went to the victim's home that night. He claimed that his delay in getting home was because he had sat outside the Sugar Shack on South Adams, listening to the music. No, he said, he didn't think anybody saw him there who knew him. Besides, he didn't go in because he didn't want to pay the cover charge, so he stayed out in the parking lot smoking a few cigarettes. After he stopped by the convenience store, he walked on home.

"In light of the testimony that has been presented thus far," I say, "I suggest that we reevaluate this theory." I point out to Bobby the obvious, that a defense based on the premise that he was not at Patty Stiles' house the night she was murdered does not appear to be rooted in reality. Perhaps, I suggest, there is a theory that includes him showing up at Patty's house the night of her murder.

"Okay," Bobby says, after several seconds of silence. "Speaking hypothetically, let's say I was there, and let's say that it was me who smoked her dope, had sex with her, then went to get some more cigarettes and beer. Let's suppose that I came back to find her dead, got scared and ran. Hypothetically speaking, that would explain things, wouldn't it?"

Neither Paul nor I responds immediately, but we are clearly intrigued, so he continues.

"Maybe someone was watching me and her do it on the couch. Someone who was jealous. Maybe this dude figured he owned her. He gets madder and madder. After I'm gone she lets him in and he confronts her. She tells him to kiss her ass, which really gets him pissed. She makes fun of him, taunts him. You know how she can be," he says looking at me. "He loses it, grabs a knife and starts stabbing." Bobby pauses, looking at Paul and then at me. "Now, Counselors, hypothetically speaking, how does that sound?"

"Is that what happened, Bobby?"

"Now, Teddy, didn't you advise me when we first met that it is safer to speak in hypothetical terms?"

"Dammit, Bobby, I need to know the truth." I can feel my face getting flushed and my voice rising. Paul reaches over and puts his hand on my arm. "Speaking hypothetically," he says, "there's a bit of a problem with that theory."

"Yeah, what's that?" Bobby is now giving his attention to my partner.

"There's the little matter of the statement you gave the police when you were arrested, Bobby. You told them you didn't go to the victim's house that night."

"They didn't read me my damn rights, though, man. Y'all got that statement suppressed. They can't use it, can they?" Bobby seems impressed with his understanding of criminal law and procedure, but he is not quite right, which I point out.

"Yes and no, Bobby. While it's true they can't use that statement against you in their case in chief, once you take the stand they are free to impeach you with any prior inconsistent statements you may have made. It would be hard enough for the jury to believe that you were at Patty's house, had sex with her, smoked dope with her, and then somebody else came in and killed her in the fifteen minutes it took you to go to the Seven-Eleven and back. If you get on the stand and say something that conflicts with what you told the police, the state will be able to show the jury that you are a liar."

"The only other possibility," Paul joins in, "is that Bobby admits that he lied to the police that night. He knew what the truth was, but he was afraid that they wouldn't believe him. Just like he's afraid the jury won't believe him now. But now he's under oath and he is telling the truth."

The three of us sit quietly for several seconds; then I break the silence. "Well, Bobby, think about it. You don't have to make a decision today. We'll talk about it some more. But it looks like Haley's going to close his case before the end of the day tomorrow, so we're going to have to get together on this thing pretty quick."

My client nods his acknowledgment just as the bailiff knocks on the door and tells us he needs to get Bobby back. As the door closes behind him, Paul and I look at each other, neither of us sure of the other one, but afraid to admit it to each other, or to ourselves. With an unspoken agreement, we get up, silently, and walk out the door, each going a different way.

TWENTY-SEVEN

Thursday—October 9th

I am tired, depressed, and agitated. During the trial I have intentionally kept my distance from my partner, from Bert, and from my client and his family. All of my energy is focused on the case, and I cannot afford the luxury of hand holding, esoteric "what ifs," idle conversation. I know that I should get more sleep, but I am too keyed up. My alco check was negative again this morning, but I am beginning to wonder if I can keep it up. With each new bit of information gained, my anxiety level has shot out of sight.

Haley starts off the morning with what he figures will be one of his best witnesses. He is wrong.

Eddie Lewis is a large, middle-aged black man who tells the jury that on June twelfth he was working the night shift at the minute market located at the corner of South Adams and Jenkins. Yes, he says, he knows the defendant, though not by name. He used to come in the store from time to time. Did he come in the store the night of June twelfth? Yes. Do you remember what time? Yes, it was a little after eleven o'clock. He is sure of the time because he remembers it was just after the eleven o'clock news had come on. How, Haley asked him, can he be so sure it wasn't Thursday night, or Saturday night, rather than Friday night. Easy, Lewis responds, he remembers because it was the night of the NBA playoffs, and he didn't work Thursday or Saturday.

"Thank you, Mr. Lewis. Your witness." Haley sits down, a satisfied look on his face.

"If I understand you correctly, Mr. Lewis," I begin, "your certainty about the date and the time is based upon the fact that the NBA playoffs were on that night?"

"That's right. You see, we've got a little TV that we keep in the store, you know, when things get slow. Well, I watched the game mostly, off and on that night."

"Was it a good game, Mr. Lewis?"

"Objection, Your Honor." Haley rises. "I fail to see how the quality of the basketball game that night has anything to do with this case."

Rowe looks to me.

"Judge, if you will give me just a little bit of latitude, I will show the relevance."

"All right," he says, "but try to tie it up quick."

"Yes, sir." I turn back to the witness. "So, Mr. Lewis, was it a good game?"

"Yes, it was. It was nip and tuck the whole time."

"In fact, didn't it go into overtime?"

"That's right."

"And, right after that, the news came on."

"Right."

"You were watching that too?"

"Yeah, it was kind of slow and, like I say, I was watching the TV off and on."

"And, it was right after the news came on, that you say Bobby Jackson came in and bought his beer and cigarettes."

"That's what I said before." Lewis gives me a look like a patient school teacher to a slow child.

"And you're sure of that?"

"Yes, I'm sure."

I walk back over to the defense table, and pull out a document from my file, hold it out in front of me. "Your Honor, I would like to show this document to the witness and ask some questions of him. But first I would like to ask the court to take judicial notice of this document, which purports to be a certified copy of the programming schedule of WCTV, Channel Six, for Friday, June twelfth of this year."

"Objection." Haley is quick on his feet and is asking for a side bar. Rowe motions us forward.

"Judge, the defense is not allowed to introduce exhibits into evidence during our case in chief." Haley is obviously surprised and annoyed. He is looking over the document as he speaks. "Nor can he introduce evidence through judicial notice."

He is technically correct, which I acknowledge. I suggest that I am merely trying to keep the presentation of evidence logical but, if Mr. Haley insists, I will be glad to recall Mr. Lewis after the state has rested.

"Mr. Haley?" Rowe looks at the prosecutor.

Haley's face makes it obvious that he realizes his predicament. Because of my long-winded request for judicial notice the jury has a pretty good idea of what's coming. I watch as his face sags visibly upon reading the document. He knows that I can get this in during the defense's case. If he objects now the jury may think he is trying to hide something which, of course, he would be. He looks back up to Rowe. He has made his decision. "Withdraw the objection, Your Honor," he says, loud enough for the jurors to hear. Rowe formally grants judicial notice of the document explaining to the jury that certain facts which are subject to verification as to their accuracy may be judicially noticed by the court and thus accepted by the jury as proven.

"Thank you, Your Honor." I then turn my attention back to the witness. "Mr. Lewis, I would like to ask you to take a look at this document and direct your attention to the slot shown for the NBA playoffs on the night of June twelfth of this year. Do you see it?"

"Yes, I've got it."

"And what time does it say that the game started?"

"It started at nine P.M., it says here." I can see that the witness is reading ahead of himself, as his head is down and he seems only mildly interested in what I have to say next. I see the surprise in his face as he looks back up to me.

"And, Mr. Lewis, what time does it show there that the basketball game ended?"

There is a long pause as Lewis contemplates the significance of his answer. "It says here that the game got over at eleven twenty-seven."

There is a slight murmur in the audience. I don't get to my next question before Lewis continues, apologetically, "Well, actually, I didn't really look at the clock. I was just going by the news. I mean they call it the eleven o'clock news. But, now I do remember. The game went into overtime. Went longer than they thought. Well, I—"

I cut him off with another question. "Would it be more accurate then, to say, upon reflection, that you saw Bobby Jackson in the store sometime a little after eleven thirty, and not eleven o'clock?"

"Yes, that's it. I don't know how I could have messed that up."

"Thank you, Mr. Lewis."

It is a small victory perhaps, but the defense table is a happier place now. Haley wisely decides not to linger in this land-mined area any longer and declares he has no questions for redirect.

The state next recalls Detective Randy Powell to tell the

jury about the arrest of Bobby and the search of his house. Bernice Jackson told them Bobby wasn't there. When they searched the house, however, they found Bobby, hiding in his bedroom closet. He identifies the shoes also found in the closet, which he sent to the lab for testing. Did they look for black pants and black T-shirt, Haley asks. Yes, they did. And? None were found.

On cross, I ask if he saw a washing machine at the Jackson house.

"I don't recall."

"You don't recall?" I ask, arching my eyebrows. "Your report doesn't indicate one way or the other, does it?" My tone is accusatory.

There is a long pause as Powell looks over his notes, then, "No."

"So, for all you know, Detective, there may have been a washer full of clothes at the time of your search."

"If there had been a washer, I am sure we would have searched it.

"And, if there hadn't been?"

Powell gets my point, but he doesn't want to make it easy, so I continue. "If there hadn't been a washer, then you wouldn't know if there was a load of laundry being done somewhere else, would you?"

"I guess not."

Powell also confirms that Bobby had an outstanding warrant for violation of probation in a misdemeanor drug case—not the best thing for the jury to hear, I know, but better that they think he's hiding from a misdemeanor, than a murder charge.

Haley's last witness puts a hole in our best defense theory. The serologist from FDLE makes it very clear that whoever may have left his saliva, semen, and pubic hair at Patty Stiles' home on the night of the murder, it could not possibly have been Sammy Smith, since his blood type was

completely incompatible. Though we have scored some
hits during the day, the final round, without question, be-
longs to the prosecution.

Just after three the state rests and Rowe denies my motion for judgment of acquittal. I am about to request of
the judge that we recess for the day when he announces
that he wants to see the attorneys in his chambers. The two
prosecutors, Paul, Bert, and I all hustle to keep up with the
judge as he steps down from the bench, through the side
door, and begins walking briskly back to his office.

We all nod to Eva as we go into Rowe's inner office. He
sits, pulls his cigar out from a holder on his desk, bites off
the end, lights it, and begins puffing large clouds of smoke
up into the air. Rowe has not indicated that we are to sit
for this meeting, and no one dares take a seat without being
invited.

"Have a seat, gentlemen," he says, motioning to the
chairs. We all sit. "Now, Mr. Haley, I understand you have
something you wish to bring up?"

"Yes, Your Honor. This is a little awkward, but earlier
today my office received word from the homicide investigators on this case that they have been given some new
information." Everyone is looking expectantly at Haley.
"This new information concerns defense counsel, Mr.
Stevens." Now, all eyes in the room, except Haley's, are
looking at me.

"Yes?" Rowe says with an edge of hardness.

"Without going into details, the information suggests
that Mr. Stevens had a sexual relationship with the victim,
which was ongoing up until the time of her death." I see
in Haley's lap a manila envelope the size, I think, of an
eight-by-ten photograph. "Detective Powell and others are
following up on this anonymous tip, and, although I am
confident that any new information uncovered will not
change our prosecution of Bobby Jackson, it does, at the

very least, point to a clear conflict of interest in Mr. Stevens representing Mr. Jackson in this case."

Rowe is leaning back in his chair, puffing away on the cigar.

"We'd rather not divulge the details to Mr. Stevens at this time, since the investigation of this information is not complete, but, Judge, if you'd like to see what we have at this point, in camera . . ."

"That won't be necessary, Mr. Haley. And anything you want to show me should be shown to Mr. Stevens as well."

"May I be heard, on this, Your Honor?" I say.

"No, Mr. Stevens, you may not. Not at this time. Somebody ought to be reading you your Miranda rights." He hesitates a few seconds, looking out the window. "Good God Almighty," he says under his breath, but everyone hears him. Then he turns back to look at all of us, but is concentrating on me when he speaks. Suddenly I feel like an intern again.

"I'm going to recess this mess until tomorrow morning at seven A.M. We're going to meet right here in my office. Detective Powell's going to be here, Bobby Jackson's going to be here, and a court reporter is going to be here. Mr. Haley, you're going to lay out everything you've got on this that you think might reflect unfavorably on Mr. Stevens relative to his representation of Mr. Jackson in this case. I mean a full disclosure. I'm going to let Mr. Jackson talk to independent counsel, if he wants to. But I'm going to have his statement, on record, whether he wants to continue with Mr. Stevens as his lawyer." Rowe pauses for a second and then says, "That's all, gentlemen. See you tomorrow morning."

We all get up and leave slowly, in stunned silence. Outside the door, as the prosecution team turns one way and we turn the other, Paul breaks the silence. "Have you ever heard of such bullshit? Listen, Ted, we'll get together later and plan how to handle this." I look into the eyes of my partner. "Thanks, Paul, but I think I need to work on this alone."

He looks confused but doesn't respond. I walk off down the hall alone.

Down in the parking garage, I sit in my car drinking the last of the bottle of vodka and smoking a couple of cigarettes before deciding what to do. I pull out the slip of paper in my pocket, the phone message from Alonzo Johnson. I pull the cell phone from my jacket pocket, punch in the number, but the battery is too weak to get through the parking garage. I think of going back to the office, but decide I just can't do that right now. I walk back up the stairs and into the attorney's lounge area. There is no one in this section of the courthouse, and the silence is rather eerie. I sit down beside the courtesy phone, take the slip of paper out again, and dial the number. He answers on the second ring.

"Hello."

"Is this Mr. Johnson?"

"Yes."

"Mr. Johnson, this is Ted Stevens. I'm returning your call from earlier today."

"Yeah, I thought maybe we should talk."

"What about?"

The pause seems to last forever. "Well, you know, when I testified today, the man asked me to look around the courtroom and see if I saw the person I had seen the night Patty got killed?"

"Yes."

"Well, I did see your client that night, like I said. But when he asked me that question, and I looked over toward the defense table, I realized that I saw somebody else that night too. About two blocks down on Meridian Street, as I was driving by, I saw a man walking, and then getting into a car."

Afraid of what I might hear, I have to ask the question: "And who'd you see, Alonzo?" I brace myself for the answer.

As I listen to Alonzo Johnson describe what he saw that night, I can feel pieces of the puzzle slamming into each other, fighting to form a recognizable picture. "Are you going to be home for a while?"

"Yeah, I'll be here the rest of the evening."

"I'll be right over."

I hang up the receiver, still stunned, thoughts ricocheting quickly off the sides of my brain as I try to determine how to handle this new information, only too aware of the implications. As I turn to leave, I come face to face with Bert Murphy, who is standing in the doorway. On reflex I jump back. "Damn, Bert, what are you trying to do, scare the shit out of me?"

"Sorry, Ted, I saw you come in here, thought maybe I'd check with you and see if you wanted me to do anything. I couldn't help but overhear. That was Alonzo Johnson you were talking to? Anything helpful?"

I look around the room, as if there might be an answer somewhere in one of the corners. "I doubt it, Bert. It sounds like maybe he's having second thoughts about his identification of Bobby. Feeling a little guilty about it. I think maybe the detectives pressured him a bit on that identification. He may end up coming out and helping us on the defense—that is, if I am still on it."

"Geez, Ted, what do you think they got? Prints? Photos?"

"I don't know, and quite frankly, Bert, I don't care. I think Bobby's going to ride with me on this, 'cause I know they don't have enough. And I've got a couple of new slants that I'm working on. I need to talk to you about it if you

have some time later on tonight. I'm going to go see Bobby
after I talk to Johnson."

"Yeah, sure. You want me to come by the office?"

"Yeah, I'll be there until pretty late, say about nine? We'll
go over your testimony because you'll probably be our first
witness."

"All right, Ted. See you then. And, listen, Teddy Bear.
You take care of yourself."

TWENTY-EIGHT

Thursday—October 9th

I swish the golden brown liquid around in the glass, take another swallow, emptying the contents, then place both the bottle and the glass back in my bottom right drawer. Just enough, I tell myself, to calm my nerves but not to dull my senses. I open my top desk drawer again, pick up the gun, check the safety, and return it to its place. I check the tape recorder once more, then looking at my watch, seeing that it is eight fifty-eight, go ahead and turn it on record. I wipe the perspiration from my forehead with a brown paper towel.

The Jackson files are spread out all over my desk, but the ones I will need are close by. I light another cigarette, take a deep draw, holding it for two full seconds, then let it out. I get up out of my chair and pace. I'm not at all sure that I have made the right decision. Maybe it's not too late, I think. Maybe I should hold my cards close to the chest, take a couple more, and see what I get. But, like my daddy used to tell me, if you don't know how to bluff, then you shouldn't be playing the game.

"Hello, anybody home?"

Bert's words startle me out of my thoughts. I look at my watch. Exactly nine o'clock. "Up here, Bert," I say as I hear his footsteps already bounding up the stairs. Three seconds later, Bert is standing in the doorway of my office.

"Hey, Teddy. You doing all right? Are you ready for tomorrow?"

"Yeah, Bert. I talked with Bobby a little earlier. He's gonna go with me on this thing, I feel pretty sure."

"What do you think they have, the photos?"

"I don't know, and I don't really care," I say, trying to sound confident. "I think I've got some new information. I appreciate you coming over, since you're going to be my lead witness tomorrow. I need to go over these new twists, make sure we're on the same page."

"Sure," he says, taking a seat across the desk from me. "You got a new angle?"

"Well, yes. I've got a new suspect, another alternative I'd like to suggest to the jury."

"Yeah, who?"

"You."

Bert tries to look surprised, but for once I think I can see behind the mask. Finally he smiles and says, "This is very interesting, Ted, but don't you have plenty of suspects already without picking on me?" When I don't respond immediately, he continues, "You're serious, aren't you? Okay, I'll bite. How does it play out, Counselor?"

"Well, when I get you on the stand, I'll want to get into why you were so eager to get on this case, why you lied about bonding Bobby Jackson out before, lied about talking to his family, since Bernice says that she hadn't talked to you before. I'll be wondering aloud why it was that you couldn't find anyone to confirm that Patty Stiles was working on a story about drug dealing, why you somehow missed Shawn Wolfe in your investigation, why you were so skeptical of the whole idea, tried to steer me away from it."

"Why, indeed? Please tell us." Bert fills the dramatic

pause I thought I had created. His tone is sarcastic, mocking.

"The reason," I say, pulling out one of the photographs of Sammy Smith and company and pushing it in front of Bert, "the reason I'm thinking, Bert, is maybe this is you." I point to the mystery man in the photo.

"Sure doesn't look like me," Bert replies, looking up at me, a small smile on his lips. "Oh, I get it. I was wearing a disguise, a fake beard, a dark-haired wig. You thinking maybe you would find a hat and a coat like this somewhere in my house?"

"Yes," I say simply.

"There must be more," he says.

I pull out the notes I had made from the pocket notebook found in Patty's house. I look at them, rather than Bert, as I speak. "When I started thinking that maybe the P.M. in Patty's notes meant Paul Morganstein, it never occurred to me that A.M. might mean Albert Murphy."

"Probably because I never go by Albert. Everybody knows me as Bert."

"Yes," I agree. "That's why it didn't occur to me before, I guess. But that is your legal name. That's how it is officially listed in the motor vehicle records, which show you as the owner of this car," I say, pointing to one of the photos that Shawn Wolfe has enlarged for me.

Bert has picked up the photo now and is looking at it intently, as I continue. "I thought that sixty-eight El Camino looked familiar, but it didn't register when I looked at the photos before. I had assumed that the focus of the shot was the men in the background, on the sidewalk. Although you can't read the license plate numbers clearly, I don't think there's any real question that that's your car.

"Albert Murphy is also the official name designated as one of the officers and directors of a corporation called Capital Hill Properties, Inc., which owns the property lo-

cated at four fifteen West Brevard Street, one of the addresses in Patty's notebook. I think Patty was referring to
this as a crack house. That would explain the C H. I will,
of course, bring out the fact that you were present when
the notebook was found by me at Patty's house, were aware
of the contents, and would probably find it relatively easy
to get back in." I look at Bert, arching my eyebrows.

"I would also suggest to the jury that your lifestyle is
perhaps a little lavish for a private investigator, even a very
good one—thirty acres on the Wakulla River, a pretty nice
spread—the vintage Corvettes, which cost a pretty penny.
Then, of course, there is the fact that you worked for many
years in vice and narcotics, made some big busts, a real
cowboy. I'm sure you learned a few things, made a few
connections, maybe like the guy with the Dade County license plate I saw leaving your office. I wonder how many
air tickets they'll find you've purchased to Miami over the
last few years. You're smart, Bert, and very careful. I suspect
that very few people who deal with you in the drug business
know your real identity, Sammy Smith probably being one
of them. How does it sound so far?"

"All right," Bert says. "Let's see how this would go." At
this, Bert begins a dialogue with himself, playing the role
of both the witness and the attorney.

"Have you ever bonded Bobby Jackson out in a criminal
case before this one?"

"Yes."

"What about the records which show that his bondsman
has always been Bill Jackson?"

"You should check with Billy. He handled the paperwork
but his company wouldn't take it, so he came to me. He
was the bondsman in name only. My company was the actual bonding company."

"Did you, in fact, tell one thing to Bobby Jackson's family, and one thing to his lawyer, in order to get into a position to be appointed as the investigator in this case?"

"To be honest, I don't really remember exactly how I got involved, who talked to who first. I might have contacted B.J.'s family first. I don't recall. But, I don't know that I would want to rely too much on Bernice Jackson's memory as to exactly what happened. I don't think she was in a real good emotional state at that time."

"And did you, Mr. Murphy, try to steer Mr. Stevens away from the theory about a connection with a drug story the victim was supposedly working on?"

"No, I did not."

"You were aware, though, weren't you, of a notebook, pocket-sized, found at the victim's home by Mr. Stevens?"

"I am aware of a notebook, but I cannot say from where it came."

"Well, weren't you there when Mr. Stevens found it in the magazine rack, as he has indicated?"

"No, as I recall, I was in another part of the house. Mr. Stevens called me in and told me he had found the notebook in the magazine rack."

"Well, Mr. Murphy, you did see, though, didn't you, the contents of that notebook?"

"Yes, I did."

"And, didn't you see in the notebook, the writings and symbols as shown on the exhibit prepared by Mr. Stevens?"

"No, quite honestly, I didn't recall what Mr. Stevens had. I suppose he has a better memory than me, which is a little embarrassing being a private detective. But, like I told him before, I didn't remember it that way."

"What about Shawn Wolfe, Mr. Murphy. Why is it that you missed this link?"

"I didn't miss the link, Counselor. Mr. Wolfe was out of the country at the time. I did mention it to Mr. Stevens, but I suppose he forgot. I might add that I did identify

Sammy Smith, right away, from the photos that Mr. Wolfe showed us, even arranged a meeting with Mr. Smith."

"Did you follow every direction of Mr. Stevens in this regard?"

"Yes, I did."

"It would have been easy for you, Mr. Murphy, to gain entrance to the victim's home after that notebook was found, wouldn't it?" Bert is being overly dramatic here, mocking me still.

"I suppose you could say that. However, I did not. You could also say, of course, that Mr. Stevens could have gained access a lot easier than I could. That's because he has a key." With this he looks at me accusingly. "Don't you, Ted?"

I break into Bert's dialogue with himself. "But how would you know that, Bert, except that you were the private detective my father-in-law hired to follow me. And you lied to me about that, didn't you? You had me chasing every private detective in Panama City, a wild goose chase. All because you planned to use it against me. Isn't that right?"

"Now Ted, you know I couldn't tell you if I was because that would be a breach of confidence. You do know about that, don't you, Counselor?"

Bert's smile is really beginning to annoy me. "Bert, I've got your damn check right here," I say, pushing a copy of the canceled check over toward him.

He only glances at the check, then says, "You're going to have to ask Captain Turner about that, Ted. I don't suspect you'd believe anything I said anyway." Bert's tone sounds as if he is hurt, disappointed. He is shaking his head.

"And how do you explain the fact that a witness saw you in the vicinity of the victim's home shortly after the time of her death?" I had thought that this question would, in fact, be somewhat startling to Bert, but if he is shocked or surprised, he makes no show of it.

"He must be mistaken. If he saw me, he's got his nights mixed up. I was at my brother's house that night, until about eleven thirty or twelve. That was the night we were watching the NBA playoffs."

I have no idea whether he is telling the truth or not, but I feel pretty sure that his brother will cover for him either way. I don't like the way this is going.

"You know, Teddy, sometimes people do things they're ashamed of. Something too horrible to accept. They try to convince themselves that they couldn't have done it. But maybe they were too drunk to remember." He is looking directly at me now, but I can't meet his stare. "Deep down inside, though, the guilt eats them alive. They begin to do things to try to get themselves caught, because they know it's the right thing to do. They leave subtle clues behind so that the issue will be forced.

"Is that what you've been doing, Ted? Bobby told me about his suspicions, about the scratches on your arm that you tried to explain away, about your piss-poor alibi for the night Patty Stiles was murdered. And, hell, everybody knows that you're a drunk. Is that what happened, Teddy? Did you kill her in one of your alcoholic stupors? And now you can't face it? Will they find your prints at the murder scene? Have you hidden the bloody clothes somewhere? I wonder if the print on the letters you supposedly received matches the print on any of the equipment in your office?"

Bert has gotten up from the chair now and is standing, leaning on the desk, looking down at me. I am looking off to the side, taking in his words, still wondering. Bert continues.

"But, hey, it's really none of my business, is it, I mean as long as B.J. doesn't go down. He's my client too, you know, and I think I owe him a duty too. Yeah, I got nothing to

hide, but, if you do put me on the stand and start asking
me questions, there's some other information that's bound
to come out that wouldn't be too good for you, Ted.

"Now, I understand that you gotta represent your client
and I appreciate that. But, if you think about it, your theory
of the new suspect, while mildly interesting, is full of holes.
Personally, I think you might want to be lookin' a little
closer to home. See you tomorrow, Teddy Bear—bright and
early." He turns around and slowly, deliberately, walks out
of my office. His last words linger in the air, reminding me
of the voice of my caller.

I open my drawer and turn off the tape recorder, click
the safety off the gun. I sit there in the silence of my office,
thinking, pondering what Bert has told me. I take the bourbon bottle and the glass from the drawer and pour it full.
I take a large swallow. Then another. I am staring absently
out the window onto the street below when I hear footsteps
coming up the stairs. A figure pauses in the doorway. I turn
my head and look directly at the face of my partner, Paul
Morganstein. He is not smiling.

Paul walks slowly into my office and up to the desk where
both of us, standing, look into each other's eyes. Finally,
he breaks the silence.

"Nice try, Teddy."

I reach over and turn off the intercom button on my
phone. "Could you hear everything?"

"Yeah."

"Well, it didn't go quite as planned, do you think?"

"He is slick and he is smooth, Teddy. But I don't think
I'd want to play that tape back for anybody. Hey, don't
worry, Ted, we'll deal with it, we have to. We'll get everything out on the table tomorrow morning. Whether Rowe
decides to declare a mistrial or not, I don't think you've
got much choice. Come on, let's go."

"Nah, I need a little time here with my files, to think. You go ahead."

"All right, but don't stay up all night. And, Ted, don't make matters worse," he says, pointing to the glass on my desk. "You want me to take the bottle with me?"

"This is my last one, partner."

"All right, see you tomorrow."

"Yeah."

Paul looks at me skeptically, but turns and walks out. I listen to the sound of his footsteps going down the stairs and out the front door. I take a sip from my glass, walk back over to the window and look out onto the city.

It had not been a good idea with Bert, I realize. I didn't have enough. Hadn't covered all my bases. There had not been enough time. And now, I had played my hand. I had bluffed, and he had called it. The chips belonged to Bert.

As I take another sip from my glass, I hear a noise, like the door opening and closing, but I don't hear footsteps. I wait a couple of seconds. Must be Paul.

"What's the matter, did you forget something?" I call down the stairs.

TWENTY-NINE

Thursday—October 9th

There is no immediate response and I am about to call out again when I hear footsteps just outside my door and the voice of Bert Murphy as he crosses the threshold to my office.

"Yeah, I did forget something, Ted." He is smiling but I notice he is wearing surgical gloves on his hands, one of which carries a handgun. Not a good sign. I think about the drawer, about the gun, and I edge slowly toward my desk.

"What's going on, Bert?"

"Teddy, Teddy, Teddy," he says, shaking his head. "It's too late to act dumb. Might have worked before, but not now."

As I reach toward the drawer to open it, he is around the desk gripping my wrist. He is as strong as he looks. He opens the drawer and removes the gun. "I'll take this, thank you." With the other hand he removes the tape recorder, places it on top of the desk, and pushes the rewind button. He smiles as he listens to me and Paul. "Excellent," he says. He punches the fast forward a few times until he gets to the end of that conversation. Then he holds his hand over the microphone and hits the play button letting it run to the end of the tape. He then rewinds to the point where Paul left the office. "That should do it nicely," he says. During this time, I have not spoken a word but have been considering my options. There aren't many good ones.

"All right, Bert, you've convinced me. This is not necessary."

"Oh, I'm afraid it is, Ted. You're too much a loose cannon now. Besides, now you've got your partner wondering. We're just gonna have to tie up some loose ends."

"So, what? You're going to kill me?"

"Well, sort of, but not really." He gives me an apologetic look, almost a smile. "You're gonna kill yourself, Ted."

"Gee, Bert, I'd like to, but I've made other plans."

There's a slight chuckle from Bert. "Yeah, Teddy, I like that. Glad to see you have a sense of humor. The fact of the matter is, though, that you've thought about suicide many times before. Here." He slides the glass over toward me. "Don't let me stop you."

"I'm not allowed to drink."

"That's true, of course," Bert says. "But you're also a drunk, Teddy. Everybody knows that. You will be drinking quite a bit tonight. More than you already have," he says, looking at the half-empty bottle on my desk. "And, in case you don't have enough . . ." He pulls out another bottle from his coat and places it on the desk.

"No, Bert, I'm not going to play. If you're going to kill me, you might as well go ahead and do it. But you'll have to shoot me from a distance, or there will be a hell of a struggle and you'll have a hard time selling the idea that it was suicide. Listen, there's no need to get drastic on me. We can talk this over. We can work this thing out, I'm sure." I'm hoping the combination of bluff and reason will work, but I see no signs of it in Bert's face.

"Afraid not, old buddy. Now, you can go ahead and make

your move, but you know, if you do, I'll kill you." Yes, this I am sure of. "There might be a struggle, and the position of the body might make it a little more difficult, but I'll take my chances. No, you're gonna go along with me, for now. Because you know it'll give you some more time. Maybe something will come to you. Maybe you'll talk me out of it. Maybe someone will come. At the very least, while we share a few drinks, maybe I'll answer your questions. At least you'll go to your grave with the pieces to the puzzle."

I hold out my glass. He pours about two ounces. I take a sip.

"Aw, come on now, let's be realistic. It'll take all night if you just sip this stuff. I figure an ounce a minute. That seems fair."

Without further comment, I down the contents of the glass. "Okay, first question. I hate to waste my time on the obvious, but best to know for sure. The scenario here is that I drink myself into a stupor, write a suicide note confessing to Patty Stiles' murder, explaining that I can't live with the guilt anymore, and then shoot myself in the head?"

"You have to admit, that's the logical conclusion to this whole sordid mess," Bert says. "Trial attorney who has everything going for him, can't believe his good luck, starts finding reasons to be unhappy. He's always been a heavy drinker, but he begins to drink too much, has an affair with one of his clients. When he comes to his senses, realizes he needs to dump the girlfriend, she decides she ain't ready to be dumped.

"She remembers some photographs she took. Photographs that will be impossible to explain to a distraught wife. She threatens to send them, even calls the wife, anonymously. He goes over to the girlfriend's house, not sure what he will say, not sure what he will do. But, while he's watching the house, he sees Bobby Jackson come up and go in like he owns the place. He gets up closer and watches through the window as she does things with this guy that he thought were reserved only for him. His rage begins to consume him.

"Bobby leaves, he goes in, confronts her. She refuses to give the photos to him. In fact, she assures him that his wife will see every one of them. He goes berserk, grabs the knife and . . . Well, you know what happens next. Here, you're not drinking." He pours another half-glass of bourbon and I take a large sip.

"But, to his dismay, it is all for naught. His wife leaves him anyway. Under the influence of her overprotective father she hires a son-of-a-bitch lawyer and declares an all-out war in the divorce proceeding. Our attorney now begins to drink more and more.

"By some sick twist of fate, he is appointed to represent the man accused of the murder. The guilt, and the conflict, are too much to bear. Everyone can see he is on the edge. He gets caught DUI. He keeps violating the terms of his pretrial release. His partner, the investigator on the case, his secretary, all of them will confirm that he seemed distant, depressed, agitated. Obviously, he is out of control when he physically assaults a news reporter. Then, when it looks like the truth is about to come out, truth that he has been hiding from himself, but now must face, he . . . Well, after he drinks himself plenty of courage," he says, pointing at the bourbon bottle, "he takes his own life, having first left a suicide note confessing to the murder, of course."

"Of course." I take a very large gulp of bourbon. "How tragic."

"Indeed."

"So, another silly question, but you did kill her, didn't you?"

Bert pulls the photograph of Sammy Smith and the mystery man out from the pile. "I was afraid you might stumble onto something, Ted, but I thought I could sidetrack you. Yes, that's me in the photo. The money is so good, and it's so easy, Ted. I've been one of the biggest suppliers for this town, and the main connection with Miami, for almost six years, and no one's come even close to tying me to it. But that's because I'm careful. You know about being careful, don't you, Ted?" He motions me to take another sip, which I do.

"Apparently not," I say.

"You guessed right about the fake beard and the wig, but nobody will find anything like that at my house. As soon as I saw those photos, I got rid of anything that might link me up. I got to admit, though, you did pretty good at figuring out that connection with my car, and the addresses for those crack houses.

"And that was the problem with Patty Stiles. I'll tell you, she found out more in three weeks than the cops have been able to find out in three years. For some reason these jerk-offs on the street don't think a skinny white lady reporter with a camera is any danger. They think they can bullshit her a little bit." Bert is shaking his head, real disappointed, as if he is about to say something like you can't get good help these days, but I beat him to it. This causes him to smile big. Then he gets serious. "She got too close is all. I tried to reason with her, put her off the scent, everything, but she was a pernicious little bitch."

I take another sip without prompting, then ask, "So, you had planned to set me up all along, using what you found out when you were working for my father-in-law?"

"No, Teddy, like I told you. You were a friend. I could have given the goods on you to Captain Turner, but I didn't want to hurt you. Besides, the guy is a jerk. So, I told him I didn't find anything on you. He was real pissed. Actually, it was just fate, I think, the way things turned out.

"I did some surveillance on Stiles' house for two or three nights, trying to figure out the best way to handle this. I didn't really want to kill her, you gotta believe that. I thought maybe I could scare her. That was my mistake, I guess. And then I didn't have much choice.

"Anyway, that third night is when I saw Bobby come over. I got close enough to see what was going on. Then, when he left, I figured this was as good a time as any. I guess, to be truthful, in the back of my mind, I was thinking if things didn't go quite right, and extreme measures had to be taken, Bobby Jackson might turn out to be a prime suspect."

"I thought you said you were at your brother's house."

Bert gives me a look, full of sympathy. "Ted, that was just for the benefit of the tape. I knew you were taping me, I knew that Saint Pauli Boy was listening in. I was pretty convincing, though, wasn't I? The truth is, Teddy, I like you. But you're no match in the wits department with me. That's not bragging, that's just the way it is. Dennis will back me up on an alibi if I tell him to, but I don't think anybody's gonna be asking about an alibi from me."

"Not when they get my suicide/confession."

Bert nods in agreement, waves his gun toward the glass. I take another sip, which empties it. He fills it back up halfway. I take another sip.

"Then Alonzo Johnson was right. He did see you walking down Meridian."

"That's right. As a rule, I park a good safe distance away from the place or the person I am surveilling, unless I need to be real close. Same with all my drug deals. The disguise was another precaution. Very few people know who is under the disguise. Sammy was one of them. And Sammy did pretty good till his lips got a little too loose."

"You killed Sammy then, too?"

"No, I didn't kill Sammy. That job was done by some

friends of mine from Miami. They wanted to take care of you too, but I convinced them otherwise. That would raise too many suspicions, too many questions."

On cue, I take another sip from the glass, emptying it again. Bert opens the other bottle and pours another half-glass. I am beginning to feel the buzz and tell myself that I must keep my mind clear. I realize that I am already at a disadvantage, physically and mentally, but, as Bert said, at least I can buy some time. Something, I hope, will come to me. Bert begins again.

"I was in and out of Patty's house in probably less than ten minutes. I had gotten into her house before, just to see what she had on me, so I knew where everything was. It was pretty easy. The bitch may have been a slob in her personal life, but she was very organized in her work. I took all of her files, the camera, all of the floppy disks, just in case. And erased the files in her computer."

I reflect on Bert's professed ignorance about computers at Patty's, and also on the state-of-the-art system in his office. Another clue missed.

"You finding that notebook was a fluke. And, had you not found that, we probably wouldn't be here today. I think I could have probably steered you away from the drug-dealing connection. You know, it's funny how those things work, isn't it. I decided to go ahead and break back into her house and get that notebook, figuring that's the only thing even remotely connected to the story that you had. And, I'm thinking you won't be able to make any sense of those notes, if you don't have them.

"But then, somehow, through all your alcoholic haze, you were able to recite, from memory, some of the stuff in there. Enough that you think you've got something. Then, of course, old Shawn Wolfe sees you on TV and brings up some photographs that he never would have thought to do otherwise.

"I did try to make it look like a burglary, just to confuse them a little. Hell, I really didn't want Bobby convicted of the murder, just the prime suspect."

"A real peach of a guy you are," I say.

Bert smiles, makes a drinking motion with his hand, and I oblige. I look at my watch and see that thirty minutes have passed since Bert came through my door. I feel tired, shaky, and it seems my speech is a bit slurred. Maybe Paul will come back. It probably wouldn't do any good if he did, though. Bert would just kill him with my gun, make it look like I did it. Then we'd have a murder/suicide. I can see that Bert is really getting into his narrative. Maybe if he gets distracted, I can hit him with a bottle before he has a chance to react. I know if I wait too much longer, I will not be able to do anything much, physically. And, the more I drink, the less I care what happens. I have to try to keep Bert going, as long as I can. I put on my best sober face.

"When did you decide to set me up, Bert?"

"Aww, like I say, fate's huge hand pushed us together again it seems." Bert shifts in the chair now, putting his feet up on my desk. "I followed the investigation, of course, from a distance. And, of course, when I saw that you had been appointed, I had mixed emotions. I knew your connection to the victim, that you were, shall we say, compromised in that respect. I knew you'd have to be careful, and, you were hitting the bottle pretty good."

"Still am. Cheers," I say as I take another sip. "You were my pen pal, I guess?"

Bert nods his head. "Well, the first one you got was legitimate. That was from former Commissioner Johnson, I'm sure, or one of his cohorts. I was kinda hoping that would put you onto him, but you never got real enthusiastic about that lead. On the other hand, it did inspire me to find another way to distract you, keep you going in different directions, play with your head. The more unsure you were, the less likely you were to discover the truth. And I figured you had your own doubts about yourself. I knew how much you were drinking, and when I investigated your whereabouts that night and some of the other details, you began to look pretty good as a suspect yourself."

"Well, it looks like you fucked me pretty good, Bert. I hope it was as good for you as it was for me."

Bert gives another big smile. "There's that warped sense of humor again. I love it. And, yeah, in all honesty, I've got to admit that in some ways I've enjoyed it. Just wish there could've been a happier ending."

"There still could be," I say hopefully, but Bert is shaking his head no.

"And Teddy, it was so easy. It was no problem for me to lift one of your keys and make a copy so I could get into your office anytime I wanted. When the police get to investigating, they're gonna discover that the print on the letters you received match up with the printer in your secretary's office."

I shake my head. "I guess I was a pretty sick bastard, huh? Generating my own hate mail. I guess it all fits, doesn't it. It was obviously an inside job. The little kitty cat, even."

"Yeah. Pretty dramatic, huh?"

"Oh, Oscar material, for sure," I say, certain that my words are barely understandable now. "And I suppose you followed me that night to the Rajun Cajun?"

"Sure, Teddy, I had to keep tabs on you. Besides, I saw you at Patty's house taking those photos. I didn't know what they were at the time, but when I dug them out of the Dumpster I realized what a treat we were all in for. Very sloppy, Ted, but then again, alcohol will do that to you, won't it?"

As Bert speaks my mind races wildly, weighing my options, seeking desperately for some plan, some out. Only if Bert feels in complete control, only when he's sure he's won will he be vulnerable. But will I be in any condition to take advantage of what he gives me? I will have to do something. Time is running out. Already I am having difficulty just concentrating on Bert's words, aware that my perceptions of the situation are probably suspect.

The idea of catching Bert off guard and overpowering him is not high on my list, but neither is blind luck, which seems the only other option, so I begin looking around the room for something I can use as a weapon. There are several heavy objects within reach: books, crystal paperweight, ashtray, maybe a chair. All are possibilities but not real promising against a guy with a gun in his hand. What I need is one of those silent alarms, like the bank tellers have under the counter. Then it comes to me. A possibility. I reach behind me where my suit jacket hangs on the back of my chair. Bert notices my movement and positions himself to deal with whatever I have in mind.

"Relax, Bert. Just getting a cigarette," I say as my hand slips into the pocket. Bert relaxes noticeably as he sees the pack of Winstons I have retrieved. I shake one free and offer it to him. He puts up his hand to decline. I take it, light it from the lighter next to the ashtray and then return the pack to my pocket. As my hand goes in, I feel for the cell phone I keep there, flip open the cover, feel for the auto 9-1-1 dial, then cough to hide the noise, hoping I have punched the correct button. Bert does not seem to notice anything unusual, a bemused look on his face, as I begin speaking again.

"You had me going pretty good with the red herring on Paul," I say.

"Yeah, I made the stuff up about the neighbor seeing him. But I knew when I saw that stuff about the P.M.—I knew who A.M. was—I thought there might be some connection there. Guess I just got lucky. Whatever I could do to keep you guessing, keep you off balance."

"Did you arrange for the DUI?"

"No, that was your own doing, Ted, but you got to admit it fit real nicely. All you needed, buddy, was a little bit of rope. It didn't take a genius to see that sooner or later the booze was going to get the best of you. I knew you didn't have an alibi. I planted the seed in Bobby's ear. He decided to follow up on it himself, like I knew he would. And then you've got things coming at you from so many different directions. I'm surprised you kept it together so long.

"But look on the bright side, Ted. At least you know you're not a murderer. I'm not quite sure what happened with you that night. It's clear you had a bunch to drink there at Harry A's. And you did fill your car up that night and then filled it up the next day at the same station, so you obviously drove somewhere. I suspect it might have been Panama City. It's about the same distance as Tallahassee. Heaven knows how you made it there without having a wreck."

And back again, I think to myself, remembering where I had awakened.

"I suspect you found another bar, drank a little bit more until you completely blacked out. You probably got in a fight somewhere, which would explain the scratches on your arm, the blood."

"So, everything points to me?"

"That's right. I was the anonymous caller to the police a couple of days ago, suggesting that they compare your prints with unidentified prints at the murder scene. I also sent them a couple of photos. I imagine your wife will confirm that she had her suspicions, that some unknown female called her and told her she would be sending her some photographs. That she left you that night Patty was killed."

"Thus giving me both motive and opportunity," I say.

"But what about the mail and the photograph to Beth. That wouldn't make sense for me to send that to her. That'd be crazy."

"Precisely," Bert says. "You are crazy, Ted. Remember, you wanted to get caught. And, how did they describe you in that newspaper article—'wound up extremely tight'?—something like that."

The second bottle is now halfway empty and I know I will not make it through. I am having trouble focusing my vision, and there is a tingling sensation in my fingers. I smile at Bert, and he smiles back. I am drifting into a zone between sleep and consciousness. I have more questions, but the words won't seem to form on my lips.

Bert is over at my computer keyboard typing away. He is talking and I am fighting to understand what he is saying. It seems as though he is reading something aloud. I try to catch a few of the words as they drift past me in slow motion:—living with the horrible reality—drunk—Beth/forgiveness—disgrace. I am thinking of all the clues I missed—was too self-absorbed to see.

I am thinking that his plan will probably work. He will wait until I pass out or am too helpless to resist. He will put the gun in my hand and pull the trigger for me. Even if the 9-1-1 call went through and they trace it here, no one will make it here in time. It will be assumed that I had second thoughts before pulling the trigger. But maybe they'll get here before Bert can leave, at least catch him. Somehow this does not comfort me. No, I've got to stall a bit longer. But I know with the few brain cells remaining to me, that I must do something now before it is too late. Not only am I about to die, but it will be a death of shame. I will be remembered as a murderer. No one will find out the truth. At least, if I struggle, he might find it hard to stage a suicide. Either way I'll be dead.

I can sense some movement in Bert's direction. I am

talking, at least I think I am talking. Bert's voice seems to
have split into two different ones, coming from two different locations. There are two of them now. I am aware of
movement again. What was I going to say? I can't remember. I've got to rest now. I'll think about that later. Must
sleep. Will I remember this dream when I wake up. Will I
wake up?

THIRTY

I awaken to the face of my partner. There is an eerie white light surrounding his body. Is this one of those out-of-body experiences I've heard about? I blink my eyes several times as the picture becomes a little clearer. There is no aura around my partner, simply the ceiling light trying to shine around him. I grasp very quickly that I am in a room in some medical facility. I can hear Paul's voice.

"Welcome back."

I can see the IV in my right arm and the tube above it. Other than a rather severe headache, I don't feel particularly worse for the wear. "Welcome back? Where have I been?"

"On the brink, fellow. You got admitted to the hospital with a blood alcohol level of five point five. This usually is associated with toxic death, coma stage at the least. The good news, of course, is you don't have a bullet hole in your head." He sees my puzzled look. "You don't remember?"

I pause for several seconds. "Yes," I say, beginning to remember bits and pieces. "I think I do. I remember Bert Murphy making me drink lots and lots of bourbon. I remember him telling me some of the stuff he did . . . but it's real hazy." I grimace as I concentrate, trying to remember.

"It's not important, Ted. You don't have to remember."

"No, it's important. I do have to remember. He was going to write out a suicide note, make it look like I killed Patty Stiles."

"We know that, Ted. But, listen, I can tell you all about that later. You probably just need to get some rest now. You've been out for almost two days."

"No, it's all right. I'm fine. What do you mean you know. Tell me what happened."

"Seems that Bert was a little too smart for his own good. He gave TPD an anonymous tip to look for your prints at the Stiles' house, and he sent them the photographs. They went to a judge and got permission to bug your office and tap our phones that same day. They heard the whole thing. Even your 9-1-1 call. That kind of forced their hand 'cause they were afraid the siren would spook Bert, so they broke up your party early."

"Waited long enough, didn't they?"

"Want to sue for reckless endangerment?" Paul smiles at me, and I smile back.

"Those little shits," I say.

"Yeah, well civil liberties aside, I don't know that you've got much to complain about in this particular case. They probably had enough probable cause to tap the phone and bug your office, if you decide to worry about that. And if they hadn't been there close by, you most certainly would be dead now. Granted they could have come a little sooner, but they had no way of knowing how far gone you were on the booze, and they wanted to get Murphy's whole story on the tape. They had your prints, the photos, and Randy Powell never was convinced that your hate mail was coming from outside. He checked the type on some of your pleadings with the type on the letters. Actually, they were ready to close up surveillance for the night when Bert came back in that second time. They got everything on tape."

"So, I've been out for almost two days. I guess the press is having a field day on this, huh?"

"Well, it's not been great, but it could be worse. I played the spin doctor for you. I got with Tom Haley, and, given the circumstances, the police were kind. They didn't give out many details about you. The slant was that Bert tried to set you up, make you out as a suspect. I don't know if it's true, but they say Bert's been under investigation on the drug thing for about a year, but they've never had anything conclusive, until now. You come off as a bit of a hero. Needless to say, Bobby's been released. His clan is happy."

"Bert, of course, has been charged with Patty's murder?"

"That's correct," Paul says, "and Sammy Smith's too. I think he's going to try and cut a deal, though."

"What!"

"Yeah, you should know—there's no such thing as an open-and-shut case.

"I've told Haley, and Judge Rowe, that you're going to check into an inpatient treatment program as soon as you get out of the hospital. Chris Carter says she's looking forward to working with you." Another smile, as he waves away my skeptical look. "Anyway, I've been talking with the chairman of the grievance committee. You're going to have a lot to answer for, Ted. But I think they'll agree to a suspension with a public reprimand, maybe some period of probation where you have to show rehabilitation, show that you've gotten off the booze. I think you can avoid disbarment."

I start to protest, but I don't have the strength, and I know that he's right. I know that I've ruined my marriage, done serious damage to my career, and it's time to face the music. I'll give Beth what she wants in the divorce. I know that I've made her unhappy, and myself in the bargain. I'll take whatever lumps are coming, then I'll start again. I tell Paul that I'll go out on my own when I get over this. I appreciate him standing by me, but I don't intend to drag him down anymore.

"Nonsense," Paul tells me. "We're all behind you. You've got a lot of people, a lot of friends in this town, Ted, who are willing to help you, to support you—if you'll meet them halfway."

I give Paul a nod, not completely agreeing, but not wanting to argue.

"Oh, by the way, a couple of those folks have been waiting for you to wake up. I had the nurse go and fetch them when I saw you starting to stir."

I follow Paul's gaze over to where Beth is standing in the doorway, tears beginning to form in her eyes, a slight smile too. At her side is my daughter. Annie drops her mother's hand and runs over to my bed.

"Daddy, Daddy, you're awake."

I embrace her with my free arm as she snuggles her head into the crook of my arm. I look back at my wife across the room. I hold her gaze for several seconds, asking her with my eyes for one more chance. Too much to ask, I know. There has been too much hurt, too much pain. She wipes the tears from her eyes, smiles again. In those eyes I don't see yes, but perhaps, maybe. It is enough for now.